Praise for *If Winter Comes*

From the outset, the reader of this luminous novel becomes Fanny Kemble's rapt audience-of-one, consciously attuned to how her marriage to Pierce Butler, a Philadelphia aristocrat, will fail. At her husband's slave plantation, where she identifies with the plight of the slaves, it's as if the utter depravity of what she encounters transforms the Fanny we knew up to this point. It is the rare reader who won't find herself gripped by the pulse-quickening chapters of this beautifully written book.

—Dennis Must, author of *The World's Smallest Bible*, *Going Dark*, and *Brother Carnival*

Where in his earlier satirical novels, Jack Smith attacked the military/industrial complex and capitalistic greed, he now in dramatizing Fanny Kemble's career, braves racism, patriarchy, and slavery as our national hearts of darkness. Kemble's first person comes alive; settings are evocative as are manners and idioms of speech. Nothing in this timely, well-paced, and provocative novel feels forced. The story is all: authentic and moving.

—DeWitt Henry, author of *Sweet Marjoram: Notes and Essays*

A fascinating novel of a young woman as strongminded and brave as she is beautiful. Every detail of 1830s America springs to life until you feel you are there: the theaters, the streets, the city slums and the interminable pain and hardship of slaves on a Georgia plantation and the drudgery of the daily endurance of a loveless and inescapable marriage. Based on the remarkable life of an actress and writer whose work is still revered, *If Winter Comes* is a marvelous addition to fiction about women who with little legal power made a huge difference in the world.

—Stephanie Cowell, author of *Marrying Mozart* and *Claude and Camille*, and recipient of an American Book Award

IF WINTER COMES

a novel
by Jack Smith

SERVING HOUSE BOOKS

Published by Serving House Books
Copenhagen, Denmark and South Orange, NJ

www.servinghousebooks.com

ISBN: 978-1-947175-42-6

Library of Congress Control Number: 2020946779

Member of The Independent Book Publishers Association

First Serving House Books Edition 2020

Cover Image: 123rf.com

Author Photograph: Mary Jane Smith

Serving House Books Logo: Barry Lereng Wilmont

This is a work of fiction, based on the life of Fanny Kemble. It's not biography. I take plenty of liberties for the sake of fiction, especially with the ending. Fanny Kemble's husband, Pierce Butler, is also a work of the imagination, though based on the real Pierce Butler. —Jack Smith

To Mary Jane Smith

Books by Jack Smith

Co-authored with Eddie J. Girdner, *Killing Me Softly: Toxic Waste, Corporate Profit, and the Struggle for Environmental Justice*, Monthly Review Press, 2002.

Hog to Hog, Texas Review Press, 2008.

Write and Revise for Publication: A 6-Month Plan for Crafting an Exceptional Novel and Other Works of Fiction, Writer's Digest Books, 2013.

Icon, Serving House Books, 2014.

Being, Serving House Books, 2016.

Miss Manners for War Criminals, Serving House Books, 2017.

Inventing the World: The Fiction Writer's Guide to Craft and Process, Serving House Books, 2018.

Run, Serving House Books, 2020.

"I have sometimes been haunted with the idea that it was an imperative duty, knowing what I know, and having seen what I have seen, to do all that lies in my power to show the dangers and the evils of this frightful institution."

—Fanny Kemble, letter to Harriet St. Leger, Branchtown, Oct. 26, 1840, *Records of a Later Life*, II, 40.

"The revelation of thought takes men out of servitude into freedom."

—Ralph Waldo Emerson, *The Conduct of Life*, 1871

"If Winter comes, can Spring be far behind?"

—Percy Bysshe Shelley, "Ode to the West Wind"

PART ONE
PASSAGES
1832 - 1834

1
Passage to America
1832

On a hot summer day in 1832, Fanny Kemble, British actress, stood aft on the packet ship *Pacific*, watching the London wharf drifting steadily away. Finally, it was but a black speck, and they were heading into open water. "Now we're truly underway," said her father, Charles Kemble. "Thirty-seven long days before us, Fanny. We shall feel like strangers to dear old England!"

This thought gave her a definite sense of foreboding but an air of excitement as well.

And how true her father's words proved to be. Over the days, over the weeks, she felt her whole world changing. She began to believe for the first time in geography, in a world much larger than England, a world that, for her, had hitherto been recorded only in history books and on maps. To her mind they might as well be traveling to a different planet. It was a world many leagues away—somewhere beyond where the reddening sky met the slate-gray edge of water.

The endpoint of their present passage was New York City, an eighth the size of London, but still a flourishing city—and America's largest. "It is there," Charles Kemble informed her, "that you shall become a renowned Shakespearean actress just like your aunt Sarah Siddons, the Tragic Muse. Depend on it. I hope you realize how important this tour is, dear."

"Of course," she said. "Of course I do."

She did, but she often wondered, silently wondered: what about things other than acting, what about living, what about life? For actually taking up her life in such a foreign place seemed, if she dwelt on it very long, but a mere phantasm, one that tended to spook her. She had more than once sneaked a look at her father's thick black ledger, with his scribblings of bookings, that string of cities where they would soon perform: New York, Philadelphia, Baltimore, Boston, Washington, D.C., Charleston, with repeated visits to these cities, and up to Canada as well—to Niagara.

She grew nervous at the prospect of all this.

Long, idle days at sea. She worked away hour by hour in her cabin, below decks, her teacup close by, writing in her travel journal, writing letters to Mrs. Jameson, her famous British author friend, and to others as well, studying German and Italian, reading Byron, reading Edward Trelawny's spirited *Adventures of a Younger* Son, and then she would go above deck for fresh air and exercise. She loved to walk the ship bow to stern, stern to bow, until her legs felt tired and tight—and she felt renewed. In the cool of the evenings, she dined on deck with her fellow passengers, sharing stories, laughing, and singing. She found such gaiety embracing, heartening.

She knew them all soon enough, and they knew her. They knew the basic facts, that is: Fanny Kemble, age twenty-two, famous British actress, setting off with her father, the distinguished thespian Charles Kemble, for a two-year Shakespearean tour on the American stage. Only three years on stage, and Fanny already a *sensation*!—this from her father. And Aunt Dall, beloved spinster aunt—surely they could see how close the two of them were. How much Fanny depended on Dall, and how much Dall depended on Fanny—the two of them a noticeable pair, Fanny fetching things for the older woman, Aunt Dall inquiring if Fanny was pleased with the meals, her quarters, and what she was presently reading, expressing interest, her voice resonating with the air of a chaperone, which she was. Miss Adelaide De Camp was surely her mother, her fellow passengers had first assumed, but no—"She's my aunt," she had to correct them. "Mother's back in England. Back waiting." Why hadn't she come—your mother? Fanny had no answer, at least none for them. *She's depressed so often, very depressed.* Could she say that? No. She must not reveal family secrets. She made excuses. She switched the subject. She talked. She loved to talk. But she could be reclusive, and they knew it. Often they saw her writing in her journal. She would catch them looking. "A writer?" she was asked. "Well, yes," she answered. "Yes, I am a writer as well as an actress." What she wanted to say was: "Really, I'd much rather be a writer than an actress," but she mustn't say such a thing with her father so close by because he would feel guilty, though he surely knew the truth. Still, she did not want to worry him any more than he already was with that enormous Covent Garden debt like a boulder about to sink him—and the whole family, too. How burdensome it was, yet how necessary, to be faithful to the legacy of the Kembles. "You must understand," her father told her. "We are Kembles, and Kembles come from a long line of actors. Theater people in and out. We must not lose that—for how tragic that would be. Do you see? Do you?" When he said this to her, he studied her closely, as though he wished her to contemplate their possible doom.

Her father often stayed up late into the night, on the main deck, drinking brandy with a small group of men. Their talk was a low hum, punctuated at times by cascading barks of laughter. She lingered about, then eventually went down below. She feared for her father stepping his way down the narrow sea ladder, all tipsy, to his sleeping quarters, one oil lantern swinging.

༄

Thirty something days sailing now, and they all began to keep an eye out for land, especially when the captain boomed: "Keep your eyes peeled, mates. You'll see a dot.

13

And then when we close in on her, a black mark, she'll be. Long Island, mates."

Fanny thought of this matter of land and water, how one might see land from the sea's point of view—its stretches mythic, its interminable reaches partaking of infinitude. We see, she thought, with the eyes of finitude, this thing or that, this building or that, this street corner or that. But the sea is counter; the sea is the dream life where anything, everything, is possible. Which takes faith, inordinate faith, to think that when you set out on this vast, immeasurable sea—yes, immeasurable, for all the official voodoo of instruments and charts!—you will, in fact, one day arrive there, at that designated place, that shore where they said you were appointed to arrive.

And then, suddenly, it was there.

"There," pointed Charles Kemble, "is where our new life begins, Fanny. You see?"

And soon, she and her fellow passengers were assembling on the main deck to witness, way off, that single dot at the edge of the horizon, over the gray Atlantic. Yes, that nearly indistinguishable mark meant this long, long journey, weeks and weeks of it, thirty-seven long days of it, was now over—America, finally.

Then the next day, New York City itself: growing larger, still larger, and larger still. The afternoon turning to evening, a pinkness enflamed by red, and then redness swelling the sea, as though a cauldron were boiling the very water, and then dusk, a gentle darkness settling on them, most of them still on deck, feeling the night air cool, the spray of seawater refreshing. And, as though inspired by some unseen, ghostly presence, her fellow world travelers burst forth with shouts, laughter, ceremony, saving it all up for now, unleashing their pent-up joy, their furious intent. They swung their wine bottles high over their heads, passed their bottles around for quick swigs and swallows.

"Glory be!" someone shouted.

Sailing, sailing, for so long, and they were now sailing in for the real thing.

2
The Tour
1832 - 1834

New York City was frantic like London, like Paris, too, but without Paris's air of sophistication, in spite of the young women in their French demi-toilette, in spite of their necks bare to the world's gazing. How they attracted attention, she noticed, in their French shuffle and their pretentions French-fashioned shoes. She herself paraded up and down Broadway with her father, who excitedly rehearsed their upcoming theatrical engagements at the Park Theater—their daily practices as well as nightly performances.

But Fanny had trouble paying attention, for she was gripped by this new city rising before her, with the evening sun streaking the deep blue sky in brilliant orange, and the fluttering pigeons on the sidewalks and the ledges of buildings and rooftops.

Now and then Broadway crossed streets with a view of the river through a line of trees, the bright sun sending fractured beams of brilliant white light. She wanted to go there, to that river, to stand and gaze, but her father insisted they stay on this main thoroughfare and not veer off course. He did not trust off-streets. Well, perhaps that was just fine, she thought, for seeing that river up close would only make her homesick for the Thames.

So this was New York.

After exploring the city, they returned to their rooms at the American Hotel. Dall herself had stayed put, resting. Fanny despaired at all the trunks they must contend with—so much to put away, so much to manage—their clothing and other personal items, plus innumerable costumes, and two whole trunks filled with scripts. They must open all the trunks, go through them, and organize everything. The costumes for the first play must be separated out and dispatched soon to the Park Theater.

It burdened her to think of all that work.

But first, she must attend to her own trunk, a new brown one for her first oceanic passage.

"The American is among the best hotels in New York," said her father. "Such French fineries—as you can see."

"Showy." But how unkempt it was overall, reminding her of hotels in Dublin. She was about to point out the peeling wallpaper in several places, but she held her tongue.

"It does have its measure of Irish untidiness," said Charles, who must have caught her scowl. He thought little of the Irish.

"We can hardly blame that on the Irish. At least I don't."

"Perhaps I misspoke."

Charles took up the newspaper. "Cholera. It's peaked, but we could still face it."

"We just escaped it back home. Will we here?"

"It's gone over the whole civilized world. No one's safe, not even a man of Hegel's stature—can you believe it? And here in this city: three thousand dead. Isn't that a fright?"

"Perhaps we'll succumb yet."

"No, no," said Charles.

The management soon brought their supper, and the three of them sat down to a meal of fish, soup, and meat, of cheese, puddings, and tarts—all wrapped in ice. "Safety measures," said Charles. "Surely."

No finger glasses, she noticed, and some sort of patched tablecloth, both of which she judged as due to a lack of taste and decorum, sadly lacking in this new country.

Before retiring, she wrote in her journal:

London is a city that remembers too much. Its history is one of blood and guilt and every imaginable act of violence and torture. How tangled its dreams, as Shakespeare shows us. I cannot help but wonder: What does New York have to remember? Surely, there is plenty.

At 7:00 the next morning, she raised her bedroom window and looked down four floors to observe the street life below: carriages and delivery wagons rumbling on the cobblestones, barkers in shrill voices calling out their bakery wares, young boys hawking newspapers. A horse pulling a fruit and vegetable cart stopped directly below her, the horse whinnying and snorting.

From here, it was but a short walk to City Hall Park, a green with white palings around the periphery, where she had strolled with her father shortly after their evening meal. They had passed many a pretty young woman with parasol—mauve, leaf green, black, with matching fringes. As much as she loved the sea, she was excited to be in a city, once again.

She swatted at bugs and mosquitoes and closed her window.

The management delivered a complimentary breakfast of eggs, bread, and coffee. Afterwards, she turned to her journal. Since being shipboard on the *Pacific*, she had been keeping a daily record of her travels. This volume, she thought, would chronicle an English woman's experiences in America. Perhaps she would become the next Frances Trollope and conjure up a book as good—and as scandalous!—as *The Domestic Manners of the Americans*.

A literary manifesto.

"I'm not one to look the other way," she told herself. "I'm one to say just what I see, hear, and feel."

She stood before the gilt-edged mirror hanging on a wall in her room. She would soon debut as Bianca of *Fazio*. "I go for tragedy over comedy," she had often told her father. "The latter is good, but the former is better." To her mind, it was because tragedy was every bit human. Tragedy was at the heart of human existence, birth being but the first movement toward death.

"A rather dismal view," said her father. "Isn't it?"

"Can you deny it?"

"No, I suppose not, but the world does have its nicer qualities, too."

He was sipping brandy.

"Is that what you mean?" she said, pointing.

He laughed.

A few days later, a hackney cab was pulling up to the American Hotel porte-cochère. The driver stepped down and opened the cab doors, and she and her father each stepped inside, grasping their scripts, with the driver shutting their doors once they were settled. A few more cabs would soon follow, loaded down with several trunks of costumes and scripts. Her father had been anguishing over their being lost—or stolen. "I'm sure they will be safe," she said.

In five minutes, the cab was pulling up in front of the three-story Park Theater on Chatham Street, with its colonnaded entrance. Once inside, Fanny took in the vastness, beauty, and elegance of the interior, which reportedly held an audience of two-thousand. Four galleries high, it was, with gold carvings all about, and a gigantic gold medallion adorning the marble ceiling. And how she loved the red silk-covered orchestra seating. Such lavish display. One couldn't help but stand and stare.

She prepared herself to take on what she had come to think of as an alternate existence, in which she would become someone other than herself—a Juliet, a Portia, or a Beatrice. Such excitement there was in this mysterious transformation, one she had felt from the start, from her two years on the London stage. She thrilled to how one could become so many different persons, one's own self disappearing and the stage character taking over. She actually became those characters. She was in their skins, saw with their eyes, spoke with their tongues. "And when that happens, I am no longer Fanny. On that stage, Fanny is no more. But where is she?" Sometimes, this thought disturbed her. "What am I capable of being, of becoming? Dear God!"

"I must admit it's a metamorphosis like none other," said her father. "Only an actor, or actress, can understand—truly understand."

"The greatest actresses must feel every bit of this," she said. "Wouldn't you agree?"

"Yes, I do. Sarah Siddons, I'm sure, did. For, isn't it true, that one has to fully immerse oneself—to be good, to be any good at all."

"I cannot help but think that's true," she said.

Her life was soon a series of dramatic performances: morning practices every day but Sunday, evening performances as many as three to four nights a week, and practices before her hotel mirror at every available minute not otherwise committed.

"You will get to know me well!" she told the mirror. And then she jabbed her finger at it. "Fanny. I am Fanny. Who are you?" She laughed.

There she was in that mirror, facing herself.

"Ah! You're ready, are you? Well, I will not be all work—no! Drudgery is not my style!"

She was rather delighted by a number of eligible bachelors attempting to court her—young men of considerable means: bankers, lawyers, and businessmen of all stripes.

"Be sure you're not overly taken with them," cautioned

Dall, "however fine a figure they cut. After all, your father, as you know, is counting on you."

"I shan't forget."

"And besides," said Dall, "there is much to be thought of concerning the marital state. Much not initially imagined."

She knew what her aunt had in mind. Long ago, the poor woman's fiancé had jilted her. "You must never broach this subject with your aunt," said her father. "It's much too painful for her."

Fanny had no intentions, she assured herself, regarding marriage, yet she did find the company of gentlemen a pleasure at dinner parties on Saturday nights, in spite of their rather lackluster table conversation—excepting, of course, Washington Irving sitting right next to her at Mayor Philip Hone's dinner party. This portly man with a distinct aristocratic bearing, fiftyish, with his clean-shaven face, curly hair draped over his ears, bent forward and inquired of her: "Do you like ghost stories, Miss Kemble?" When she smiled, and assured him she did, he smiled, then said, "Well, then, in that case," and he proceeded to recount his tale of Sleepy Hollow as though he'd rehearsed it and rehearsed it, his voice practiced but mellifluous, enchanting. She was full of rapt attention, the story playing out in her head, the dark Autumn night, the ghostly rider. Her father tippled brandy in a final flourish, then clinked glasses with America's most famous author.

"I could fall in love with such a man," she thought, "if he were but thirty years younger!"

Yet the high point of the evening was, as usual, when they danced the waltz. She felt utterly swept away! In every limb of her body, it was as though her partner were whisking her about in the very air itself, so that she hardly knew where her feet had gone! The waltz, she assured herself, is innocent despite the cautionary words of the sullen minister who lurked about at Mayor Philip Hone's party, his myopic eyes like a scourge on the entire festivities.

And then that self-same minister made a point of show-ing up at the parlor of the American Hotel to warn her of a woman's indiscretion in getting so close to a man—as was the case with this particular dance, he stated, which, in his opinion, should have been left back in corrupt Europe from whence it sprang. This was something God did not smile on. "An unwise promiscuous arrangement," he declared. "Quite indecent, in my humble opinion."

"Well," she informed him, "I am only interested in the liveliness of the music itself. I have no ill-advised notions of the kind you refer to!"

"Please do consider what I have, in all good faith, spoken of," he said. And then he rose to go, put on his top hat, and gave her a final nod.

I will not, she told herself. "And I will never give up the waltz—never! It is not indecent as this gloomy Puritan divine thinks!"

Horseback riding—this was her true thrill. Aunt Dall, acting as chaperone, had little to fear, indeed, for Fanny did not feel romantically inclined toward any of the gentlemen she rode with. In her opinion, something decidedly essential was missing in them, and in the womenfolk too: culture, or sophistication. Breeding. These Americans were simply too coarse, too plain. She wanted, had always wanted, a poetic existence, and she did not see in them the least bit of that. In the country houses of England, one could enjoy the best of culture and learning. There one could revel in the society of aristocratic and learned ladies and gentlemen who knew of Wordsworth and Coleridge, of Sir Walter Scott, of Byron and Shelley, and, of course, Shakespeare. These Americans, what did they know? Yes, they were constant theatergoers, yet they could not speak at any length on art, music, and literature, as their English counterparts demonstrably could. What did they really know about her plays? She suspected not very much at all. They could do little more than repeat the plot! "Perhaps," she thought, "I will have to expect much less of them. This, after all, is not England."

One afternoon a man, thirtyish, with a ruddy complexion, with bushy side-whiskers, a pug nose—a very short man with very small hands—showed up in her hotel drawing room. He had parked his top hat on his knee, and between his legs rested a black cane with a gold knob. The expression he wore on his fat face suggested that he was more than happy with himself, and he expected others to be as well. This, she saw, mainly in that distasteful grin creeping over his thick, rubbery lips.

He was busy stirring a cup of tea on a mahogany tea table. He stopped to take a puff on a cigar, sending swirls of gray smoke into the air, toward the white ceiling medallion.

"You're Miss Kemble," he stated.

"Yes?" She stood a short distance from him, and did not take a seat.

"I am Edward Hamilton," he announced, his voice booming. "Of course I know of you. Perhaps you've also heard of me. You've been in New York three weeks now, according to the papers, and so it's very possible, perhaps likely. I'm a lawyer. A senior partner of Hamilton, Brown, and Thompson."

She wanted to say, "So? Why would that interest me in the least?" But she said, "I'm sorry, but I haven't."

"Ah, but do please sit," he said, and motioned at a chair somewhat close to him. Aunt Dall was sitting not far away, next to her father, who was reading a newspaper.

She took a seat, but not the one this boor had pointed at. A young woman brought her tea, set it on a small tea table close by, along with a creamer and a bowl of sugar and a spoon. Fanny meanwhile watched Mr. Hamilton's face to see if it gave her any ideas, but she could think of nothing to say.

"I have often wondered," he said, "what an actress does

with her time—when she is not acting, that is. Perhaps you can educate me."

"One does what one ordinarily does. As you might expect."

She glanced at her father, and he glanced back, raising his eyebrows a little.

"And what would that amount to?"

"What? Well, I read when I have time. Do you?"

"Yes, of course. Much of what I read amounts to legal documents."

He went on to speak of his professional labors over many kinds of legal entanglements, and then spoke of a recent divorce proceeding he had handled. "Being new to New York, the case wouldn't be familiar to you, but it was a rather famous one."

"I see," she said.

"Divorce cases are rather cut and dried," he said, puffing on his cigar. "The husband wins out usually as long as he doesn't abandon the wife. Financially speaking, the husband, of course, owns everything—there's really nothing very complicated about that aspect. What I suppose I've learned in the way of the holy bond of matrimony is, if you're a woman, don't abandon your husband!" He laughed with a noisy rattle that rose from his throat. He again blew out smoke.

"Interesting work, I'm sure," she said.

"But that's not all my work, Miss Kemble. Enforcing the rights of slaveholders is one specialty of mine, I guess you could say. Despite the abolition of slavery in New York—which goes back a few years—a man has a clear legal right to his fugitive slaves—his legal property."

She said nothing. She again exchanged glances with her father.

"Perhaps you disagree?"

"Yes, I most emphatically do. I find that decidedly appalling."

He sat forward. "Oh? You do? How so?"

"Slavery!"

He shrugged. "Well, I myself don't find it so. Property is property. A man of the law, such as I am, has deep respect for property. A man's property is his own, and he has a right to claim it with the full force of the law behind him. Read your John Locke—your very own, Miss Kemble."

"I have a different idea of property than you," she said, "and I think you're wrong about Locke."

He smiled. "He was up to his neck in it—now wasn't he? Actions speak louder than words, n'est-ce pas? But let's turn our attention elsewhere. I note from the papers that you ride horses. On Sundays principally. I look forward to seeing you next you ride. I myself find much amusement in saddling a horse."

She again said nothing.

"And now," he said, "I must part company. It's been a distinct pleasure, Miss Kemble." He rose, bowed, placed his top hat on his head, and took up his cane. "Good day to you."

She watched him saunter off in that top hat. It nearly swallowed the man, and, she thought, what a laughable but noxious Tom Thumb!

She dreaded seeing this pompous fool when she rode next, and almost decided not to ride, but could not give it up and certainly not just because of him, and so she headed for the stables on Long Island that Sunday afternoon, as usual. Aunt Dall accompanied her.

She had been riding perhaps a half hour when Mr. Hamilton came upon her, thrashing his reins, and tipping his hat.

She slowed.

"I was hoping," he said, "to find you. I suppose you noticed from our little parlor conversation the other day that I was rather taken with you."

"No. I didn't."

"Well, I was. Indeed I was. I found you . . . well, rather fetching, to use a Southern manner of expression—I deal with many a Southerner, you see—and I was hoping we might meet again. Is that your chaperone back yonder?"

"My aunt."

"Aha! Well, I am quite sure she will not notice anything untoward. Perhaps, though, you would like to come to my apartment, one of the finest townhouses on Broadway, for a drink of one of the finest wines New York imports. There will be others in attendance, of course. I'm not asking for anything scandalous, not a rendezvous—indeed not. There will be my brother, his wife, a few of my friends, and a few young ladies who come from distinguished social backgrounds . . . I will give you the address—"

"You needn't."

"Oh. And why not?"

She took a moment. "I don't feel we are quite right for each other."

"And why is that?"

She shook her head. "I'll leave that for you to imagine on your own."

He laughed. "You're a hard woman, Miss Kemble. But I suppose that comes from your trade, does it not? Those in your profession must have seen the world, seen plenty of it."

She glared at him. "Perhaps you'd like to tell me exactly what you mean."

"I'll leave it to your imagination to discover," he said, and rode off.

Tom Thumb on a horse, she thought. But a painful perversion of her English fairy tale character.

Of late, ever since Edward Hamilton, she'd had the fugitive slave law in mind. Then, one late afternoon on Broadway, she spotted two hefty white men, two hulks, manhandling a black man, shackled, into what appeared to be a black police

26

wagon. A silver object glistened in the sun.

She started to interfere, but before she could speak her mind, the horses were trotting off.

This, she told herself, is the underbelly. Under New York's civilized veneer, this is what you see. You must keep this in mind as you prance around up on that stage—and doing what? What are you really up to, up there, showing off your cute little self before a few thousand anxious faces, lusting for entertainment? And all that primping you do beforehand—is it worth even a penny when it comes down to it? "But," she thought, "what can I do about it? I can feel bad, utterly anguished even, but what good will that do?"

❦

It was time to move on to their second city, Philadelphia.

She was excited about the prospect of a new place, but her father said it would be a full day of travel. They would have to rise early in the morning, about four or five, in the dismal dark.

"I won't be able to sleep very well," she said, "knowing that. I wish you'd just grabbed and shaken me!"

"Have some brandy," he said. "It will relax you."

"No thank you." But then she went ahead and accepted it, and she and her father had an hour together, sipping. She had a cordial glass, filled nearly to the brim, and she fell into bed, seeking pleasant dreams.

The next morning, around six, they set off at the bottom of Barclay Street to take the steamboat to the New Jersey shore. There they boarded a coach over a road one could hardly call a road, with tree roots sticking straight up, and at other times, it was more a bog or marsh. The three of them—herself, her father, and Aunt Dall—were endlessly jostled, jarred, tossed about, and banged against each other

27

so hard that she feared their falling out through the leathern sides and being run over. How backward!

Eventually they changed from coach to rail, pulled by a team of horses, unlike the rail from Liverpool to Manchester, where trains were now steam-driven. Finally they boarded a three-story steamboat over the Delaware. It was almost identical to the one that had pulled alongside their sailing ship, the *Pacific*, to take them ashore on their first morning in New York. Her father remained above decks with the men, while she and Dall were dispatched below to the dimly lighted women's quarters. After a length of time, during which she read a book, or tried to, and Aunt Dall stitched together a garment, they were ushered up to the main deck, and behold: the brilliant blue sky hovering over the downtown of four- and five-story buildings, and the sundown fiery red like a conflagration.

She stood at the bow. "How I love the sundown."

The three-story Mansion House Hotel was set back half a city block from Chestnut. A waist-high brick wall ran along this street, with hitching posts spaced every ten feet or so for carriages and cabs. With the assistance of two porters, they made their way into the hotel, then up the stairs to their suite of rooms, where she immediately noticed the decor: American Empire furniture, with marble Regency fireplaces and fine silk chinoiserie wallpaper.

"Elegant!"

"Yes," said her father. "The Mansion House is Philadelphia's finest. Much better than the American, I think you'll agree, and, as you see, the management has afforded us a pianoforte."

He winked. And then he and Dall disappeared into their respective rooms.

In spite of how tired she was, Fanny went straight for it.

She settled herself on the bench. She sat still, waiting, listening. Mendelssohn. She could hear him somewhere deep within her before she began to play. Like a mountainous ascent, or—the very opposite—a descent into a pool of rich blue lake water. "I'm an undine," she thought. "I'm a water creature." Now she felt the music all about her, within and without.

She stopped, resting her fingers on the keys. She moved to a desk and wrote in her journal:

> *I do not think I could do without music because I was never meant to live in a world that left the soul to dry. And how it does dry when it isn't touched by poetry and music, music and poetry! The two are one and the same really.*

The next morning, they were off to the Chestnut Street Theatre. This playhouse made for a rather grand entrance with its arcade supported by four gigantic Grecian columns and two statues of the dramatic muses recessed into the façade: comedy on one side, tragedy on the other. And how provocatively situated it was betwixt the Melodeon Troupe Dancers and the Shakespeare Bowling Saloon—rather urbane, surely, for this Quaker city. She would never have imagined Philadelphia as diverting with such abandon from its narrow Quaker morality, yet this was, after all, the theater—and its surrounds.

What about the rest of the city?

Staid.

She saw that in the uniformity of the buildings, the respectable-looking shops—somehow there was an air of propriety, of fitness and correctness, about it all. And the Mansion House itself was a study in decorum and decency.

She wrote to Mrs. Jameson:

> *Philadelphia is much different from New York,*

which has pretensions of Paris, of frivolity, of aban-
don, though nothing of the sophisticated, nothing
of the urbane. It is, when it comes down to it, all
gesture. Philadelphia feels utterly conventional,
and yet there is something about it that attracts me.
Perhaps it's a feeling of security and safety. I cannot
imagine mayhem in this town the way I can in New
York.

Meanwhile, my father holds court in the Shake-
speare Bowling Saloon—as you might well imag-
ine. Often at noon, but sometimes at breaks. I do
worry about him with all that brandy. Sometimes I
fear he'll spring a leak—he wishes to be a ship, but
is actually a boat!—and we'll all go down! But, as
you know, he's got a staying power about him. And
so I suppose I can trust that.

Once again, the days seemed to blur one into the other.
Practices and performances filled nearly every waking hour—
other than brief afternoon interludes with gentleman callers.
Sometimes, late of a night she read Tennyson's *Poems, Chief-*
ly Lyrical, which the poet had given her after her last performance in London. There he stood, that tall, thin man, with
such an expressive face, clean-shaven, and that mop of dark
hair. "For you," he said. "I hope you enjoy it—as much as I
enjoy your acting."

This is poetry! It is the work of sheer genius, Mr. Tenny-
son, she wrote him, but then to herself she couldn't help but
wonder: "Don't I prefer Shelley? Don't I relish Byron? It's so
hard to know!" Sometimes, after reading late into the night,
she tried to write her own poetry, but it fell so far short of
her expectations. Against the poetry of the greats, how utterly amateurish it seemed, and how utterly embarrassing!

Sundays she went horseback riding on Forester, a spirited

bay horse her father had bought her. And she thought: "If he is buying me off, I cannot help but be bought off—with a horse of this caliber."

Aunt Dall mounted an old mare, falling far behind. Fanny rode furiously. Sometimes it was as though she could not ride fast enough, and she tended to dare herself not to slack up, but to increase her speed beyond what she could safely manage. She thought of her beloved Forester and herself as bonded together spiritually, two palpable bodies, yet unconfined somehow by the constraints of ordinary matter. Such energy—she felt she could almost fly. "How good it feels to break so free!" she told her aunt.

"I'll not ride with you if you behave so," said Dall. And then she laughed. "But I suppose that's just youth. At least you're not wasting that."

"Oh? Am I not bound to the theater like an indentured servant? Am I not a slave even? Do I not crave freedom, sheer recklessness?"

She gave it all a flourish, swinging her riding crop above her.

"Shush," said Dall. "Your father would be hurt to hear such as that."

"I will hold my tongue, then," said Fanny, but she fell to laughing.

"Child, child," said Dall. "You must be careful what you say—and do."

"I suppose I will have you to tell me," said Fanny. "To restrain my impulsive nature."

"Not always," said Dall.

"Oh, dear Aunt!" cried Fanny.

In the hotel parlor, there sat a young man talking, with animation, to her father. Fanny stood nearby as this man said, "Of course I'm for states' rights. It's essential to democracy in my opinion. The federal government has no business

31

telling a state what to do. It's tyranny if it does."

"Ah!" said her father, a man not geared to politics. "My life is the theater," he told her and others. "I'll leave the running of the state to those who are more inclined to the quotidian."

He rose and placed his hand on her shoulder. "This is Fanny Kemble, my daughter. This is Mr. Pierce Butler."

The young man also rose, brushing down his frock coat. "Hello, Miss Kemble. It's a great pleasure to make your acquaintance. I've seen every one of your plays—in Philadelphia, that is. I've seen and enjoyed them all."

"Mr. Butler plays the flute in the orchestra. At our own Chestnut Street Theater," said Charles. "Perhaps you've seen him—or will see him."

"Not yet."

"And in Washington and New York, on occasion."

"I do love the flute," she said. "It seems so . . . haunting . . . so ethereal."

"Indeed," he said.

"Mr. Butler also has a great love of horses, perhaps equal to your own. He's a committed equestrian, are you not, sir?"

"Indeed I am, sir," said Pierce Butler. He smiled at her. "Where do you ride?" He ran a finger lightly on his elongated sideburn.

"Along the Schuylkill."

"I will join you if you will have me."

"Pardon?" Yet she smiled.

"I am a man who makes up his mind quickly," he said, and once again stroked his sideburn.

"Oh!" she said. "Well!"

She soon had much to commit to her journal. She wrote about this Mr. Butler and his equestrian abilities:

Perhaps Mr. Butler's horse is not quite as good as

my plucky Forester, for he continually falls behind me. Or does he lack a complete and full knowledge of horsemanship? I think he tends to think of me as competitive. A woman, I realize, is never to compete with a man. How red his face grows! I suppose I should be ashamed of myself, and yet I fail to be so. I'm sure I should be if I want this man to enjoy my company. But do I—do I really? He plays the flute in the orchestra! Still, I cannot decide. It's so hard to know one's own heart!

Nonetheless, she allowed him to take her on carriage rides about the city. And then, after very little passage of time, he began to take her to little shops to buy her pieces of jewelry and books of poetry. She read poetry to him in her best speaking voice, articulating each syllable so that she picked up the rhythm just right, just so. Poetry, she thought, must be read with careful attention to beat, to pacing. If one delighted in the words themselves, savoring them, then one wanted to speak them just so, speaking them into existence. And she did, with her favorite poets: Tennyson, Byron, Shelley. Sometimes he would read, and she couldn't help but be amused by how he tripped over the words, and yet she thought it becoming, and a credit to him, that he would read poetry at all. She had not met any American men yet who did, though she knew there must surely be some—mustn't there?

Pierce Butler lavished her with flowers at the Mansion House. At first he had signed them "an admirer," but then he soon confessed to being that very admirer. "I wish to make you happy," he said.

"How I do love flowers!"

One Sunday afternoon, his driver drew up before a three-story mansion on the corner of Eighth and Chestnut. They remained in the carriage staring at this townhouse.

"Do you like it?"

"Yes. It's beautiful. It's quite . . . majestic."

"It was my grandfather's. Major Butler's."

"Oh, my, a major!"

He looked at her rather oddly. Had she offended him?

The Butlers, he told her, had roots back to Ireland, and from the time of Major Pierce Butler had accumulated considerable property and money. This townhouse rising before them had been empty for the past ten years since his grandfather had died, in 1822. As soon as his great aunt died, and she was getting quite old and infirm, he stood to inherit it and several other properties. But it was his whenever he wished it to be.

"My aunt is a reasonable woman," he said. "And wouldn't it be better to be occupied? It's always better for a house to be occupied. By the right people, of course. Good caretakers, I guess you might say. Otherwise, it falls to ruin—it deteriorates. That's the way it is with houses." He gave her a long look, as though he were expecting a response.

"Yes, that must be true," she said. She asked to see inside.

"Oh, it's not ready for showing. Not at this time. It needs a bit of work."

They remained staring at it, as though they could imagine their way in.

And she could: the library, the drawing room, the front and back parlors, the bedrooms and other spaces. How elegant and refined it would all be. She saw herself on the third floor, looking out a window—perhaps the one in the center. It reminded her of London townhouses. Charming was the word that came to mind.

"There's a garden spot to the rear," he said. "Shall we have a look?"

"Yes, please," she said, and he signaled the driver.

The sere Autumn air blew through the leafless trees. Brown, brittle leaves scattered along the cobblestones. She liked the clattering noise they made.

That evening, she wrote Mrs. Jameson:

This Mr. Pierce Butler I have become acquainted with will inherit a fine townhouse and other properties. He's a Philadelphia aristocrat. He's studied the law, but does he practice it? I do not know. He's an aristocrat, a learned one, as one might expect and demand, and I rather doubt he needs to work. I'm rather sure Aunt Dall would consider him a good catch, all in all, though, as she reminds me, I am obliged to do my father's bidding, which is, of course, to be a faithful Kemble, an actress, and save the family from that dreadful Covent Garden debt! What a curse that's proven to be. And so I must not think of marriage. But what if I become like my poor Aunt Dall, a spinster—a stern, sometimes lugubrious, old woman! I'll not have it! Though it must be said that I love her so. She is, after all, a good woman, and a very wise one. On an entirely different note, I must say how much I treasure the book you sent me—Shakespeare's Heroines. I shall read it with great interest!
Your dearest friend,
Fanny

In January, just back from Washington, D.C, they once again took residence in the Mansion House. A letter awaited her from Mrs. Jameson. It was a lengthy one, much of it mystifying with the woman's subtleties and paradoxes. *I do hope you find* Shakespeare's Heroines *valuable. You, of course, know the Bard's women characters from the inside out, having become so many of them.* In closing, she inquired: *Does he have a country house as well as that fine townhouse?*

Fanny couldn't help but ask.

"Indeed. Butler Place. Six miles north."

She wanted to see it.

"Well, it's also in need of repair."

"If you'd rather not," she said.

"I suppose just to look and not go inside," he said, "would be all right."

One snowy afternoon, he took her by carriage.

It was on Old York Road. It was a three-story, white frame farmhouse, with white columns and front porches, on both first and second stories. It was certainly a far cry from an English country home, situated, as it was, betwixt a cornfield to one side and an apple orchard to the other. A huge stone barn rose on the edge of the cornfield. There was no lawn to speak of, just a riotous growth of weeds. Two tall oaks stood sentinel.

"That land across the road is in the family also," he said, pointing.

She saw the fence and the deep, wide fields. "Is that so?"

"Yes, it is. Well," he said, "you've seen both. Which do you prefer?"

She paused. "I suppose I like the townhouse more."

"Of course," he stated.

She said nothing to this. She had surely misspoken.

"Do you like America?" he asked.

"Pardon?"

"America. Do you like it?"

"Yes and no."

He stared at her, his eyes intense as though what she'd said entirely mystified him. And then he said, "Is that so? Why ever is that?"

"Slavery—to state the matter in one word. How can one tolerate such an abomination? How can one live in a country with that always there, like an open sore?"

His chin jerked. He shook his head. "Indeed. Well, I suppose every country has its problems. Consider the misery of the working class in your own country. The miserable poor."

"I know. And it's the same here, isn't it? But to put people in bondage because of the color of their skin—that's an atrocity, isn't it now?"

He took a moment. He was lighting a cigar. He blew smoke out. "What about England and its slave colonies in the Caribbean?"

"William Wilberforce, 1807," she said. "And much more will happen soon, I do believe—and, from what I hear back home, perhaps next year. I'm an abolitionist. Where do you stand?"

He seemed jarred by this pointed question. His eyes grew large. Had she been too blunt?

Then he gave her what she thought of as a tolerant grin. "Here we call it the 'peculiar institution'. We don't speak of it in polite company."

She felt her face growing warm. She felt a quiver in her stomach, and her body shaking, just slightly. But she said, "Maybe you should."

He didn't say anything for a few moments. And then he said, "I would hate to see the conflict over this matter destroy the Union. But it could."

She had not had such a conversation with him before, and she felt embarrassed about overstepping customary boundaries. Perhaps, she thought, that's why her father avoided politics.

In February, they returned to New York. This time, she met the prominent novelist Catharine Sedgwick at a dinner party, after a Friday night performance at the Park Theater.

Fanny felt drawn in by this literary woman, authoress of *Hope Leslie*, which she'd recently read. She had much to share about this novel, but also, of course, her acting tour, its joys as well as woes. As to the latter, she spoke of the cloddish Philadelphia audiences who irritated her when they failed to rise at the curtain call. There they sat like absolute dolts! At least New Yorkers knew better than that! But, all in all, it was her life, her calling. And she doubted she could do without it.

"It is your calling," said Catharine. "And you do it so well."

"Thank you. But I write poetry, too," said Fanny. "And I'm keeping a journal."

"Is that so? About what?"

She explained.

"I am sure that will be quite a treasure," said Catharine, smiling knowingly at her.

"I guess you can say I have hopes of being a travel writer and a social critic."

"Indeed! You will undoubtedly encounter resistance, being an Englishwoman with such views. Or, should I say, being a woman with such views?"

"I suppose I will." And then, somehow, the subject of Pierce Butler came up. She found herself claiming that this Philadelphia aristocrat had obvious designs on her. She had not intended to say this. She was only speaking of her life, but it was true: she had spent much of her free time of late with Mr. Butler.

Catharine looked long at her, sipping her wine. Then she said, "This Mr. Butler, what kind of man is he?"

She took a moment or two. "He's very kind, I guess you could say. And accomplished, with interests matching my own." She spoke of his love of horsemanship, but more to the point, his playing the flute in the orchestra, though she hadn't yet witnessed his doing so. Mainly he liked poetry. He had bought her books of poetry to share with him. They had spent time reading Tennyson together—and Shelley and Bryon as well. "An American man liking poetry I find rather pleasing." She smiled. "He is different in that respect from the other gentlemen I've met—so far, that is." Perhaps, she thought, Catharine Sedgwick could help her solve the riddle of Pierce Butler—the riddle of her heart, that is.

"What do you mean by 'kind'?" the novelist asked.

This rattled her. She temporarily froze.

A distinguished looking man was now approaching them. "Good evening, Miss Kemble. I'm Ralph Emerson." He made a little bow, dexterously avoiding tipping his red wine goblet.

"A poet, he should call himself," said Catharine. "And a very fine one. Perhaps you know of his winning the Bowdoin Prize at Harvard."

"That's been some time ago." He smiled. There was an eloquence about him which she immediately liked. Such a calm voice. And what a firm jaw!

Fanny felt his attention completely on her. She grew embarrassed.

Catharine turned the topic to Mr. Emerson's loss of his wife at the tender age of twenty due to consumption. "I feel such compassion for you," she stated. "I think of her always, and you, and your great loss. Please accept my deepest condolences—in person. A letter isn't the flesh," she said.

"One must deal with life's slings and arrows," said Emerson. "One does the best one can."

"Mr. Emerson," said Catharine, looking from him to her, "is one of my dearest friends, along with the Reverend Ellery Channing, whom you must also meet."

"Are you familiar with the Reverend?" asked Emerson.

"I've read some of his sermons and essays."

"They display a rare talent, do they not?"

"Ralph is off to Italy soon, aren't you?" said Catharine.

"Yes, I am. And then to France and England, as well."

"Bon voyage," said Catharine, smiling.

"I trust that this passage will be beneficial to me—in some way," said Emerson.

"You can tell us what they're all about in all three places."

"I hope to learn something—a skill, no less."

"Perhaps," said Catharine, "you should go on the lyceum circuit. As I've been urging him to do in many a letter," she said to Fanny, smiling.

"I shall strongly consider that," he said and gave them both a smile.

When Emerson drifted off to speak to others, Catharine turned to her. "What do you know of this man? This Mr. Butler?"

Suddenly, under the older woman's scrutinizing stare, she felt she knew absolutely nothing.

"I really don't know very much," she said. "And he hasn't proposed marriage. I do fear his proposing, though, for I'm an actress—with serious commitments."

"That you are." She paused, seeming to reflect. "I hope you don't feel that I've singled you out, but perhaps I have. I do feel it my mission, of sorts, to speak to women such as you who have great talent and who might, just might, fall into the clutches of some domineering man—and especially one of lesser intellect and talent. Marriage, my dear, is so often a trap. Or at least it's proven itself to be."

Fanny couldn't speak for a moment.

"I hope I haven't offended you."

"I sometimes doubt that I will ever enter that state," said Fanny, thinking of her mother and her sorrowful lot.

"Well," said Catharine, smiling, "I didn't myself, but I wouldn't be totally opposed to it. My sister-in-law, Elizabeth, finds marriage an utter blessing! But one must draw lines. You see?"

"What lines?"

"Between male power and female power."

"I know there's a difference."

"It's knowing where those lines are, or should be, that is crucial for a woman," said Catharine. "And I speak not of marriage only, but of life in general."

Shortly afterwards, she met the Reverend Ellery Channing in Boston at the Federal Street Church. They sat in the minister's office, filled with books: stuffing the shelves, stacked on the floor, mounted high on his desk. He leaned back in his desk chair, with his hands folded. "My good friend Miss Sedgwick has spoken very highly of you, Miss Kemble. I know you're an accomplished actress. Naturally I read the papers."

"Thank you."

"But, if you will permit me, I do wish to speak to you about a rather important matter—regarding the theater. That particular profession. This has been on my mind ever since Miss Sedgwick spoke of our arranging a meeting."

"Yes? What is that?"

He looked closely at her. "It's this, and I don't wish to offend, but I must speak frankly, without equivocation, that I believe the theater to be a corrupt influence. Only consider, Miss Kemble, the diverse set of characters paraded across the stage—some utterly vile. They are the worst of moral influences, are they not?"

She started to object, but he raised a hand.

"Bear with me but a moment, for I wish to propose an alternative. Instead of presenting whole plays, adopting roles, and all that, you might instead pick and choose certain noble passages from Shakespeare, elevated ones, and read those. The moral component would then, you see, become quite apparent. You would avoid stirring up the rank passions and base desires of your audience. If one is to present a good moral influence, I see no other way. And you?"

She couldn't speak immediately. What he had said swirled about in her head. But then she could speak—and did.

"Absolutely not. No. Please."

"I beg your pardon?"

"Do you not see that drama provides a context for the moral center you speak of? Do you not see that any audience worth its salt will come away opposed to the base behaviors you speak of, whether murder, adultery, or any other form of iniquity? And besides, Shakespeare—he is pure poetry. What is life without poetry?"

He smiled. "Perhaps we had better move on. We are not likely to agree on this matter. We are only likely to offend each other, and I do not wish to risk that, at least on this one particular subject."

"I see," she said.

"But surely," he said, eyeing her, "we both oppose the wrongness of slavery. As a British woman, you surely do."

"Yes. I am quite opposed to it. I don't see how anyone could not be."

"It's perpetually on my mind, from sunup to sundown—ever since my visit to the West Indies a few years back. It should be on everyone's. Such a plague on our land. Let me explain why."

And as he did, she found herself attentive to his voice, attentive to everything about him, his gestures, the way his eyes stared straight at her, not flinching. This was a man with a conscience, she thought, however flawed his understanding of drama.

"How can such a monstrosity go on in a civilized country? Yet it has. We are the inheritors of this wicked, corrupt institution, and yet it is our duty to change it. It is God's charge to us to do so. Every single individual must feel this duty. Every single individual must not only speak out against it but do something to end it."

She flinched. "How can one manage to do that?"

"That, my dear, is not easy. I grant it."

"No," she said. "I'm sure it's not."

"That's right because in doing so, one faces danger—great danger in some cases. The forces aligned against us are very powerful."

"And so we must put our heads on the chopping block?"

He gave a little laugh. "I don't think of it quite that way, but yes. Yes. In this world, if we own up to our moral responsibilities, our heads will always be on the chopping block."

She shook her head. "I'm sorry, but I must say I recoil at such an obligation. I wouldn't make a very good martyr, I fear. But I do wish to be of service."

"We must find good models. And they do exist. William Lloyd Garrison, with his new *Liberator*, and Lucretia Mott, a Philadelphian, with her strong, demonstrated Quaker morality. And there are others."

"Well," she said. "I feel . . . overwhelmed to think of it. It's right to take a stand, but I feel overwhelmed."

He nodded. "Yes, it is a terrible burden. It takes courage, and yet those who give up their lives for abolition will have served the good. How can we serve the good, the right, if we do nothing? We serve evil if because of our non-action, we become complicit."

She said nothing. She found herself looking at him, trying to formulate a reply.

He waited.

"I suppose I am complicit, then," she said. "And a sinful woman."

"There are degrees," he said.

She wanted to disappear into her own life. She wanted to be happy. Nights she lay in bed imagining the Major's townhouse. She saw herself in the library, taking down a book from a high shelf, then dusting it off. She saw herself sitting with a book of poetry on her lap, looking out the open window onto shady, tree-lined Eighth Street. She was having a cup of tea, and she was watching carriages rumbling by. The noise of horse hooves on the cobblestones, their neighing, the reins jingling—she was alone in the library, it was dusk, and it would soon be dark. She imagined the scent of spring in the cool April breezes through the greening trees.

She wrote Mrs. Jameson on what she called her latest "news" in this strange, strange land. Mr. Pierce Butler had, prior to their moving on to New York, been taking up most of her time. *He writes that he will soon follow me here to Boston! I fear I am falling into a whirlpool. I fear I shall drown—utterly! What is wrong with me?*

Spring was in full bloom when she heard back:

You speak again of Mr. Pierce Butler. I would advise caution in matters such as this. One wants restraint. You hardly know this new world, at the other end of the Atlantic. You hardly know its customs, its dangerous proclivities, its temper. One thinks of wild red men and Negroes. Slaves. One thinks of tyrannical masters. But of course you must decide. I am half a world away and cannot offer anything very useful.

She did not dare take up this topic with Aunt Dall. She must hide the matter from her as much as possible. Sometimes she questioned herself over the prospect of ever being a married woman. Sometimes she told herself that she was fine, just as she was, and she need not bind herself to a man, no matter the man, for she had a life ahead of her that was satisfying, fulfilling. Performance was her life. Was there any other? She wrote in her journal:

I am who I am because of performance. Who would I be without it? I am myself, and not myself. I am many others, and no one. I am, in a way, pure spirit, driven by any vagrant puff of wind. Give me a

part, and I'll take it. Ah, perhaps I am utterly im-
moral? Think ye it's true?

Nights she read Mrs. Jameson's *Shakespeare's Heroines*, and when she was finished, she wrote the authoress a long letter. She concluded on this note:

*I fear that it has taken me too long, much too long—
an embarrassing length of time!—to read your
wonderful book. It has been calling me, though
I must, as you might imagine, blame it on something besides myself, and so I will blame it on my
overly busy schedule, which gives me hardly any
time to do anything. Yet I regret missing reading
it earlier, for I find your analysis of Shakespeare's
women truly insightful. This is a book, in Bacon's
inimitable words, to be "digested." Hereafter I will
never play Shakespeare's women the same way, for
I know them even more deeply now for having read
your book. You see them as a woman does, and I
know that Shakespeare, could he comment, would
applaud this work for having understood the depths
of his insights into each and every one.*

It was late summer when she received Mrs. Jameson's response:

*Naturally I am thrilled by your letter. When you re-
turn to England, and I hope you do so soon, we can
talk further about the greatest master of literature
the world has ever known. Is there any other?*

Back in Boston, Pierce took her horseback riding at Mt.

Auburn, a cemetery but a public park as well—an odd combination, mused Fanny. It was a garden cemetery, Pierce told her, and ran over a hundred acres.

Her rented horse galloped over the green, rolling hills. Several times they passed Aunt Dall, who stood talking to a middle-aged couple next to a huge marble monument. It seemed a serious conversation, for she saw not a hint of a smile on any of their faces. In fact, wasn't that a look of stupefaction on Aunt Dall's face, her mouth sagging to one side, her head shaking.

"What?" wondered Fanny. "What?"

Finally, when Dall was alone, and meandering about, Fanny rode up to her and stopped. She dismounted and held the reins tightly. "Who were those people?"

"New Yorkers."

"Oh. You looked so serious. So sober."

Aunt Dall nodded. And then she whispered, "Yes, dear. Yes. You see, they told me something . . ."

"What?"

Aunt Dall raised a hand. Pierce was now dismounting his own steed.

"Never mind," said Dall. "Perhaps later."

They were off to Niagara.

Her father had invited along Edward Trelawny.

He was tall, broad-shouldered, with a dark, Moorish face, with a prominent scar, a man with long black hair that hung to his shoulders and a wiry mustache with the ends curled up. Such eyes—how they flashed!

She found herself alone with him. She was enthralled by his tales, just as she was when she'd read his book on the passage over—but more so now, as he seemed to reach right inside her, to capture her very being. There was no way she could not listen.

In a slow, measured voice, yet impassioned, Trelawny spoke of how his Romantic hero, Shelley, had drowned at sea, in a squall that occurred off of Livorno, Italy, and of how he had built a funeral pyre on the shore of Viareggio, on the Tyrrhenian Sea—and, when the poet's heart refused to burn, of how he had saved Shelley's heart for his poor, wretched widow. As he spoke, as the fervid pitch of his voice rang out, Fanny could envision that funeral pyre, see the blazing fire, hear it crackling, see the blue water, feel the night wind blowing sand on the beach.

"How tragic to die so young."

"Yes, and the same for Byron, too."

"But for the cause of liberty," she said. "Was it not?"

"Yes. There are things worth dying for, and things worth living for."

He placed his hand on his mid-region. "I took a bullet here, the fragments of which are deep inside me, beyond the surgeon's skill, I'm told. But one must not be fearful. One must put certain things on the line. Greek liberty, to me, was one of them, as it was to my dear friend Lord Byron."

She grasped his hand. She had not meant to, but suddenly it was happening.

He smiled at her, and squeezed hers.

Five nights into their journey, on a boat steaming up the dark canal to Utica, with the chir- of nightjars and throaty calls of owls, Trelawny whispered, "Ah, Fanny, you are a kindred soul, a sister spirit to Shelley and Bryon, my own tribe."

His arm went around her shoulder. She could not resist him. Yet she warned herself: "He is almost old enough to be your father!"

Pierce was a short distance away, drinking brandy with her father. He had joined them in Utica. He did not like this

Mr. Trelawny. He had hardly spoken a word to him. Sometimes she caught a scowl on his face.

Several miles before Niagara, making a narrow curve, their coach hit something hard in the road and suddenly flipped over, square on its side. At first she couldn't react. She couldn't even think, only feel, only hear: moans, whimpering. She struggled to free herself. She now saw the others: her father, his face contorted; Aunt Dall with a huge, bloody gash stretching the length of her forehead; Trelawny, his complexion utterly wan. All of them jammed together, a pile of bodies, suffocating each other.

Up above them, she could make out the face of Pierce Butler looking down through the open coach door.

Now her father was crawling out, his feet kicking her. She cried out. She soon followed, worming her way up. Once she was out, there was Trelawny emerging.

Pierce was standing off to one side.

Her father and Trelawny were now reaching down, going for Aunt Dall. Soon they were pulling the old woman out, helping her to stand.

"We must seek help now," said her father. "We mustn't delay a moment."

Trelawny, with her father, assisted Aunt Dall in walking. Pierce went ahead of them all. "I'll find a suitable place," he yelled back. She walked behind Dall, just in case the woman lost her footing—and, if she did, perhaps she could help catch her.

They soon came to a tavern. There was Pierce at the door.

The host appeared and assisted Dall in getting inside.

Men were sitting at tables bent over drinks, smoking, laughing, carrying on.

"She's been hurt," said her father. "She needs help. Hurry, please."

"Ah, yes. Indeed." The host called out, and two large, strapping men suddenly appeared.

"Help this woman up to a guest room," he said. "But be gentle." He turned to her father. "And the rest of you?" He was looking around.

"We'll make it," said her father.

The two men carried Dall up the narrow stairs to an upper room. They laid her on the bed. A woman soon arrived with bandages, and Trelawny set about bandaging her forehead. Fanny administered salts and eau de Cologne. A house servant appeared with a large carafe of water, along with a goblet.

Her aunt complained of a bad back. "Something's happened . . . something terrible inside me."

"You must heal, Aunt," said Fanny, bending down, stroking her cheeks. But she recognized in her voice a distinct doubt. There was something broken about this poor old woman, something which neither bandages, perfumes, salts, food nor water were likely to aid in her healing.

As the night wore on, Fanny continued to minister to her, urging her to sip water. A house servant delivered hot tea and warm broth.

There was a soft light in the room from the yellow moon. The night breeze felt good through the open window.

It was growing near midnight, and Dall, her voice barely audible, beckoned Fanny closer. Her hands were cold, but her forehead oddly warm, moist.

"Yes, Aunt?"

She was struggling to speak, to breathe. "I hope . . . that you will have a good life, my dear niece . . . I hope you will make good choices . . . for a good life is one of making . . . good choices."

"Oh, Aunt, you'll be all right."

"No, my dear . . . I won't. One knows . . . when one's time is up."

"But it's not—"

Dall beckoned her.

Fanny moved closer.

Dall whispered, "I am not acquainted with this man—this Mr. Butler."

"I know."

"Even your father . . . hasn't spoken of him."

"Well," she said.

"Do be careful. Careful."

"I will. But why do you say that?"

Dall stared at her, swallowing, gripping her hand. And then she said, "That couple . . . from New York . . . I spoke to . . . in Boston. Perhaps you remember?"

"Yes."

Dall closed her eyes. "They said something . . . about your . . . Mr. Butler. Something not good. Something that makes one despair . . . at the thought."

"What?"

"Fanny, dearest . . . I'm an old woman, and my time is at hand . . . I feel I must be honest. Do you wish me to be honest?"

"Yes, Aunt."

"I'm cold . . . so cold."

"You're shivering. More blankets. I'll get some."

She did and returned to her aunt's bedside.

The woman seemed unable to go on, but then she did: "Well, then, I will. Fanny, your Mr. Butler . . . this man went to houses . . . of ill-repute . . . in New York . . . I was told." Her breathing was exceedingly heavy. "He was meanwhile engaged . . . to a young lady from Philadelphia . . . Emily Chapman, her name was, from a good family . . . a terrible thing, just terrible, dear."

"Were they sure? Were they? How could they—"

"Yes."

"But what were they like? Can we trust . . ."

"I must sleep now, dear, for I'm so tired . . . oh, I can see. Oh, dear, I can see . . ."

"What? What, Aunt?"

"Pictures. Pictures."

"Tell me—"

"I'm so, so very tired."

"Yes," said Fanny. "Yes. I know."

She patted her hand.

She did not make it to the morning. There she lay, not looking dead, but just asleep.

But cold, very cold.

They arranged for the burial.

It was but the following afternoon when they conducted a short funeral.

"It should have been England," said Fanny. "She belonged to England."

"We as well," said Trelawny. "Dear old England."

"Indeed," said her father. "She did not wish to come, but felt . . . she felt it her duty."

Fanny did not ask.

☙

She stood with him at the Falls.

What thunderous cascading! It partook, she thought, of the eternal in its never-ending roar—its roiling, gushing, its battling of huge boulders, spraying up white foam. An orange-red sun enflamed the sky above them, piled high with jagged gray clouds. She could hardly think. She could only feel, feel, *feel*.

"Table Rock, Fanny. The very altar of Nature."

"Yes," she whispered. "Yes . . ."

"Ah, Fanny, dear, it's the sheer sublimity, isn't it? It's sort of like God, isn't it?"

But how fathom it? She started to take a step—a foot forward.

His hand restrained her. "No—oh, no, Fanny. That's the real thing. It gets no more real than that."

51

"I know," she said. "I know—"

She closed her eyes. She wanted to absorb it in her silent, dark theater—every bit of it.

"Do you really want him?" he asked. "This Mr. Butler?"

This took her off guard. "I don't know," she whispered. "I cannot—"

"Listen. Listen to me."

"Yes?"

"You must forget this man. You must break off any ties."

"Why?"

"Because he's wrong for you. The man lacks character. He's of a very low caliber. One can spot that right off."

"How? How do you know?"

"I just do, Fanny." His head was next to hers, her wet cheek next to his.

She started to pull away, but she couldn't.

Autumn brought crisp weather, with the heat and humidity gone.

"Which do you prefer?" asked Pierce, "were you to become my wife? The Major's townhouse or Butler Place?"

She looked steadily at the Major's townhouse but said nothing.

"Well?" he asked.

"You assume too much. Much too much."

"I beg your pardon, but which do you prefer—outside of that question. I'll ask it that way."

"The townhouse."

"I see. Well, I'm quite sure that can be arranged. It could be ready in a month, I venture to say. Six servants would be about right for a house of this size. Wouldn't you agree?"

She didn't answer.

"It would require at least that many," he said.

Several times he had asked her to marry him, but so far she had not led him to believe, in the least, that she would. Was he a man who went to immoral women? Was he? Could she believe what she had received second-hand from her nearly delirious dying aunt? He did not seem the kind of man who would go to harlots. But what if he did? He was a single man. She supposed that single men did such things. Yes, they were sometimes reprehensible in that way, but there were other aspects to their character, and not that alone. Wasn't that true?

Meanwhile, she had received a letter from Edward Trelawny. It read:

My dearest Fanny,
If you will be my bride, I will take you wherever you wish to go. We will go where nature is pristine, and sacred, and where poetry thrives. Be assured that I will take good care of you. If you like the mountains, that is where we will go. You like the sea, I know, and we will go there. You love the water, and we will go to Venice. Ah, Venice, a place of mystery and romance! I can see the two of us in a gondola, Fanny! And the haunts of many a scholar, there we will go, too. Paris calls us both. There is life in Paris, Fanny, more than here, or in America, and I know you know that. Do be my love.
With my sincerest affection,
Edward

"Perhaps," said Pierce Butler, "you would like a June wedding. For our wedding journey, we could go to Newport, which you will find quite fashionable."

"Were I to marry you," she said, "I might be pleased with

53

that."

"Ah, but aren't you tired of toiling on the stage? I would think," he went on, "that you surely could not remain an actress forever."

"Perhaps I will. One cannot be sure."

"You surely do not mean that."

"Why not?"

"I think you would find life at the Major's townhouse quite comfortable." He laid a hand on hers. "You would find everything about it very much to your liking."

She withdrew her hand. "I do not like to be forced. Why do you push and push?"

"I only mean to coax."

"You coax too hard."

She wrote in her journal:

I am pulled in two different directions. One by Edward Trelawny, who captivates me in every imaginable way but is, without question, too old for me and, to boot, something of a pirate, and how would a civilized woman live like that? Would he be all over the world, driven by his wanderlust, and meanwhile, where would I be? But how I love the dreadful romance of it! Mr. Trelawny is a romantic man, and I'm unable to say that he is not mine, and I am not his, in spite of our age difference. Perhaps it's the childish dreamer in me. This other man, this Mr. Pierce Butler, is stable. That's what I think when I think of him: stability. He is a man of property, a man who would offer a life of ease, wherein I could read, write, be the writer I've long imagined myself to be, just like Mrs. Jameson. And, of course, Catharine Sedgwick. But to do this I must give up, yes give up, my life as an actress. How can I? Yet it is becoming undeniably burdensome, in spite of my love of it. I do tire of such continual effort. It has, in fact, become close to drudgery. I must correct myself: It is drudgery, in spite of my love of theater, drama—the great ideas, the grand beauty of expression. Pierce Butler is a way out of that life, which has become so tiring to me—isn't he? But is he an immoral man, seeking the services of women of the night? Even if that were true, surely that's in the past. At least, one hopes it is. Dear god, I must not torment myself over such a matter as that!

She wrote Mrs. Jameson. Should she go with her emotions or her reason? Should she think pragmatically? How could one possibly decide? In a few months, she heard back:

I'll be spending the winter in Edinburgh, and I will carefully think on this matter. But for the most part, I am given, at least at this time, to believing that one can make mistakes when one ignores one's heart, one's feelings. To depart from what we feel, and feel deeply, this, my dear, is to invite trouble. But you must give me more time to reflect on this matter, if you please.

Troubled by this response, Fanny wrote Catharine Sedgwick. She ended up writing and rewriting her letter several times, but finally she had it down just as she wished. It seemed to state her problem quite well:

I cannot judge my feelings all that well, but marriage, I do think, is at least in some respects a legal settlement made for the benefit of both parties. Must one be passionately in love? You do see what I mean, don't you? I am in love, I am quite sure, with another man, but that love seems to me to be utterly foolish. Shouldn't one be levelheaded about a matter such as this? My heart tells me Mr. Trelawny. My head tells me Mr. Butler. I confess I am thinking mostly in material terms! For with the latter, I can live the life I truly want. How can I possibly decide?

Catharine wrote back:

If by levelheaded you mean without emotion altogether, then I fear this is risking your happiness. Do not forget that we are flesh and blood creatures, that we have heads for rational thoughts, but we also have hearts that cry out for love and affection. Will the needs of the heart be met in this union?

She did not know how to answer. She decided it best to put the matter aside and allow herself time to come to some sort of decision. Pierce Butler was a good man, after all— or at least mostly, if not entirely—and that, it seemed, was enough for now. She asked herself this: "Who knows how many men such as Pierce Butler, or how many men period, have given into their lustful side and gone to women of the night? Surely, if he did, he is not alone. I will put that behind me forever," she decided.

When the spring of 1834 arrived, she had been touring for a year and a half. They were back in New York. It was rainy and windy, a succession of cold March days, and she felt closed in, utterly bleak. Would warm April days never come? She was struck by a grim feeling of emptiness. She felt the weight, more than ever, of bearing up under a continual round of practices and performances. And she wondered, "Where am I headed? Where am I going?"

Perhaps, she thought, absolutely nowhere.

She had come to think of her life as utter "sameness." And yet she knew that most people's lives were a matter of routine, varying very little from day to day. She did require a certain amount of sameness, and no matter what she did, or where she went, she would undoubtedly fall into certain predictable patterns. "Yet I think I would like to start afresh," she thought. "I would like to fill my days with the things I love, and not feel so driven about." She had come to think of her life as a continual journeying, back and forth, from hotel to theater, theater to hotel, from hotel to stage, stage to hotel. "I am homeless," she thought, "for how is a hotel, even a very fine one, a home?"

She told these things to herself, but not to her father. She continued to be as committed to being a Kemble as she could, and she never once flagged, but made sure that her father could see in her absolute commitment and devotion.

Late one night, when the weather had improved, she walked along the gas-lighted poles at City Hall Park. Despite the clement weather, she was feeling something mournful down in her soul. She had come to an impasse. "I am utterly drained," she said aloud. "Is there anything left in me? No, there is not. I cannot go to rehearsal tomorrow. I simply cannot." Tomorrow they would begin Sheridan's *The School for Scandal*, which had failed miserably in Philadelphia, and her father wanted to make it a success in New York. He swore that New York audiences, being more cosmopolitan, would be more open to it. She wasn't as optimistic, for audiences here, as elsewhere in America, were basically dull and uncomprehending when it came to the least little subtlety. And how could she play Lady Teazle? That took an abundance of energy, and that she had left at the Park Theater today, what little there was to begin with!

She returned to the hotel, feeling a distinct sense of futility.

Her father appeared. "Fanny, Mr. Butler, I am told, wishes to see you. He's down in the parlor."

"At this hour?"

"It does seem a bit odd to me that the man would come at nearly midnight."

"I'll not see him," she said. "It's much too late. I look a fright."

"I do think it's not sound," he said. "I'll let the porter know."

But suddenly she changed her mind. Her father was at the door.

"No," she said. "No. Tell him I will be down momentarily."

"Pardon?"

"Please," she said.

He said something through the half-opened door, which she didn't catch. And then he closed it.

He was back in ten minutes. "I've done as you asked," he said. "But it is dreadfully late to be seeing anyone."

"You mean a man, don't you?"

"I'll not judge such a thing as that," he said. And he stepped into his bedroom, and the door went shut.

She saw him as she entered the parlor. He rose from a settee.

"Hello," he said. He held his silk top hat before him. "Would you wish to sit down with me, for a short spell? I just had to see you."

She nodded. "All right. I suppose I can."

He didn't speak immediately. He seemed to be struggling to form his words. It was as though he were picking out a book from a shelf and couldn't decide. But finally, he said, "I've come to ask you, once again. Perhaps I shouldn't, but I can't help but ask."

She said nothing. She just stared at him.

"Please," he said. "I've come to plead with you to accept my proposal of marriage. You see, I am beyond merely asking. And so I plead that you will not wait a minute longer, but to accept it right now. For I am quite serious. I can offer you much. A good life. Surely you know that. Surely you realize that I can make you quite happy."

He went on for a little while, and she heard him out, and then it was her turn. "No. I really cannot. I really cannot do as you please. I have commitments. Very important ones."

"To your father."

"Yes, but also to the stage."

"I know this. I understand this. But I'm asking you to choose me over your father—and the stage." And then he mentioned the Bible, and how one chose a wife and cleaved to her, and she to him, for it was the right thing to do—according to God Himself.

She couldn't help but laugh. "Well, I know that. But I'm not ready for that choosing. And thus there is no mandate such as you mention."

His lips trembled just slightly. His complexion reddened. "As you wish, then." He rose.

She rose, too. "It has to be this way," she said. "This is the way it must be."

"Naturally," he said, "I am disappointed. Quite so." His eyes leveled on her. "I don't particularly like—I mean it seems to me—"

"What?"

"Nothing. Nothing at all."

She watched as he placed his top hat on and made his way, stiffly, out of the parlor. She saw him outside hailing a hackney cab. She sat back down, and then she couldn't help but leave the hotel and take a walk, again, in the moonlit

City Hall Park, despite the very late hour.

Later, up in her room, she hurriedly wrote Catharine:

I've broken it off with Mr. Butler. Or at least I assume he thinks so. He again proposed marriage just an hour ago, and I declined. I declared that I was not ready for such a state. He gave it a biblical footing, of cleaving to each other, but if one cleaves to another, one must first choose that other. I don't choose him. At least I cannot choose him right now. I want a different man, a man I have dreamed of ever since Niagara, and yet this man I cannot have, for he is wrong for me. What is wrong with me? Must I be so dreamy, so untethered to reality, that I cut the ropes altogether and try to float in the beatific blue? Surely, a time will come when I regret this penchant for the unreal, the lofty, the ethereal. I find a man of my own adventurous soul in this other man, Mr. Edward Trelawny—but so little in Mr. Pierce Butler. Yet he, I know, would be better for real life. And isn't that what we must all live, at some point, real life?

When she had finished writing, she sealed the letter and took it down to the desk clerk. A courier would post it first thing in the morning.

That was coming too fast, and she must hie herself to bed!

But she felt relieved, satisfied to have spoken her mind. She had not flinched. She had said exactly what was on her mind.

A week later, she heard back from Catharine:

Dearest Fanny,

I see that you are still pondering this plight regarding your suitor Mr. Butler. I am struck by your penchant for the "unreal," and your feeling that you must somehow abide by the "real." For me, the unreal, so-called, is, so often, rich and wondrous. But we do live in a mundane world, and we have but little chance of escaping it anywhere or at least for very long. Surely one must keep this in mind when choosing a marriage partner. Even so, if a man is substantially "real," he might be a great bore to a woman who needs, desires, and simply must have the "unreal."

I do wish you success in being who you are—and in remaining so.

Sincerely,

Your dearest friend, Catharine

Meanwhile, they had moved on to Baltimore. One balmy spring evening, a short, thin man with gray eyes, dark hair, olive complexion, and a thick, dark mustache stood before her in the parlor of their hotel. There was air of the unhealthy about him, the ashen. But there was an air of mystery about him, too, a faint sense that at any moment, he would speak of something deeply mystical, spiritual, visionary.

"You are a magnificent actress, Miss Kemble," he said, his voice rushed. "And I think I have fallen in love with you." He went on, one hand clutching a book, his second hand limp at his side, a faint smile forming: "You see, I myself come from an acting family, English like yourself. I have been informed that my name comes from Edgar in *King Lear*, which my parents performed about the time I was born."

"Oh? How delightful."

"I am Edgar Poe." He made a slight bow.

"Please," she said. "Please sit."

And now she was not sure of what else to say, but he was handing her the book he'd been clutching, and her eyes focused on it.

"A copy of my recent volume. I hope you will read it. Look, please, please take a look." His voice was almost frantic.

It was a very small book of forty pages with a dark brown cover. It was entitled *Al Aaraaf, Tamerlane and Minor Poems*, authored by "A Bostonian." She turned to him. "You didn't take credit for this. Why not?"

He shrugged. "Perhaps you will find this volume to your liking. Perhaps the language will appeal to you. I was influenced by the great Lord Byron."

"Oh! I do love Byron!" She read the opening line of "Tamerlane" aloud: "Kind solace in a dying hour!"

"But the rest," he said, and there were those eyes again, dark gray, but full of intent. "I do hope you like the rest. There were but fifty copies printed of this volume, and not very many left. This one's for you."

She could not read it in his presence. She felt the weight of those dark eyes, heavy like lead on her. She kept the book open. She sensed that she must not close it until he had left.

"I shall," she spoke. "Please be assured."

"A poet lives by the dying light. Each breath he takes finality measures against eternal night. Words. Each word is measured by the principle of beauty."

"Yes. Yes, it is."

"I bid you Godspeed. I will be in attendance at your next performance."

And then he left.

She was shaking. She had, she felt, been in the presence of Lord Byron himself, though a more mysterious, inscrutable version.

She wrote Catharine about this strange guest to her hotel

parlor, and Catharine wrote back:

I know little of him, but Ralph Emerson speaks doubtfully of the man. Apparently Mr. Poe sent him a copy of his book, the same one he gave you. His letter to Mr. Emerson was a bit befuddling, to say the least, though, as Ralph Waldo assured me, not altogether so, and there was something deeply somber about him. Emerson felt a sort of presence even in the letter, and that's but a pale imitation, of course, of who he might be in the flesh. You say he claimed, forthright, to "have fallen in love with you"—my, but that's forward. His literary criticism, says Emerson, who's read him in the magazines, is unparalleled. Are you falling in love with this gentleman? Is this more of your "unreal"?

Fanny wrote back:

Were I to fall in love with Mr. Poe, whom I saw only once—and that, a very abbreviated visit—I might count myself an impulsive woman indeed. Impetuous. But I can certainly imagine a woman falling in love with this strange, enigmatic soul. I can imagine a woman like myself—with a soul for poetry—utterly lost to him!

By May, she had completed her journal. She had included what she felt was right to include, right to say. There were things to love about this country, but there were things to deplore as well, as she wrote Catharine Sedgwick.

Catharine wrote her back:

I would not be too optimistic about this work being

published, or, if it is, of its meeting with a favorable reception. Keep in mind that you are an English-woman. You could be considered an unwelcome in-terloper. But I insist on your publishing it anyway. What democratic country worth its salt is so myo-pic as not to take criticism—and even welcome it?

It was but a few weeks when the publisher she had sub-mitted to wrote her back:

Dear Miss Kemble,
With great enthusiasm, I welcome this book to our list. I read it over this past weekend and could not put it down. As an Englishwoman, you have devel-oped a thorough, acute rendering not only of your travels, but also of your many observations and judgments.
We welcome you as an author. You will herewith find two copies of the book contract. Please sign one and forward it to us at your earliest conve-nience.
Your Humble Servant,
Mr. Henry Carey
Carey, Lea & Blanchard

Whom could she share this great news with? She informed her father. She wrote Mrs. Jameson. She wrote Catharine. She debated sharing it with Pierce Butler, but decided not to. She wrote Edward Trelawney.

It was late May, with the fragrant spring air refreshing, and Pierce Butler continued to pursue her, with an abundance of aromatic flowers, and with a volley of short, passionate letters.

She felt pestered, but she also felt needed. Here was a man who wanted her. And, he was saying, they would take up residence in the Major's townhouse as soon as they returned from their wedding journey—in Newport, if she so wished.

"Do think about it," he said. "Do consider it."

"I haven't even met your family."

"There is plenty of time for that. There's no rush, is there?"

"What are they like?"

"What's anyone like?" he said, and laughed.

"Who are some of them?"

"My aunt, whom I mentioned."

"Yes?"

"And my brother, John, and his wife, Gabriella."

"And more?"

"Other relatives," he said, evasively, and smiled.

She let it drop.

She spent a few miserable days working all this over in her mind.

If her aunt was still alive, she would see her. She would seek advice. Perhaps she should finally speak to her father. Perhaps he should know that she was exhausted with being an actress. She did not want to resent him, but she was beginning to, for she felt like she was being used, used, a body bouncing all over that stage, from morning to night, from practice to performance. "I do not wish to entertain any longer," she told herself. "I wish to be only me, Fanny Kemble. I wish to disappear into something. Some thing or another."

She approached her father: "I do not wish to be a bad daughter. But I must say what I've been feeling—what has been on my mind for some time."

He directed her to take a seat.

She informed him, forthrightly.

He sat staring at her. Then his expression softened a little. "How long," he asked, "have you been feeling this?"

"For some time," she said, wishing to say no more.

"Is it something else?"

"What?"

"A man perhaps."

She felt her face grow hot, and she knew she was reddening. She was not wanting to speak to him about that. Perhaps a woman, but not him.

He sat there, quiet for a little. Then he said, "I cannot demand of you any more than you've already given. But I do wish you would continue. You will be sadly missed. I am not sure how I could ever replace you."

"I will stay my two years," she said.

"I count on your doing so," he said.

She continued to see herself in the Major's townhouse, the carriages going up and down the tree-lined street, the library, which she'd stock with books to be read, to be studied. Most of the time Pierce Butler was not in these daydreams. She was alone. He was elsewhere, where men tended to be, taking care of business, smoking a cigar, oblivious to most everything else. She imagined long walks on her own. She imagined spring, like the season before her, the summer, the fall, the coming of winter with snow, the coming, once again, of spring with balmy weather and bird song.

Something was working in her. She did not wish to analyze it further.

She again approached her father. He was working at his ledger. They were coming to the end of the season. From her nearly two years on the American stage, she had over thirty-five thousand dollars saved in the Bank of New Orleans. Her father also had, he had told her, a handsome amount stored up himself. "We are doing quite well," he had assured her from time to time. "And we'll have our great successes to take back to England. And there, Fanny, we can begin again."

It had become abhorrent to her—those words. Well, they were beyond that matter of beginning again. But even finishing up the two years—that was more than she could handle. Why had she promised it?

He looked up from his work. "Fanny," he said.

"I wish to say something to you."

"Please—do sit."

She took a chair next to him as he placed his pen in the gutter of the ledger.

"As you know, my book is soon to be published."

"Yes, quite. And that is truly an honor." His voice was a bit shaky. He took a sip of brandy.

She knew not how to go on, but she must. She spoke of wanting to be a writer more than an actress, of wanting to go on to this other career soon, very soon, and of considering marriage to a suitable man.

"To Mr. Pierce Butler, I presume."

"Yes."

"Well, then."

"You do not approve?"

He shrugged. "I hardly know the man. And therefore I will not offer an opinion one way or the other."

"You think him—unworthy in some way?"

"I pride myself on knowing about men—and women as well. I've done a long study of my fellow creatures on this earth. I cannot be sure about Mr. Butler, but I'm not certain that you're making a good choice. I do feel you are making a bad one giving up your acting career."

"I realize that."

"I do fear for you—a little."

"Fear? Why?"

"Because I don't know the man."

"How could you, though, really?"

"It would take time, of course. But Fanny, you must be sure. Are you quite sure?"

"Yes," she said, but she wasn't. She had given up on being sure. One must take chances, mustn't one? Wasn't life one big chance?

"Well, then," he said.

She then spoke of her earnings. She would leave some to Dall's poor sister, who, as a governess, was after all in need of a bit of help, but he could have the lion's share. She herself would not lack for money. By doing so, she said, she could remain faithful to the Kemble name—to some extent, at least. "It's for that debt—you must have it."

"A very good daughter, you are," he said.

She thought she saw tears in his eyes.

"I mean to be. Though I do realize—" She couldn't go on.

"I, of course, do wish you well."

"I cannot stay the whole two years . . . a few more performances at most. I was wrong to have promised it. I'm not . . . able to. I'm simply not—"

He nodded. That's all he did.

He would not oppose her. The matter was concluded.

She left, feeling oddly empty. That thirty-five thousand gone. After all that work. But how could she grudge her father that? She would have plenty. How could she keep that money for herself, not really needing it?

"Do you love him?" she wondered. "I like him. Mostly. But perhaps that's not the issue. Perhaps, it's at least convenient to marry him. I am choosing for life, for a life, and not for my yearning heart, at least not for him. My yearning heart for what he can provide. Yes, that. Be honest, now. Yes, I am being honest."

She stood before the mirror. It seemed important somehow to look at the person she was about to speak to.

"This is a marriage of convenience—I fully admit it. I'm in love with another man."

She stared at herself.

"I am not going to fool myself. I am demanding absolute honesty. He's a fine man, a good man, but I feel nothing deep for him. He might as well be a friend, a companion. Yes, that's right, and so what's wrong with that?"

She jabbed the mirror with her finger.

"Speak to me," she snapped.

It snapped right back at her.

"Do you understand? I speak the truth. This is Fanny. This is not some stage character. I'm not practicing. This is the real thing! This is Fanny speaking to you. Do you understand: I enter this marriage a woman seeking a good deal. All right?"

She waited.

"Oh, dear God," she said, turning away, "what am I about to do?"

"You are being honest with yourself," said the mirror. "That's what you're doing."

"Yes, I am. I am being absolutely honest."

"Will you be happy?" said the mirror.

"I'll have some sort of life. How can I not have some sort of life in the Major's townhouse? Dear God, I would surely think so!"

"Yes," said the mirror. "You will. And you must."

"One thing is true: I will be a drudge no longer!"

Though rather reluctantly, though somewhat confused, she accepted Pierce Butler's marriage proposal. And shortly afterwards, on a stifling hot summer day, they were married in Christ Church in Philadelphia. She found herself crying, almost uncontrollably, in front of her new husband, and in front of the minister.

And then everything went black.

She awoke to soft slaps on her cheek. It was the white-bearded minister staring down at her.

"Ah! A woman's emotions! Or this dreadful heat!"

He helped her stand.

Pierce was eyeing her, with a frown on his face.

The reception followed.

Joined in holy matrimony, they immediately left for Newport for their wedding journey.

3
Wedding Journey
Summer, 1834

When the coach arrived at Newport, the red sundown had streaked the sky with blotches of purple like bruised flesh. Under the porte-cochère, two porters assisted Fanny and her new husband out of the coach. Pierce took Fanny's hand, and they entered the three-story beach hotel, two porters hefting their trunks into the lobby.

They then carried them upstairs.

Up in their room, Fanny lay down for an hour and then dressed for supper. Pierce lingered before the vanity, brushing his bushy sideburns. Now and then he would draw up close to the mirror, studying himself. He adjusted his frock coat. He turned and beckoned her. "Come," he said. "We're running late."

In the hotel restaurant, Pierce ordered halibut, John roast duck, and the men decided on the rest of the order and two bottles of wine. From their narrow window, which looked out on the broad Newport Bay, Fanny could see a black bathing hat bobbing, gradually disappearing into the deep blue distance, where the sun smoldered like red-hot embers. How far? How far would that woman go?

"Are you with us, Fanny?" said Pierce. "What are you gazing at?"

She turned to see.

Two young black waiters were serving their food, a third pouring wine.

"Sir," said the third one, his head bent low.

"That will do," said Pierce. "Do not spill it. Do you hear?"

"Yessir," the black waiter said, his head bobbing.

"Be about your business now," said Pierce. "But watch for my hand. I'll raise it when I require more. Do you hear?"

"Yes, sir."

"*Massa*," said Pierce, sternly. "You call me *massa*, boy."

"Yes, *massa*."

The black waiter went off.

"He's not a slave," said John. "He's free black."

"I know that. But he needs training. He needs to learn the proper respect."

Fanny watched the black waiters delivering plates of food, and pouring wine, from table to table. This was a side of her husband she hadn't seen before, this coarseness, this ugliness. How had he managed to hide it from her? He had, and she wanted to slap him. She had already slapped him once on this trip, but he had caught her by the wrist and twisted it with his chubby hand until she had cried out. "Don't you ever," he warned her.

And she had warned him: "I will be seeking an annulment—soon."

He laughed. "Don't be so theatrical. You deserved it."

"What?"

"Look," he said. "Just keep a civil tongue with me."

"I don't know you," she told him.

"*What?*"

"You're different than before."

"I am who I am," he said. "And you are my wife. Do keep that in mind."

Now they all began to eat.

John had his ruddy face down shoveling in the food.

Gabriella, his wife, was picking at hers. "This meat isn't tender," she said.

John did't bother looking up. "It will do, though, won't it?

"No, it will not. It's not to my taste." Her voice had

grown petulant, whiny. Her lips, puckered downward, had a look of expected doom.

"Eat it, and maybe we'll order something different next time," said John.

"Look. It's the Wilkersons," said Pierce.

Fanny looked up from her plate. He was motioning at a distinguished looking man in a dark frock coat and a woman with dark hair and finely sculpted features. She had rich, full lips. She was fashionably dressed in a light blue ball gown.

"Ah," said John.

"Who are the Wilkersons?"

"They're from New York."

"Is that all?"

"No, of course not, Fanny. We know them. They're important people."

"They have much to recommend them," said Gabriella. "You will not find a woman more cultured than Mrs. Wilkerson. She hosts many, many dinner parties and balls. And she can tell you all about Shakespeare. I would think a former player like yourself could profit from her instruction. And her person."

There was that sneering look on Gabriella's lips. She disdained actresses—players, she called them. And Fanny had realized at the wedding that the whole Butler clan thought Pierce Butler had married down. A theater woman! A gypsy! He had not once, during their courtship, or their short engagement, introduced her to his family—not to any member of it. Now she knew why.

One old woman with red lips and a scowl had hobbled toward her and asked, "Are you a player, Miss Kemble?"

"*Mrs. Butler*," Pierce corrected her. He had quickly intervened, positioning himself between Fanny and the dowager. "She was until recently, Aunt. But no more. I assure you."

"I see," said the old woman. "Then I suppose that will have to do. Won't it?"

Afterwards, in the coach to Newport, she had confronted him. "How could you treat me so? Why didn't you defend me? From such ugliness? From that horrible aunt of yours!"

He was looking out the coach window. When she repeated her question, he turned slowly toward her. "They have their principles," he said. "They're not the same as yours."

"Principles."

"Yes, Fanny."

"I see you're suddenly ashamed of me. How dare you!"

He adjusted his top hat, and lighted a cigar. "Let's put the matter to rest. Shall we, dear?"

"No. You have just married a woman you're ashamed of—how could you?"

He was silent a moment. And then he raised a finger. "Fanny, I will not be interrogated in this manner. I'm your husband now. Please show some respect."

"Respect!"

He whirled around. He removed his cigar. "Don't forget whom you're speaking to." He jammed his cigar in his mouth. "We are no longer courting. You'd best learn to obey me."

And that's when she had slapped him.

John saw it and his face flushed red. "*Pierce. Goddamned.*"

And that's when her new husband grabbed her wrist and twisted hard. The red embers of his cigar glowed in the darkening coach.

Fanny now steadied her eyes on Gabriella, who was still looking at her, a fork raised tentatively. "Then I suppose I owe it to myself to become acquainted with this Mrs. Wilkerson. Is it not true? She will be such a fine influence. What about Mr. Wilkerson?"

"He's a gentleman all around," said John.

"I don't particularly like him," said Gabriella.

74

"He pays enough attention to you," said John. "More than enough for my taste."

Gabriella looked away. "Well, perhaps I don't like that."

"Ha!" said John. "Then I suppose he's wasting his time." He went back to his duck.

"I don't care for that remark," said Gabriella. "In the least."

Later that evening, they entered the hotel ballroom, a gargantuan space with a long row of tall, wrought iron-grilled windows, through which one could view the white moon suspended over the dark bay. Fanny was dressed in a mauve silk taffeta dress with gigot sleeves, Gabriella in a pale blue silk evening gown. Party snacks and drinks were being carried about as groups of revelers indulged, chatting away.

A string quartet was playing the Allegro movement of Schubert's *Death and the Maiden.* Such emotion, and yet a very odd choice, quite ponderous, thought Fanny, for this gathering of partiers drinking, snacking, chattering, and laughing.

But how fine, how deeply moving.

Pierce pulled her along, ushering her into the fold.

"Mr. Wilkerson, Mrs. Wilkerson, I present to you my bride, Mrs. Fanny Butler. We are here on our honeymoon."

Mr. Wilkerson made a slight bow. "My congratulations. A pleasure to meet you, Mrs. Butler."

"Fanny," said Mrs. Wilkerson, smiling. "I want to say Fanny Kemble. A famous couple by now. In all the papers. My," she said to Pierce, "we wouldn't have imagined that you, sir, would ever tie the knot."

"Indeed I have," said Pierce, grinning, taking Fanny by the arm.

Mr. Wilkerson turned to John. "The John Butlers! Well, now. It is very pleasing to see both of you again. Accompanying the Pierce Butlers on their wedding journey, I presume."

"Yes, sir," said John.

"Gabriella," Mr. Wilkerson noted, smiling.

"How are you, Gabriella?" asked Mrs. Wilkerson.

"Oh, I am quite fine," said Gabriella.

"Splendid, dear."

And now the string quartet was, of a sudden, playing Mendelssohn. Yes, and the very piece, Opus 12, Fanny had thrilled to several years ago in London. How haunting that music, so much so that she began to sense a radiant beauty transforming all—the commonplace as well as the ugly—to sheer poetry.

If, she mused, if one could only lose oneself, one's whole being, in such a reservoir of power. If one could only fuse oneself, shedding flesh, becoming spirit only.

"*Fanny.*"

"Yes?"

"Be attentive. Is that asking too much?"

"The music. It has utterly cast a spell over me!"

"Dull to my way of thinking. But they'll be playing a waltz soon, surely."

He turned to Mrs. Wilkerson, and then he moved closer, his lips flat against the woman's ear, and whispered something, a sly grin extending to his bushy brown sideburns.

Mrs. Wilkerson laughed, and blushed. "Ah!" she said. "Aha!"

"What?" said Fanny.

"Nothing," said Pierce. "Ah, here comes the Colonel. A man who knew my grandfather. An old friend of the Butler clan."

A slim, white-haired gentleman gimped toward them.

"Hello, Colonel, and how are you, sir, this evening?" asked Mr. Wilkerson.

"I am wonderfully well, sir," drawled the Colonel, who wore a navy blue tailcoat, and white trousers. "And I trust you are the same."

"Life meanders," said Mr. Wilkerson, "but we do the

best we can."

"Life plods along," said Mrs. Wilkerson, "doesn't it? But nothing much ever changes is what I've noticed. Man is man. Woman is woman."

"How philosophical we are tonight, madam," spoke the Colonel.

"I certainly have no intention of being so," said Mrs. Wilkerson.

"But it comes naturally?" A flicker of a grin played on the Colonel's narrow lips. He fingered his white beard.

"If we aren't philosophical, I suppose we suffer, don't we?" said Mrs. Wilkerson.

"We do anyway, don't we?" said the Colonel. "But yes, one must be philosophical—stoic, I suppose. War teaches us that."

"And this is Mrs. Fanny Butler," said Mrs. Wilkerson to the Colonel. "I want to say Kemble."

The Colonel bowed, with a bow more pronounced than Mr. Wilkerson's. And then he turned to Pierce. "You have tied the knot, then, sir."

"Indeed."

"Did I hear correctly?" asked the Colonel, "that you, madam, have given up your acting? Your Shakespeare?"

"For now."

"Forever," said Pierce, exchanging glances with her.

"Which is it?" asked Mrs. Wilkerson, her eyes glinting.

"I suppose you must rely on my husband," said Fanny, "who seems to know better than I."

"The stage is hardly suitable for a married woman," said Pierce, flatly.

"But you were such a stage presence, my dear!" cried Mrs. Wilkerson. "It must be exceedingly difficult not to be so—anymore."

"Yet you didn't come down to Charleston," said the Colonel.

She did not wish to explain Charles Kemble's cancellation. How could they go down to Charleston in the midst of a nullification crisis over that federal tariff? Her father would have none of it.

"I regret that," she said.

"My wife and I loved you in New York," said Mr. Wilkerson.

"You made Shakespeare Shakespeare," said Mrs. Wilkerson. "You were absolutely divine! The Tragic Muse all over!—according to the papers."

"According to my father."

Mrs. Wilkerson was looking at Pierce expectantly. "And so, where will you and your beautiful young bride take up lodgings?"

"Philadelphia."

"Oh, I must insist on New York," said Mrs. Wilkerson, her eyes dancing.

Pierce shook his head. "No, ma'am, we belong in Philadelphia. It's a family town."

"No man belongs in Philadelphia," said the Colonel. "New York's the future, sir. Unless you choose Charleston, which is, of course, the finest of all cities. And what is better than the South for fine cities. And families?"

The Wilkersons laughed.

"Otherwise, New York," said the Colonel. "Unless you intend to follow in the footsteps of your grandfather." He smiled at them. "The Major became a propertied man in Philadelphia. Once there, he seldom made an appearance down South."

"To his plantations," said Mr. Wilkerson.

"That is correct, sir."

"Well, now," said Mrs. Wilkerson.

"Yes," said Pierce. "And so it's Philadelphia, at least for now."

"Not forever, I do hope," said Mrs. Wilkerson, her voice

saucy.

"My dear wife," said Mr. Wilkerson. "My, my."

She seemed oblivious to him. "*Well*, I don't suppose you'll perform in Philadelphia, at the Chestnut Street Theater—is that but history?"

Fanny started to answer.

"It is," said Pierce. He turned and motioned at the string quartet, which was now playing a waltz. "As I promised," he said. "Shall we?"

The evening wore on, with the waltz, and John came into view. She soon found his arms encircling her, his eyes intent, his touch intimate, and she kept pulling away, trying to keep her distance. She looked about for Pierce.

"Madam?" said John, when the music stopped.

"Yes?"

"Have you been here before—to Newport?"

"No."

"But you've traveled extensively, haven't you?"

"Not so much."

"You think you can abide Philadelphia?"

She didn't answer immediately. Finally, she said, "I like Philadelphia."

"But do you love it?"

"Why do you ask?"

"Well, my dear, Philadelphia isn't London."

She gave him a look. "I'm well aware of that, John."

Pierce placed his pantaloons on a hook. Fanny put her clothes in a drawer.

They were soon in bed. And suddenly he was upon her. "John goes for you," he said, "but you're mine. All mine. Not his. You're damned right."

In the moonlight she could see his nose twitching, his eyes squinting, his mouth hanging half open.

She smelled the liquor on his breath, and she didn't want to.

He was running his hands all over her.

He wasn't touching her. No. He was marking his territory.

He got on her, in her, and he moved quickly. He was done in less than a minute, a fierce rhythmic plunging, and he suddenly flopped over, sighing, panting.

She lay there, staring at the dark ceiling. She soon heard his snoring.

Afterwards, the summer heat sweltering, the air in the room became wet, drippy.

The next morning, she stood at the window, watching the swimmers, the blue water chained with puddles of brilliant white light. A middle-age woman, her bathing dress tight against her hefty body, was waddling toward two young girls busily splashing each other. The woman adjusted her brown bathing hat. She barked something at the two young girls, who looked bright, cheerful. It was impossible to make out much about the mother. One couldn't hear her words, and one couldn't read her lips.

After breakfast in the hotel dining room, Pierce and John sat smoking cigars.

"You go where you want," said Pierce. "John and I have business to attend to."

"What business is that?"

"*Fanny.*"

"Cards," said John. "If you must know."

"Cards. I suppose you will have much fun."

"We will indeed," said Pierce. "Now please go."

"I hope you don't mind a gambling man," said John, leering at her.

"Not if he wins."

"Ah, there's the rub," said John. "Pierce rarely wins. Do you?"

"I goddamned do win," said Pierce. "And you know it."

"Occasionally," said John, his rubbery lips clenching the cigar.

She left them.

Down the grainy, sandy slope, she made her way toward the Bay. Wispy, pale clouds rose about the rich blue water like white birds in flight. The wind had picked up, and there was a heavy scent of salt in the sea air and the raucous screeching of sea gulls. Men in Nankeen tights and straw hats, clutching life preservers, leaped about. An omnibus was making its way down from the hotel, hands waving out of windows, the glistening Percherons trotting in the sand.

A sign announced times for swimming. The men had the water until noon.

How free they all were. The men, the birds.

In the afternoons she read books. He caught her with *Faust* one evening just before supper. "That's not even English," he said.

"No. You're right. It's German."

He grabbed the edge of the book. "Why in the world would you be reading such a thing as that?"

She had no answer for such a question. She just looked at him.

"Goddamn. Can't you think of anything better to do? Here in Newport?"

"What else would you have me do?"

He shook his head. "Have you no imagination?"

"Yes. I do. I'm going back to acting. I've decided on it."

His eyes went black. "The hell!" he cried. "The righteous hell you are."

"Yes. I am, in spite of your cursing."

"Are you trying to antagonize me?"

"Isn't it the other way around?"

"Everything you want to do," he said, swinging a finger at her, "has nothing to do with me. This will change. I warn you. This will, without question, change."

The look she saw in his face was sheer resolve. As though he had settled on taking a rod to his child and that was that.

"Then why don't you change it? Why don't you spend more time with me?"

"Doing what?"

"Doing something. Anything."

"Don't nag. I hate a nagging woman."

"Maybe you married the wrong woman," she said.

He raised a finger. "I'd think you'd act more like a woman. Like a real wife."

"You didn't court a wife," she said.

"No! A madwoman!"

He paced the floor. He stood at the window, looking toward the water.

She watched him.

He finally spoke. "Oh, they praise your acting, but—"

He was silent. He did not go on.

"What?" she finally said.

"You are hardly a woman, hardly a wife! Goddamn it!"

He started to cry.

That evening, the moonlight on the beach was opaque and vague. Up ahead a short distance, a man was leaning into a voluptuous looking woman, his hand now on the woman's waist, his hand now lowering.

There was a jerkiness in the man's movements.

Then the movements stopped, and the couple stood motionless in the sand. Looking in her direction. She left after she'd watched them for a full minute.

Nights they went dancing. She was swept about the floor, in the light of six-branch chandeliers, the walls flickering by in American landscapes of mountains, forests, and rivers. She was passed from Pierce to John, from John to Pierce, to Mr. Wilkerson, to the Colonel. "My dear, but you do dance wonderfully well!" exclaimed the Colonel.

She spotted Pierce, his hands about Mrs. Wilkerson's slim waist, the waltz lifting the gorgeous woman about with such delight and grace that she might, at any moment, float off in the magical flow of musical streams.

In bed he went for her.

"No," she snapped.

"What?"

"No. Go to that woman of yours."

"What woman?"

"You know what woman."

"You'll not," he said.

"What?" she said. "I'll not *what*?"

"You'll not challenge me. I'll have none of it!"

"Oh, but I will!" she cried.

He shoved his fist against her face. He ground it against her lip. "Goddamn it, you shut your mouth!"

She moved quickly away, her lip hurting. She was sure it was bleeding.

"You hurt me," she said. She hated to whimper, but she was whimpering.

"I apologize. But you angered me. You shouldn't anger me like that."

When he again made his move on her, she pushed him away. Hard, she pushed him hard. "You will get me with child," she said.

"Would that be so bad? Would it?"

"For me, it would be."

"This is what I want, Fanny. And I am your husband."

"And so?"

"Don't you say that!" He went for her nightgown, but she again resisted him. She wouldn't let him get close, and then she got up out of bed and sat on a chair in the dark.

After a while his voice came from the bed. "I do hope you will learn to respect my wishes. Like normal wives do."

She said nothing.

"This is a period of transition," he said. "From courtship to marriage. You should think of it that way. I do."

She still said nothing. She stared into the blackness, the quiet. Through the window she could see the lopsided pale white moon.

"Think of Newport in that way."

She could hear him moving in the bed. Then he was standing before her, a hulking male body.

"It shouldn't make a difference *what* I ask, Fanny. You should respect whatever I ask of you." His voice was stern now—harsh.

She felt his hands now on her shoulders. She shoved him away.

"You do what I say!" he shouted.

She was up, dressing now. "I'll do what I wish!"

"You'll goddamn repent of it!"

"I already do!"

Once dressed, she was out of the room and onto the beach, the night sky swirling with a cloud of bright stars.

The next evening in the dance hall, Gabriella was saying to Mrs. Wilkerson, "Will you host your annual party again this year?"

"Of course. The invitations will go out in about a month."

"We're so dreadfully bored in Philadelphia," said Gabriella. "There is nothing there—absolutely nothing." Her white porcelain cheeks seemed about to crack.

"Philadelphia is no place unless you're a Quaker," said Mrs. Wilkerson.

"Quakers don't dance," said John.

"New York isn't everything," said Pierce.

"Well, you've gone there enough," said Mrs. Wilkerson, grinning. "Have you not?"

"What?" said Pierce, sharply.

"One never knows with my wife," said Mr. Wilkerson. "Does one? She's a woman of studied innuendo."

"And yet in spite of it, one must surely learn to see one's way about," said Mrs. Wilkerson. "Mustn't one?" she said to Fanny.

"The light breaks?"

"Well. Surely an actress knows."

"An actress is many people."

"Indeed. But which one is the real one, dear?"

"They're all equally real," said Fanny.

"Oh, my!" said Mrs. Wilkerson. "You *are* a prize." She gave her a long smile. "What is in that actress head of yours?"

She walked the beach, evening after evening. She watched, readying herself. When the light grew opaque, then gradually failed, extinguished like a snuffed lamp, she knew she'd see the two of them. Him, her, their salacious joining, illuminated by the misshapen moon. She knew this: how she'd feel, more and more, the weight of her not knowing—followed by her terrible knowing. She knew the warm breezes off the dark water would soothe yet chill.

4
At John Butler's
Fall, 1834

They entered John Butler's townhouse on a late August evening, after three days of a miserably hot coach ride, and Pierce, leading the way said, "Didn't I tell you it was a fine townhouse?"

He directed her down a hallway, papered in emerald green, with green birds springing into flight. Chinese wallpaper decorated the dining room wall.

They gathered at the supper table: Pierce, herself, John, and Gabriella. Two servants were bringing boiled ham, roast potatoes, and custards. A third was pouring water from a large carafe.

Fanny ate, then excused herself, and went on up to her room. It seemed only reasonable to her that a newly married couple would have their own home and not be forced to live with relatives—and worse, for her, ones who thought she was a hussy, or a tramp.

He had told her only that afternoon, with but an hour's ride left to Philadelphia, about taking up residence at John Butler's.

"What? What about the Major's townhouse?"

"No—that's out."

"What? You promised me. All along. And now you tell me this?"

"Things change," he said. "One must be flexible."

"Oh? Then what about Butler Place?"

"It's not ready yet, Fanny."

But she pushed the matter. She confronted him face to face.

"It's but a temporary delay. Besides, you'll love John's place."

She shook her head. "How dare you?"

It was quite nice, she had to admit, but it wasn't hers. She needed her own place. She needed to make an important connection. She needed to root in like a plant.

Mainly, he had lied. All that time, he had lied to her. What kind of man would do that? What kind of husband would maintain such a lie until almost the last minute?

"How could I be so gullible?" she wondered.

The sky was darkening. Pierce showed up at her door, locked it, and removed his frock coat. "I would appreciate it," he said, "if you would be of a mind." He directed her to one side of her bed. He patted it.

"No, not tonight. I'm much too tired. And it's too hot."

"Even so," he said. He again patted the bed.

"No, please. I must rest. It was a very hard journey."

He frowned and began pulling at her clothing.

"No!"

He motioned a finger at her. "I'll retire without it tonight, but I will surely take it amiss that you are treating me so. After all, I am your husband. Do not forget that, my darling."

"How can I forget it?" she wanted to say. But she didn't bother to respond. She wished him to leave—if only he would.

"As you wish," he said, heading for the door, "but I cannot help but be disappointed. After all, it's been a while. Too long. Much too long."

"I dare say it will be much longer," she wanted to say.

He left, slamming the door, and then she heard his hard boots clomping in the hallway, all the way down to his room. She heard that door slam shut.

"I want the townhouse," she informed him the next morning. "You led me to believe, from the very first, that this was mine. What happened to that promise? I demand an explanation."

"You demand, do you?"

"Yes, I do demand. I have a right to it!"

"I'm sorry, but it will have to be Butler Place."

"Why?"

"Don't be impertinent. Butler Place will have to do. Now that should conclude the matter."

"Because of your aunt?"

He glared at her. "Please," he said, "attend to your own business, and let me attend to mine."

"Isn't it? It's your aunt."

His face reddened. "Yes. Yes. Yes. Now leave me alone about it."

"It was very wrong of you to mislead me like that. How could you do that? I at least want to see Butler Place."

"Not now. As soon as it's renovated."

"And when will *that* be?"

"You are not to question me in that insolent tone about such matters," he said, and went for her arm, but she swung away.

"If you want a willing wife," she said, lowering her voice, "you will take me to Butler Place."

He studied her. He grinned, just slightly. "I can show you all right, but it's not ready to be shown."

"I wish to see it anyway, in spite of that. I think I have a right to see it. And a right to know when we'll occupy it."

"You and your rights," he said, eyeing her.

"You would prefer me to have none?"

"New Year's Day."

"Well?"

"All right," he said. "Fine."

That afternoon, he took her to Butler Place. The carriage pulled up in a drive that circled to one side of the house.

They entered, and she went about it from floor to floor, room to room. She loved the marble fireplaces, but she despaired at the much-needed repairs and refurnishing: splintered molding, broken windows, soiled wallpaper, threadbare carpeting, the brown Rococo furniture worn, faded, and misshapen. All about the place wafted a foul odor of mold and mildew. She felt sick. She felt faint.

But she collected her wits. "I doubt that you can make so many repairs by New Year's Day. Can you?"

"It's all quite minor."

"Then why haven't you done the repairs?"

He bristled. She had offended him, his dignity as the man of the house. "Leave the repairs to me. That's my domain. You can purchase the household goods."

"Oh? Well, I will certainly do that. But I'll need a little money."

"What for?"

"Lunches, and so forth."

"Yes, yes, I'm sure. I'll need a list—of furnishings and whatnot. But not too long. And nothing extravagant."

"Perhaps," she said, "Gabriella can inform me where she purchased hers."

He said nothing for a few moments. And then he glared at her. "Paris—if you must know. When they were there."

"When was that?"

"When their child died."

Something sunk in her chest. She swallowed hard. "Oh, dear God, no."

"Perhaps you've wondered why she's so grim."

He came to her again, and she went ahead and allowed it. She tried not to think about it, looking up at the ceiling as he rammed himself inside of her, and afterwards she was glad to see him dressing, and then leaving her room. "I'm not a cold woman," she told herself, "but I am cold toward a man who's so cold and unfeeling toward me. And why shouldn't I be? What if I weren't cold? What would that say about me?"

~

For a few weeks, she spent time shopping, making lists and redoing lists. She divided her lists into several categories: furnishings, dishes and silverware, linens, and miscellaneous items. She spent whole days in stores, pricing things, comparing, sitting down in cafes to eat lunch all by herself, happy to be alone with her own thoughts. She tried to imagine Butler Place decorated with the finest, a place that was presentable and worthy of guests. She imagined the many guests that might come: doctors, lawyers, judges, the mayor perhaps, men and women of distinction. And, of course, when visitors came from England, actors as well as writers—she would make them feel welcome, acting as a good hostess. She would invite Catharine Sedgwick, Ralph Waldo Emerson, and the Reverend Ellery Channing. Perhaps she would even invite Edward Trelawny—secretly, of course.

But, society or not, at least she would have a place of her own, a place to decorate to her heart's delight.

Thinking of her new life in this way made her feel a little like salvaging her marriage, or trying to. Perhaps she wasn't acting the way a married woman should act. Perhaps she wasn't submissive enough. Perhaps she was too argumentative. She would try to do better. She would try to be understanding. Perhaps if she were more forgiving and gentle, he would be so as well.

Daily, she began to look forward to her new life, come the New Year.

When he came to her room one evening, she handed him the various lists she had made per category. He gazed at them for a moment or two, and then he folded them.

"Is that all?"

"I'll give them some consideration," he remarked.

"I spent a lot of time making those lists."

"As I said, I'll give them consideration. All right?"

He went off. He closed her door.

"Why?" she wondered. "Why? Why trouble yourself?"

She found herself crying.

But it was out of anger, not sadness. "I feel nothing, absolutely nothing, for him in my heart," she said to herself. "But contempt. Yes, I feel that."

She removed her wedding ring and held it up before her. She opened her secretary and dropped it in, among her pen nibs and ink. "Perhaps he will notice the absence," she thought. She sat before the window and watched a squirrel moving along a limb toward her. Across the street were several townhouses. They had no trees growing up before any of their windows, as John's place did. The squirrel was now at her window. "I will feed you," she said. "And we will be friends."

She saw that she must find ways to occupy herself to keep from thinking of Butler Place. Perhaps she could fix up her room.

She went shopping and came back with some colorful cotton fabrics: red, green, brown, and purple. She set about hanging them on the walls—a few to one side of her bed, a few to the other, a few directly over the headboard of her bed—and a few on the wall opposite her bed, placed where she could lie on her bed and take in the color.

How spirited!

He came in shortly afterwards, when she was busy feeding her squirrel.

"My god! What is this? What, Fanny?"

"Why do you ask?"

"Why would you do this?"

"Because I like it. They're wonderfully zestful, don't you think?"

"No. They're silly. This is what you spend your money on?"

"Well, you don't have to like them. But I do, and it's my room."

"No. It's not. It's John's because it's John's house."

"Does John inhabit this room?"

"Look. I want them down, Fanny. All of it!" He tore the red cloth free from the wall by her bed. "Now!"

And then he left.

She took the other cloths down herself since he had ruined what she had enjoyed. How could she feel good about it now?

What is possessing me? She had been shopping again, and now she was dressing in a pair of Turkish trousers. She would soon mount her Forester. She stood before the mirror. *Don't I look a sight?*

She had to laugh, but at the same time, she felt energized.

She knew he would arrive soon, for he must check: Was her room respectable now? Or had she done something else untoward? Had she desecrated it with more garish accents?

"Only what I'm wearing," she said, aloud.

He came in, just when she'd predicted he would.

At first he just stared at her, and then a grin formed.

"What?" he said. "What *are* you doing?"

"It's pretty apparent, isn't it? I'm about to go horseback riding. On my dear Forester. You used to like horseback riding. Would you care to join me?"

He was staring at her trousers. "Are you trying to rile me? Do you wish to annoy me?"

"Tell me," she said, "what is wrong with my trousers?"

His grin went to a laugh. "I think you know. You'll not leave the house in that fashion. Indeed not."

"No?"

"No."

"Well, all right. I suppose, in the future, you'd like to pick out my clothing for me. Would you?"

"I think I'd better." He started to leave, and then he stood at the door. "You know, Fanny, you really are a joke sometimes." He shook his head and laughed. "Go down and show John. Let's see what he thinks."

"Go away," she said. "Just leave me be."

"You are a silly woman. Utterly foolish." And then he left, banging the door.

Perhaps I just need a change. Yes, I do need a change.

She wrote letters to Mrs. Jameson, as well as to other friends in England—and to Catharine Sedgwick: *I am about to drown in a morass of sameness. I must find something of my own in this house where I do not belong. I feel an enervating sense of ennui—and believe it or not, doom.*

She dreaded Friday nights when the Butler relatives gathered in the back parlor.

Pierce insisted she entertain their guests with piano playing or accompaniment. If it were the former, he said, it should be nothing too frivolous, please, and nothing too somber. "Something fitting for an informal gathering. Isn't that right, John?"

"That's right. Something fitting."

"Please, and not too loud," said Gabriella.

Though she liked traditional parlor music, after complying with their wishes on several occasions, Fanny began to feel like a trained monkey. She wanted something more complex, richer. Something passionate, haunting.

One evening she suggested Chopin's Études, Opus 10. She held up the sheet music.

Pierce glanced at it. "I don't hardly think so, Fanny."

"Once, at least?"

He shrugged. "John?"

"If she must."

Permission granted. And so she took her seat at the pianoforte and began to play. She wanted to be alone with the music—entirely to herself. Soon she began to feel it. It was as though the keys were obeying her every feeling, sense, need, her fingers gliding over them, gliding and pounding, pounding and gliding. She had entered a doorway now, a doorway into the music itself. Alone, inside it, she was in a different room, her own room. It was a room full of sound and color. There was room for only one soul here, hers. The others— they seemed to have utterly vanished.

Afterwards, she sat on the piano bench, saying nothing. She could not find the words, nor would they be interested in what she had to say, were she to speak. She felt quite certain of that.

She returned to her chair.

The relatives began to clap. But their applause suddenly ended when Gabriella took a seat at the piano. John joined her, and Gabriella began to play. The two of them sang "I Know a Bank Where the Wild Thyme Blows."

John's ruddy cheeks glowed. Gabriella sang mournfully, as though what she had chosen were a funeral dirge.

"You've had your moment now, Fanny. But no more. Do

please keep this in mind for my sake, and for our guests as well."

"My dear husband," she said, "you couldn't appreciate it?"

"No, I couldn't—and don't. Nor could our guests, in spite of their clapping."

"I'll not bore you the next time."

"See that you don't."

"You're in my room," she said.

"I'll take some first." He pointed at the bed.

"No, you will not."

"Fanny."

"Out!"

"Don't lock that door. I don't appreciate that."

"Then treat me better."

"I treat you just right," he said, with a pained look. "How am I so bad? You make me out to be so bad, but how am I so bad?"

"Please," she said. "I'm going to bed. I'm tired."

"Just like a woman. Not to discuss it."

"What is there to discuss? Have you looked at my lists?"

"I believe I assured you I would."

"But have you?"

"I will, Fanny."

"Why should I trust that you will?" she said.

At that he left and when he was gone, she snuffed out the two Argand lamps.

On Saturday nights, a special guest would arrive, someone important in the community, someone John and Pierce wished to impress.

"You see, Fanny, one does well to make as many business acquaintances as possible. Good ones, my dear."

"I'm sure," she said.

They settled in the front parlor, which was much more decorative than the back. The room had a genteel atmosphere, with etagères filled with glittery objects, gold in one corner, imported Murano glass in the other, and large potted plants rising from the wool carpet accented with Turkish rugs.

One Saturday night it was the Oxnards.

Mr. Oxnard maintained an air of self-importance, though there was something decidedly charming about him, the way he would seem to ponder a question or comment. She liked that meditative look that frequently came over his brow, the way his eyes lifted and dropped as though he were juggling an idea. But more than that, his voice had a smooth, melodious quality to it, like that of a French horn, and Fanny sometimes closed her eyes, just momentarily, to listen to it. She did not wish to appear to be dozing off, so she looked away, as though she had taken notice of something in the room. To her mind, Mr. Oxnard seemed in the wrong profession with such a remarkable voice. She tried to find a word for it. Mellifluous. Yes, that was it. He had character, and he made such a fine physical presence. Would a man such as he like poetry—and not just feign an interest in it, as her husband clearly had during their courtship?

His wife, Molly, though, was grossly overweight and utterly insipid, spending an inordinate amount of time on the subject of silverware. The cleaning of it, that is. The woman went to great lengths to provide a full commentary on its proper care: the many directions one must be sure to convey to one's servants should one wish to keep the "finest ware." The details soon overwhelmed Fanny, and when Pierce asked her to play, she hurried to the piano, but all the while she had silverware on her mind, and she hit a few false notes, which embarrassed her.

"You'll have to ignore Mrs. Oxnard," said Pierce. "None of us is quite clear on why Mr. Oxnard took her as his wife."

"I suppose she had something to offer," said Fanny. "Silverware, I suppose."

"It's certainly a mystery," said Pierce, grinning. "But I do think he regards her as a good wife, a helpmeet of the first order in spite of her offensive appearance."

"Helpmeet?"

"It's a biblical word, Fanny."

"Yes, of course, I know of it."

"I would expect my own wife to be more careful of what she ate," said Pierce. "I cannot imagine such a woman as my wife. And she's only forty!"

"You needn't worry," she said.

"Oh, I didn't mean . . ." he said. And he looked genuinely concerned.

For a moment, she thought, this was the man who had courted her. She warmed to him.

"I took no offense," she said. "I quite agree."

He nodded.

She told herself that she would never be such a boring woman—or so fat. She would not let marriage do that to her. She would do whatever it took to avoid both.

"Tonight?" he said. "Without further delay?"

"All right," she said.

But a few days later, when she once again asked about the lists, he said, "I don't appreciate a wife that nags. If I deem the items on the list to be worthy of purchase, I will purchase them. Otherwise, I won't. Is that clear? I hope it is. I don't wish to be harsh, but a wife, as I see it, must not be so overbearing, but know her place—and I think I have made that abundantly clear enough by now, haven't I? If not, I really do not know what else to say."

Something dropped in her chest.

She felt her face flushing. Her right hand was about to go up, to slap this man, but she gained control. "I think you've said enough," she said. "Yes, you've said quite enough."

"Now then," he said. "The time has come again. Has it not?"

"Go away."

"What?"

"Go. Away!"

He left, slamming the door.

"I'll drive him off to other women," she thought, "but what choice have I?"

And then she thought, "He must repent of his unloving behavior to me. Of his wrongful treatment. I must hold out for that, or I'm a fool. A silly little woman."

She no longer wanted him in that way, not after Newport. She often imagined a different man, him, that dashing adventurer. She had more than once thought of him when her husband was on top of her. But this made her feel terribly guilty. She should not be thinking such thoughts. Still, she could not deny whom she truly wanted. And perhaps, she thought, just perhaps, I will one day have him. It's possible, isn't it? Sinful to think of, but possible.

During her honeymoon in Newport, Catharine Sedgwick had written her a letter which she kept in her locked secretary and sometimes consulted. The letter came at a time when she was wondering about what she had done, about her "great mistake." Catharine had written:

> If you are to be a married woman, you must decide between two opposing poles: that of your husband and that of yourself, the wife. Who will win out? If you lean too much to your own pole, he will depart. Sometimes, of course, that is indisputably the best for a woman. What you must not tolerate is

dictatorial behavior on his part, driving you to his male pole. If you do, there will be nothing left of you.

She had written Catharine back, stating how she did not know what to do. Marriage was a contract. She had signed papers. Her father was back in England. Where could she go? Whom could she turn to?

You can turn to me if you so wish. Come to the Berkshires, to Lenox, before it's too late. Give up this mistaken marital bond. It was not made in Heaven, but apparently in the other place. Do you love him—at all? If you do not, please do not stay with him another minute.

But she had. Perhaps, she had thought, he would change. And now, she thought, come the New Year she would have her own place. Yes, he would want what she did not want to give, and she would have to make concessions from time to time, and perhaps she was making herself a whore in doing so, but she would have a place where she could live on her own terms, separate from him. It was big enough. She could avoid him entirely in that house. But if she went to Lenox, she would be a mere hanger-on, and an old spinster like her poor dead Aunt Dall, God rest her soul.

"You could go back home," she thought. "You could follow your father to England." And then she began considering that. It was an option, wasn't it? And perhaps she would do so. She must think on it more because she would be once again facing that drudgery of acting, acting, acting. "I will settle for Butler Place," she thought, "and he can support me in my artistic endeavors. A patron, he will be. Yes. That's what he will be, and *all* he will be."

On Sundays they attended the Unitarian church.

"I'm not a Unitarian," Fanny had first objected.

"I'm aware of that," said Pierce. "But if you wish to attend church with me, this is where I go and where my family attends. I do assume you want to attend with me." They had pews up front, he informed her, paid for, and therefore he could not consider moving.

"I suppose I must, then," she said.

It was on Tenth and Locust, a spacious octagon-shaped building, filled almost to capacity, with nearly three hundred people.

One Sunday Reverend Furness spoke of his good friend William Ellery Channing and of their mutual friend, Ralph Waldo Emerson. "I see great promise in both of these men," he said. "They are visionaries. We need visionaries in this young country. We need visionaries who are alive to the world around them! We must not stagnate like the Old World!"

And then he paused and spoke very softly. She had to strain to hear.

"There will be things I will be telling you," he said. "But there is a time to keep silent, and a time to speak, as we find in the Good Book. This is not yet the time to speak."

She wanted to speak to Reverend Furness. She wanted to speak to him about Reverend Channing and Emerson, too, but her husband was already on his way back to the carriage.

When the carriage was on its way, she told him how much she liked the Reverend's sermon. Did he?

"I suppose it was just fine," said Pierce.

"That's all you have to say?"

"I don't agree with everything the Reverend says. Naturally."

"What, for instance?"

"Must I?"

"Please."

"Well, dear, I find some of what he says a bit trying, I guess you could say."

"What do you mean?"

"Fanny, Fanny. If you like the Reverend, that's good. That's very good." Pierce let loose a volley of cigar smoke and turned to her. "It's best that you like the man's sermons. For that way, you won't decide to attend a different church."

"That wouldn't please you."

"No, it would not. A husband and wife should be yoked together, and that of course means attending church together. I think others would look dimly on us were that not the case."

"Others."

"Yes, yes, Fanny. Others."

❧

The city rose before her in red and brown against a pale white sky streaked in blue. Carriage wheels rolled and rattled on the cobblestones, splotched with horse manure. The smoke from cigars came at her in blasts. Women in bonnets milled about the shops, and men in top hats hurried ahead with apparent determination. Some bent over to spit. She found this disgusting, abominable. It was American, though, and she'd given some space to this revolting habit in her journal, which, according to her publisher, she should be receiving soon—the galleys, that is.

Black people congregated, murmuring with heavy, indecipherable accents. They would not look directly at her or at other white people. No whites spoke to them.

"They belong to themselves," Pierce had told her. "They belong in Southwark and Moyamensing. If they don't stay put, we'll have some very bad trouble, just like that riot last summer. Keep clear of them. Don't speak to them. This you need to understand. Because it would be a lowering of you to do otherwise."

"A lowering? How is that?"

He grimaced. "You will do just fine if you simply ignore those people."

"Is that biblical? Is that what you learn from church?"

He shook his head. "Fanny. You are a very trying woman, sometimes. How do I manage to put up with you?"

"Please explain yourself."

That stern voice came. "They are hardly people. Dirty, stupid, disgusting."

"They are poor."

"They are black."

"What color would you have them?"

"You have much to learn, don't you? Much. My god, Fanny, when will you grow up?"

"I suppose you're grown up," she snapped back.

She watched as these black people lingered before shops but did not go in. It was as though they were not members of the human race, but of some other species altogether. Her husband apparently thought so. She imagined white men herding them about with sticks, off the sidewalks, into the streets, and out of the city altogether—into the countryside with the animals. And these were free blacks, not slaves.

She was feeding her squirrel friend when a knock came on her door. She opened it to a servant handing her a package. "For you, Mrs. Butler."

"Thank you."

The young woman curtsied.

She took a seat at her desk. She ripped into the package. She was soon looking over her proof sheets.

The door opened. He arrived. He stood peering over her shoulder.

She waited for a few moments. "What is it you want?"

"What is it we have here?"

"We don't have anything. I do."

"A manuscript, it seems."

"Yes, that's right."

"Yours?"

"Yes. A book I wrote, Pierce."

"Book? Is that so? Now when exactly was that?"

"On my tour."

"Your tour. And you said nothing?" He took hold of it. "May I?"

She gripped the pages. She kept her back to him.

"Fanny."

"I suppose. If I must. For a moment." She turned around and handed it to him.

He stood there, thumbing through it. Now and then he would gaze long at a page before moving on, his fingers rubbing the pages.

She watched him, her stomach churning.

He spent a good half hour gazing at the manuscript, taking a seat on the bed, flipping pages back and forth, and then finally he handed it back to her.

She saw that look. "What?"

He shook his head. "No."

"Pardon?"

"No."

"What do you mean 'No'?"

"Just what I said. 'No.' You may not publish this. No, you may not."

"Is that right? Well, I *am* publishing it."

A tolerant, patronizing grin. "No, no, you're not. It would require vast changes."

She gave him a long look. "What changes do you have in mind, Pierce. Do enlighten me."

"Don't be sarcastic."

"Tell me."

"Many. Many! My god, Fanny, I would have to go through it all. It would take time. I received but an impression in so short a space. But it was enough that I was quite displeased."

"Displeased," she said. "You."

"Yes. Me."

"Name one specific thing."

He grabbed the manuscript. "All right, I will." He turned pages. He stopped. "Listen. Listen to this: 'We must hold that slavery is the institution of tyrants. What else are we to conclude?' My god!"

He shoved the manuscript back at her. "Do you want other examples?"

She placed it before her on her desk. "This, my dear husband, is my book, not yours. So, henceforth, kindly keep your opinions to yourself."

He laughed. It was a spiteful one. "Well, darling, you are mistaken. You are very, very mistaken, I assure you."

The next morning when she went for her proofs in her locked secretary, they were gone.

She searched. And searched. Gone.

She hurried down to his study. She banged hard on his door, yelled out his name.

No response.

"Are you in there? Are you?"

The door came open—just a crack. Yes, he had them. Yes, he had taken them from her desk. Did she think she could hide her desk key so well that he wouldn't find it? Of course he could, and *did*, while she slept—*Yes, John, has a key to the door*—and he would soon be finished with the proofs, and he would be up to see her with his comments and criticisms. She must allow him a few hours—perhaps more. Yes, it might be more, so patience was in order—did she understand? Was she comprehending?

"Listen here!" she cried.

"No. *You* listen," he said, swinging a finger at her, "If you make every single one of the changes I've noted, or at least the most important ones, perhaps, just perhaps, you can publish this thing. I cannot make any promises. But perhaps." He shut the door.

She grabbed the handle and pushed at it. Hard, she pushed at it.

"You!" she shouted. "You bastard!"

She hurried up to her room and locked the door.

She would lock this man out. He would never come through that door again!

Later that night, she heard a key turning in the lock, and then a metallic rubbing. In the darkness, she couldn't see who it was, but she saw that there were two of them in the half light of the orange moon. And then she heard John's low, ribald snicker—"Looks like she's ready for you, Pierce."

"*Hush*," he whispered, snorting. And then Pierce's familiar boots clomping on the hardwood.

He was standing now at her bedside. "Are we calm enough now to have a decent talk? Or must we throw yet another tantrum?"

She could see the proofs clutched in his hand, swinging at his side.

She rose from the bed and rushed for the door in her white linen nightgown, brushing against John, and down the stairs. In the dark she almost fell, but she caught herself on the newel post.

In the front parlor she found her way, step by step, to the mantel and the Argand lamps. She carried one of the lamps into the pitch-black kitchen and lighted it. She found leftovers in the icebox—some fresh bread and boiled ham. She ate and poured from a carafe of water.

She wanted sleep, but she would not go back upstairs to that room. If she did, she might meet him on the stairs or the landing. Perhaps, she thought, she could stay up and read all night, but this would mean going back up to her room to find a book. To her knowledge, there was not a library in this house. John and Gabriella were not readers.

Back in the parlor, she stared out the window at the dark night. No stars. The moon was pumpkin orange, floating in a feathery, white mist of cloud cover.

She lay down on the horsehair sofa, and after a while she fell asleep.

Her dreams were unsettled, agitated. She was in a place of blue mist, a slippery place where she felt she could slip, or slide, at any time and go under, under.

She awoke to the sun streaming through the window, making a wedge of light on the salmon and sage tiles of the wool carpet. Her muscles were tight and aching. Her head was throbbing. She crept up the stairs.

Her proofs were stacked loosely and sliding on her desk. She restacked them, banging them top, bottom, and sides, straightening up the pages. She sat down and went through them, shocked at the inky, scribbled notations and sentences, whole paragraphs slashed through, his words replacing hers. She felt violated, like she'd been raped.

The door suddenly opened. He advanced on her, a nervous, jittery grin on his face. "You've seen it—I see. Good . . . it's time we talked, Fanny. Are you ready, finally? Can you control yourself a little now? Is that possible?"

She grabbed up her proofs.

He came at her and tried to wrest them away. "Fanny . . ."

"Go!" she snapped.

"Now, listen here—"

"Go!"

He blocked her passage. "You *cannot* publish that goddamn thing! It is not befitting a lady, and it will be a huge embarrassment, one we can ill afford. And you will certainly take out those ill-advised remarks about slavery, too—oh, do be assured! Oh, indeed you will!"

"You mean *you*."

"What?"

"*You* can ill afford." She pushed past him. She was at the door. She was on the landing.

"What are we to do?" came his cry.

She spun around. "*We* are to do nothing, Pierce. If anybody does anything at all, it will be me."

"I'll go to your goddamned publisher!"

She hurried down the stairs, and out into the city. Free, free, she thought. *Free.*

⁕

Sometimes he was gone for several days, and she was content to be alone. If it was business, he did not tell her about the nature of his business, nor she did ask. She would not inquire about his business, but he must not impose himself on her writing. She had little interest in his business, whatever it was, except she expected him to make enough that he would follow through on his promise to do the many repairs at Butler Place and purchase the new furniture—and purchase the other things she had noted on her various lists. That was the least he could do, given his inexcusable lies.

As to her book, she swore that this man she called husband would not change a jot or a tittle of it. This was her book, and she would edit it line by line to please herself— and, of course, her publisher. But not him. "He has nothing, nothing to do with that," she told herself. "At least I have this, if I do not have a real husband. It's something anyway. Now isn't it?"

She wrote Catharine:

In reading my American Journal, I feel like I'm a second Fanny Trollope. I don't wish to think too highly of myself, but really it seems to combine social criticism with wit. My tone could be harsher at times, but it is, after all, something of a travelogue—if not that entirely. I do like the female voice. I find myself brash at times, but it pleases me so. I find myself lyrical when the mood calls for it. I find myself acerbic when it's fitting. I will send you a copy when it's published, next spring, or at the latest, next summer, according to my publisher. I do hope you like it.

⌒∿⌒

She had moved to the front parlor of an afternoon to play the pianoforte. It was a fine break, she thought, from the labor of poring over her proofs. How laborious that work had become in spite of her excitement at seeing her work in print.

One afternoon Gabriella stood in the doorway. Fanny stopped playing. "Is something wrong?"

"Yes, please. We do not use the front parlor unless we're entertaining."

"Oh. Then I do apologize. May I use the back parlor?"

Gabriella eyed her for a few moments. "Well, you may if you will not be so loud and boisterous. But perhaps back there, they will not hear you three houses down. This isn't the stage, Fanny. It's not the opera."

"I realize that."

"You're our guest. I do hope you will pay us that respect."

"I will most assuredly do so," she said.

On sunny days, the afternoon sunlight gleamed against the red and brown brick buildings to the rear of John Butler's townhouse, and on gray days came rain, fall rain, dribbling down the window panes. This was a second space for her. She would no longer feel so confined to her room.

Sometimes when she stopped to rest from her playing, she could hear a hum of voices, droning from down the hall, from Pierce's study. She opened the parlor door to listen. She heard spurts of furious talk, then short stretches of silence, then more lively talk. She imagined John leaning on Pierce's desk, cigar in mouth, and Pierce gazing up at him, cigar perched in his. Business, this was, the manly sphere, scented with Turkish tobacco, with thick gray clouds of smoke billowing before them.

One morning she heard loud noises like dog barks.

That was John. "Goddamned place!"

She listened for a few moments. She tried to make out what they were saying.

She crept down the hall. She stood outside the study with her ear to the door.

"We're doing fine." That was Pierce.

"Profits up?" That was John, his voice deeper, gruffer. Rowdy, robust.

"Some."

"Could be better, couldn't it?"

"She asked about the overseer. Funny, isn't it?"

"It is. Still interested in what goes on down there, isn't she?"

"I told her all is fine down there—and so no need to worry."

"Old and sick, and you'd think she'd not be thinking much about that—not anymore."

"Won't be long now, judging from appearances." That was Pierce, his voice higher-pitched, with a nasal whine.

"Why does she give a damn about it, anyway? She gets her big fat share."

"Old people. They live in the past."

"Ha! You're certainly right there."

The door suddenly opened, and a blast of smoke hit her. She coughed. She backed up.

"Fanny . . . what the almighty hell are you doing?"

"I've come to see Pierce."

"What?"

Before he could block her, she pushed by him. She was in that study of his for the first time.

There he was with a thick black ledger opened before him, pressing down the pages with his short, stubby fingers, a cigar stuck between two fingers of his right hand.

"Hey, now! What do you think you're doing?"

She pointed at the ledger. "What is that—exactly?"

He rose from his desk. "Nothing to you, Fanny." He pointed at the door. "Go."

"What business is it you're conducting, Pierce? Let's hear it."

He advanced toward her. "How dare you speak to me in that fashion!"

"I do dare. What business?"

Now he was in her face. "A man's business, Fanny, is his own business. Need I remind you of that simple fact?"

"It's not a fact to me."

"It is a fact, and you had best march yourself out that door! Now!"

He had her by the arm.

But she got free of him and was at his desk now, grabbing the thick, black ledger, spinning it around, then taking it up, the pen dropping from the gutter of the book to the floor. She held the ledger before her.

He grabbed at it, but she swung free. "What is this?"

"Listen, you! Give me that goddamned thing!"

"No. I'll have my look."

He was suddenly on her, grabbing her by the neck, but not before she'd already seen the words *Butler Plantation*—

110

and the words *Slave Expenses* . . .

"You're a slave owner. That's what you are!"

"No. I am not."

"Oh? Well, it certainly looks like it to me!"

He stared at her, then at John, who was lingering in the doorway. "I but manage it. That is all, Fanny. Now, march yourself out—"

"Butler," she said. "Butler Plantation. Will you inherit it?"

He took a moment. "Yes, Fanny. I will. Are you satisfied? Is that what you want to hear?"

"It's a terrible sin you're committing."

"The sin," he said, "is yours. Goddamn you!"

She left him there, red-faced, shaking.

She wrote Catharine Sedgwick a lengthy letter. In the final passage, she stated:

> *I have just discovered that my husband manages a slave plantation and that he stands to inherit it. I did not see, until now, just how much of a mistake I really did make. I am fully complicit. I must redeem myself somehow.*

She soon heard back:

> *As to your "mistake," it was, after all, a mistake. To rectify it, you must do everything in your power to bring your husband to an understanding of his guilt in being part of such a monstrous enterprise. Moral suasion is the way. We must believe in it, Fanny. Every man has a soul, and it's just a matter of finding ways to reach that soul. To find the conscience, as it were. It is true that most slave owners, or those who profit from such a horror, are, of*

course, very difficult to reach. But it is possible. Do
the impossible, Fanny. We must believe the impos-
sible is possible.

One late October evening, Pierce came to her door. "Mr.
Edward Trelawny is in the parlor, waiting. Were you aware
of this visit?"

"No."

"Well, John is making preparations. Your presence is, of
course, required—and soon."

She spent a few minutes fixing her hair, and then she went
below to the front parlor. This wasn't real. It didn't feel real.

When she entered the front parlor, two servants were
pouring tea from the tea service.

John and Gabriella sat on the horsehair sofa. She took a
seat by Pierce on the red settee. Trelawny sat before them in
a straight-backed chair. He was a large man, even larger than
she'd remembered. A strong man, one who filled the room
with his remarkable presence.

He looked closely at her for a long moment or two. There
was a knowing smile on his face.

He inquired about everyone's health, about Philadelphia,
spoke of the weather and how it had eased up. October, he
said, was nature's justice. Certainly one needed reparation
after the terrible heat of summer.

"Indeed," said John. "Philadelphia summers can be quite
hellish. Of course it's not as bad as the South." He looked at
Pierce, who nodded.

When an uncomfortable silence followed, Fanny made
mention of Trelawny's book. "Would you speak of it?" she
asked.

"Ah," he said. "Would you, any of you, like to hear of an
adventure on the high seas? Would that constitute permissi-
ble parlor talk?"

"Go ahead," said John. "We'll let you know if it doesn't."

"It must be suitable for women's ears," said Gabriella.

"We shall hope," said Trelawny, "that it is." And he began telling of his attending to the body of the great English poet Shelley on the beach of the Tyrrhenian Sea. He spoke of skirmishes on the high seas. He spoke of an attack in Madagascar against the pirates—and of the princess Zela, an Arabian sheik's daughter, who died afterwards, so tragically.

"How sad it must have been," said Fanny.

"Yes," said Trelawny, "but we find sadness wherever we find beauty. They go hand in hand, do they not? And so one must expect this."

And then he spoke of the Edenic beauty of the Isle of France, Zela's most beloved spot, a faerie land, it was, and how he'd put her remains there on a funeral pyre. He had watched it burn. "Battles I could survive, but that? How could I? How in the world can a man survive such a thing as that?"

His plaintive cry brought glances from both Pierce and John. Gabriella looked on, her porcelain-finish face about to crack.

"Don't you have something more pleasant to speak of?" she asked. "I feel like the dead have been laid out before us!"

"My apologies," said Trelawny. "I do, in fact, have something more than pleasant. I would call it powerful—supernatural, almost."

"Ghosts?" asked John.

"No, I do not want ghosts," said Gabriella. "Please!"

"It's not ghosts. It's Niagara."

John laughed.

"That's hardly supernatural," said Gabriella, her voice brusque. "It's quite . . . beautiful. Isn't it, John?"

"Indeed."

"Even now, I can see it," spoke Trelawny. "I can hear its roar! A roar that never stops. Can you hear it? Listen, if you would. Close your eyes. Listen."

"Of course not," said Gabriella. "Don't be foolish."

"Fanny?"

She tried to. She closed her eyes as the room went quiet. And then something came to her. "Yes . . . yes, I think I do . . . I think so."

She saw it, did hear it. And for a moment, just for a moment, she stood there before it.

"Ah, such a lovely place!" said Trelawny. "I could hardly leave it. I continued to linger there long after everyone else had left. And do you know why?"

"Why?" said John.

"Because, you see, an idea had come to me. It was not an idea a sane man would have, but then by the world's standards I'm not exactly sane. And so here it was: 'I must swim that river. I must swim it.' That's what came to me. Yes, swim it. One would not be so foolish as to swim it above the Falls. One would not be that insane—at least I'm not, but below it, yes, I would think about that. But it's still quite treacherous due to whirlpools that can pull you straight down, swirling, swirling into a watery abyss."

"You jumped in the river," said John.

"Yes, sir, I did."

"No, sir, you did not," said John, grinning.

"Indeed I did," said Trelawny. He lightly rubbed his mustache with an idle finger.

"Witnesses?" said Pierce.

"Oh, yes. Of course. The witness of nature herself. I leapt in and went down deep, deep into that river and felt the mighty pull of it—I felt those cold, unforgiving undercurrents pulling me, grabbing me, yanking me straight toward a whirlpool. It was the river, you see—what it wanted. It does want, you know. We think of it as a mere thing, but the river is not a mere thing. It feels. It feels greatly. It's brimming with life forms, and it's living. It *knows*. It knew me, and it wanted me. But I wouldn't let it have its way, you see. I set about asserting my own power. We do have power, you know—and this is why we live in the first place—to come to know that power. To know our very soul. A man who does not know his soul, that man is a dead man."

Trelawny paused, looking about.

"To know your soul, you must drown yourself?" said John.

Trelawny laughed. "That's not exactly what I had in mind, Mr. Butler."

Pierce was saying something, but Fanny couldn't make it out.

"I once bought a black man out of slavery," said Trelawny. "Name of John. It was a gesture. It was a gesture that felt just right."

"No relation of mine," said John.

"I dare say he wasn't. He was very, very black, sir." Then he rose from his chair.

"Not all gestures are good," said Pierce. "What kind of black man was it that you unleashed on the world?"

"Good. Very good. Better than many a white." He rose. "Now I must bid you all Godspeed."

The Butlers rose. Fanny rose.

Trelawny made his way through the wool-carpeted entrance hall to the outside door.

Fanny followed him out the door, onto the sidewalk.

He touched her hand. "I have something for you, Fanny." He reached inside a traveling bag and pulled out a small package. It was in green paper embossed with butterflies, brown, green, and gold.

"How lovely!"

"I think you will find it a good companion," he said.

He gave her a quick kiss on the cheek and was gone. She saw him step into a hackney cab that had pulled up just a few townhouses down.

She went back inside. Pierce and John were waiting in the entrance hall.

"He said nothing of that visit of his," said Pierce. "Are you sure you knew nothing of it?"

"No. I did not."

"What is that?"

"A present."

"Allow me," he said, and reached for it. But Fanny yanked it from his grasp and quickly took the stairs up to her room, clutching it tightly.

She opened the package, wrapped neatly in white tissue paper. It was Shelley's *Posthumous Poems*, a handsome edition, printed ten years previous, in London. How gorgeous it was. There, inside, on fine stationery, was a note carefully penned in Trelawny's baroque script.

> *Dearest Fanny,*
> *I wish to meet you when Miss Martineau comes to town, which, as you've probably noted in the papers, is very soon. I hope that you will come alone, for then we can speak more freely. And then, perhaps, we can partake of some fine wine at the Hotchkiss Inn. Would you bless me with your company?*
> *Yours affectionately,*
> *Edward Trelawny*

She tucked the letter in the bottom of her secretary and locked it securely away. "Oh, Edward," she thought. "What am I to say?"

❧

She had somehow missed seeing the imminent arrival of Harriet Martineau. She searched a pile of recent newspapers in the entrance hall and spotted it in a brief announcement. Harriet Martineau, writer and scholar, was coming to Philadelphia. This famous Englishwoman, touring America, was not on a tour such as she herself had made but a speaking tour—principally on slavery. On Friday night, but two nights off, the woman would make her appearance.

Fanny quickly made arrangements. She would go alone, leaving Pierce to those visiting relatives yearning for parlor music. His driver would take her in the carriage. She would say nothing to him about it.

Here she was, returning to the Mansion House Hotel, but not as a guest, rather as an attendee. She had never been to the ballroom. How classy, with its apple-green colored walls, white ceiling medallions in the shape of gigantic roses, Ormolu-mounted mahogany sofas, and a few dozen mahogany chairs scooted to the walls to make ample standing room.

She looked around for Edward Trelawny, but she didn't see him.

On a small platform centered in this spacious room was Harriet Martineau, tall, slender, with an imposing demeanor. Several women were crowded about her. A hush had fallen. They waited while the distinguished looking woman stared at them, looking from one to another. Finally, she spoke.

"I will go down to the South. I will go down there and see if I can do any good—any good at all. It will not be safe. It is not safe what I am doing here, in Philadelphia, this City of Brotherly Love! It is not safe for you to be here. But this world is not safe. Nothing good in this world is safe."

A woman was gesticulating at her.

"Yes!" shouted Martineau. "Come! Step forth! Speak!"

Martineau positioned her speaking trumpet in her ear for the woman to shout through. "What kind of good can actually be done with such a system—with its being so deeply entrenched?"

"What can be done?" asked Martineau, removing the

speaking trumpet. "What at all? That's the question before us. The answer is plenty! Good can always be done. You must believe it. Never doubt it. We have powers—powers in us, waiting to be released!"

Much clapping. It went on and on.

Martineau raised a hand, and quelled it. "Powers," she sang out. "Powers of both head and heart."

Fanny felt a touch on her arm. She turned to look, and she faced a woman garbed in a gray cape with a white bonnet, with piercing brown eyes.

"Aren't you Fanny Kemble?"

"Yes. And you—"

"I'm Lucretia Mott."

"Oh, dear God," said Fanny. "I've read about you. I—"

"Bless you," said Lucretia Mott. "Yes, I do make the papers occasionally."

"I'm very pleased to meet you, Mrs. Mott. Of course, I've heard of much of your good work."

"Call me Lucretia. Our local Female Anti-Slavery Society?"

"Yes, of course."

Miss Martineau was now saying, "A woman does not need a man. A woman needs to be directed by her own power, not patriarchal power."

A lull, and Fanny excused herself, then rushed forward and positioned her mouth against the speaking trumpet. "Do you think slavery will end in our lifetime?" she asked, half yelling it at the woman. She felt silly, embarrassed, to be yelling in that manner, but what choice had she?

Miss Martineau looked about. "The question, my dear people, is whether slavery will end in our lifetime, and I must say, unequivocally, that I do believe it will. There is a surge of blood in the people of this country. There is circulation now, and it increases day by day." She pointed. "Look over there, and you will see a valiant worker in the cause—Mrs.

Lucretia Mott, a founder of the Philadelphia Female Anti-Slavery Society. Because of people like her, the spirit of abolition is quickening and quickening. But it may take more than this. It may take a bloodbath to end this terrible inhumanity against our fellow brothers and sisters. That is my prediction. And ladies and gentleman, let me be blunt: If I were you, I would rather see the American Union dissolve than make devilish compromises with slavers. Yes, I know, I am an Englishwoman, but my fellow worker in the cause, your own Mr. Lloyd Garrison, believes the Constitution is a pact with the devil!"

"Thank you," said Fanny, into the trumpet.

"You are most welcome," said Harriet Martineau.

A voice from an enclave of men: "Do you advocate amalgamation, woman?"

Miss Martineau held up her speaking trumpet.

"Do you advocate *amalgamation*?" the man shouted.

"I hear you not!" shouted Miss Martineau, beckoning him to come forward.

"I will not use that ridiculous instrument!" yelled the man.

Miss Martineau tapped her speaking trumpet. "Speak," she proclaimed.

The man shook his head.

And then Fanny spotted Edward Trelawny. He was making his way back to her; then suddenly, he shifted his direction. He approached Harriet Martineau.

"Speak!" Miss Martineau again implored the man.

Trelawny meanwhile took up the speaking trumpet. "Miss Martineau, please speak of the conscience. Tell us of moral suasion, if you would."

A brief pause. Fanny watched as Martineau nodded. Then nodded again. Then: "Ah, moral suasion! Indeed. A man is not a man, but a rock, or a stone, who does not have a conscience. My mission, and it should be yours, too, is to transform that heart of stone to flesh—that is, we must set out to find a soul! That which will animate it!"

"If there is one!" said Edward Trelawny. "Is there?"

"Ah, yes! The big question, isn't it? It is sometimes encrusted in ice, I will grant you. But it's there, I do believe. And so it behooves us to break through that ice."

Lucretia Mott placed her hand on Fanny's. "I do hope to see more of you. I sense something about you, that you are very strong. Resist this evil of slavery, a curse on our land. Resist it with all your soul. A woman of your standing must do this. I'll speak frankly—I do not approve of the theater, but I know you are very educated, and that I do approve of. And so I say again, do everything, everything in your power, to destroy this monstrosity. We could use important British figures like you fighting for our cause."

In this appeal, she had grown passionate. Her face was flushed.

"I will," said Fanny, "if I can only discover how."

"Oh, there are ways."

"Yes? Tell me, then."

"Join our anti-slavery society. We are very busy doing good work. Necessary work with the goal of abolition on the horizon."

"Yes, I know. But I'm not much of a joiner. I'm rather . . . to myself, I guess you could say."

"I wouldn't think of an actress quite in that way."

"An actress can be in her own little world."

"We are all different. Find some way to do something of value, whatever that is."

"Such as?"

"Boycott, for one. Boycott slave products. That option is open to everyone."

"How?"

"Go to Southwark. You'll see places to purchase slave-free goods. If we all did that, where would the profit be?"

"Yes, of course."

"You'll do something," said Lucretia. "Unfortunately, it's not enough merely to be against slavery. We must be weighed in the balance and not found wanting."

"Yes. I know that."

"You'll of course encounter resistance. I must warn you."

"My husband—I just recently discovered that he manages a slave plantation and stands to inherit it. And so . . . I'm at a loss, Mrs. Mott."

"Dear God, no."

"Yes, it's true."

"Poor child. Well, you must do something. Indeed you must."

"I will. If I can. And as much as I can."

Miss Martineau was again holding forth. She was speaking of the certain collapse of this unjust system. "A house with a rotten foundation is bound to topple!" she shouted. "But will we ourselves, each of us, topple right along with it?"

A woman approached her, and took up the speaking trumpet.

"Yes?" said Martineau.

"What do you mean by us toppling—exactly?"

"Exactly this," said Martineau. "There will be nothing of good in us, if we hide our talent under a bushel. Isn't that true?"

"Yes," said the woman. "Yes, it's true."

"Amalgamation," shouted that same man. "Amalgamation, plain and simple!"

Lucretia Mott bid her goodbye.

She was left with Edward Trelawny, who had just approached her.

"Shall we take a hackney to the Hotchkiss?"

They arrived at the Hotchkiss Inn, a three-gabled white-frame dwelling, freshly whitewashed, with a second-floor wrap-around porch.

There he was; there she was.

"I prayed that you would come with me," he said, flashing a smile.

"Was that to God?"

"A sort of God."

He led her, grasping her hand, to a table next to a window. Through it, she could see men and women in eveningwear strolling the sidewalk. In the light of gas lamps, she could make out their faces. She could not hear their voices, but they seemed happy.

Trelawny ordered red wine, bread, boiled mutton, and custards. He spoke of Mexico, of his plans there—hiking up into the rugged mountains, getting to know the locals, eating their food, imbibing their spirits. Wasn't that better, he asked, than returning to England? For his heart was set on Mexico.

"Perhaps," she said.

"I would like to take you with me. Will you go?"

Those eyes. She could not seem to resist them. But she said nothing.

"Will you?"

"How can I?"

"You can. So much, Fanny, so much passes us by as we live out our ordinary lives, doing our ordinary things, seeing with our ordinary eyes, feeling with our ordinary hearts—and there will be much *pleasure* there—in the Mexican heartland, the mountains . . ." He paused. "Do you recognize—?"

"Wordsworth?"

"Yes, of course."

"With me," he said, laying a hand on her arm, "you will always have Wordsworth close by, but this Pierce Butler, what do you have with him? What can he possibly give you? What has he given you? Have you repented your decision? I cannot help but think you have."

She started to say something, but then she didn't.

"Have you?"

"Please," she said. "I cannot speak of this. Don't pressure me."

"Let me speak, then, for the two of us. Because I can. I can see it. He doesn't look at you the way a man looks at a woman he's in love with."

"No? How then?"

He peered at her, and she fell into those eyes, like deep, dark pools of water. He again placed a hand on her arm, gently. Should she resist? Should she move her arm?

"Like a man who's in possession of a woman, and owns her body and soul."

"Mr. Trelawny."

"Edward, please."

She gripped her wine glass. "You know that? You are certain of that?"

"Yes. I am quite certain."

"But how?"

"Do you want this man, Fanny?"

In her mind, she was thinking, "No. No, I do not." But she said to him, "Perhaps I'd better leave."

"You never really wanted him, did you?"

"Edward."

"Tell me. Speak. It will be good for you."

"At one time, maybe. At one time."

"Up at Niagara? Did you want him then?"

His question froze her. "I don't know. I can't be sure."

"A man like him will bury you, Fanny."

"I won't allow it. I will not allow such a thing."

"Fanny, let me take you to a place where there is mystery, enchantment, where the pure air stirs the soul. To the heights and depths. To Mexico. A soul dries up in a place like this. In this dull Quaker city."

"You keep forgetting," she said. "You keep forgetting."

"What, my dear?"

"I am a married woman. I've made a holy commitment."

"Holy? It's an unholy alliance. Is it not?"

And in her mind, she was thinking, "Yes. Yes, it is. How can I deny it? I do not deny it."

"I'm staying here at the Hotchkiss. If you wish to see me, contact the desk manager. I'll be waiting for you, Fanny, dearest."

She nodded. She hadn't told him of Pierce, the slaver. Not yet. But she would. She must.

⌒

She set out early one afternoon. She wore her bonnet because if she came back late, in the dark, it was common wisdom that a woman without a bonnet on at night might be arrested as a streetwalker. How scandalous!

She passed rundown houses, with gray, rotted boards, porches collapsing, windows broken. Trash littered the streets.

She came to a small store, next to a Methodist church rising up on a grassy knoll.

She saw the sign: FREE PRODUCE.

She hesitated. Did she really want to do this? This felt so unlike herself. She did not get involved in movements of any kind. She was ready to offer her opinion, and she was ready to argue a position, but this?

She went in anyway.

A tall black man approached her. He had a kind, smiling face, and he looked at her as though he knew her already.

"Hello, missis—somethin' you a-wantin'?"

"I'm just looking. Thank you." She saw clothing on hooks and pegs, shoes on shelves, dry goods of sundry kinds, including soaps.

"You needin' some sugar, maybe?"

"Sugar—no. I don't know. Not really."

He pointed. "Yes, ma'am. A barrel of it right o'er there. Right there—see?"

He led her to it. She stood looking. She rested her hand on it. They could use sugar back at the house, but only a little, not a lot. What good could this possibly do?

"How about five pounds of sugar for the lady?" said the man. "These here products, they's guaranteed slave-free, ma'am. Means no whippin' went into this here sugar. No black man got big welts all over his back to produce this barrel of fine sugar. Maple sugar, raised up north. Don't it look fine? Be good in your tea, wouldn't it?"

"Yes, sir, it would."

His face went all funny. He looked surprised, shocked. "'Sir'? You don't need to call me that, missis."

"Oh. I'm sorry. I didn't mean to offend."

"Oh, no—no offense, missis. No offense. To the contrary!"

Her face grew hot. "I—"

"It's okay. It's okay, missis. You wantin' that sugar, then?"

She struggled to find her composure. "Yes. Can you deliver?"

"Deliver? Oh, sure, missis, we can. We sure can. We can deliver right to your door. You bet."

"I'll take it, then." She gave him John Butler's address, which she'd written on a small piece of paper.

She paid him.

"Slave-free. You come back now, ma'am. You buy more slave-free. You welcome here."

He seemed so familiar. "Do I know you?" she asked. "I feel as if I know you—but from where?"

He gave her a quick laugh. "No, ma'am. I don't reckon so."

"I think I've seen you before," she said. "But where—I don't know."

"Out and about in the city, maybe," he said, smiling.

"Yes," she said. "It must be. Certainly."

She bid him goodbye and walked back all the way to John's house. Her legs were so tired when she arrived that she had to go upstairs to rest. Supper would be in an hour.

Her squirrel friend was at her window, and she took a moment to open it, then feed him. They she lay down.

It was as though she had passed out. It was as though she could sleep forever.

An absolute darkness seemed about to engulf her.

When a raucous commotion occurred from down below, she could not come to her senses enough to understand it. Loud yelling. Shouts. Outrage. She got herself up and made her way to the door. She opened it a crack, and then all the way—then she stood on the landing. Then she began to make her way quickly down the stairs.

"Now you hear this, nigger. I never ordered that goddamn stuff!"

A patient, high-pitched voice, pleasant but persistent: "The lady, sir, she order it."

"I don't give a good goddamn—lady? *What* lady?"

"Nice lady. I hear she was a real nice lady."

"*I* ordered it!" shouted Fanny, hurrying down the stairs. She pushed past John to collect the box from the black man. He was a different black man, older, and slightly bent over.

"Thank you. Thank you very much."

"You real welcome, missis."

She bid him goodbye and shut the door. She held her box against her chest.

"*You* ordered it?"

"Yes, I did. It's slave-free." She hurried up the stairs with it.

From below came John's shouts: "Well, my God, Fanny! What the almighty hell?"

Pierce confronted her. "This business of slave-free

goods—this has upset John very much. It's an insult. And from a guest!"

"John loves slavery, does he?"

A tolerant, husbandly grin. "Fanny, Fanny. He knows it's the law, it's the custom, and there's nothing we can do about it. So don't try to change him. You'll never do it. Where is that sugar?"

"Over there," she said, pointing at the window sill. The squirrel was gone.

"I'll take that," he said, and he went over to the window and grabbed it.

"What exactly are you going to do with it?"

"Never you mind. Now, that book of yours. Where is it?"

"Why?"

"Let me see it."

"No."

"It's not at the publisher's, is it?"

"No."

"Well, then. I will see it before you send it to the publisher. Understand me?"

She said nothing.

"Did you hear me?"

"Yes, I heard you. I can't help but hear you. All the time I'm hearing you!"

"Damn you," he said, and he left with the sugar.

One November morning, she vomited in the chamber pot. The following morning, she did the same. She said nothing to Pierce, for she must think about this matter on her own.

When he came to her bed, she shunned him. "Leave me alone," she said.

He glared at her. And then a nasty grin worked on his

lips. "Maybe I will."

"What do you mean?"

"Just use your head. Use it for once."

"Oh?"

"Where's your ring, anyway?"

"Where do you think it is?"

"You tell me."

"It's where it is. That's where it is."

"I don't appreciate that attitude. It's quite unnecessary. And it's ugly."

The next morning, before everyone had risen, she packed her trunk. In a light handbag, she carried her book manuscript, her pen, and pen nibs. She took her wedding ring out of her secretary and dropped it in her bag. She left a note on her desk:

> *Pierce,*
> *It is quite obvious to any rational creature that we have made a very serious mistake. We must end this ill-conceived union posthaste. I will send for my trunk. I am returning to England.*
> *Fanny*

She walked out, her bonnet on, carrying her reticule, John Butler's townhouse now behind her. She would begin a new life on her native soil, one not beholden to Pierce Butler any longer, one not beholden to anyone. She would go back and see what she'd see.

The morning air felt cold and damp. After several blocks, she came to a jewelry shop. It was filled with jewelry of all kinds, displayed in glass cases. Elegant looking boxes held elegant looking pieces. Her own ring was not of the finest quality. Her husband had informed her of that fact. "I suppose I could have spent more," he had told her, a few days into their honeymoon. She didn't ask him why he didn't. When she didn't, he said, "But, then, what is a wedding ring, anyway? Really? What is it?"

They'd been fighting, but she couldn't remember what about. She had objected to his tone of voice. Since their wedding, he'd adopted a new tone, not heard even once during their courtship. No, she had not been subjected to that stern, acerbic tone of his, the one that meant: *You are my wife. You are now to listen to me, to heed everything I say, and to obey. Obedience—this is what I expect of you.* This is what that new tone meant. That's what it meant when he wasn't saying that very thing directly.

She stood before the jeweler. He sat at his desk in the light of two flickering candles and studied her ring closely. He was a pudgy-faced man, perhaps fifty, with a thick black mustache. He looked up from his work and squinted at her. "Why do you wish to part with this, ma'am? Are you not pleased with it?"

"Because I have no use for it."

"Why is that?"

"Please. What will you give me for it?"

"Your name, ma'am?"

"Fanny Kemble."

"Ah, yes. I see. But not Kemble, is it? Butler, isn't it? Your husband is Mr. Pierce Butler, is he not?"

"Why is that important? He's no longer my husband."

"Indeed. Why didn't he ask for this ring back?"

"Because it's mine."

"Well, ma'am, I must have his permission to purchase it."

"No. Surely not."

"Yes, ma'am. I'm sorry, but I must know his disposition in this matter."

"Then I'll sell it elsewhere."

He shook his head. "No. I don't think so. I really doubt you'll be able to, Mrs. Butler. I think you'll find it's the same with other jewelers in this city."

"Perhaps. But perhaps not." She dropped the ring in her reticule and left.

She walked about Philadelphia, shop to shop, the ring unsold.

It was now eleven o'clock. She walked toward the Hotchkiss.

Across the street was a restaurant, and she decided to sit and have a cup of hot tea. She chose a seat near a window where she could observe and consider the hotel.

A young woman served her. Fanny stirred in sugar, then sipped.

She sat observing the Hotchkiss. Perhaps that fourth-floor room, two windows from the corner, would be Edward Trelawny's. She imagined being in that room with him. "An adulterous woman, I am. What does the Good Book say? Merely to think such thoughts is adulterous. I am committing adultery in my heart."

An older couple noticed her. The woman said something to her husband, and then she looked again at Fanny. She knew what the woman was thinking: *What is this woman doing here alone? Doesn't she have a husband? Is she decent, respectable? Or is she the other kind?*

I am wearing my bonnet, she thought.

She reached into her bag and removed *Religio Medici* by Sir Thomas Browne. She engrossed herself, immersed herself in it. It was a religious book, one for the soul, a philosophical one, but it was also an exceedingly personal book, and it was as though, at times, the author were speaking directly to her.

She ordered another cup of tea.

She soon stood before the desk clerk in the lobby of the Hotchkiss.

"Some lunch, perhaps?" asked Edward Trelawny.
"Yes, I'm very hungry."

They sat in the same place as before, at the window, and she could see walkers hurrying to and fro from shops.

"You have decided, then? Your trunk—should I arrange a courier?"

"No, not yet. Let me think," she said. "I must think."

He nodded. "Of course."

She thought of her ring—not sold. She thought of Pierce, John, and Gabriella back at John Butler's house wondering about her. She had left a note. She was glad she'd left a note. She thought of her father, what he would think. She thought of her mother. She thought of Aunt Dall, what she would have thought. She thought of Mrs. Jameson. Of Catharine Sedgwick. Of Lucretia Mott, a holy Quaker woman, highly principled.

Still, none of those people could possibly know what it meant to be married to a man like Pierce Butler. A man such as that.

"Perhaps," she said. "But not just yet."

"Ah, Fanny, do allow me to make your life better. You're an Englishwoman. You're not meant for American soil. You're not meant for some Philadelphia aristocrat. Some tyrant. And a dunce to boot."

His hand was touching hers.

"Apparently I'm not," she said. "I know I'm not."

"And so, you must choose. Choose me, Fanny. Choose Mexico. For now, anyway, and then we'll see about later. Perhaps back in England, we'll make further plans. I'll take care of you. You can put an end to all this. But do it now. Wait no longer!"

She let his hand clasp hers. She saw the age in him. And he had killed men. He had taken lives. Although this fact did not show in his eyes, perhaps she would see it yet.

They ate, and he again spoke of arranging for a courier. Her trunk could be delivered in a matter of an hour. He would see to it. And they could then set out by coach and eventually board a ship bound for the South, perhaps Charleston, where they could then take coaches to points south, then west, and on down to Mexico. It would be many days over rugged roads, of course, but she was a traveler, wasn't she? He could see that on their trip to Niagara. She was not like that husband of hers who bellyached at every jostle of the coach. "Remember how we, the two of us, couldn't help but laugh? Remember, Fanny? 'Ah, Mr. Butler. Life demands so much, doesn't it?'"

"I can't go," she said. "I can't go with you."

"Why, darling?"

"I simply cannot. It wouldn't be right. It would be immoral, wrong—evil."

He shook his head. "No, it wouldn't. Evil is what you are suffering under right now. Save yourself. You can still do that, you know."

"No," she said, "I must try to make it better. He was once a good man, when we courted. Perhaps if I were a different woman . . . perhaps. Perhaps he would be a different man."

He shook his head. "It's not your fault. It's him. It's his fault."

"I can't," she said. "And don't ask me again."

"All right."

And then she found her voice, enough that she could tell him what had been on her mind, deeply on her mind. "He's a slaver. What am I to do?"

"A slaver."

"Yes."

He nodded, slowly. "I knew it. Somehow I knew it. I could tell."

"You could?"

"Yes. I could."

"I must leave him," she said. "Somehow."

"Yes, you must. And the sooner, the better."

She was about to tell him about her condition, but she

didn't. She couldn't. Not right now.

Edward Trelawny signaled a hackney.

She boarded.

Out the window, she waved at him. He waved back. How sad he looked. Forlorn. She wanted to go back. She was about to signal the driver, but then she didn't. The cab went on, bumping over the cobblestones.

From downtown, she walked the six miles north to Butler Place and stood there before it, imagining. She paced the yard. She thought of what she might do with it, how she might plant trees, grow flowers, grow vegetables. And upstairs, where that window faced the road, she could read and write. She could write a volume of poetry. And sometime in the following spring, her book would be released. Her first appearance as a writer. It would be published in London, too. An international writer she would be, and perhaps it would make a lot of money.

When she set out for home, it was growing dark, chilly, with a sharp wind. She had six miles to go. When she finally entered the city, almost two hours later, she still had a distance to go, and she was tiring. It had been a long day. She must get there, somehow.

A dead pig lay rotting in the street. A dog barked.

John let her in. "Fanny, Fanny. Fanny, our poor silly Fanny."

She took the stairs quickly, gripping the banister as she made her way up to the second-floor landing. She felt unsteady, queasy. Sick—she felt sick. When she came to her room, she stood outside the door, momentarily, and then entered.

She lighted a lamp and began to undress.

In a few moments, the door burst open, and there he

stood.

"I'm sick," she said. "Please—please do not speak to me. Do not upbraid me."

He came to her. He lay a hand on her forehead. "Surely you *are* sick. But you have embarrassed me greatly in this city, Fanny. I do not know that I can ever recover from it. Why? Why? Why do you treat me so?"

"Unlace me," she said. "And please, please be still. Just please do that."

"I will for now, but we must speak of this matter soon."

"I must sleep," she said.

"Tomorrow morning," he said, "we will speak of it." He seemed to be staring at her from a long way off, but he was right next to her.

"We will not speak of it ever," she said. "And you had better prepare Butler Place. If you want a wife."

"I told you," he said, "New Year's Day."

"It had better be ready," she said. "And I do mean it. I'm soon to have a child."

"What?" he cried. "What? How wonderful!"

"Do remember what I said," she said.

"But aren't you excited? A boy! I know it will be a boy."

"I must sleep. Please go. Please just go."

PART TWO
BUTLER PLACE
1835 - 1838

1
At Butler Place
1835

New Year's Day, a bitterly cold day, their carriage pulling up into the winding drive, with a light snow powdering it. A slant of bright sunlight illuminating the front of the house, making the snowfall glow yellow. In a second and third carriage, six servants following close behind, servants soon to occupy the third-floor rooms.

The house was still in need of whitewashing, the exterior repairs not done, the eaves still hanging down in several places. They stood on the porch. Pierce inserted the key. He entered first, then Fanny. Moments later, here came the servants, six young women giggling and laughing. "Third floor," said Pierce, pointing. "You'll be sharing rooms. Go on up now, my dears."

Off they went.

She watched him. How he watched those young girls.

She went about the house, from floor to floor, room to room. No repairs, and the same threadbare furniture.

Afterwards, she stood in the parlor, looking at the dumpy furniture. A deep sense of despair worked at her. What was that odd smell? It was different somehow than before. It seemed more poisonous. Was it?

He placed his hand flat against her stomach. "My son," he said. "I'm quite certain it will be a boy. Aren't you, my dear?"

She moved away.

"My, my," he said. "It *is* mine, too, you know."

"Not a thing has been done to this house. Not a single thing."

"Well, now. I aired it out. For a full two days."

"What is that smell, then?"

He shrugged. "Give it time, Fanny. I must see about the fireplaces. We have a manservant who will attend to that matter. Oh, and supper will be in a few hours, I'm quite sure. Depend on it."

Repaired or not, newly furnished or not, smelly or not, it was hers. She would get used to it, perhaps. At least she was no longer an unwelcome guest in John Butler's house. But why had he made her wait for four months when he had made absolutely no repairs or changes at all? She knew the real truth, didn't she? He never meant to fix it up. It was all a big lie. But why should that surprise her?

After supper, she spent her evening in the parlor, alone. She felt comforted by the warmth of the fireplace. It was quite pleasant having the piano right by the window, with a view of the snowfall. She felt at peace. Soon she would go up to her room, where the fireplace would also be ready.

The next day more snow.

And the day after.

For three whole days, it came in heavy, wet flakes, the sun glistening on it, filling it with a soft light. She went out into the front yard and scooped up handfuls. There was a joy in it. How pure white it was, covering the roof of the house and the barn, filling the limbs of the pines beyond the fencerow across the road, covering the fence railing—and the sheer stretch of it from hill to hill.

The snow let up for a few days, and then more came. And still more. The roads were impassable. The outside world had shut them in, but she loved the feeling of being immured in the house with her books and writing. Her husband lived one life in his study on the first floor, she another in her room on the second, with a window facing Old York Road. It was just as she had imagined.

She had turned in the galleys to her book shortly before coming to Butler Place, and so she had settled that matter. He knew nothing of it. It was her book, and she had kept him from meddling in it, ruining it. In that, she felt a great accomplishment.

A new life lay before her. She would enjoy it somehow.

After all, not only did she have her own place now, but she had a child coming that would make her happy. "I will educate this child," she told herself. "Whether boy or girl, it will be strong, and it will learn to do justice. It will most likely live long enough to bring in the new century, when things, one hopes, will be better." No slavery by then, she thought. Surely, no slavery by then. How awful to feel so compromised—so complicit. It felt like a cancer in her soul. She must, like the surgeon, cut it out from her very being—but what would that take, short of getting her stiff-necked husband to renounce any part he played in this terrible thing—and especially his inheritance? How unlikely that was, and so meanwhile, how could she feel right about anything with the underbelly of her daily existence so rotten, so wicked? She had never felt that way in England because it was so far away, so remote. But no longer—not here.

Still, she thought, I must find happiness in spite of this.

The snow tapered off, then stopped, and the snow plows came. From the front parlor, Fanny watched as they cleared the roads, the snow swirling in the morning sun, the horses pulling hard, their nostrils steaming in the cold air, the drivers cracking whips. She opened the front door and, one foot at a time, stepped carefully over the porch, then down the steps, and into the yard, and trudged to the end of their carriage drive, which the snow plows had left clear of piled snow.

She looked up and down the road.

South was Philadelphia, the theater, shopping, and restaurants. She longed to go see a play, shop in a bookshop, or sit in a restaurant. Even though she loved being in the country, loved the space and the quiet, she couldn't help miss being in the city. But she would find a way to go as much as she could. She would walk the six miles if need be and the six miles back. Hadn't she already proven she could? Yes, she was presently with child, but at some point, not all that long from now, she wouldn't need to depend on her husband, or even a servant.

On Sunday, they took the carriage to Philadelphia to attend the Unitarian church. Fanny sat on two quilt blankets to protect her and the baby from the hard bouncing against the rutted, snow-packed road.

The Reverend Furness preached on the subject of renewal. His cadences continued to delight her, and she thought him a poet, with a grandiloquent voice. He spoke again of Emerson, a friend from his youth. "Ralph Waldo Emerson has a vision, my friends—a vision of newness. He is presently writing an essay called 'Nature.' When it's published, you can be sure I will read it! Devour it whole!

"Think of it this way: Each day is a new beginning. Life itself is a new beginning, once we align ourselves with Universal Being, circulating in us and in Nature. I capitalize that word, as does Emerson. It's a matter of each man's coming to know his own, unique vision. We seek a vision, we must each of us do this, and we must make sure that our range of vision is wide, and yet not diffuse."

Then he leaned against the podium. "What is beauty? What is the ideal? What is justice? What is the nature of the good? All the great thinkers from the past have posed these very questions. And we still pose them today if we're thoughtful, do we not?"

His soft eyes rested gently on the congregation. He paused for a considerable time. He looked about. And then he said, "Is slavery just? Is it? Search your soul. Is it right to own another human being? To extract labor from this human being as if they were but a horse or an ox?"

He waited, with his eyes once again moving across the congregation, now and then resting on one section, then on another. He was now looking at her, and then at her husband.

"And in owning another human being, what atrocities do we commit? Are there any limits?"

Afterwards, Pierce hurried her out to the carriage. "It looks like more snow. We must get back to the house."

But snow did not come immediately. A week went by, and then it came, and came again, giving her whole world an unreal feeling. So much white. So pure white. By February, snow lay two feet on the ground. "I don't know what to think of it," she thought. "It stirs my soul. I try to understand it, but I cannot. I feel I'm in the presence of sheer being, and I am overwhelmed—yes, overwhelmed."

She wrote Catharine:

> *I sometimes feel buried. Perhaps the snow will rise to the tops of the windows, and in that case, I will be. Or to the top of the house itself. The baby will be coming in May or June, my doctor informs me. By then the world will be luxuriant with green—the grass, the leaves springing forth life on the trees, and the lilacs blooming. How I do long for that. Am I not always wanting change? If cold, hot. If hot, cold. Surely I am a restless soul. What does it take to satisfy me? But in that, am I not human?*

She wrote in her journal:

I fear childbirth. Perhaps I will die. Perhaps this time next year, I will be buried under a foot of snow. Or more! But no, I must not think such thoughts. I must be courageous. I suppose I must see it as a test. Will I pass?

Spring arrived with cold, wet weather. It had been raining for three days straight, a steady drizzle. The roads were mud and muck. Fanny stayed inside, in her room, trying to stay warm, tending to the fire, sipping tea. Her window view of the road worked at her.

She wrote in her journal:

I have trouble composing poetry with this view of a drenched world. This steady drizzle is like a wetness in the heart, only to be redeemed by the promise of summer. How I long for that more than anything. But then I think of my lot, and then the lot of others. I think of those seven hundred souls down there on my husband's plantations. He claims their lot is easy. "They have a very kind overseer," he says. And so, yesterday, I asked him: "Do they look forward to sunny days with blue skies?" His answer: "Don't bother me with your impertinent meddling. They are who they are. They know their place and they don't expect more. It's as simple as that."

She had been saving newspaper articles on the subject of slavery. She locked them away in her secretary to keep them from her husband's prying eyes.

Pierce came down with a bout of rheumatism.

He entered her room, moaning. "Cod liver oil, please. I must have it. I must have something."

"Check with the servants," she told him.

"I'm unable. I can't move."

"Stay, then," she said, directing him to her chair.

She went downstairs, where she noticed Jane Hannigan dusting. She directed her to look for the needed remedy.

Jane looked about in the cupboard. After a few moments, she shook her head. "We have none."

When she entered Pierce's room, he lay there whimpering. "It's going to kill me. I can't do a single thing. It's going to kill me."

"What exactly do you want?"

"Some cake and tea, please."

"I can't take those stairs again, Pierce. I really cannot. I'm with child, or have you forgotten?"

"But I need something. I desperately need something."

She stood on the landing, deliberating. Well, she guessed she could. There were so many steps, and a woman expecting had to watch each and every one, and for the past few days, she had felt woozy. She gripped the banister hard. She took one careful step, then another.

There was Jane Hannigan again. She told her to bring cake and tea up to Mr. Butler, who was not feeling well. Where were the rest of the servants?

"Molly's not feeling well. The rest are cleaning."

"Where is Molly?"

"In bed. Shall I tell her you want her?"

"No. Certainly not. We must not disturb her."

"Yes, missis," said Jane.

"You needn't call me 'missis,'" said Fanny. She tired of having to telling the girl this.

"Fanny."

"Yes, that's right—thank you."

As she so often did, she recalled Pierce's warning about this matter of familiar address. "You will get no respect from a servant who calls you by your first name, I assure you. Don't you realize that?"

"Even so," she had replied, "I loathe being called missis."

"As you wish," he said. "If you won't listen, I suppose that's your prerogative."

Back in their room, Pierce started to sit up, then fell back on the bed. "It's here, here, and here. It's here too," he said, grasping his knee. "And here," he said, gripping an ankle. "It's like I'm being broken on the wheel."

"Dear God—if you would, I'd prefer not to think of such a thing as that!"

"But it's true."

"Act like an adult. And quit complaining so much."

He glared at her. "You don't show once ounce of sympathy, do you? Not one."

"You will be better soon, I'm sure. If a servant takes ill, will you give this person time to rest and heal?"

He laughed. "Servants have all sorts of excuses, Fanny. Most of which you cannot trust."

"Then I suppose you'll not want to hear that Molly is lying in bed sick."

"Sick, is she? Well, I'll deal with her later."

When Jane Hannigan arrived with the cake and tea, Pierce sat up in bed and reached for the tray she held with her pretty, girlish hands.

The young girl settled the tray on his lap, balancing the cup, with the steaming hot tea. "I hope you feel better, Mr. Butler . . ."

"Thank you, Jane."

She blushed. Those blue eyes, how they flashed.

"You're a good girl," he said, and lightly touched her hand.

144

"Thank you." She gave him a quick curtsy, then left.

He began to eat his cake, staring at the door.

"She's gone, Pierce."

He grinned, shaking his head. "She's such a sweet little child," he said.

In a week's time, Pierce went back to his study. Fanny began reading and taking notes on William Ellery Channing's recently published pamphlet, entitled *Slavery*, which Catharine had sent her. Step by step, Channing set forth why slavery was unequivocally wrong. "He cannot be property in the sight of God and justice, because he is a Rational, Moral, Immortal Being; because created in God's image . . ."

One has one's duty, stated Channing, to oppose slavery with its myriad forms of shocking cruelties. And she now thought: "If I cannot join an abolitionist group, being heavy with child and six miles from the city, I can at least write my own defense of the abolitionist position." This, she saw, would amount to much more than the sporadic comments she had included in her journal. If she couldn't boycott slave products, with her husband managing the purchase of all their store-bought goods, she could at least urge the purchase of slave-free products. And eventually, she thought, she would somehow purchase them herself.

She spent long days rereading her backlog of newspaper clippings, writing, and thinking. She scratched through several drafts of an argument and finally, with a new pen nib, produced one that pleased her. It was in a careful, neat hand.

She wrote Mr. Carey. Could he possibly publish her anti-slavery piece, herewith enclosed, simultaneously with her journal?

In but a few days, he replied:

Dear Mrs. Butler,

Indeed, we would be interested in publishing your anti-slavery piece. But I do feel I must apprize you of the fact that doing so could be dangerous for our publishing company as well as for you, the author. There could be serious repercussions. Only recently, in New York, as you might recall, a mob hurled Mr. Arthur Tappan's furniture out the windows of his home and burned every bit of it. Mr. Tappan is a prominent citizen. Yet one must face one's fears. We respect your work and your conscience, and you will not find that our publishing house is too fearful to do the right thing.

Now, I feel I must take this present opportunity to apprize you of another occurrence. I feel it incumbent on me to do so. I have been remiss, I fear, in not informing you about a particular action your husband took several months back. To wit, your husband declared all proceedings from your book to go to him. When he came to me last year offering me money to cancel the contract, I refused to do so. The contract is binding. Since then, I have been debating whether or not to enter into a fray between husband and wife on a monetary matter, but by law, the money is your husband's. I regret having to inform you of this fact, yet I feel obligated to do so. This, I am sure, is not pleasant news to an author, but given the law, I am constrained to follow it.

I trust that you will understand. I greatly regret having to be bearer of this bad news.

Your humble servant,

Mr. Henry Carey

Carey, Lea & Blanchard

She saw now what had happened. She saw now why her

husband had not bothered to mention the book again. She was on her way down to his study to inform him that, legally or not, she would not permit this wholesale thievery of her earnings—and then she stopped herself. Why give him the pleasure? There would be other ways, surely, that she could settle things. She would study on it. She would devise a plan that would even the score. She would not be the victim of such high-handed treatment! "You think me so weak, do you? But I am not weak. And you shall find that out."

※

In late May, on a bright, sunny day, she felt the cramps coming, and she knew. The time had come. She sent Pierce for the midwife.

She lay in bed waiting, hurting, the pain building. It was four hours before the midwife showed.

The midwife gripped her hand and then said, "Let us see how we are advancing." She pulled Fanny's nightgown up and examined her. She said, "It may be some time yet. Your husband has asked for hot water and cloths, and these will be brought up to me soon."

The woman sat down at her bedside and watched her.

She was a Quaker woman.

Jane Hannigan brought up the cloths and a pan of heated water.

The midwife said, "Put them right there." She motioned at the night table where the lamp light was flickering.

Fanny went into a spasm of pain, gripped the cover, and let out a prolonged cry before it ended.

"This is all to be expected," said the midwife. "You must accept this as divinely ordained. It's a trial, and a tribulation, but afterwards you will have a beautiful child."

"Hold my hand," said Fanny, "the next time—please."

"I will," said the midwife.

It came again. She felt the grip of the woman tightening against her palm as her paroxysm of pain became worse and worse, and still worse, and then subsided, and she breathed finally, and the woman let up, and removed her hand.

"Thank you. How kind you are!"

"God will bless you," said the midwife. "I am certain of it." She rubbed Fanny's forehead, just lightly. She wiped it with a damp, lukewarm cloth.

She felt comforted. There was something about this woman, the way the light streamed through the Venetian blinds, refracting, and causing a glow that lit up the woman's face—this made her think of a divine light, a glow of God's very presence. She felt comforted. Her eyes filled with tears.

It went on and on. And on. It grew so much worse that she began to think of this midwife as part of the pain itself, of the feeling of being ripped apart. There would be nothing left of her body, of her. The baby would come, but she would be lost, lost, lost to utter blackness.

"I cannot abide this," she thought. "I cannot endure it. Not another moment of it. I cannot stand this torture!"

"Push, push," said the midwife, sternly. "You must push!"

"I can't!" cried Fanny.

"You must," said the midwife.

She kept at it. All night, all the next morning, and late into the next afternoon. Such misery, such horrible, terrible misery. "No one deserves to suffer like this," she thought. "No one! Dearest God, why do you punish me so?"

On the evening of the second day, the baby came. A girl. She was so tired, exhausted, everything in her utterly weak. She could hardly feel a thing. But she wanted her baby. She must have her baby. She motioned at the midwife. She could hardly speak.

The midwife brought the baby to her, and she held it against her naked bosom. "I will always, always love you," she whispered to the baby. "You are mine, and I will always, always love you."

"What will you call the baby?" asked the midwife.

"Sarah."

"A fine name. For Sarah of the Bible?"

"Yes."

"No. In fact, it's my mother's name," said Pierce. He stood to the side of the midwife, staring at her, and then at the baby.

"Oh—I see."

"Sally," she said to the baby. Such beautiful blue eyes! Such dark hair! Such perfection!

"Sally?"

"For Sarah."

"Oh, no," he said. "No, I don't think—"

"Yes," she said, glaring at him. "She's mine. I suffered enough to name her what I want. She is Sally, not Sarah. I will refer to her as that. Do you understand?"

He said nothing, but she saw that look. It was a look that told her he did not intend to let her have her way. But it didn't matter because she would have it, regardless.

Here it was early June, and when she stepped to the window with Baby Sally, breaking her doctor's lying-in orders, she couldn't help but be enlivened by the sunlit morning, the green grass, a breeze scented with daisies and clover making the curtains billow before her in the open window.

She lay on her bed rereading Channing's pamphlet on the wrongness of slavery, marking key passages and taking marginal notes.

The doctor stepped in, with Pierce close behind.

He bent over her and took her chin in his hands. He gripped tightly. Then he placed his wide hands on her cheeks, again gripping, and stared long at her. He relinquished his hold and stood before her. He motioned at her pamphlet, reached forward, and took hold of it. "Ah, what have we here?" He squinted at it and turned pages. He stopped and looked long at it. Then his eyes leveled on hers. "My! My! I would not think a woman who has just given birth would find this material tolerable reading. I must say, I am rather shocked."

"Why is that, Doctor?"

"Because. It's too much of a stress, a strain. Is it not?"

"No, sir."

"Well," he said, handing the pamphlet to Pierce. "I'll leave the matter to your husband." He winked and reached to shake Pierce's free hand, and then he was gone.

Pierce scrutinized it. He shook his head. "How disgusting. What must the doctor think?"

"Think? He knows, I take it, that at least one of us finds slavery an appalling, wrongful thing. Give me my pamphlet."

"I should burn it."

"Give it to me!"

He threw it across the room. It hit the wall and landed on the floor, the pages splayed.

She got out of bed, bent over, and picked it up. Suddenly, she felt like she'd injured herself.

One morning two servants delivered a crate, set it on the floor by her bed, and pried open the top.

Finally. Here it was, her own book, with a dark red muslin cover, published by Carey, Lea & Blanchard. 1835. Author: Fanny Kemble. And here, too, was a stack of pamphlets, her anti-slavery piece, all here, and released to the world.

In a week, she received a letter from Catharine:

Your book sold eight hundred copies the first day in one New York bookstore alone! It is certainly a sensation. I would not be too depressed about the reviews. I know they are not favorable, but this is a matter every writer must deal with—on each and every book. The pamphlet? You have officially joined the abolitionist movement, my dear friend! And I see that Lloyd Garrison has run your piece in The Liberator. *How wonderful! The Reverend Channing sends his highest regards. He is distributing it to his congregation.*

Catharine had included several newspaper clippings. Fanny read through the reviews of her book, rushing through them. Fragments flashed at her:

Vulgar, with writing not fit for a genteel lady.

Not worthy of her gender

Not worthy of her class.

Even the young Victoria, an English woman of the highest rank, scorned her book as unbefitting to her high station as England's most notable of thespians. She stated: *What would the noble Sarah Siddons, if she were alive today, say in regards to this particular production?*

I have been sabotaged by my own countrywoman! Fanny wrote Catharine. *This could send me to bed for a month! Why get up? Why rise to meet the day?*

But there was one from Mr. Edgar Poe, in the *Southern Literary Messenger*, which was a mixed one. On the one hand he lauded her "vivacity of style," but then—how contradictory of him!—he found it quite unpleasing for her to use such coarse words as "dawdled," "gulped," and "pottering."

"Is that not vivacious, Mr. Poe? But then, am I not ladylike enough for you? For any of you?"

"Well," she thought. "Well. Perhaps I am not a lady. Perhaps you are expecting something I cannot give—that I will not give. You take exception to my voice? You wish to fit me to a mold, to make my voice like all other female voices? You wish to tame me, do you? I will not be tamed!"

⌒∾⌒

One evening he came to her red-faced, his jaw trembling. She smelled the stink of alcohol on him.

She gagged.

"Fanny, goddamn it! Do you realize what you've done! 'Nigger lover!' That's what they're calling you! And me—married to a nigger lover! Having a wife like you—so goddamned uncontrollable!"

His voice was breaking.

"I am speaking out for justice," she said. "That's all."

"*Justice.* You want them to burn our goddamned house down?"

She was still in her lying-in, and she wasn't up to it. She had no defenses. Here he was lording it over a woman who wasn't ready to do battle, still enervated by giving birth, and already half-sick with despair. "Please," she said. "Please, just please—"

"Please *what*?"

"I am very weak. I have just given you—"

"A baby? A goddamned baby! Why couldn't it have been a boy? That's what I wanted! Why can't I ever get what I want—ever? You tell me!"

"You don't like little Sally?"

"Don't call her that!"

"I *will* call her that. That's her name."

"No, damn it—it's not!"

"You have no say in this matter. None whatsoever."

"Trouble!" he cried. "That's what you've given me. Trouble! Nothing but trouble since the minute I met you!"

"Married me?"
"Yes!"

Darkness falling. She awoke. Where was she?

What was that noise?

Then she saw: There he was in the deep shadows of her room, bending down. Breathing, breathing heavily. Snorting.

Now he had something up against his chest. Her crate of books.

"Goddamn."

"What are you doing?"

"Goddamn it."

"No! You put that down!"

"Put it down . . . put it down. Sure! Sure I will . . ."

He got out the door, onto the landing, then made boot noises down the stairs.

She got up, going after him. She got down to the first floor and made it to the front door. She stepped on the porch, gripped the railing, and then moved as quickly as she could off the porch and into the grass.

Her knees felt weak, like they would buckle.

The smell of smoke was strong here, and she knew. In a few moments, she saw it: a huge fire, her husband standing back, flinging things into it, feeding it.

"Dear god!"

She advanced on him, too fast, causing her to stumble. She fell flat. She lay there, sure she was injured. Then she pulled herself up, stumbling again. Now she came right upon him, flinging her pamphlets, and she tried to shove him away.

He shoved her back.

She started to topple over, but caught her balance.

There, on the ground, was her crate of books.

She went for it.

But he suddenly had it, circling around with it, blocking her off. Then he moved toward the fire and flung it in. It landed on a pile of burning pamphlets.

"Now!" he shouted. "Now! Right there! See? See it? Goddamn it—do you see it?"

"You can't burn them all."

"What?" His face was rollicking red.

"You. You are a horrible bastard!"

❧

A few days later, Miss Hannigan came to her room and presented her with a card. "A Mrs. Williams is awaiting your presence in the parlor."

"Is that so? Well, I'm hardly presentable."

"Should I tell her—?"

"No. Tell her I will be down momentarily."

"I will, Mrs. Butler."

She began to brush her hair. What should she put on? A cape?

"Now I look like a matron," she thought. "How staid this attire!" But at least it was a light green color—the color of summer. "Still," she thought, studying herself in the mirror, "I do not like the way I look. Fat, plain, matronly."

She knew who this Mrs. Williams was. She knew what to expect, having read about her and her organization in the newspaper.

When she entered the room, Mrs. Williams rose. She was a heavyset woman in her fifties, with plump, rosy cheeks, and a massive bosom. She wore a chocolate brown day dress with matching shawl. She looked ultra-conventional. The woman wished her good morning and hoped she hadn't come at an inconvenient time.

"No," said Fanny, "it's not inconvenient."

The woman began by asking about the baby, and Fanny, hoping to hurry on, made short work of that, assuring her that the baby was just fine, thank you.

Molly appeared with the coffee service, with cream, sugar, and napkins. This she knew to do, and yet it would extend the meeting. It was necessary, of course, to learn Mrs. Williams's disposition on sugar or cream—or should it be both? The woman was quick to choose cream, and when Fanny chose cream also, this prompted Mrs. Williams to say: "Ah! It appears we have something in common, then, do we not, Mrs. Butler? We both take cream in our coffee!"

Fanny said nothing.

Molly curtsied and left.

"Such nice summer weather. Isn't it quite pleasant?"

"Yes, it is. Very much so."

Mrs. Williams adjusted herself on the scuffed rosewood settee. What must she think? But Fanny didn't care.

Mrs. Williams now fixed her eyes on Fanny.

"Yes?"

"Mrs. Butler, I've spoken to your husband, and he has suggested that I see you—about a particular matter. And so I've come to do so."

"Indeed."

"Yes, ma'am. I've come to collect for a very worthy cause."

"Oh? Which cause is that?"

"The American Colonization Society. You've heard of us, I presume."

"Yes, I have."

Mrs. Williams held her coffee cup, positioned on her saucer. "Our local chapter is particularly disturbed by the rioting last summer. We feel that colonization is the best measure to address such a problem. Western Africa, as I'm sure you've read—this is where we're sending them. But it's an expensive undertaking, and the Society does need ample funding. And so I come to you seeking a donation for this good cause."

She took a sip of coffee. Her chubby hand gripped the cup.

Fanny shook her head. "Thank you for your visit, Mrs. Williams, but I do not wish to contribute to this cause."

"Pardon? May I ask why not?"

"May I ask why you wish to send black people to Africa?"

Mrs. Williams drew in a large breath. "Yes, of course." She set her coffee cup down. "Yes, you should indeed ask before making a donation. You must, I quite understand. The Pennsylvania chapter—"

"No—please. I'm well aware of the Pennsylvania chapter and its goals, Mrs. Williams. But you—why do you yourself wish to send these blacks to Africa, a country they've never known."

A pause. A pursing of the lips. "Mrs. Butler, surely you know."

"Please remind me."

The woman's lips trembled, or appeared to do so. But then she seemed to gather her resolve. "If you will but permit me to do so. You see, it is the thinking of many rational discussants on this subject that these people, if you could even call them such—well, they can never acclimate themselves to American ways. To civilized ways, that is. How can they possibly do such as that? It boggles the imagination, does it not?"

"They certainly can't if you send them to Africa."

Mrs. Williams laughed and raised a napkin to her lips. "My, but you are very witty, Mrs. Butler. And being an actress, I would expect it. I saw most of your plays here in Philadelphia, incidentally, and I enjoyed them very much. I even saw you in New York once when Mr. Williams had business in that city. You were quite—well, invigorating. I must say that I thoroughly enjoyed them. As did Mr. Williams."

"I'm glad you did. Thank you."

"You are an actress par excellence," said Mrs. Williams.

"That's in my past, of course."

"Yes—now that you're married. Of course. But to answer

your question, Mrs. Butler, for my own part, I hold that there is an element of moral laxity in these people that contributes to their criminal behavior. What if this spreads and influences . . . do you gather my meaning? It was an unfortunate set of circumstances that brought them here in the first place, the peculiar institution, I am quick to grant this, but now, having no solution to this matter, there is little else we can do with them."

"Sweep them away, then?"

She smiled. "Ah, again, the witticism. But truly, Mrs. Butler, free blacks do present a danger to the city and even to outlying areas, as we've recently seen. And were they to creep further, you see—"

"I do not wish to contribute to this cause, Mrs. Williams."

Mrs. Williams nodded. She raised her coffee cup for a sip. "Very well. I don't mean to pressure or impose—or offend. But you see, your husband—"

"My husband doesn't know everything. There are, in fact, many things he does not know. Or wish to know."

Mrs. Williams took a moment or two. "Umm. I see."

"It's a very bad idea. The answer is employment and opportunities for these poor people."

"Amalgamation? But how? Reasonably speaking?"

"Perhaps you should put your efforts into that question."

She grimaced. "My coachman awaits me. I must be leaving soon. But I do wish you well in your new home, and I wish you well with your new addition. My visit's purpose was threefold—to make those two wishes and to collect for the Society."

"Thank you."

Mrs. Williams slowly sipped her coffee and then set down her cup, gingerly. She rose. "Do keep us in mind. Perhaps you will see things differently at some point, and then, assuming you do, please contact me for a donation."

"I am quite certain that I will not."

Mrs. Williams's face now grew red. She began to shake. "But Mrs. Butler, they are inferior in so many respects— to say the least—these blacks! Don't you see that this is a very serious, an absolutely terrible, problem we have on our hands?"

The woman had grown strident.

Fanny gathered herself. "*If* they are inferior, it's because of what has been done to them. Do you dispute that?"

"But nonetheless, they *are* inferior, and how can they ever be ordinary, decent citizens? I do not think they can. I cannot imagine a way that this is possible."

"How would you have them be?"

"Civilized."

"Perhaps if they were white?"

The woman's eyes grew large. "Well, dear, I suppose my coachman is getting anxious. I must be getting back."

"Good day to you," said Fanny.

"Mr. Williams says his wife visited you yesterday."

"Yes, she did."

"They're prominent people in the community, Fanny."

"Is that so? What is it you are trying to say, Pierce?"

"You would not contribute to her cause. I suppose you think you can outwit me. But you didn't—and you can't."

"How is that, my dear husband?"

"I did so in your name, my dear wife."

"What?"

"Yes. I did. And so, you are now a contributor to that cause."

"You horrible—!"

He grabbed her. She shoved him away.

"You want to drag us down in the dirt!" he shouted. "That's what you want. But you won't!"

"We *are* in the dirt!"

She decided to speak out against this matter of colonization. All morning, she worked away at an editorial for the local paper. She made three points:

Colonization isn't emancipation at all, but deportation.

It's man-stealing, unless one chooses it, but how can a poor black person really know what he or she is agreeing to?

Colonization is meant to keep down the number of free blacks, perceived as a threat to that horrible institution of slavery.

On this final point, she wrote that free blacks were, after all, a living symbol of freedom, and they could also work to free their enslaved brothers and sisters. She wrote: *If you have read* The Liberator, *you have seen the endless litany of daily atrocities committed against black people held in bondage. Do you wish to do even the smallest thing to keep alive an institution responsible for such barbarities? Do you wish to see more innocent black people flogged, starved, and worked to death?*

When she was finished, she left Margery with the baby and began the six-mile trek into town. It took her two hours, and she was utterly exhausted by the time she arrived. Her stomach felt queasy, and her legs felt weak and wobbly.

A woman, fiftyish, with drab eyes and short, stubby fingers met her at the counter. "Yes, ma'am? May I help you?"

"I wish to see the editor."

The woman eyed her. "He's busy right now, ma'am. May I help?"

"Yes, you may." She handed the editorial to the woman.

The woman glanced at it. Then she squinted at her. "You wrote this, ma'am?"

"Yes, I did."

"Well, you must see Mr. Holder about such a matter as

this. Please wait there." She pointed at a row of walnut open armchairs.

"May I have a drink of water, please?"

The woman looked long at her. "Surely," she said.

Fanny took a seat.

The woman came with a drink of water.

"Thank you."

She drank it down. She would be all right now. She could use another glass of water, but she would feel obtrusive to ask for it.

She waited for a few hours, but no editor. She waited another hour, and then she re-approached the counter.

"Yes?" said the woman. Her drab eyes lifted.

"Is the editor available yet?"

The woman turned and looked toward the back, to an office where a balding man with a thick brown beard sat hunched over his desk, his pen poised over something.

"No, Mr. Holder remains busy."

"Then I will continue to wait."

"As you wish, ma'am."

She waited for two more hours, and then the woman raised a finger, signaling her to step forward. "He's ready for you now," she said.

"Thank you."

She made her way back behind the counter, through a narrow walkway, through a sea of desks, where several young men were busily working away, jabbering at each other, and she entered the editor's office. He motioned her in.

She stood at his desk.

"Please sit, Mrs. Butler. Please do sit." He drew in on a cigar and let smoke seep between his lips.

She took a seat facing him.

He studied her for a moment or two. "You're an author, are you not? You wrote this—what I have before me. On the matter of colonization."

"Yes, I am. And I did."

"A rather controversial author, aren't you? From what I've read and heard."

"I suppose you could say that."

"Rather inflammatory."

"If you think so."

He sat forward. "I regret to tell you, Mrs. Butler, but we will not be able to publish this." He thwacked it with his pen.

"Too inflammatory?"

"Indeed. Our readers would most likely be offended. They would surely take it amiss. That is the long and short of it. I cannot risk offending our readers in that way, and I trust you will understand."

"I suppose I do. But do you understand that you are missing an opportunity?"

He offered her a smug smile. "No, I don't believe we are. Perhaps you'd rather seek a place in the abolitionist literature."

"You're advising me to do this?"

He set his pen down. "No, no! Indeed not! I'm not advising that at all."

"Why then did you suggest it?"

"Mrs. Butler."

"Yes?"

"It does not belong in our paper. Or anywhere else, among decent folks, in my opinion."

"It does belong. It belongs in as many publications as possible. It belongs here because your paper reaches many Philadelphians, readers who need to understand how wrong colonization is. How it's a travesty of justice."

He leveled his eyes on her. "I don't wish to be preached at, Mrs. Butler."

"On this topic?"

"On any topic."

Something suddenly came over her, a tremor. She could

hardly speak. For a moment she thought she would faint. "I'm—" she said. "I'm—"

"What, ma'am? What? Are you all right, Mrs. Butler?"

"I don't know. I don't—"

"Mrs. Butler—can I be of any assistance?"

He rose from his desk.

She sat there, staring at the floor. Her whole body was quivering. She could hardly breathe. He was still speaking to her, his deep voice grating on her nerves. There were no words, only that jarring voice. "I'm ill. I'm very ill," she said. "Something has come over me."

"Oh, my," he said. "Then perhaps you'd better lie down."

"Yes," she said. "I think I'd better."

He went to her, took her by the hand, and helped her up. And then he walked her slowly out of his office to a door, a fatherly hand on her shoulder. He opened the door, and a small room with a sofa appeared. He led her to the sofa and assisted her in lying down. "I will see about some help," he said. "Some female help. Please lie still."

In a minute or two, the woman from the counter was standing there, staring down at her. She had a glass of water in her hand.

Fanny raised herself up and took a drink. And then she lowered herself and lay back down.

"Sleep," said the woman. "It's the best thing. It's the birth, isn't it?"

"Yes. I think so. But how did you know?"

"I read the paper, Mrs. Butler," said the woman, smiling.

"Oh. Of course." She paused, again feeling very sick. "I shouldn't have walked. I should not have."

"You walked? From where?"

"From Butler Place."

"Butler Place. Oh, dear God! That's miles and miles from here, isn't it?"

"Six."

"Dear Lord, such a thing to do," said the woman, "such a thing as that. It isn't wise." She patted Fanny on the shoulder, and then she left.

She awoke to a soothing voice.

The woman had taken her hand. "Mr. Holder will give you a ride home in his carriage whenever you're ready. You mustn't walk back. Absolutely not."

"No," said Fanny, sitting up. "No. I cannot."

Mr. Holder stood in the doorway, his top hat pulled down over his forehead. He was leaning on a cane, half-smiling. He had a kind face she hadn't noticed before.

With the woman's help, they were soon in the carriage. Mr. Holder said little on the ride back. The carriage eventually rolled to a stop in the carriage drive of Butler Place.

As she stepped out, he said, "Say hello to Mr. Butler for me. Please do give him my kind regards."

"Thank you," said Fanny, "for your kindness."

"It's much too far to walk for a woman, Mrs. Butler, especially one who has recently given birth. A woman needs to ride in a carriage, and not do such a thing as that." His voice was remonstrative. But then, as before, he half smiled.

"I will keep that in mind," said Fanny. "Thank you again for your kindness, and good day."

He nodded, and the carriage went off, the horses trotting back toward Philadelphia.

"Can't you keep your tongue still?"

"Perhaps I will wag it until it falls off."

"You do try my patience. And I do have my limits, you know, as any man does."

"I myself have no patience with a slaver."

"Ha! You make me laugh! What do you know about slavery, about black people, about colonization? Other than what you've read and heard?"

163

"I've read enough and I've heard enough."

"Yes, I'm sure you have, and it's all lies."

"I suppose slavery is good for the slaves."

"Better than an African jungle."

"Have you been there?"

"I know what I know."

"That's what I thought."

Dear Fanny,

You speak of an odious husband. You speak of the imminent summer heat. Do come to the Berkshires, my dear friend. You must come to where the clime is much better, where the northern air refreshes and you will enjoy the freethinking of educated, cultured people, where artists and writers abound—and, always the prospect of such notables as Alexis de Toqueville, who graced us with his wonderful presence only a few years back. In the evenings, we gather around and listen to such notables as Ralph Emerson, reading from his poems, or from his essay on Nature, soon to be published, and we are all stirred, stimulated. No one interrupts. No one says anything for a little, and then we all talk. This exhausts one after a while, but it's a very good exhaustion. You will adore it and profit from it. And when you do come, you must stay long enough that you truly get Lenox into your blood. Come anytime. Don't feel you need to write. I won't be traveling at all this summer, or this autumn. The Berkshires are suffused with a soft, gentle light. Emerson speaks of it as only Emerson can.

And there was more, said Catharine, much more to relate. There was Elizabeth, her sister-in-law, who ran a school for young girls. And so not only was there the ethereal beauty of the Berkshires, and the pleasant, spiritual benefit of being in contact with thinkers, writers, and artists, but there was also a very progressive school for the young. This school promised to develop young minds, of young girls, in the practice of self-reliance. Emerson had been lecturing on self-reliance, intending an essay on this subject at some point, and they had spent whole evenings discussing it. *He often repeats what he says on his lecture tours: 'Whoso would be a man must be a nonconformist.' But I add, "Whoso would be a woman must also be a nonconformist!"*

Yes, Fanny wrote, *yes, conformity is a bane that destroys every moral fiber in a human being, man or woman.* She would certainly find a way to travel up to the Berkshires. She wanted to visit Elizabeth's school because she needed ideas, as many as possible, to educate her little daughter. She wrote:

> *I must see to it that she is an independent woman. I will raise her on poetry! On philosophy! On all the great ideas of the past! She will learn how wrong some things are in this world—and how right other things are! She will learn about the terrible wrongness of slavery.*

When she posted that letter, she at first left it on the small entrance room table, but then she thought better of that and asked a servant who was going to town to post it. It would be safer that way. It would be sure to find its way to Lenox.

> *Dear Fanny,*
> *I read your letter with great interest. And I want to say more about Elizabeth's fine school. What you will find there is a marvelous industry meant to improve the lot of women. The young girls learn much in the way of study, not just how to play the piano, or guitar, or dance, or draw, or become skillful in archery, but how to pursue ideas, to take*

them to their logical conclusions. They work inde-
pendently, but with Elizabeth's guidance, of course.
It's marvelous how much a young girl can learn.
You speak of slavery. Elizabeth is a staunch aboli-
tionist. She reads from Garrison's Liberator *to her*
students. You would be surprised at what she has
accomplished with her young charges. I'm quite
sure you will want to visit her school room.
Your friend,
Catharine

Fanny spent much of July, when the summer heat began to stoke up, wondering if, or when, she might be able to visit Catharine. When August came, it was getting dreadfully hot, and for health's sake alone, she and her baby needed a more northern clime.

When Pierce rolled in one day in a new black barouche, she was excited at the prospect of more money. Surely, if he could afford such a carriage as that, he could afford the pittance it would cost her to go up to Lenox.

She knocked on his study door.

She waited. She heard the rustling of papers. She waited some more, and then she knocked again.

The door opened.

"I've been waiting out here. What took you so long?"

"What exactly do you want?"

"To take a trip somewhere, to relieve us from this heat."

He leaned in the doorway. "And where is it you intend to go?"

"Saratoga Springs, perhaps."

He shook his head. "No, no. Too expensive—no."

"Well, then, somewhere less expensive."

"And where is that?"

"To the Berkshires, perhaps, to visit my friend Catharine."

He shook his head. "That's not advisable with Baby Sarah, is it? Coach travel? Consider what happened to your aunt."

"Even so, it would be better traveling in a coach than battling with this heat. Would it not?"

"I don't think so. I think we should hold back on that presently." He lighted his cigar and started to close his office door.

"Don't you care about your baby's health?"

"Yes, yes, but let's not be so dramatic." He shut the door.

In the evenings she tried to cool off little Sally, fanning her, but the air was so humid and close, with absolutely no breeze. They simply must go to a more favorable climate, to the north preferably, or perhaps to the coast. Mountain air or a sea breeze would cool off the baby and them, too. She did not see how they could remain here at Butler Place in such insufferable heat. What if the baby were overcome? What if she died?

He was busily wiping off his new barouche. She brought the matter up again.

"One can always imagine disasters," he said, not looking at her.

"This heat is killing our daughter. Look at her!"

He stopped wiping and looked at her, then at the baby. "It seems to me that you exaggerate. The baby looks fine to me."

"No. The baby is not fine! Don't you see? Look how red she is! How blotched her skin—look right there. And how sweaty!"

She held the baby up to his face.

He glanced at it, then shook his head. "I really don't see a problem, at least not a serious one. Besides, we must watch our spending."

"Spending! What about this new carriage? Did you watch your spending on that?"

He stiffened. "That's my business. It hardly concerns you."

"Does this baby concern you?"

"I have spoken my mind on this. The subject is closed. Keep the matter to yourself."

She wanted to say "You have taken my money—stolen it," but again, she did not want to give him the satisfaction of knowing he had legally swindled her.

She went off with little Sally and continued placing cold, wet cloths against her forehead.

One evening when he was sitting in the front porch swing, she once again brought the matter up.

"You are too insistent. Much too insistent. Why are you so insistent?"

"Look at this baby, Pierce. Just look at her." The heat was truly oppressive this evening, worse than ever, and she did not see how it could be more stifling. She feared the poor thing would expire at any moment. What if she went to sleep and did not wake up? Their thermometer on the front porch was sitting at one hundred and nine degrees, and the sun had already gone down.

"My friend Catharine could take us in at no cost."

"Is that right?"

"Yes. She wants us to visit. We have a standing invitation."

"She's an abolitionist, isn't she?"

"That's right. She is. And so?"

"You certainly don't need a female like that stirring you all up."

"I will be stirred up nonetheless, but at least you won't have a dead daughter to mourn over—if you care even a whit about her."

He looked away. He was quiet for a few moments. And then he sighed. "How long? How long? Spell it out. How much time are you wanting?"

"A month. Probably."

"A month?"

"Yes, and I will need a little money."

"Yes, yes. Of course you will. How much?"

"Enough for the travel, meals, and for a night's lodging—both ways."

"No clothes?"

"No."

He stood up. He paced for a few moments. And then he turned to her. "Well . . . all right. All right—fine."

She walked about the porch with little Sally. "How much will you give me?"

"Whatever I decide. It will be on your writing desk by tomorrow morning."

Early the next morning, a man servant gave her a ride in their older carriage into the city. In Philadelphia, she waited in the coach house for a half hour, then departed for New York.

By now, the sun had risen in the clear blue sky. She rested her eyes and tried to avoid the elderly couple who sat across from her, and who now and then looked at her and smiled. She didn't feel very talkative, and what would she have to say anyway to these two strangers? She stared out the coach window at the passing countryside, the houses, the barns, the cows and pigs. Horses leaned over fences, going for the thick green grass. The rough ride shook her insides, and she held little Sally against her to comfort her.

Finally, the elderly woman spoke to her. "Are you visiting in New York with your little one?"

"In Massachusetts. In the Berkshires? And you?"

"We're traveling to Paris. It is so far away, and I greatly fear ocean travel."

The man smiled. "We've done it before. It's nothing to fear, not really."

"Well, I myself fear it," said the woman. "You don't sound American."

"I'm British."

"Well, that's nice," said the woman. "To travel about so. But ocean travel—oh, dear."

Fanny resolved not to engage in more conversation. She did not wish to share her life story with these two strangers.

At a coach house in New York, she ate a meal of bread, oysters, custard, and coffee. She found a convenient place to nurse her baby. Soon she was boarding another coach. By the time they came to Connecticut, it had grown dark, and she watched for lighted lamps in small clapboard houses that leaned toward the rutty road. In some houses, she glimpsed women knitting or holding children. In one, she got a quick glance at men and women gathered around a piano, singing, gesturing, and laughing. At another house, a man was in a side yard, coming down hard with an ax on a stump of a tree. His chops rang out.

They came to a two-story stone house set back from a giant oak, and they were soon inside taking their supper. There was very little to eat, a small portion of fried ham, mush, and coffee, and she soon made ready for bed. In her assigned room on the second floor, Fanny found only one wet towel. She was to share this and the bed with a woman about twice her age and twice her size. She feared the woman rolling over on little Sally. She had trouble falling asleep when the woman went to deep, loud snoring, and shaking, but finally she awoke when the morning light streamed through the curtainless window.

She hurriedly dressed and made her way down the creaking stairs.

At a long table, she had her breakfast with a group of travelers—bread, a scorched egg, and burnt coffee.

The coach bound for points north was filled to capacity. She was sandwiched between the fat lady whom she'd had to sleep with and the coach door. Across from them was a woman with three children, who bounced up and down and giggled. The woman, fortyish, kept shushing them. She wore a grim look on her face.

By mid-afternoon, the coach had emptied out, and she could rest and enjoy some peace of mind, save for the continual bouncing and jarring of the vehicle over the rugged terrain.

When evening broke, the sun set with an orange halo of light. They arrived on the outskirts of a small village of well-kept cottages, and the driver sang out, "Lenox!" The coach rolled into a drive in front of a small coach house and came to an abrupt stop. The horses whinnied and snorted.

A cabbie approached her. "Cab, ma'am?"

"Yes. To the Sedgwick place, please."

"It will be but a moment," he said. He led her to the hackney cab. She climbed aboard, nestling her baby against her. Soon, the cab was on its way down the main street, when suddenly it turned sharply to the left and headed past the courthouse. Then it turned a corner and came to a two-story, white frame house. Fronting it were Greek pilasters and a fanlight in the center gable of the second story. The driver helped her down out of the cab, then wrestled her brown leather trunk to the front door.

She stood there a few moments, apprehensive, and then she knocked, lightly. She heard noises inside, and suddenly the door opened, and a tall young black woman greeted her and invited her into a small entrance hall. "It will be but a moment or two," she said.

She disappeared, and then, moments later, Catharine herself was coming, at first with a shock of recognition, and then with a warm smile. "Welcome to Lenox, Fanny. I feared you would never come! But at last, you are here . . . and you've brought your baby, I see." And before Fanny could answer her, she said, "Shall we slide the trunk inside?"

171

Then, when they'd accomplished that, Catharine said, "I suspect you must be starved. Please—come."

⁂

After supper, Catharine led Fanny, with Sally in her arms, to the front parlor, where they sat down under a spell of softly glowing lamps. The parlor was tastefully furnished, with a mahogany center table laden with a bowl of apples, a fireplace with the mantel decorated with fine cut glass, and a brass clock.

A servant brought a tea service, including a pot of tea, two cups, an Oriental blue creamer and spatterware sugar bowl. While they sipped their tea, Catharine spoke of "little things," as she called them: a recent storm when, a few nights ago, harsh rains had beat down on them for hour upon hour, of sunshine for the past few days, of a white cat she had seen just this morning in the wet grass. "I suppose this cat lives close by," said Catharine. "I always feel so anxious about any creature who has no home. Does this cat have one? I wonder. I had never seen the poor thing before." And then her eyes fell on Sally, who was now asleep. "Does she always sleep so profoundly?"

"Not always," but Fanny mentioned that much of the time her nursemaid, Margery, looked after her, when she wasn't nursing her or lying down to nap with her, and often, at these times, she read to her, which little Sally truly enjoyed, judging from the peaceful, contented look on her angelic little face.

"Even at that age," said Catharine, "it's very good to read to a child, as I'm sure Elizabeth would agree. The earlier one starts the better, generally, though we both hold that learning Greek by age three, Latin by age seven, as was the case for your own John Stuart Mill, is a bit extreme." She smiled. "If you wish, we'll go visit her school tomorrow. It's in a little

172

house to the back, on the edge of a very productive garden. Elizabeth writes her own texts. As I'm sure you'll note, she's a very educated woman—a rarity in this country, I regret to say."

"Yes, unfortunately."

"You'll be impressed, I think, with her school."

"I do wish to see it." And then she said, "Would you read from your new novel?"

"Now? Well . . . I suppose I could."

"We'd both enjoy it."

"Ah!" said Catharine. "Then of course I must." She rose from the settee she had been lounging on, went to a book-shelf close to the mantel, and returned. She opened the book and began to read: of two young girls just two or three years before the Revolution, two girls going through a wicket garden gate from the rear of a mansion reeking of royal favor, to enter Broadway. The older girl, a teenager, had dark hair and seemed "born to empire," with "the step of a young Juno." The younger one seemed "framed for all tender humanities." "A black servant in livery" followed the two girls.

Catharine stopped reading. "I hope I'm not boring you."

"Oh, no! Certainly not!"

"I'm delighted," said Catherine. "But let's talk instead." She placed the book on a small table next to her, and then she sat forward. "Tell me more about your husband. About his pecuniary interests in slavery, though I suppose that to do so will smack of the tautological?"

"Yes, it will. To put it mildly, he looks forward to his inheritance, which I fear he'll receive very soon. And so I agonize over that—daily."

"What will you do?"

"What can I do? He's not inclined to change, not in the least. Certainly I can't influence him to change. For one thing, I'm a woman, and to his mind, I have no right to offer an opinion that differs from his, and second, he is a staunch supporter of this devilish institution."

"You can only try. I must say that I feel remiss about this matter myself. Because I do know that we are our brothers' keepers. And we *will* be judged. With that in mind, I'll be attending the meeting in January of the Massachusetts Antislavery Society. I hope I can do some good through that means. Not enough good, though, I fear."

"Perhaps slavery will be the end of this country. Perhaps whatever one does, and however much one gives to the cause of abolition, it will mean nothing at all."

Catharine stared at her. "You really think so?"

"I fear it's true."

"Even so, we must exert as much effort as possible. We must do justice. But at the same time, we must do what we can to save the Union. It's a good Union. It's vital, as I see it."

"There are those who disagree with you, for instance Harriet Martineau."

"Yes, and William Lloyd Garrison. But I'm not quite there. Perhaps I'll come to that, eventually."

"I'm an Englishwoman," said Fanny. "I've not become fully acclimated, and so talk of the Union, or its being dissolved, means much less to me than to you."

"And yet you *have* made your home here."

"That, I fear, was a mistake."

"Perhaps so. Perhaps it was, though I'm certainly glad of your company, and your friendship. And I think great things will come of your being an American."

"Why? How so?"

"Your pamphlet was a good start, regardless of how it was received."

"My husband burnt it. Along with my book."

Catharine sat forward. "How dreadful."

"How predictable. He would burn anything that he didn't agree with."

"And you're saddled for life with such a man?"

"I must find a way to leave him. It's the only way."

"At some point, one hopes you can. I assume you will take your child."

"Yes. Of course."

"Then, Fanny, he will hunt you down. You will be like a runaway slave with the law entirely on his side."

"I know. But what other choice have I—ultimately?"

The next morning they went down a path through a garden filled with marigolds and zinnias. "This is a flower garden, and earlier in the summer a vegetable one as well, but at this time of year, only the marigolds and zinnias survive."

They came to a one-story building.

Catharine knocked lightly, and there was but a moment's delay before a tall, slim woman with dark hair, curled in the same manner as Catharine's, stood before them. Her eyes were very blue and penetrating. In a hushed voice, she welcomed them into the schoolroom, where a dozen young girls were working quietly away at their desks. "They are busy with rhetoric right now. Soon they will be turning to eloquence, then to history, then to physiology." She grabbed a book from a set of shelves. "And you will be glad to know that they read Shakespeare, practicing their recitations—and, of course, searching for and discussing among themselves various meanings they apprehend. I demand some memorization, but they must not stop with this, but train their minds. Perhaps you would like to read to them."

"I would be pleased to."

They stood at the back of the room before an arrangement of plants. Fanny watched as the girls wrote with their cedar pencils, with black lead.

"My charges," said Elizabeth, "will, above all, learn self-confidence and personal dignity. I direct each of their studies toward their own sense of power, which they must develop early on. This means a well-rounded education.

175

Without this preparation, should they fall into the hands of a man who treats them like a mere child, it will be too late. But should they enter into the marital union, I do emphasize the importance of this bond, which I view as sacred, and thus not to be treated lightly."

After a short while, Elizabeth said they should gather at four o'clock, after classes had concluded for the day, to take tea in the parlor and relax and speak their minds. "I'm so pleased you've come at last. Catharine held out hope that you would. And so did I." She clasped Fanny's hand warmly.

"You might find it interesting that Elizabeth descends, on her mother's side, from Jonathan Edwards, who came out to Stockbridge to preach to the Indians. Are you familiar with him?"

"Yes. I regret to say I am."

"That infamous sermon? We, neither I nor Elizabeth, go for such a vision of damnation as Edwards had, though one cannot say that he invented this on his own. He had deep roots, you know, in Calvin, Aquinas, and Augustine. I myself cannot see the blessed in Heaven looking down on the pits of hell rejoicing over the punishment of the unsaved, especially their unsaved loved ones."

"How horrifying."

"Of course Edwards also had his Puritan forebears to thank for that ghastly vision of his. Are you familiar with *The Day of Doom* by Wigglesworth?"

"No, I cannot say that I am."

"Well, one might say that it's Edwards in verse. Shocking, really."

"Do you believe in damnation?"

They were on an early morning walk, which Catharine took daily, and had now come to the Housatonic River. The morning sun through the trees colored it gold and green. The woods were bathed by the early morning light.

"Well, I certainly don't believe in infant damnation, like Edwards, who found such a thing as that 'sweet,' given the Puritan emphasis on God's sovereignty above all else. I question Original Sin if it means that. Like my fellow Unitarians, I am, I guess you might say, more enlightened—if that's the right word. I'm, in fact, a lapsed Calvinist. However, I do hold out the possibility of damnation for those who devote themselves to the devil's work, though I can't say exactly what such damnation would be like."

"Cast into outer darkness—perhaps?"

"I must believe," said Catharine, "that they *will* pay for their terrible iniquities in some way. I hold out for some sort of justice. Don't you?"

"But is it possible that some might be utterly incapable of being different? Because of who they are? Or who they've become?"

"Are you thinking of your husband?"

"Yes."

"Some slavers *have* come to see the light."

"From whence has such light fallen on them?"

"Ah! It's a mystery," said Catharine.

"It takes a soul?"

"Yes—it does."

"Perhaps that soul can be so lost that there isn't one at all."

"In that case, one struggles all the much harder. Isn't it true?"

"I don't know. I don't see how I can bear that burden. I can bear some burdens, but that one? I don't see how."

Catharine studied her. "We do bear the burden of reaching those in their ignorance and evil, however difficult that is. Edwards held that we have no freedom of the will. I don't accept that."

"Nor do I." Right now, she had nothing further to say. Not regarding Pierce Butler, she didn't.

One September afternoon Ralph Waldo Emerson arrived. Fanny watched from inside the parlor as he stepped down from a hackney cab. He was met by Catharine and Elizabeth, who ushered him into the parlor, and he brushed off his frock coat as Elizabeth mentioned a spot of tea.

That evening, he spoke of poetry. "Of late, I've been considering a piece on the role of the poet." He drew out a leather-bound notebook. "I'll read from this early start, if you'll permit. It's been circling around in my brain as I write in my journals. But do please keep in mind, it's just a start." He took a moment, and then read:

> *For poetry was all written before time was, and whenever we are so finely organized that we can penetrate into that region where the air is music, we hear those primal warblings and attempt to write them down, but we lose ever and anon a word or a verse and substitute something of our own, and thus miswrite the poem.*

"You see it as metaphysical, then," said Catharine.

"Yes. I must say I do. And having a strong moral component. A few years ago when I went to England, as you know, I was apprised of something the notable Shelley said about poets. It's been circulating among poets and writers of various stamps in an essay which he never published called 'A Defence of Poetry.' I hope it does see the light of day, for what it says answers to much of what I myself believe. Namely, this: 'Poets are the unacknowledged legislators of the world.' Poetry, you see, pierces the veil. Of Maya? Poets, I want to say, are liberating gods."

He spoke further of this, and then of his recent poems.

"Perhaps you'd like to speak of your antislavery work," said Elizabeth. "For Fanny's sake."

He nodded. He looked directly at her. "I will, of course."

"Please," she said.

"Well, to put the matter succinctly, in Saint Augustine, Florida, last decade, I was considerably revolted by a slave auction I witnessed—in the yard outside the meeting of the Bible Society. Seeing it with my own eyes made me realize the importance of coming out against it in both word and deed. As pastor of the Second Church in Boston, I opened my pulpit to those who would speak out against such a plague on our land. I saw that we must end it, absolutely, or it would be our own end." He looked away for a moment. "Incidentally, I recently met a very enterprising young man at Harvard—one Henry David Thoreau. I was impressed about his strong position on this matter. I see great promise in the man."

"Mr. Emerson is about to get married," spoke Catharine, "in less than a month. Aren't you, Ralph?"

"Yes, I am."

"To Lidia Jackson, an abolitionist and a fierce contender for women's rights."

"She is."

"You speak of the poet," said Elizabeth. "And Shelley. In my opinion, literature must have a moral component to it, not merely an aesthetic one. Yet didn't Mr. Poe say something to you about the poem for the poem's own sake?"

"Yes, he's been thinking along those lines. And it's a seductive principle, I grant it, but I do hold that the poem is transcendental and thus moral—always moral. "The moral law lies at the center of nature and radiates to the circumference."

Catharine smiled. "We do await the publication of your essay, Ralph."

"Ah, that will be soon. It's scheduled for next year."

"And now," said Catharine, "perhaps Fanny will play the

pianoforte."

"I'd be pleased." She rose and made her way to the piano bench. Every night it was the same, and she relished the chance to play—before them, she did. This night she sat down to Beethoven's Seventh Symphony, the *Allegretto*, or Second Movement. She felt the presence of Beethoven himself in the room, her own presence shared with his, but the others' presence as well. It was a community of listeners, a pleasure dome unlike any she'd known in America, more like what she'd known in country houses back in England. She despaired of leaving Lenox, but the time had come, and she must soon go back to her regular, everyday life.

It was mid-September when she returned to Butler Place, the air crisper, the fierce heat of August over. She went back to her studies and writing. She spent time reading Shakespeare to little Sally. "By the time you are a young girl, you will know Shakespeare in and out," she said, kissing the child. "And then, you will go up to Lenox, to Elizabeth's school. I will miss you, but I will visit there much—I promise!"

And then she thought, "But how can I do that? I would want to go with you. Perhaps we will just move to Lenox!"

And then it struck her, as it always did, that her dreams were dependent, utterly dependent, on what her husband would allow. She could not have her own life. She could not pilot her own ship. She had made choices earlier on that had cut off choices she could make now or in the future.

In a few days, she noticed something different—the absence of Jane Hannigan. Where was she? Was she sick?

No.

The young girl had been fired.

She inquired as to her whereabouts. None of the servants knew where Miss Hannigan lived.

In a boarding house, said Margery. "That really ramshackle one, down by the river, close to the ship joiner's. There's a tavern right close by."

"Thank you."

She went in search.

She trekked the six miles to Philadelphia. Down by the Delaware River, she located the boarding house with half of the front windows boarded up. Catcalls and whistles came from a knot of men gathered in front of that nearby tavern.

She hurried into the boarding house.

Inside, it was unbearably hot and stuffy. How could one possibly breathe in here? She made her way down the first-floor hall. Then she retraced her steps and went down the opposite way. She came to the last door, where, in whitewash on the brown door, was sloppily painted: Mrs. White, Landlord.

She knocked, and waited.

She had to knock again and again.

"Yes, yes, yes. I'm coming, coming, coming," a hoarse voice croaked.

The door jerked open, and a woman of about sixty stood before Fanny, running her hand through her grayish, tangled hair, covered in part by a white bonnet.

"And what may I do for you, ma'am?"

"I'm looking for Jane Hannigan."

"Is that so? What do you want with the girl?"

"I was her employer."

"She owe you money or something?"

"No."

"What then?"

"It's a matter of private business, Mrs. White, and I'm not at liberty to discuss it with you."

The landlady scowled. "Well, she's on the third floor is where she is. Three Sixteen."

The door slammed.

Fanny took the stairs. Dusty, dirty, with refuse scattered all about. A smell of coal. Of garbage. Noxious fumes of every sort, a study in effluvia.

When she got to 316, she stood there. Should she? What did she want? What did she hope to gain? This is silly, she thought. No, she thought, it's silly to hesitate. That's what's silly.

She knocked. A few light knocks.

The door jerked open. A man appeared with one cheek bulging. She stepped aside, and he let loose on the hall floor. He barely missed her shoe. She saw the revolting brown puddle, and she gagged.

"What're you a-wantin'?" he said, leaning toward her. Brown juice leaked out both sides of his mouth, dribbling down his chin.

"I'm Mrs. Fanny Butler. I need to speak to your daughter—Jane."

"Jane!" the man yelled. "That lady you a-worked for—she's here to talk at you." He turned to Fanny. "You had no business a-firing my daughter."

He disappeared, shutting the door on her.

It was a little while before Jane Hannigan opened the door. When she did, she looked like she'd just gotten up from a nap. Her eyelids were puffy, her eyes red and swollen, and she seemed to have trouble focusing.

"What is it you want?"

"Why did my husband fire you?"

"It was wrong—what he done."

"But why?"

"You don't know?"

"No, I don't."

"I don't wish to say it. It's not becoming a lady."

"Tell me. Please."

182

The girl shook her head.

"Please, Jane."

The girl said nothing. She looked away, down at the floor.

"Jane."

The girl looked up, then leaned in toward her and spoke in a whisper. "Okay, if I must. You stand there and ask, and want to know, and so I just will. See, he was all the time a-wanting to . . ."

"What?"

"He was all the time—"

"I heard you. *What?*"

"For the longest time, ma'am—"

"You tell me, Jane," she said softly.

"He wanted to. He did. That's what I'm a-saying, ma'am."

Fanny drew back. "I hope you're not making this up."

"No. I'm not a-making a single thing up, ma'am. I'd swear on the Holy Word of God."

"You needn't do that."

"And when I wouldn't anymore, he fired me."

"Anymore?"

"That's right."

"Are you telling me the truth, Jane?"

"Yes, ma'am, I am. He offered me money."

"Did you take it?"

The girl paused. She looked away.

"Did you?"

Silence.

"Did you?"

"Yes . . . I couldn't help it."

"What?"

"I couldn't."

"And why is that?"

"It was a lot."

"Dear God," said Fanny.

"Yeah?" said the girl.

"That makes you a whore, Jane. That's what that makes you!"

"I needed it. I needed the money."

"Needed it! You have wronged me. Terribly."

The girl's face went red. "Blame him! Not me!" She stepped back into the apartment, slamming the door.

Fanny stood there for a few moments.

And then she went down the stairs, holding her nose against the stench, and came to the bottom floor. She stepped out into the evening.

The men were no longer there in front of that tavern.

She looked down to the river.

A three-story steamboat was on the Delaware. The sun was down, and it would be dark before she got back to Butler Place. But there would be a moon, and she would be guided by that.

As soon as she got home, she immediately went to her husband's study. She knocked hard, several knuckle-hard knocks.

"Who is it?"

"Let me in. We must talk, Pierce."

"What is it?"

"I want in. Do you hear me?"

She heard things being shuffled about, papers, an object of some kind against wood, then boots on the hardwood. He appeared at the door with a scowl on his face, and he cleared his throat two or three times. "Yes? What?"

"Let me in. I must see you—in private, please."

"And why is that?"

"I cannot answer that out here, Pierce."

"Why not?"

"Because it's a private matter, as I said."

"Well, all right. Come in. If you must."

He opened the door a little wider, but he blocked her further passage into the study. He fixed his eyes on her. "What? What now?"

"You wish me to take it up here—like this?"

"Yes. Why not?"

"Well, all right. I will then. The Hannigan girl. Jane."

"What about her?"

"I went to see her. At her boarding house."

"Oh, you did? Now why in the world would you do that?"

"To see why you fired her."

"Why didn't you ask me?"

She ignored this question. "She told me things."

"Things? What sort of things?"

"She said, Pierce, that you seduced her. And that you paid her money. You have made her a whore—this is what you have done. One of our servants, in our own home. A whore. And while I was gone."

He laughed. "Fanny, Fanny."

"You think it's funny?"

"Yes, I do. Don't you understand? She's a common, low-down, base servant. She wouldn't do her work, at least not up to my standards. Lazing around, taking my money for nothing. So what would you expect her to say? I fired her, and she retaliated. It's as simple as that."

"You are denying this then."

He stared at her, but then his eyes wavered, and he looked about. "There's not a grain of truth to it."

"I'm having a hard time believing that, Pierce. Convince me that I should."

His cheeks flushed. "You are pathetic! That's what you are. If you want to believe what that little tramp said, that's your prerogative. There's not much a man can do to change a woman's mind once she's made that mind up, but it's wrong to think such a thing about your husband. To believe the word of a vile little servant!"

185

"Not if it's true."

His eyes twitched. "It's time you left. I'll not abide any further accusations. Get!"

"You've been told," she said. "I am wise to you." When she was halfway down the hall, she heard something bang hard against the wall. And then she heard yelling.

The next morning, he came to her desk and planted his hands on a newspaper she'd been reading.

"Yes? What is it?"

"I've come to talk."

"And what do you wish to speak of?"

"To put it plainly, it's this problem you're having and have had for some time now."

"Oh? What problem do you speak of, Pierce? Enlighten me."

"Well, it's obvious, quite obvious to me, and it should be to you, too—it's that of adjusting to the marital state. Quite frankly, I don't know what to do."

He looked about, as though seeking an answer on the floor, the walls, or ceiling.

"You're just stumped, aren't you?"

His stomped his boot on the floor. "No sarcasm! We can ill afford it!"

"That might be a bit hard for me. I'm just brimming with it, apparently. My cup overfloweth."

He got that look on his face, of husbandly tolerance for a wife who was hysterical. And then he said, "You're not happy, are you? As a married woman, you've never been happy, have you?"

"I wanted to be, Pierce. But this isn't what you wanted."

"You're wrong. I did want this."

"Given that, it's strange how you've behaved."

"Me! You!"

"Any objective witness would disagree," she said.

He paced the floor. "There is no reason, absolutely none at all, why you wouldn't be the happiest woman in the world. You've got a husband of considerable means. You've got a fine home. You've got a beautiful daughter. But that imagination of yours—you blow things up so. There's really nothing there at all, but by the time your imagination works on it, it's some huge monstrosity. It's disturbing, quite disturbing, and not at all healthy for you, me, or our child. And so it's come down to it—I have but little choice."

"Oh, and what is that?"

"I must seek outside help."

"And what kind of help is that, Pierce?"

"An expert in the female area, Fanny. One Doctor Hegstrom, a man who knows and understands women."

"Ah! And so I'm to go see this Doctor Hegstrom, am I?"

"No, he will be coming here to see you."

"How thoughtful of him."

"We shall see," said Pierce. "Shall we not?"

"See what?"

He ran a finger over one sideburn. "Whether or not you are capable of adjusting. That is what we shall see."

"And if I'm not?"

"First, the doctor, please," said Pierce. "Let's hold off judgment." He left her room, and she watched as he closed the door very softly. It was hardly audible.

It was a brisk fall day with a gentle, dry wind. Soon, the leaves on the two oaks would be turning burnt orange, red, and yellowish. Fall winds would scatter them across the yard. It was her favorite time. She sat on the porch waiting. The carriage arrived, bumping up to a stop on the drive right behind Pierce's new barouche. A tall, broad-shouldered man in a black frock coat, wearing a black top hat and carrying a black doctor's bag, stepped out and slowly made his way across the yard. Pierce met him as he gained the porch.

"Good morning, Doctor. I'm Pierce Butler."

"Doctor Hegstrom." He stuck out his hand, and the two men shook.

"And this is Mrs. Butler," said Pierce, nodding in her direction.

The doctor tipped his hat. "A pleasure to make your acquaintance, Mrs. Butler."

"Why thank you, Doctor."

"You may confer with Mrs. Butler in my study," said Pierce.

"Oh, I think right here is quite suitable," said Fanny. "The Doctor and I can enjoy the fall weather together."

"Don't be ridiculous. My study, Fanny." He snapped his fingers.

"In your study—ah. Well, then, if we must."

She watched as the two men exchanged glances.

Pierce opened the door and stood there. The doctor entered, and Fanny followed him and Pierce down to Pierce's study. Her husband opened the study door.

Dr. Hegstrom stepped in.

Fanny stepped in.

The door closed, and it was just the two of them.

The doctor settled down behind Pierce's mahogany desk and leaned back slightly as Fanny took the chair positioned in front of it. This chair had not been there before.

And then he settled back gradually, easefully.

"How is your health, Mrs. Butler?"

"My health? Why it's splendid. Thank you for asking."

"Very good. What would you say is on your mind, mostly? What stirs your daily thoughts?"

"You come right to it, don't you, sir?"

He eyed her sharply. "Indeed. This is, after all, a doctor's appointment. It's not a social call."

"I appreciate the house call."

"Your daily thoughts, Mrs. Butler. Let us proceed."

"If we must. Well, I suppose I have thoughts like anyone else. Like you, for instance."

"And what thoughts do you imagine I have?"

"Normal thoughts. Do you not?"

"This is not about me. It's about you."

"Well, my thoughts are quite normal—if yours are."

"And what are normal thoughts?"

"What do you think they are?"

"No, Mrs. Butler. I asked you. I would appreciate an answer, to the best of your knowledge."

"Normal thoughts? Well, Doctor, I would say normal thoughts are thoughts that are geared to the occasion. They are prompted by something we can name as happening or existing, and they follow squarely on the heels of that something and are rationally, or emotionally, connected to it. Wouldn't you agree?"

"Emotionally?"

"Yes . . . indeed. We do have two sides to our nature, sir. Is it not true?"

"Can you provide an example of something happening or existing, as you say?"

"A particular occurrence?"

"Yes."

"And what would you have in mind, specifically speaking?"

"Well, Mrs. Butler, please use your imagination. Perhaps a meal that tastes bad, or water that tastes bad, or a horse that balks—or a husband who doesn't come up to one's expectations?"

Fanny laughed.

The doctor's eyes went dark. "Mrs. Butler."

"The last of your four is quite different in kind, isn't it, from the first three?"

"Please answer the question. Let's do keep our minds on the matter at hand." The doctor folded his thick hands on the shiny mahogany surface of the desk.

"All right. I think the latter is much too general. You would surely need to be more specific—to make your point clear. Wouldn't you?"

The doctor's lips tightened. "If I must." He was quiet for a moment. Then he said, "Let us assume, for instance, that your husband went to the barn—that barn to the rear of your house. Grant this, shall we?"

"I suppose we may."

He frowned. "Very well, then. Let us now imagine that he didn't come out—and yet a whole hour had passed. Would that be an event of the kind you are referring to?"

"It might do in a pickle. Though I would need to know a little more in the way of details—to be able to judge."

"Yes. Well, then. Let us say that you made certain suppositions from having witnessed your husband's going out to that barn. Let us say you concluded that he was intending to hang himself." He worked his tongue against his thin lips.

"Oh, my," said Fanny.

"Well, now, Mrs. Butler, would this conclusion follow reasonably 'on the heels,' as you put it, of his being in the barn for say a full hour?"

"Certainly not. Unless one knew that he was intending to hang himself. But it would still be mere speculation. Wouldn't it?"

"Yes," said the doctor. "It would be."

Fanny smiled.

"You're a very clever woman, are you not?" said the doctor.

"I hope so."

The doctor readjusted himself in his chair. He sat forward. "I do not doubt that you want the best for your husband, but you must be sure that you don't let flights of fancy guide you in your perceptions and judgment of him. For instance, let us say that one of your servants said that Mr. Butler was talking of hanging himself. Would you believe her?"

"That would depend."

"On what, Mrs. Butler?"

"If other evidence suggested that he might do this terrible thing, I might well believe her."

"Evidence such as?"

"Something I'd seen myself."

"Do you generally trust the word of servants, Mrs. Butler?"

"I generally don't trust the word of anyone, sir. Not on its own steam. I go on my own eyes, my ears, and my best judgment."

"Isn't it true that servants might not be trustworthy?"

"They might not be. Just as others might not be."

"But does it make sense to trust them over your husband—ever? A man whom you chose to wed and to be obedient to for your entire life on this earth?"

She shook her head. "If I agreed to the latter, I was greatly in error."

"Pardon?"

"That is correct, Doctor."

The doctor leaned on his elbows, his chin resting on his fists. "And so probably some of the time, you take the word of a servant just to confirm what you want to believe about your husband, this man God has set over you in the natural order of things—this man you don't wish to obey. Isn't that right?"

"I don't believe I said that."

"You are a willful woman, are you not?"

"The will is important, Doctor. What are we without it, sir?"

"A woman must be sure her will does not carry her away.

Mustn't she?"

Fanny rose from her chair. "A man must also. Well, I'll be excusing myself at this time. I have work to attend to."

"Work? What sort of work?"

"I am a writer, sir. If you must know."

He nodded. "Yes . . . I am well aware of that. And I must say that I do not approve of what I've seen and heard."

"That's unfortunate, isn't it? Our meeting is concluded, Doctor." She had her hand on the doorknob.

He motioned at her chair. "Please, Mrs. Butler, we are not finished, not at all."

"Oh, I quite disagree. We are indeed finished." She left, with the door swinging half open.

Up in her room she waited at the window. Soon the two men stood in the yard. Pierce talked, and the doctor nodded. And then the doctor talked, and Pierce nodded. With the window raised, she could hear only a muffled babble because they were talking very softly. Soon, the doctor left and Pierce mounted the steps to the porch. She heard the front door screech open and shut.

A few days later, spread before her was the Philadelphia newspaper. On page three was an article about *a local businessman, Mr. Pierce Butler, who had recently run afoul of one Mr. James Harness, a New York businessman, over an alleged impropriety with Mr. Harness's wife in Mr. Butler's hotel room.* It happened on September 8, when Mr. Butler had been spending time in New York on business. To defend his honor, Mr. Harness had invited Mr. Butler to a duel. They had settled the matter on Long Island, but neither party had been wounded. Yet Mr. Harness had filed a suit in a New York court for divorce. He had also filed a damage suit against Mr. Pierce Butler in that same court.

"Vindicated. Am I not?" She made her way down to his study.

She knocked. Waited. Knocked again. Waited.

When he opened the door, she shoved the crumpled newspaper at him.

He took a glance. Then snorted. "There isn't an ounce of truth to that story. Mr. Harness is a very competitive businessman, utterly savage, and this is the way he gets even when he loses out on a good deal—which he did. He spreads flagrant lies."

"You were gone to New York while I was visiting the Berkshires?"

"Yes—and so?"

"What did you do in New York?"

He gave her a sharp look. "Is that any business of yours?"

"Did you see that woman?"

"Which woman?"

"Mrs. Wilkerson."

"I beg your pardon."

"I expect you did, and I expect you certainly did what Mr. Harness claims, didn't you?"

"No, Fanny, I did not, and I do not appreciate your suggesting that I did."

"Did you see other women?"

He slammed a paperweight down on his desktop. "I will not tolerate this line of questioning. Didn't Dr. Hegstrom do you any good at all? Must I invite him back for a second session?"

"Ha! That was for *you*, not me. Perhaps Dr. Hegstrom was fooled, but I certainly wasn't."

"Get out!"

"Give me that newspaper."

He stared at her. He began ripping it up.

"That won't change a thing," she said.

It was a two-day coach ride over rugged roads, and she was very tired when she arrived.

She took rooms at the American Hotel as she had two years earlier, at this very time of the year, though it was almost October and the air was dry and cool.

It was late evening when she looked out of her open hotel window to observe the street life below, the evening strollers, the pedestrians wading through flocks of cooing pigeons, the carriages rumbling. She could hear the continual cacophony of river traffic. Voices she didn't recognize, in foreign tongues, rang out.

That night, she stayed up late writing letters. She wrote Mrs. Jameson. She brought her up to date on her life since her last letter—which had been some time ago, for which, she said, *I do apologize*, and then she stated what had just happened regarding her philandering husband. *Clearly I have made a mistake. Clearly I should have thought harder and longer. I am married to a philanderer and a slaver. Quite a combination, isn't it? And I know not what to do. Here I am laying this at your door. Forgive me for this, but this is where I am, and what's on my mind. Someday I hope to be free, free, free of both burdens—were that possible. But here on American soil?—I see not how. But I mustn't burden you any further with my problems.*

And to Catharine and Elizabeth together, she wrote: *If my husband's latest behavior hasn't reached you yet, via the newspapers, I will notify you here.* She did, at some length. And then she said, *I don't think 'mistake' is quite the right word for what I did, what I entered into. And what I now face daily. I know not what to call it, nor what to do. I am trapped, it seems. Sometimes I wonder what is wrong with me. Why don't I just up and leave? Why don't I? A woman who was not so foolish would surely find a way. I must do so. I absolutely must!*

194

She also wrote in her journal:

We shall see what exactly my husband has wrought. What damages? How many marital infractions and how extensive?

The next morning, once she'd had a breakfast of eggs, bread, and coffee, she went directly to see Mr. Harness at his Broadway business address.

The receptionist kept her nearly an hour before she was able to gain entrance into the man's office.

He rose to meet her. He was a large, beefy man, and well-shaven, except for his thick, brown mustache. He had a puzzled looking smile on his face. "Mrs. Butler. Well, I was not expecting you. You of all people, I was not expecting."

"May I have a moment of your time, sir?"

"You may. Certainly. Please sit."

"Thank you." She took a chair.

"Yes, I am a bit surprised, to say the least, that you decided to come all the way from Philadelphia to our fair city—to see me, of all people."

"I wanted to hear your side of the story, from you, directly. I read the newspaper article, but is there more?"

He nodded. "Indeed. Yes, there's more. Where shall I start?"

She waited.

"Well," he began, "including the raw pain of realizing that your husband put my wife in such a compromising position—and yet she participated in this odious act. I could not describe that pain fully in print, nor was I inclined to do so. She was certainly not guiltless, but I do feel entitled to blame most of it on your husband. She is a weak woman, and he made promises. That part wasn't included either—it was somehow left out, and perhaps it's best that it was—but she told me of several promises the lowly wretch made. Ex-

195

cuse me, I realize that I'm speaking of your husband, but really—"

"What promises?"

He leaned forward in a confidential manner. "Well, Mrs. Butler, that he would marry her. She's a very beautiful woman, you know. Well, you don't know. How could you? But he promised her a much better life than I could afford her. He spoke of vast fortunes soon coming his way. I must say I am glad they did not include such grandiose promises in the newspaper, for I wouldn't want such as that out for public consumption since it would make me look rather mediocre in comparison—Mr. Butler, a highly successful businessman, me—well—something of a failure. I've got a reputation to uphold, you know, and this scandal is harming me greatly. Or at least I fear it will. But I wanted it in the newspaper because a man like your husband should not be able to get away with wrecking another man's life. Which is what an adulterous affair does, as I'm quite sure you know—and what has undoubtedly prompted you to come and speak to me."

"He took her to his room?"

"Yes, ma'am, he did. That's what led to the duel. My honor was at stake, you see."

"You did duel?"

"Yes, we did."

"But neither of you was wounded?"

He grinned. "Both bad shots, as it were. Both very bad shots. But fortunate, I suppose, don't you think? Though, and I hate to confess it, I was set on killing him. I was set to shoot him straight through the heart. Or the head. It's a terrible thing to admit, but I was."

She said nothing. She just looked at him.

"But I didn't. I couldn't do it. I'm not a violent man by disposition."

"Then you intentionally—"

"Yes, ma'am. There are precedents for this sort of behavior, you know. But I took a risk. Now didn't I? However, it would have looked bad . . . well, I don't have to spell it out for you, do I?"

"What do you know about my husband—beyond those embarrassing details?"

He was silent for a few moments. "Well, I don't feel very comfortable sharing such things with a woman, especially a man's wife."

"You've shared some rather compromising details already, haven't you?"

"Yes. I have. Indeed. You see, Mr. Butler and I go back several years. He used to do business here in New York. He would come up and stay for a few weeks, and he and I would go hunting on Long Island. Playing cards, too. He's a terrible card player, but he doesn't know when to give up. And he seldom pays his gambling debts—fully, at least. All this is before we were both married, you see. Your husband was quite the blade, Mrs. Butler. He was seeing a married woman back then, but of course, not being any relation to me, I didn't much care."

"What was her name?"

"Name? I have no idea."

"And . . . what else?"

"I'm not one to gossip, especially when it comes to degraded behavior."

"Please tell me what my husband did besides seeing that married woman."

"Ah! Well, to put it bluntly, ma'am, he had this habit—some men do—of seeing women—how should I put it?—of questionable morals. And having said that, I suppose now you'll want to know if I did, too."

"No, that's your own business."

"He went constantly. And since I am not feeling very kindly toward your marriage, given what he's done to my own, I will let you know that this is a habit that he has kept up ever since. You see, when he comes to New York, when that happens, he goes to the red light districts and he satisfies his needs—which are apparently great, as he's told me on many an occasion. I suppose, with more reflection, I'll realize I shouldn't be saying all that to you, and it's not your fault you married such a poor excuse for a human being, but really you would be better off if you thought about the things I've said and break that marital bond. You'll get nothing in terms of pecuniary resolution, but you'll at least be shut of such a bad man. And he is a bad man, Mrs. Butler. You've been married how long?"

"A little over a year."

"And you have a child."

"Yes."

He sat back in his chair. "He will get the child, but you, at least, will have your freedom. Do give it some thought, ma'am."

She rose from her chair. "Thank you for everything you've told me."

"It's no bother. I guess you know I'm suing the bastard."

"Yes, of course. I read the newspaper article."

"That you did. I won't likely get anywhere with it, but it's a gesture. And I do hope it pains the man to be dragged into court. That's some bad publicity for him—at least there's that, or at least I hope so. I'm not usually a vindictive man, Mrs. Butler—but in this case, well . . . " He rose from his desk. "Good day to you, ma'am."

She bid him good day, and she went back to her hotel room.

2
Inheritance
1836 - 1838

Winter was once again upon them, a long January immured in the house, the continual snow somehow the security of oblivion, but she despaired of it, too, of those interminably long days of being shut in. She wrote in her journal:

> We seek, where we presently are, or where we might someday end up, in the deep reaches of the world, some sort of happiness, some sort of meaning. Despair and happiness are so inextricably linked. They are indeed cousins. How we yearn, yearn, yearn for what we might have had, or still could.

Many years later, she would reflect on this time and think of these lines from Christina Rossetti's poem "In the Bleak Midwinter":

> In the bleak midwinter, frosty wind made moan,
> Earth stood hard as iron, water like a stone;
> Snow had fallen, snow on snow, snow on snow,
> In the bleak midwinter, long ago.

But that was many years hence. Now was now, and she turned inward more than ever, dwelling on memory, thoughts of her childhood in England, of her young womanhood, of being what she once was, an actress, a Kemble.

All of it gone now. Gone.

How the bright winter moon inspired her, yet she must pull the curtains tight against it to somehow see, with an inward eye, and hear, too—her younger self, back in London, back on stage. Behold Juliet, in her elegant velvet, at her inaugural performance at Covent Garden, standing there before the vast proscenium arch, the audience crowding the long rows of boxes, four levels high, on both sides of the theater—with two thousand or more in attendance, her limp voice barely audible, her stomach jittery, her hands shaky.

Tis but a name that is my enemy.
Thou art thyself, though not a Montague.
What's Montague? It is nor hand, nor foot,
Nor arm, nor face, nor any other part
Belonging to a man. O, be some other name!
What's in a name?

Up closer now, behold her, deathly wan in the gas lighting of the theater. Her young, sweet voice, rising, falling. A fledgling player aghast at the prospect of falling off the stage into the orchestra pit! See how she trembles!

Yet how diligently she had practiced. She had gone over each and every passage, each and every line, committing every word to heart—even Romeo's lines—learning the whole script in three weeks' time, her mother such a martinet, demanding, correcting. "No, Fanny. Say it again. Again. Get it right this time." Her father? "How grand, how fine, Fanny!" But did he mean it? In the earliest of her early days, did he really mean it then?

Sometimes she could see her younger self, her accomplished self, for stretches of a half-minute or more—as if she were dreaming. How melodious her voice, how measured each syllable, uttered with timed precision! She could become others. She could become anyone. Look now: Juliet, a real flesh-and-blood person, not just a voice, not just a series of gestures—no! Juliet! Juliet herself! And Fanny—who was Fanny? Where was Fanny? Fading, fading. Ah, how she did so feel it, this being another, being completely another, feel it in every respect. And that's what it took, did it not? That's what it took to be a sensation.

But then, as she watched and listened now in her silent, dark theater, her voice would begin to fade out, her presence on that stage fade, the stage itself disappear, and she was left with her lonely self, married but not married, a wife but not a wife.

One night, Niagara came to her in a rhapsody of radiant color, though blurred so she could hardly see with any clarity. There she stood in her white bonnet and parasol, green with white fringe, and close by Mr. Edward Trelawny, a shadowy figure in top hat with wide shoulders, his mustache ends curled up.

Close together, so close.

A bonding—a true bonding of heart and head.

And before them both: the raging Falls.

She carried them deep in her heart.

One February afternoon, she sat at her desk with a view of the immense, pure white snow, covering the yard, the road, the land as far as she could see, the sky gray and promising more. Why not see it for what it was, the freedom of escape? Hadn't she wanted this? Hadn't she wanted a quiet life, a contemplative life, alone, to disappear into her own head, and have surrounds such as this, a snow-blanketed land, to charm her, to fill her with pleasure?

How peaceful. She longed for the night when she could, once again, dream back.

This remembering, this seizing of the now-gone past, so irretrievable yet not so when grasped by the transformative imagination—how beguiling! She began a letter.

Dear Edward,

I have come upon something of a distinctly myste-rious nature. Perhaps I am going mad! Perhaps I am already mad! I am half certain that I must be, though I entreat you to tell me that I am not—you, who were confessedly mad over Niagara. But per-haps madness is not such a terrible affliction when it yields such joy, when it yields such pleasure of soul and body, too. I can feel my fingers tingling against my forehead when it begins, and when it continues, my arms tingle. What is this "it" I speak of? I fear saying anything, anything at all. Yet I will. What it is—I'll begin here—is the visual and au-ral perception of my presence, my very being, on stage—that of my first performance of Romeo and Juliet, *certain treasured lines as I stood delivering them at Covent Garden but a child of twenty. How I remember that halcyon October day in 1829, so long ago, it now seems, though it isn't in actual years, and something, I know not what, is compel-ling me to relive it. And I do. This is the part that disturbs, yet also excites, me the most—"enthralls" is perhaps a better word. I actually do relive it. I can see myself. I can hear myself. I can see others. And not just this play but more. I see, hear, myself as Portia. I see, hear, myself as Beatrice. Dear, God, is this some sort of witchery? Are you acquainted with such a thing? And now I must ask: Did you actually "see" Niagara when you motioned your hands in the air at John Butler's? Did you actually see and hear the roaring of the Falls? I did. Twice now. For but a moment or two. It was suddenly there before me. I nearly wept at its incalculable, incomprehensible beauty—remembered, so fondly remembered! No—experienced! I do want to say*

that I cannot do such a thing merely on a whim. The act calls for more than that—an actual being "there." Is it possible? Do you comprehend what I am asking you? I feel that you are the only one I can trouble with such a question. Somehow, I am compelled to go back, back, and, on occasions, I am actually there. Perhaps you know what I speak of?
Your Undying Friend,
Fanny

She would have to wait a week to post the letter, a week for the roads to become passable. And then, as she knew full well, it would be a few months before she heard back from Edward Trelawny, all the way back in England, assuming that was, in fact, where he was.

Madness, she thought, is *not* a welcome affliction. She knew her mother to be half-mad, crushed by depression, a burden over the years to her father and to her poor dead Aunt Dall. Many times, with very little apparent provocation, her mother would descend into a great gloom, casting the whole house in a cold darkness. She would speak but little. She would not speak even if spoken to. She would undergo bouts of anger and rage. The gleam in her eyes frightened Fanny. "Am I now my mother?" she asked herself. "Or will I soon be?"

Her mother was not always given to such erratic behavior. When Fanny was practicing for her debut at Covent Garden, she was quite talkative, though business-like. She spoke of her family's duty to help deliver her husband from his ruinous debt, to prevent him from hiding out in France. "Away from us," said her mother, "leaving us here, all alone, to fend for ourselves. And yet what is to be done? The creditors are becoming exceedingly impatient, aggressive. They want money, and now. We must help. It is incumbent on us to help. You, especially, dear one," she said, her eyes steady on Fanny. "Perhaps you are the only one, my daughter, who can manage to help the poor man do that. I myself am not equal to the task—if ever I were. Yet I did, I must say, have an impressive start."

Of course her mother was speaking of her childhood dancing, and especially before the Prince Regent, who was exceedingly amused by her childish antics. "How delightful I was," she enthused, "and then it was all over. My own actual stage performances at Covent Garden were exemplary, excellent, in my own opinion—but not enough, I suppose. They were lacking in style, I was informed. In the proper 'flair.' I was not, my dear daughter, the Tragic Muse. But who can be? I did not pretend to be."

Fanny knew what disturbed her mother the most—not her failed acting career, but the London climate and being cramped up in that city with all the foul odors of horse manure and factory smoke, and unrelenting noise. "I cannot be happy in such a place as this. I find it quite hellish!" Raised in rural Switzerland, which she had always referred to as "home," she wanted the fresh air of the country, and so she acquired a residence in Weybridge for the summers. There her mother did indeed seem to find respite from her depression, and even when Fanny and her sister got the smallpox, she said, "We are so vulnerable to such terrible diseases. What is it about the human lot? But we shall triumph over this. You will not die, my darlings."

"She is a strong woman, in ways," Fanny thought, *"as am I."*

Yet she could not continue to live like this, not in this Butler Place, so utterly isolated. This place, she assured herself, was her second choice. She had wanted the Major's elegant townhouse on that tree-lined street with its fine garden. What sort of life was this, even though she had once idealized it—even though she continued to try to do so? True, she had her

204

daily rituals of reading and writing, but she felt alone, with no future. Her youth gone now, what did she have to look forward to but growing older and older? She would end up, before her appointed time, a white-haired, shriveled-up old woman, a husk of her former self when she was beautiful—a radiant beauty, if one believed the papers, with raven-black hair, and a comely figure.

∞

She wrote Elizabeth Sedgwick: *Here I am, in a wilderness, almost, and I must somehow plan for my daughter's education. I will not have her manipulated by such a man as I've chained myself to! Where can I turn?*

In a week, she heard back: *If you wish to educate your little daughter, you must cultivate her with as much reading as possible. A fully-prepared young lady will be a hedge against ignorance and tyranny. And then consider enrolling her in the Hive. Perhaps as early as age ten.*

Each winter morning once she had taken a circuitous walk about the land, which the tenant farmers would soon return to farming, she entered the house from the back door, had a spot of tea, and then took the stairs to the third floor, to take little Sally from Margery.

And then, with her baby in her arms, she took the stairs down to her room and, with books already spread before her, she settled Sally on her lap. Yes, she had discovered, babies love the sound of good language, which is pleasant to the ear. Her child would imbibe great passages from literature, and that is why education must begin early. And so she read Wordsworth's "Tintern Abbey" to her, reading with her best speaking voice, the voice she had perfected on the stage, having learned to relish each syllable as though it were of pure gold. She read and reread those most lyrical of passages:

Five years have passed; five summers, with the length
Of five long winters! and again I hear
These waters, rolling from their mountain-springs
With a soft inland murmur.

In her arms, little Sally's warm body against her own, these lines, she believed, would nourish her baby like the milk from her own body, meanwhile her gentle voice softly lulling Sally to sleep.

She thought ahead. Sally must, early on, by the age of five or six, begin making her letters, doing her arithmetic, learning to draw, paint, and play the piano.

But the Hive by age ten?

I have no money, she wrote Elizabeth. *And no hope of ever having any. My husband has denied me the money from my own book. It's the law. I am a victim of an unjust law.*

Then you must make him see the wrongfulness of this law, Elizabeth wrote back.

How naïve you are! How is that suggestion any help at all? Fanny wrote back, but then she tore up the letter. She did not see how anyone could expect her to convince Pierce Butler, a thick-headed, egoistic, clod of a man, of any wrongdoing, regardless of what it was. Perhaps there were some wrongdoers who were capable of self-knowledge, but he was not one of them. The question, for her, was what the future held for her with such a man. And what about her daughter? She despaired, imagining that.

She was sure that by now he had stolen hundreds of dollars, perhaps a thousand or more, from her, all the while gloating over his legally sanctioned crime. She did not want to know about it or hear him speak of it. She did not want to know how ruinous his taking her money had been or would be. She sometimes imagined stealing the money back—if one wanted to call it that. How was it stealing when it was *her* money, rightfully hers—from a moral point of view? She had written the book, not him; she had done all the hard work; she had earned the money and was still earning it on each and every sale. She could visualize herself entering his room when he was down in his study. If he had locked his door, she knew where an extra key was. Once inside, she would go to his desk and try the drawer. Locked, of course, but she would have a sharp kitchen knife with her, stowed in her purse. She would remove it, and she would pry the drawer open, breaking it.

And then she would plunge her hand in the drawer, looking about, raising noises of different kinds: the tingling of metal, the dull rubbing of wood, the rustling of paper—noises she must not make for fear of being heard.

But then she would spot the key—yes, the key that would open the padlock on the trunk. She would take it and quickly go for the trunk, situated to one side of his bed. She would grip the padlock in her hand and then insert the key. The lock would open, making a slight click. She would lift the lid off the trunk, emitting a screech.

She would eye the door. She would watch and wait.

And then the money.

She knew where he kept his stash of bills and coins because she had seen him, in Newport, stow it in that leather bag of a night, just before retiring for bed. It was at the top of the trunk, and so she need not dig for it. She would spot it: that bag tied with a string of cowhide. She would loosen the string and dip her hand into it, going for the cash, both paper and coin. His *ready cash*—that's what he called it. For things of this kind, or that. "Do I trust banks? Not entirely, my dear."

And then it would be a matter of getting out of his room without being caught. Perhaps he would see her just as she opened the door into the hall.

A common thief. "I would be caught in the act. Caught and delivered to the sheriff."

But you, you sold my Forester.
I tell you, we can't afford the likes of that horse.
Is that so? How much did you get?

She sat before her window. She composed a letter. Here she was appealing to him, her would-be lover, in a way she had never done before. *Please come—come now. Deliver me, please.* "I am courting him," she thought. And then she imagined him appearing in a hackney cab. She imagined carrying Sally out to get into the cab next to him. She imagined the ride into Philadelphia over the snow-packed road, the snow falling. She imagined him now and then looking at little Sally. She had trouble imagining anything beyond that.

She put the letter in her fireplace and watched it burn. She cried as the fire consumed it.

She wrote her father: *I miss being an actress. I left a part of myself back on the stage. Perhaps I'm still there, on one stage or another. Perhaps*

She tore this up. She wrote again. She wished him well. She assured him she was doing well. She asked about her mother. She tried to find a way to end the letter, but she had so little to say, so little to tell him, or could tell him—if she were honest, that is.

She wanted to say: *I made a mistake in giving you all that money. Why did I not keep some of it? I have such great needs, surely matching your own. And here I am contemplating being a thief.*

She wrote this. She tore it up. She pitched it in the fire.

Pierce Butler came into his inheritance. The Philadelphia newspaper ran a full page on Pierce and John Butler, on their vast inheritance from a great aunt: two plantations in Georgia, the combined size amounting to the second largest slave-holdings in that state.

Seven hundred men, women, and children in bondage.

The Butlers are among the most notable of landed gentry in our fair city of Philadelphia, the newspaper reported.

She wrote Catharine:

> *My husband has now come into his slave plantations. I feel like a knife has been inserted into my heart and twisted. You mentioned asking Reverend Channing to come speak to him about this anathema—whence it occurred. Please do so. My husband must reject this inheritance. He will surely lose his soul were he not to. And I along with him? Each dollar I spend is from filthy blood money. Is it not? Your everlasting friend,*
> *Fanny*

Pierce spoke of going down to Georgia to attend to his new properties. He was ebullient. He had a new lightness in his step.

"Did you see that article? Did you notice the attention? My god, Fanny, isn't that something? Something to be reckoned with?"

"It is surely something," she answered.

"Well, regardless of what you say, it is something. We are rich! Never before have I been so rich! I'm tired of poverty. I'm tired of not having enough. And then John . . . well, never mind! I'm rich—finally!"

She received a letter from Elizabeth:

> *Dearest Fanny,*
> *You wrote Catharine. Consider this letter as a missive from both of us.*

You must understand what you're facing. Your husband's slave doctrine undoubtedly comes from his foundational belief in Southern honor, in white privilege, in hierarchy. You will surely face an uphill battle changing such beliefs—but you must try. We must depend on moral suasion. Some speak of violence, but violence is wrong. It must not come to violence. We are both with the Quakers on that. The Reverend Channing speaks of coming to visit you, to speak to your slaver husband. Perhaps that will, in the end, prove auspicious.
Your friends in the struggle for justice,
Elizabeth and Catharine

Fanny watched daily for the appearance of Reverend Channing. Finally, one balmy May afternoon, his carriage pulled up in front of the house. Could this gentle Northerner, this scholar, this lover of humankind prevail against her husband, who denied the inalienable rights of every human being who wasn't white? That is, a white male?

She wanted to speak, but decided against any interference.

He settled down, and at first he engaged in small talk.

Pierce Butler seemed to relish his being there. His eyes sparkled. He continually smiled. She could tell that he wanted to get to the matter at hand, but he would allow the Reverend to begin on his own steam, and then, at that point, he would take issue. He would take issue with everything the Reverend said.

She watched and waited.

Molly brought in the tea service.

Brewed hot, steamy.

This subject of slavery, it too is brewing, she thought. She felt it hanging heavy in the air.

Finally, Reverend Channing did speak of the Butler inheritance.

"And?" said Pierce.

"This is wrong. Morally wrong. Do you not see that?"

"Seven hundred slaves, Reverend, seven hundred Negroes to serve white folks like myself and Mrs. Butler. I see nothing wrong with that. Negroland, I call it. It's in God's Word. Do you dispute God's word?"

The Reverend took a few moments. And then he shook his head. "No, I do not. But what is in God's word is treating others as we would wish to be treated. It's called the Golden Rule."

"I think you're forgetting something."

"And what is that, sir?"

"These are not really people, as such. They are a lower form of existence, and must be treated so. They are like cattle and pigs. Or oxen. Just look at them, Reverend, and tell me it isn't so."

One could read the Reverend's exasperation, though he was not one to raise his voice. "I've heard such conceptions before. But don't you see how appalling they are?"

"Appalling or not," said Pierce, "truth is truth."

"The color of one's skin doesn't have a thing to do with one's being a human being, precious in God's sight."

"A pig is a pig. How can you deny it?"

Fanny exchanged glances with Channing.

"And so . . . you have, at your command, seven hundred pigs?"

"Well put, Reverend. They may not look like pigs, having a human form. But they are the same—and as dirty as pigs. Perhaps more so."

"I suppose you are quite satisfied that Congress has just passed a gag rule on this matter."

"Indeed I am. The subject of the peculiar institution should be squelched. And it is in civil, polite circles. Why not in Congress?"

"If it's such a nasty subject as not to be discussed, then

how can you support it?"

"What's nasty, and divisive, Reverend, is the continual lying of the abolitionists!"

"I see," said Channing.

Plainly, Fanny thought, Channing's words could not cut through Pierce Butler's cloud of obfuscation. The poor man saw it. He sat there for a few more moments, and then he rose from his chair.

"Good day, sir."

"A fine spring day it is, too, Reverend," said Pierce.

She wanted to slap him for his self-satisfied air, his obnoxious smugness.

Channing soon bid them both Godspeed, left, and headed for his carriage.

She followed him outside. *I would like to go with you. Let me go get my child and nursemaid, and can I go with you?* She heard those words, but she actually said, "I would like . . ."

He stopped and turned toward her. "Yes, Mrs. Butler?"

She hesitated. "Thank you for coming."

"I fear I've not done a whit of good."

"What can I do?"

He stood there, his eyes leveled on her. "Make him see the error of his thinking. If that were possible."

"But how can I do that?"

He paused, his eyes still leveled on her. "He needs to be caught in his contradictions. Can what he's saying hold up to logic?"

"No."

"I am a student of Immanuel Kant. Perhaps you noticed that from my writing on this subject. But I fear your husband's self-serving nature won't allow him to discover or follow the dictates of moral truth."

"What then?"

"What, indeed? Take risks. To stop slavery, we must take

risks."

"Yes," she answered.

Soon, his driver was taking him away, and he gave her a perfunctory wave. The carriage rolled out of the drive onto the road toward Philadelphia.

&

She would have none of it. She would not permit herself to be married to a man who owned seven hundred men, women, and children, a man who so cavalierly disrespected their rights to their own bodies. And their minds? Were those, too, for their master's disposal? Did he know what they were thinking? Could he see into their heads and hearts and require thoughts pleasing to master? No. No, they could think what they wanted. He would never know. Their minds, at least, would be free from his tyranny.

She wrote Catharine and Elizabeth about the dismal meeting with the Reverend Channing, but thanked them for their efforts in getting him to come. She spoke of her one hope for those seven hundred slaves—at least they would be free in their minds. That was something of a slight comfort to her.

Elizabeth responded—rather quickly.

> You do not know what a master is capable of. To restrict every movement of a person would certainly, in the final sum, restrict thinking itself. One becomes afraid to think thoughts contrary to master's wishes. One begins to check each and every human feeling and impulse. Is this what master would want? One becomes afraid of oneself.
> I would like to be more encouraging, but we are, after all, speaking of the work of the Devil himself. Nonetheless, there are, of course, exceptions—there

213

is, after all, the love of freedom in us all. Now and then that love surfaces, rising, rising, and one cannot help but hope and dream. And where do dreams lead? One travels at night and hides out days. Every slave who breaks free, were that possible, is an immense success for our movement. For humanity itself.

Fanny wrote back.

You mention things which disturb me greatly now that I find myself yoked to the owner of over seven hundred men, women, and children. A man of property indeed! Yet why should that surprise me? Wasn't the plain truth squarely before me? His grandfather, the major, a South Carolinian? What else could I think? Isn't it odd how we can fool ourselves? Isn't it quite odd how we can pretend we do not know something that we do, in fact, know?

Elizabeth: *We have, it is true, a great ability to rationalize, to fool ourselves at every turn. Isn't it so?*

She soon heard from Edward Trelawny. He spoke of things in England, in France, and his concern about her well-being under her worthless excuse for a husband. And then he closed, taking up her question: Was she mad to have such real-to-life experiences as she plunged, through memory, into the past?

Or is it the imagination? Ah, if so, "What the imagination seizes as Beauty must be truth," sayeth John Keats. If that's madness, you can count all the great poets mad. And you can count me mad for hearing what I am not actually hearing, seeing what I'm not

actually seeing, sensing what I'm not actually sens-
ing. You are not mad; you are the sanest woman I
know.

1837

On New Year's Day, the sky was gray, the roads packed hard with snow. She watched her husband preparing to leave in the carriage for Philadelphia. On down to Georgia he would go. It would be several days, he said, and John would be going. "Just like my grandfather, only he had a mansion there." That was long gone now, though, he'd told her. Burned to the ground.

She stood there on the porch.

It wasn't that she would miss him. She would not miss this man.

But she had wanted to go. "Why are you not allowing me to go? Inform me, please."

"It's hardly a place for a woman—a mere shack with the barest accommodations," he said, blowing smoke. "And what about Sarah?"

"I will take her with me, of course."

"No. That won't do. That certainly won't do."

"I intend to go. And I *will* go. You'll not stop me."

"Indeed I will. You must stay here where you belong." He paused. "Do you want company? Do you want Gabriella to come and stay?"

"No. I do not."

"Tell me if you do. And if so, it will be arranged."

"No." But perhaps she could go to England?

He shook his head. "Definitely not. That would require too much expense."

"With your new wealth, you can't afford that?"

"No. I cannot. Bye now," he said, and she watched as two man servants carried his trunk out to the waiting carriage.

He was gone now, and except for her servants, she was in this three-story house all alone.

She wanted to be alone. But not lonely.

The winter gloom, she knew, would soon descend on her. If only Edward would come. If only he could stay for a month or more. "If only he could stay permanently," she whispered to herself.

She wrote in her journal, January 10, 1837:

I think of Edward here at Butler Place, filling the whole place with his charm. I hear him speak to me, in a soft, manly voice. He says: "Fanny, my dearest, shall we take a long walk over the snow-covered hills? Shall we have bread and wine when we return? Shall we then sit in the parlor as dusk falls, with me tending the fire, and you sitting before it? We will read together. We will talk together. And your husband? He is gone to the South. Gone, gone, gone to Georgia to his Negroes. Hordes of them. I could shoot a man like that. Nonetheless, it's just us, the two of us, dear Fanny."

I am wrong to have such thoughts, but I do. But perhaps it's not him, so much as not wanting my husband. After all, would I really wish to travel to Mexico with him? Would I wish to go to France, or Italy, to Rome or Venice, with him? I search my heart, but I cannot find the answer. But then I think yes. Yes, I would. Oh, I am a sinful woman to have such thoughts!

One afternoon, when she was looking out her upstairs window, her pen poised over her journal, she saw a black carriage draw up, then the driver getting out.

She felt a fluttering in her chest.

And then she saw. A woman was getting out.

Gabriella. Dear God.

She must go downstairs. She closed her journal, stowed it

in her desk, and locked it away. And then she swiftly made her way down the stairs.

She approached the front entrance.

A servant was letting Gabriella in.

"Your husband thought it best if I keep you company. I thought it best, too."

A second servant was taking her coat.

"Thank you," said Fanny, "though it's not necessary. But you're certainly welcome." And then she added, "It is, after all, my turn."

"Well," said Gabriella.

That evening, after darkness had fallen, they sat in the parlor, with the fire glowing hot.

Molly entered. "Would tea and cake be appreciated?" she asked.

"Yes, please," said Fanny.

Soon Molly was bringing the tea service of blue and white porcelain ware. A second servant brought the cake and then left Molly to pour the steaming hot tea in each cup. "Sugar or cream?"

Gabriella shook her head.

"Cream for me," said Fanny. "Thank you, Molly."

Molly curtsied and left.

Gabriella was quiet as she sipped tea, but it was clear that something was on her mind. When Fanny asked, she said, "I wasn't completely honest. I wanted to come myself. It wasn't just Pierce and John."

"Oh? Well, then, I'm very glad you came."

She wondered why she'd just said that. But in a way, she was rather glad. Perhaps, she thought, perhaps, this is a good thing.

She waited for Gabriella to speak. The woman was watching out the window at the snowfall.

"I could not be alone in that house any longer."

"Oh?"

"No, I couldn't." She waved her hand around, as though she were still back there, motioning at the parlor's shadowy spaces. She spoke of the sounds in the house at night, of the dark places where the moonlight didn't reach, in corners of rooms, and elsewhere. She feared the dark, of being alone in it. Yes, she had her servants, but she did not trust them, not completely. With John gone, who knew what they might be capable of, what they might end up doing? What dangers might a woman face with four servants, one of them a man?

"You fear them?"

"You have six servants, I'm told. Do you trust them?"

"Actually five. If I don't count the regular man servant who tends the fireplaces. As to the females, I have no reason not to, not yet anyway." She did not wish to mention Jane Hannigan, who had proved herself a menace, a disgrace, even though what she had done had not been entirely her fault, though clearly she was culpable. Just consider what she had made of this house, how her low behavior had degraded it. Not to mention *his*.

Gabriella motioned at the piano. "I suppose you still play, don't you?"

"Yes. Of course. It's truly my passion, as I'm sure you know."

It was a clunky piano, out of tune, and Fanny wondered if Gabriella would hold it in low esteem. Surely she would scorn the shabbiness of Butler Place, as a whole, given the fine townhouse she and John lived in. Yet she decided to put this out of her mind. It was, after all, Pierce who had not made the repairs, bought the decent furnishings, and ignored the time she'd spent developing her lists. Would he make amends? No, she assured herself, he would not.

"Out here," said Gabriella, "you can play as loudly as you wish. Isn't it true?"

"Yes."

They smiled at each other.

Gabriella gingerly forked her cake and then took a bite. "I know we haven't gotten along, Fanny, and I suppose that's my fault. More than yours."

"I suppose we are different."

"Yes. I suppose."

"It's no matter," said Fanny.

They were quiet for a spell. Finally, Gabriella said, "What was it like being an actress? Was it . . . rather manic? Frenzied, I mean?"

"Ah! In ways. But mainly it was hard work. Continual hard work. But, yes, there was an element of frenzy about it—and the manic. But that's art. Isn't it?"

"Ah," said Gabriella, "I suppose it is. But I wouldn't know. I'm only a playgoer, so I wouldn't presume."

When they'd finished their cake, Molly entered the parlor and wanted to know if they wanted anything else.

"No," said Gabriella. "Well, perhaps more tea. Yes, that."

"The same," said Fanny.

They said little after that. Fanny searched for something to say, but she felt, as she had always felt, incapable of making small talk. And she felt uncomfortable speaking of her abolitionist ideas, though she thought she should, for it was wrong to be silent about serious matters of conscience. But how could she introduce the subject without feeling like she was preaching? And the second thing on her mind, her marital problems—what could she say about those? Clearly, she must not mention them, any of them, to her sister-in-law. Wouldn't it get right back to John? And then to Pierce. But then she thought: "So what if it did?"

When they had finished their tea, Fanny said, "You can have the guest room on the second floor down the hall from me. I will make sure the servants meet whatever needs you might have."

"Thank you for that."

"You're very welcome."

❧

Each morning she had coffee and eggs with Gabriella, sitting in the back parlor, looking out on the backyard, and beyond that to the snow-covered farmland that seemed to go on forever. Sometimes, short on conversation, Fanny spoke of little things, like butter from the farmwife and the way these people, most of them of Quaker descent, wouldn't drink wine but had only water with their meals. Somehow she couldn't help but see such behavior as overly pious. "Last summer, I was thinking," she said, "of having a picnic, a real spread, replete with all the fixings, including wine, but Pierce says they would never go for that. They are not, in the least, imbibers of that foul brew!" Still, she said, her midwife was Quaker and a very good woman.

Having said all that, she felt like a terrible gossip. How silly of me, she thought. I should speak of more substantive things and keep my dignity.

Gabriella said nothing to her prattle. She looked away for a few moments, nodded, and then she returned to her food.

Then Fanny found herself speaking of Lucretia Mott. She felt wrong not to have mentioned her. "Perhaps you know of her. She's an abolitionist, and I find her a very good woman." She felt prompted to push the matter a little further. What was the point of small talk, after all, when serious matters confronted them both: their two husbands away, down in so-called Negroland, lording it over all those poor black people in bondage? Why ignore the most obvious subject at hand?

"What are your feelings about slavery?"

Gabriella's teacup rattled as she stirred her tea. Her hand was visibly shaking. Then she said, "That's my husband's

220

business. Not mine."

"You're from Charleston, aren't you—originally?"

"Yes."

"Yet you have no opinion?"

How blunt I am, she thought.

Gabriella shook her head. She again stirred her tea. "No, Fanny. None that matters. I don't wish to interfere in my husband's business. I was taught better than that."

"But what about the inhumanity? To own another human being—to treat them like mere property—and to tyrannize over them. How can that be right?"

The woman looked away. Then she settled her eyes on Fanny. "As long as John himself is humane, I see nothing wrong with it. After all, it's legal."

"Do you think John *is* humane?"

"That's really none of my business, Fanny. And, to speak frankly, it's hardly any of yours either. Is it?"

"Oh, but it is, isn't it? I live by slave labor. And you do, too, don't you?"

Gabriella's jaw grew firm. "May we please close this subject? Might we speak of other things? More pleasant things?"

"Yes. I suppose we might."

When Margery arrived with little Sally, she held her on her lap.

Gabriella paid little attention to the child. She sometimes looked off in space, apparently lost in her own thoughts.

When not at meals, Fanny left Gabriella to her own devices, spending her days in her room, as usual. On occasion, they sat in the front parlor, and at Gabriella's request she played the piano. One night, Gabriella requested that she play something serious. "If we were entertaining, I would not make such a request, as I know you know," she said, "but since it's just the two of us, I would prefer that you did. If you don't mind."

"Beethoven, perhaps?"

"Yes, that's fine."

"Certainly," said Fanny, and she thought for a moment on what she might play. Through the window she could see the winter moonlight spilling on the snow, the black sky immense with bright stars.

She began to play *Moonlight Sonata*. And as she played, she began to feel as though the space in the room were being shared by her, Gabriella, and the ghostly presence of Beethoven himself. It was just as it was up in Lenox. She could almost feel him at her side, and she imagined that if she looked away from the piano keys, she would see him. Would he speak? Would he appreciate her performance? Was she doing justice to his composition?

When she had finished, she retook her chair, and she still felt the presence of the master. How the music lingered on, past the hearing of it. She thought that perhaps it had always been there, like Emerson spoke of poetry, played or not played, composed or not composed, as an underlying substance to be discovered, then relished, worshipped almost, surely partaking of divinity.

She spoke to Gabriella of it. "I appreciate the principle of eternity in what he said. If we could but reach that . . ."

"I fear death," said Gabriella.

Fanny was silent for a few moments. "Death? I don't think of it much—perhaps I should. But I did when having the baby."

There was a long quiet.

And then, finally, Gabriella spoke: "Perhaps Pierce told you of my child. Of the loss of my precious child—in Paris."

"Yes. He did. And I am so very sorry. I felt very sad to hear this. I wanted to say something. I just could not find the time, or the place."

A silence—again.

"I saw how easily we pass from this world to the next. The things of this world, how easily they are gone. I saw the child clutching on to me for its very life. But it could not hold. It could not fasten."

"How tragic. How utterly—"

"John tried to comfort me, but he's not one to give comfort."

She had no idea what to say. "Perhaps this is true of men in general."

"They will be gone for the whole winter, John and Pierce. One wonders, doesn't one?"

"About what?"

"Nothing."

⁂

For the next few days, Gabriella made no appearance. It was as though she were not there at all. When three days had passed, Fanny knocked on her door. The servants were delivering meals up to her room, Margery had told her.

She appeared at the door, her forlorn eyes leveling on Fanny, then dropping—to look where? The floor?

"Is something wrong?"

"No. Nothing's wrong."

"Are you sure?"

Gabriella was in her nightgown. "No. I just need to be alone."

⁂

She received a letter from Pierce. He would not be home until March, until late March most likely. But that would be it. He did not intend to stay into the summer due to the threat of malaria. *Black people don't get it like white men do*, he wrote. He was pleased, he said, to hear from John that Gabriella was staying with her. He did not ask about the baby. She wondered if he ever thought of the baby. What was little Sally to him?

The winter days wore on. She began to spend more and more time with Gabriella. One night, the snow was falling hard, swirling in the heavy wind, covering the windows in the front parlor. She would have to go outside and brush it off if she wished to see outside when playing the piano.

"I fear John's being down there. He could die in a place like that. Then I will be all alone. For if I wish to inherit what he leaves behind, I cannot remarry. He has made that quite clear in his will."

"Why ever?"

"It would be the same, he says, as abandoning him."

"Pardon me, but how could you abandon a dead man?"

"That's John."

"That's quite unfair, isn't it?"

"It's legal."

"The laws are wrong," said Fanny. "They protect men, but what about women?"

Gabriella shrugged. "Once John comes back, we'll be going to New York to see the Wilkersons. I do very much like Mrs. Wilkerson."

"That woman? My husband abandoned me for that woman. On our wedding journey, of all times. Did you know this? Were you aware of this?"

Gabriella's jaw grew firm. "She has quite a pull on men. On John, too."

"Why do you like her so much, then?"

"She has taste, great taste. She's very cultured. She throws the best parties in New York."

"What about John? And her?"

"Well, she's not interested in John."

"I suppose you're lucky in that regard, then."

"Perhaps I am."

And then she couldn't help but ask: "Is John a faithful husband? Does he honor his vows?"

Gabriella looked closely at her. "Reasonably so, I think."

She didn't bother to pursue the matter.

◦◦◦

It sometimes came to her, over these winter months of 1837, of deep seclusion at Butler Place, how much she despised her husband's infidelities, yet relished her own imagined ones. Yet over that winter she began to lose interest in Pierce's infidelities. What were they to her? Perhaps she had grown to feel vindicated by them and even wanted more. "Perhaps," she thought, "I want to see him descend into the hell of sin and iniquity as much as possible." And then she thought: "Perhaps it's the icy winter of my own heart that makes me want this. I have grown cold, cold."

When she wasn't with Gabriella, she spent much of her time writing letters, ones that took great pains, for she had need, great need, to speak of what was troubling her, to share it with an intelligent mind and a heart capable of sympathy.

She wrote Catharine: *How I long to find who I once was. How I wish for the love of a man who feels deeply, knows the tender shoots of joy, and feels the ragged edges of sorrow. And one who does not trample on the souls of others.*

Letters warmed her winters more than the fireplace in her room, especially Trelawny's appeals for her to come to England: *Come and stay. Come and be with me.*

And Catharine's:

225

Come to the Berkshires, once again, to dissolve your very soul in those sublime hills overlooking idyllic blue lakes, to partake of Emerson's Nature— notice that I capitalize the "N." Have you read his essay? You must read it. Steep yourself in it, Fanny. You must find your own "I" in Nature itself. Ah, that "transparent eyeball" he speaks of. Well, it's an image that's not all that appealing at first glance, but I must say that it does grow on you in the most powerful way. Emerson recognizes the harmony of the soul with all creation! Yes, he shows himself a pantheist, but what a spiritual awakening for a dead materialist! And there are so many of those in the North. And of course not just in the North.

Fanny wrote in her journal: *I must seek such a vision. How material I am! I must lose myself in my natural surrounds. Have I not a soul?*

⁓

That March, after Pierce returned from Georgia, the roads went, as usual, to mud and muck. Pierce once again moaned over his rheumatism. "I need a doctor," he said. "I need relief! Why am I being tortured so?"

They could not get to town over those roads, and so no philandering for her husband. She watched the servants. There was Molly, who wasn't quite as pretty as Jane Hannigan, yet she was certain he was seeking her affections in spite of his ailment.

She no longer denied her husband the marriage bed. It was just easier, she found, to allow him to come to her bed whenever he so desired. She tired of his continual badgering. She tired of his forcing his way into her room, having removed the doorknob. She tired of his forcing himself on her.

She would not show even an ounce of pleasure. "You will not get the idea that I'm in the least pleased!" Pleased or not, it was what a wife was supposed to do, said her Aunt Dall. "Otherwise, you can be certain," said her aunt, "that you make him a whoremonger." But what if, she wanted to say to her poor dead aunt, you do not love your husband and question if you ever did? And she thought, "Go ahead and be a whoremonger! I know you are!" *Why do I allow you my body? I don't! I have the bruises to show you that I don't!*

That fall she was, once again, with child. And yet, she thought, I will love the baby. Of course, I will love the baby. Perhaps the baby will free me up for greater happiness. Isn't it possible? But do I deserve happiness? Yes, she thought, I do—if I prove myself worthy of it. Somehow, I must do that.

1838

She went through a long winter, all alone, Pierce once again down South. Sally came down with a bout of scarlet fever. Her tonsils grew large, too large, and the doctor stated that she must undergo a particular procedure. "That infected tonsil could end her life," he spoke, stroking the child's cheek.

"What procedure? Please."

He described it. How they would use a double-barreled silver tube, through which he would then pass two wires, fix a loop, tighten it around the tonsil, and leave it for a full day of twenty-four hours. This would, of course, be miserably uncomfortable. "I will not lie to you."

"My little baby," said Fanny. "Oh dearest God."

"It's the only way," said the doctor, placing a hand on her shoulder. "It will rot and fall off of its own accord should we do this particular procedure. This I can tell you."

She looked at little Sally. Why so vulnerable? *I'll not let you die,* she told herself. *I suffered untold torture to bring you into this world.* "Do it, then. Do it."

227

She stayed with the poor child the full twenty-four hours, trying to comfort her. Finally, the doctor arrived. He removed the contraption and Sally stopped moaning.

Then she herself came down with a sore throat, but her life itself was not in jeopardy. Still, it would not go away. The doctor came and applied leeches. When these had little effect, he applied more leeches, and still her throat ached and ached.

"It's not helping," she said.

"It's all we have," he said. "We might try blistering."

"No."

Eventually, it did go away.

When spring came, her husband was back home, moaning over his rheumatism, of being horribly tortured.

"Please consider," she said, "that I did not say a thing when my throat was killing me. I did not speak of being tortured. But you. Oh, you!"

"You have no compassion," he said. "None whatsoever. I thought a woman was supposed to have compassion. But you? Not a lick of it."

"What can I get you?"

He grinned. "I'll take some of you right now. Close that door."

"I am with child," she said. "Or didn't you notice?"

"I suppose that lets you off."

She left him to himself.

She began to fill whole days with plantings of flowers, bushes, and a variety of trees. Why, she wondered, do I do this? Because it's for me, not for him. I am not decorating Butler Place, which is his. *I am making my own little world here, making it as livable and as delightful as I can.*

She wanted to say: "Go to the South—go permanently.

Give up being an absentee landlord. Do you think I will miss you? No, I will not."

In early May, though heavy with child, she began more ambitious abolitionist work. She persuaded their man servant to take her into Philadelphia. She left detailed instructions with Margery for the caring of little Sally. Sometimes she would stay overnight at Lucretia Mott's, making arrangements for her servant to bring her back the next day.

As the spring advanced, she began going door-to-door with Lucretia to gather signatures for an antislavery petition. In this way, she was helping prepare for the upcoming meeting of the second Anti-Slavery Convention of American Women planned for May.

Some nights they attended meetings. "I want you to understand," she told Fanny, "that I do not agree with those in our movement who oppose women speaking out. Nor do I oppose the mixing of men and women in meetings—the so-called 'promiscuous' gatherings. The Grimké sisters are stirring up much opposition not only for their ideas, but for their reckless effrontery—as the protestors see it. Naturally I don't see it that way."

"Nor do I."

"I have been accused of splitting the abolitionist movement. But one must see the women's movement as part and parcel of the other—don't you think?"

"Yes. I do."

One evening a mob descended on them. Clubs came down on heads, with screams and cries. "Out the back door," whispered Lucretia, and she pulled Fanny along, until they came to a door which opened into an alley. From there they hurried away until they hailed a hackney cab and rode back to Lucretia's.

Fanny was shaking. "They could have been in that alley."

"It was the work of Providence that they weren't. The next meeting will have to be in a church if we can find one. At least, until Pennsylvania Hall. That should be soon."

The next day, Fanny read from *The Philadelphia Inquirer*:

Last night our fair city witnessed some disturbing violence. These abolitionists are perceived as "amalgamators," who are a distinct threat to men and women who are trying to earn their daily bread. What will happen if more free blacks enter our community, as hordes come from here and there, freed from slavery, and take the very jobs that these poor Philadelphian whites rely on for their daily sustenance? Isn't it enough that the city just weathered a financial panic? And what if these free blacks set out to marry whites? Black men preying on white women? Must we sit still for this? The so-called Pennsylvania Hall, now being built, funded by eager abolitionists—when this building is completed, we'll likely see more mixing of the races. And, as far as that's concerned, the two races will, we've been informed, do so in a conspicuous manner at the upcoming wedding of two abolitionists—one Angelina Grimké, a Southern traitor to her whole heritage—and family—and one Theodore Weld, a despicable abolitionist agent. Mightn't we have expected this sordid behavior from abolitionists? Isn't abolitionism, though it pretends to be a moral cause, actually a very immoral one—a plague on our society? Where is the surgeon with his skills in cutting out these buboes? What, we may well wonder, will descend on this city with the upcoming Anti-Slavery Convention of American Women?

On the evening of May 13, a dozen people were gathered at Lucretia Mott's three-story stone house with ivy-covered porch, women from the Boston Female Anti-Slavery Society and other guests, including two black women and William Lloyd Garrison. Over coffee with cream, white cake with raisins, and coconut pudding, Lucretia introduced Fanny to Garrison.

He was not much older than she, with rich brown hair, expressive blue eyes, and lips.

"I am extremely pleased," he said, "to have published your very . . . what shall we call it . . . *spirited work!* And so I hope you will fill *The Liberator* with more rabble-rousing literature. We need a raising of conscience, don't we now?" he said, turning to Lucretia. "We must be as harsh as truth."

"Yes, we must do so with a vengeance."

"I fully intend to send you more. I intend to go down to my husband's plantations—and soon."

"Indeed. You are unequally yoked," he said. "It is a very difficult position you are in. But I look forward to publishing what you do write. For now, let me say that the child you are about to bear will, in his or her lifetime, bring in an age of peace and justice. I fully believe it."

"As do I," said Lucretia. "As do most of us in the abolitionist movement, or we would not struggle as we do."

"We must keep alive the seeds of rebellion against this institutionalized horror," said Garrison. "I have vowed in *The Liberator* not to retreat a single inch, to be as uncompromising as justice. Yet violence might, in the end, be the only solution—the powers we are pitted against are deeply entrenched, in both the South and the North. I don't think we can disallow that."

"I reject that as a solution," stated Lucretia. "As Mr. Garrison is fully aware."

"I know you do. And of course it's not my starting position. That's the same as yours—moral suasion. Otherwise, why put out *The Liberator*?"

"Fanny can supply plenty of words, can't you, dear?"

"I do hope so."

"Meanwhile," said Garrison, "we face serious opposition here in Philadelphia with this upcoming convention. We are viewed, if you've been reading the papers, as nasty 'amalgamators.' We are indeed amalgamators, so-called. We will not shy away from blacks and whites mixing. In point of fact, we welcome this with open arms. For this, we will be persecuted. And we must do everything in our power to protect our black brethren as they arrive at and depart from the Hall."

"Behold," said Lucretia, "Built from honor and integrity."

Pennsylvania Hall was a two-story building, with pillars on all sides, and compared, in *The Philadelphia Inquirer*, to a Greek Temple. As the newspaper reported, it was one among several neoclassical looking buildings, including the Second Bank of the United States. The mayor wrote:

We can thank Nicholas Biddle's travel to Greece for this fine, impressive architecture. True, it has strong abolitionist leanings, with the poet John Greenleaf Whittier's Pennsylvania Freeman *housed on the main floor, along with a storehouse of slave-free products. But do let us keep in mind that this building is open to groups of sundry kinds and not just to abolitionists, regardless of the funding behind it. Those with abolitionist proclivities must keep this in mind and respect the citizens of their community and not incite*

violence of any kind. They must restrain their pen-
chant for divisiveness as much as possible.

Emblazoned on the front of the new building were the words VIRTUE, LIBERTY AND INDEPENDENCE. On this May day, a soft light fell on it from the setting sun. Fanny and Lucretia Mott took the stairs up to the second floor where there was a large hall, replete with multiple galleries, the walls blue and white in color, with gas lighting.

Lucretia directed her to a front row seat, in plush navy blue velvet, sat down for a moment with her, and then said, "I must be about my business."

Fanny watched her as she headed up to the front of the room, to a podium. There stood Whittier and Garrison.

When the huge audience settled down, Lucretia spoke calmly, with what Fanny recognized as her typical self-assurance. "Good evening. I welcome you to a significant movement forward for those who have worked, and continue to work, assiduously, for abolition. I welcome you to a significant movement forward for women. I welcome you to a significant movement forward for the city of Philadelphia, this City of Brotherly Love, which abolished slavery in 1780 but had vestiges of it for a while afterwards, and still, to this day, I regret to say, is anything but abolitionist. I welcome you to this wonderful new building, for which we are indebted to the hard work of courageous abolitionists for their monetary support!"

Applause followed and went on for almost a full minute, until Lucretia raised a hand. "Today we celebrate the Anti-Slavery Convention of American Women—its second national meeting! And please do note. Look about you. Three thousand, it must be—for this great hall holds three thousand. Do you see any empty seats? I do not as I look from floor to gallery, from gallery to floor. And we are not just white. No, we are not! We are of more than one color. We are just God's people!"

Applause again. But it was more than clapping. There were loud shouts, and whistles, and Fanny suddenly grew fearful of this massive assembly. She grew claustrophobic. She began to shake. And she couldn't help but wonder why. After all, she was an actress and she was used to huge theaters filled to capacity. But here it was different. Here it was people mobilized against something. She, too, wanted to be mobilized, for it was a sacred cause, but the child filling her belly made her afraid, somehow.

Eventually the clapping began to die down, and Lucretia spoke of the Convention's plans, one being ending slavery in the District of Columbia. "But many others," she said. "Many. And now I turn the podium over to our guest speaker, Mr. William Lloyd Garrison!"

More applause, but he soon quelled it. He spoke of their great cause. Of *The Liberator*, now seven years old. He spoke of the risks of doing what they were now doing—opposing slavery, how he had come close a few years back in Boston to being tarred and feathered, or, his voice rose, "lynched!" He said nothing for a few moments and then again spoke: "If not for the intervention of the Boston mayor, who gave me protective custody in a jail cell, I would not be here today. You see, we are hated in both the South and the North. Perhaps you'll recall how last fall, in Alton, Illinois, a newspaper man, Elijah Lovejoy, paid with his life for his antislavery position. For him, slavery was a *sin*. This past winter the protestors against our noble cause have continued to wreak vengeance. But we have truth on our side. Don't we? Yes, we do!"

Shouting and applause.

"What is the truth? It is this: Slavery *is* a sin. Therefore, I applaud every effort to stop it. The Reverend Channing, you may well recall, sent an open letter to Mr. Henry Clay urging him to do everything he could to prevent Texas from being admitted to the Union. The Reverend predicts a dark future for our country if Texas is annexed—another slave state! We have much to do. Our work is large and demanding—nay, unending. Yet we will prevail. I feel quite confident that we *will* prevail!"

More shouting and applause. When it ended, Garrison shouted out: "Read *The Liberator*! We will not stop until slavery is at an end, not until this heinous crime against our brothers and sisters is no more!"

Garrison made a little bow, and then moved to the back.

And then John Greenleaf Whittier, a man about her age, with abundant dark hair down his forehead, took the podium. He waited until the applause quieted down, and then he began to read:

> *Not with the splendor of the days of old,*
> *The spoil of nations, and of barbaric gold;*
> *No weapons wrested from the field of blood,*
> *Where dark and stern the unyielding Roman stood . . .*

Fanny fell into the rhythm of it as Whittier read on and on, and finally, caught his breath, and slowed, enunciating, with great emphasis:

> *But calm and grateful, prayerful and sincere,*
> *As Christian freeman only, gathering here,*
> *We dedicate our lofty Hall,*
> *Pillar and arch, entablature and wall,*
> *As Virtue's Shrine, as Liberty's abode,*
> *Sacred to Freedom, and to Freedom's God!*

❧

"I must be at my end," said Fanny. "I will have to keep up by newspaper. The birth is any day now."

"Yes, you must indeed hie yourself back home."

"My carriage awaits me."

"*Will* you be going to the South?"

"I promise you that I will."

"Good," said Lucretia. "You will be a witness."

Fanny read the newspaper coverage of the May 14 dedication meeting, as well as the activities that followed on May 15 and May 16. On May 15, a resolution was passed to end slavery in the District of Columbia. On the next day, on the door of the Hall was posted, in large black letters:

REGARDETH YE!
PHILADELPHIANS WILL NOT TOLERATE
AMALGAMATION!

The mayor, reported the newspaper, urged conference leaders not to allow blacks to attend this conference. Citizens, he stated, were very disturbed when they saw black women entering and exiting the Hall, especially when accompanied by white women.

The next day, May 17, they stood in the front yard of Butler Place, she, Pierce, and their five female servants. There they witnessed a gigantic column of billowing black smoke rising high in the red sky from somewhere in Philadelphia.

A conflagration.

A city on fire.

"Burning, burning," said her husband. "Burning, burning."

The servants chattered, pointed, chattered.

They all stood watching, and then, as the sun set in a blaze of orange and blue, went inside.

The following day Pierce held up the newspaper, thwacked it, then shoved it at her. There it was: the pillars of Pennsylvania Hall swept through with a firestorm.

"Consigned to the flames—where it belongs! Finally, finally! Justice!"

He thwacked it again.

"Let me read it, please."

Seventeen thousand protestors. The words of the mayor: *I have been eminently fair, I do believe. I consulted with the abolitionists and requested that they put a stop to the attendance of black women at this convention. But they would not compromise. I had no choice but to terminate this convention. It was too divisive. It was a serious threat to the safety of our city.*

And then the arsonists.

According to some eyewitness accounts, rowdy firemen stood by, chortling and hooting, as the building blazed away. But the mayor and other city leaders disputed this, that this was abolitionist lies and slurs—that the fire simply got out of control.

She shoved the newspaper back at her husband.

"Don't you see?" he said. "Don't you?"

"What am I to see?"

"More of that will happen if your goddamned meddlesome abolitionists don't stop with their antagonizing. This is what comes of that."

She didn't speak immediately. She stared at him.

"You have a choice!" she said under her breath. "You should think carefully about that. You've made a very bad choice. You're doing it now."

She wrote Mrs. Jameson: *Isn't it odd that in a country that professes freedom, and in this City of Brotherly Love, that a building devoted to free speech would be so quickly torched?*

And to Catharine and Elizabeth: *I despair when I think of the hatred against abolitionists in this country. I despair when I think how so little comes of speech. But it's all I have, at least for now. I do not think I will take up a weapon, though if one were to do so, I could hardly blame them.*

❧

On May 28th, born on the very day her little Sally was born, at the very same hour, three years to the date, she bore little Fan. How understand that timing? Was it prophetic in some way? No mistake, it was a product of her fidelity. She was a faithful woman to her husband, who was unfaithful to her. She relished adultery in her heart, but not in fact.

She now had two children, wrapped in every pore of her heart, a corrupted heart, she told herself, unless one found redemption in meeting straightaway what one had not yet met face to face: seven hundred black men, women, and children toiling daily not only for him but for her as well.

❧

The fall set in, and then the winter.

Baby Fan, how she loved that child, even though she was from an unfortunate, wrongful union. But you love your own flesh, don't you? She stroked the child's cheek. Where did this mysterious affinity for one's own come from? But there it was, and she could look at Fan and not think of him at all. *Mine*, she thought. And Sally, mine too.

She would not spend this winter at Butler Place alone. She would follow him down, a bit later. She would take her children, and she would ask Margery to go along as nursemaid.

She wrote Lucretia: *As promised, I will soon be off to Georgia to discover, fully, my part in this horrific thing soiling the country—and soiling me. I care not a whit that my husband won't permit it. What will happen to me? Will I be shot as a dirty abolitionist? Will I be eaten by alligators? Will*

I die of yellow fever? Nonetheless, I will be going, myself, my two little ones, and my faithful nursemaid.

She wrote Catharine and Elizabeth, jointly: *When I think of Lenox, I think of a kind of paradise on earth. What about my husband's so-called Negroland? What will I make of that?*

Just shortly before Christmas, they set out for the South.

It was an interminably long journey, several days of it, most of it by coach over rugged land, and the worst of it over corduroy roads through North Carolina swamp, but then, finally, at Doboy, Georgia, they were boarding a boat, her trunk being loaded, a boat paddled by two black men, that would take them to Butler Plantation, where her husband had told her to write if there was anything important enough to write about—but, no, she wouldn't be writing him. No, indeed not. She would be there soon, without any notification, and they would see what they would see.

PART THREE
BUTLER PLANTATION
WINTER, 1839

1
At Butler Plantation

As the boat glided over the river toward Butler Plantation, it seemed as if she had gone back, back, to some primitive, primordial, wild land. She began to grow fearful. One imagined cannibals and poison darts. Yet there was much natural beauty to see in the lush growth of trees and shrubbery: the oak, the Magnolia bay, the wild myrtle, the Magnolia grandiflora, the spiked palmetto, garlanded with evergreen creepers. There was a sad beauty in the saffron sky that set over the river and the gray, moss-covered trees.

When they stepped out of the boat onto the pier jutting out into Butler River, Margery went on ahead, holding Baby Fan in one arm and guiding Sally along with the other. The overseer's dwelling was up ahead, just as Pierce had described it, a two-story, slatternly shack.

When she entered, bringing up the rear of her little party, Pierce stood before her, looking aghast.

Margery was waiting with Sally. "Up that way," said Pierce, pointing to the narrow stairs. "But be careful."

Margery, holding Fan, led Sally up the steep flight of stairs.

A man in a tan hat rose from a table.

"This is Mr. Oden," said Pierce, "the overseer. This is Mrs. Butler, my wife. You will probably recall my speaking of her."

The man nodded, just slightly, grinned, then gave a little bow. "Mrs. Butler. The pleasure is mine."

"Thank you."

Supper would be on soon, Pierce told her, but meanwhile they must go outside, for he must have words with her. "Now!"

She followed him outside.

The two of them stood with their backs to the front door.

"You brought your trunk?"

"Yes."

"I'll have it brought up," he said.

"Please do."

Then he wanted to know what in the devil's name she could be thinking in following him all the way down here to Negroland when he thought he had made it quite clear—hadn't he?—that this was no place for a woman, and certainly no place for children. What was wrong with her? His voice grew stern.

"I have explained it enough," she said. "And since you chose not to bring me, I came on my own."

"Is that right? Well, you will be on the first boat out of here tomorrow."

"No. I will not."

"We shall see about that. I think you'll discover that down here, my word is law."

"Isn't it back home, too?"

He gave her that look. "Yes, it is, Fanny, though you've chosen to be disobedient. You'll not do so here. Think of me as a captain of a ship. Do you comprehend?"

She said nothing.

He went back inside. She followed.

The three of them gathered around a small table with a beige tablecloth. A black woman delivered roasted duck, with rice and cabbage to their plates. Several times Pierce or Mr. Oden called for more food or drink, and the black woman hurried back and forth from a sideboard to the table.

Meanwhile, Fanny asked about the children: When would they eat? What would they eat? They were surely hungry.

Pierce looked up from his plate. They would eat a little later, he informed her.

"How much later?"

"I'm sure they won't starve, Fanny, and so please don't harp at me on this matter."

Fruits and vegetables, she reminded him. The children must have fruits and vegetables.

"Vegetables, fine. Fruits—that's a different matter. Fish, though."

Fish. She supposed that was all right. She ate slowly, deliberating on what it was like to be here, finally, and to meet Mr. Oden, who now and then stared at her, sometimes with a grin that rather disturbed her. Even without that grin, she could hardly imagine trusting this man. There was something about his narrow lips, his hawk nose, and his tight cheeks with a jagged scar down to one corner of his lips that made her uneasy. His huge chest and arms worried her.

They finished their supper.

The black woman began carrying plates of duck, rice, and cabbage up the stairs. "Make sure they get everything they want!" said Fanny.

"Yes, missis."

She stepped outside. There wasn't a hint of flowers or shrubs around this clapboard shack, but all about a vast, swampy wilderness, with cypress trees, draped in gray moss, rising high among the pines.

She took a short walk about, and then she returned to the overseer's shack.

Pierce was standing outside, lighting a cigar. When she approached him, he reminded her that she did not belong here. There was absolutely nothing she could do here, but, he said, "I suppose you'll find that to be true on your own."

"I didn't come here to entertain myself."

He shrugged. He would go ahead, he said, and appoint Jack, a young slave, to canoe her over the river and around the four settlements. At least she could learn something while she was here. She would do well to do that. Jack, being smarter than your average Negro, could tell her everything she needed to know about Butler Plantation. "If you could open your mind some, you'll recognize the falsehoods spread about by these abolitionists you're so taken with," he said.

"If he's so smart, why are you enslaving him?"

He took a long draw on his cigar, letting smoke curl slowly between his thin lips. "That's impertinent, Fanny. It's confrontative. Have some decency, and please don't ask such a question."

She went on inside and settled herself at a small writing desk behind a partition where there was one small bed. She would have to sleep with her husband. She did not know how she could do this. She wrote her first entry on Butler Plantation:

> *I have come here, down below into the nether regions, it would seem.*
> *There will be plenty to note. Especially about Mr. Oden, overseer.*
> *I suspect there are places in him that are filled by the Devil himself. That grin!*

She lay in bed watching the white wisps of cloud cover through the high, narrow window. It was New Year's Day. They had been married for almost five years. Her slaver husband was lying beside her, snoring; her two children were asleep upstairs, almost directly above her, with Margery, their nursemaid. Mr. Oden, overseer, lay in his little room in his narrow bed. He was so close she could hear his wheezy exhalations.

The next morning the sun was a brilliant orange globe rising forth from a band of pink sky. She walked along a dike between the river on one side and the swamp to the other, riotous with enormous sedges that trembled in a slight wind. She stood appreciating a thick growth of shrubs. A hawk circled above, then disappeared in the direction of the landing, where the boat had delivered her and her small group the evening before. Once beyond this settlement, the dikes were all there was to walk on.

She headed back.

She stopped off at the rice mill, a short distance from the overseer's shack. She watched the steam engine doing its work, a mammoth machine-deity threshing the rice from the fields worked daily by the slaves. Efficient, highly efficient, yet she quivered at such feverish, mechanical fury.

When she entered the overseer's shack, Sally was speaking to Mary, their personal cook.

"I'm free," said Sally. "Are *you* free?"

"No, child."

"Why aren't you free?"

"Because me no want to be free, honey."

"Why not?"

"Because how would all the work get done here if me get free?"

"Will you be free in heaven?"

"What? Yes—me be free then . . . sure, sure . . ."

"But why not here?"

"Me can't be free here."

"Then not in heaven either," said Sally.

"Hush," said Fanny. "That's enough. Go with Miss Margery."

Margery took her by the hand. Sally went ahead of her up the steep steps. Fanny watched carefully, fearful of her child missing a step, but then Sally disappeared, gaining the next floor. She turned to Mary. "I'm very sorry," she said.

"Oh, missis, what for you got to be sorry for?"

"For what my daughter said. I will attend to her—this will not happen again."

"Oh, missis!"

Mr. Oden was suddenly there. He tipped his tan hat. "I trust you had a pleasant sleep after such a long journey."

"I got some—thank you."

"Oh, you'll sleep plenty here. Once you settle in. The place has an effect like laudanum. On Mr. Butler, anyway. Not, I'm sorry to say, on me."

She looked at Pierce. "Soporific, is it?"

He grimaced.

At the breakfast table, Mary began delivering the food to their plates—eggs, bacon, and mush. Then she poured coffee.

She turned to Mr. Oden. She must know a few things about slave life. Could he please answer her various questions?

"I'd be happy to, Mrs. Butler, if I know the answers."

"Thank you." She quickly read them from a sheet of paper. "What is the average slave day like? When do they begin work? When do they quit? What exactly do they do? And when and what do they eat?"

"That's a lot of questions, ma'am."

"Even so," she said, "please inform me. I crave answers."

"You will find," said Pierce, "my wife to be a general annoyance. So please be warned."

"I think I am owed some sort of explanation being this man's wife."

"Um. Indeed. Well, ma'am, you want to know when they begin work—and when they quit. Sunup to sundown's your answer. But it is task labor. Let's say if they complete their quotas and have a spare hour or two, well, they can make their own money—assuming they're not too lazy. Build and sell boats, gather moss for bedding, and sell this kind of thing in Darien. They can make good money—and have."

"Quotas," she said.

248

"Yes, Mrs. Butler, they do have quotas. But it's a fair system because, as I say, once they meet those, they're free to make their own money. You don't find that on many plantations—not in Lousiana, ma'am."

"What do they do with their money?"

"Whatever they wish. They get time off once in a while, on a Saturday, say, to go blow it in Darien."

"But not on liquor," said Pierce.

"No, ma'am—if you were thinking that was my meaning."

"I approve," said Fanny. "Can they buy their freedom?"

Mr. Oden looked long at her. "That's not my affair, ma'am. It's your husband's. Isn't it, Mr. Butler?"

"If I think they're a good candidate. Only then."

"And what does that amount to?"

"If they're not troublemakers," said Mr. Oden. "That's it plain and simple, isn't it, Mr. Butler?"

"Yes. And if the price is right. Most of them don't have that kind of money. A slave brings a considerable sum on the market. Freedom costs."

"Oh, does it?" she said.

"They usually squander what they do have," said Mr. Oden.

"What do you mean?"

He forked his eggs. "Every which way a Negro ends up pitching his money to the four winds."

"Could you be more specific?"

"I could, but I won't."

She ate for a moment or two, and then said, "When do slaves eat?"

"Noonday and evening, ma'am."

"No breakfast?"

"No, ma'am."

"Why not?"

"Ask your husband."

"You've asked enough questions," said Pierce. "Find out on your own."

"You have no answer, do you? None you want to declare."

He exchanged glances with Mr. Oden. "If you must know, they don't require it, Fanny. If they required it, they would be fed at that particular time. But since they don't, they aren't."

"They toil out there from sunup to noon without breakfast?"

"That's right," said Mr. Oden.

"How in the world do they make it?"

"They're a hardy stock, ma'am. They're used to it. Aren't they, Mr. Butler?"

"Yes, they are."

"You look hardy yourself," said Fanny. "But you eat breakfast, don't you?"

"Fanny."

Mr. Oden fingered his chin. "Believe me, ma'am, they get along just fine. No one starves around here, do they, Mr. Butler?"

"No, they do not."

"What is it they eat in those two meals?"

"Indian corn. Rice mush."

"And?"

"They raise a little fowl—if they're a mind to."

"That's usual?"

"It's up to them, ma'am."

"That's enough questions," said Pierce. "Entirely enough questions. Let's leave Mr. Oden to his breakfast. And be about your own business."

Mr. Oden was sticking a piece of bacon in his mouth, chewing slowly.

"Thank you for your answers," said Fanny.

"It's no trouble," said Mr. Oden, and he took a sip of coffee. "And what is it you will do with your first day on Butler Plantation, ma'am?"

"I will take a little tour of the place, I expect."

"You can walk on the dikes, but don't fall in. And watch out for rattlers. They're likely to be crawling when that sun stokes up. And it most likely will this afternoon. At some point."

"Rattlers."

"Yes, ma'am," said Mr. Oden. "Rattlers."

Pierce escorted her to the blacksmith's shop.

"Jack!" he called out.

A young black man, about nineteen or twenty, came forth, holding a large hammer. "Yes, massa."

"This is the missis," Pierce announced, and she would require him to take her about in the canoe. "To suitably occupy her time." If Jack was busy, said Pierce in a stern voice, he must drop what he was doing and immediately obey. The missis would send a slave boy to notify him. She would certainly not come herself. But he was to be at the overseer's shack once notified. Immediately. No delay. Did he understand? He was not to make missis wait for him. He was to turn his work over to the other blacksmiths. "Do I make myself clear?"

"Yes, massa."

He turned to Fanny. "Do you want Jack to take you in the canoe right now?" He snapped a finger at Jack. "Ready, boy?"

"Yes, massa."

"No. Not this morning. But thank you," said Fanny, turning to Jack. "I do appreciate your willingness to take me about. Thank you, sir."

She waved and turned to walk back to the overseer's shack.

Suddenly her arm was being grabbed. "What was that 'sir' about? What are you trying to do? What do you think

Jack thinks of that? He is not to be called *sir*—my God! Have you lost your mind?"

She pulled loose. "No, I haven't, and I'll thank you not to you treat me in this fashion. You are to lower your voice, or do not speak to me at all. And you are not to touch me!"

"You are to leave!" he snapped. "I'll make arrangements."

"No, you won't."

"We'll see what the sheriff says," said Pierce, eyeing her.

She laughed. "I think that would be a mistake. That would not go well for you."

"Bitch," he said.

She returned to the shack and to her small room. She took up her journal and dated her entry January 2, 1839:

> *Jack is a very interesting young man. He's very handsome, very well-built. I can see he's a young man of great strength. And I'm quite sure he has a good mind and wit to go with his physical qualities. One can always tell. There is something in a person, regardless of skin color or race, which announces itself readily. Like so: "I am keen in intelligence. I know something about people and the world." This is Jack, and I will not apologize for calling him "sir." I will never apologize for that. I was not prepared to say it, but I am delighted that I did.*

The row of slave quarters began just past the overseer's shack. These were little wooden hovels the size of a small storage shed, built closely together. When she came to the end of the row, roughly a city block long, she approached a two-story, whitewashed building with the sign INFIRMARY.

Two orange trees rose in front of it.

She circled back to the rear of the slave shacks and walked along a wide drainage ditch. In the yards behind the shacks, wild ducks quacked, honked, and ran about, flapping into the air. She assumed they would be slaughtered and eaten soon, to add to the daily ration of mush.

She passed the overseer's shack and headed out to the fields, where the sun was already a blinding white sphere through a thick stand of pines. A short distance away, she could see droves of black people on the flat land. A man rode a horse about. Now and then she saw a dark line rippling against the pale blue sky, and a crack like a gunshot. A hawk soared above.

Quotas.

She hurried back inside to work on her journal.

She found herself writing:

Here, they set quotas. In our ordinary lives, we set quotas for ourselves. We want to accomplish something, and so we set forth our expectations. We'll read a book a week. We'll write a poem a day. We'll plant a dozen trees, or this or that patch we'll populate with a host of flowers, and we'll be as industrious as we can, and we'll finish a given project by such and such a date. But we do all this on our own steam, unless we, poor things, are in a factory in some company town like Lowell, Massachusetts, where work is imposed on us, where we might as well be slaves, for the unspeakable drudgery and low pay. But even in such a hellish place as that, are we fearful of the whip at the end of the day?

They sat down to supper. Mary came with fish, rice, and coffee.

Through the front window, Fanny watched as several

black women, young and old, tottery-looking, were lining up outside.

"Who are they?"

"Ah!" said Mr. Oden. "They've come to see the missis. Isn't that right, Mr. Butler?"

"Indeed," said Pierce. "They've come to see the missis, the curer of all ailments. My, my, what if you had not come?"

"I must go out, then."

"And leave your food?" said Mr. Oden.

She paid him no attention. She hurried outside and stepped into the crowd of sick, desperate looking slave women.

One old woman was shaky, sweating, her eyes bleary. "Me see missis. Missis help."

"Please. What can I do for you?"

"Me head hurt. So bad. Right here."

Fanny felt it. Her skin was very hot. The woman's facial muscles relaxed as Fanny kept her hand flat against her forehead. "Go to the Infirmary. Right this minute. You need medical attention. You're quite ill."

"Me been Infirmary. Mr. Oden, him say me not sick no more."

"Oh, but you are. You have fever. I'll tell him myself. What's your name?"

"Abigail."

"Thank you, Abigail. I'll remember that."

"Missis help," said the old woman. "Missis help Abigail."

"I *will* help, but right now you must go to the Infirmary. Please. This instant."

The old woman shambled off. A dozen more women had lined up. They crowded about her and touched her, pulled at her clothes, and told of numerous afflictions: headaches, sore throats, toothaches, stomach ailments, aching backs, neck aches, leg aches, knee problems. They spoke all at once, frantically. She could hardly hear or think.

"You the missis," said one younger woman, moving forward, "you help niggers. Mr. Oden, him no listen. You help. You good woman. Meat, missis. Need meat."

"More mush," said a woman behind her.

"Meat," said another woman. "Need meat. Lotta meat."

"Meat," said several women.

Another woman, perhaps forty, leaned toward her, supporting herself on a willow branch. "Back," she said. "Back real bad."

"What is your name?"

"Teresa."

"Thank you. Can I have your names? I need all your names," said Fanny.

They told her. She said them aloud over and over, rehearsing them, trying to remember as many as she could. They told her again, and again, of their ailments, and she said she'd tell Mr. Oden and Mr. Butler, too, and she'd see what could be done. Something could surely be done, and she would see to it.

One younger woman, with a broken front tooth, clutched her arm. "Please, missis help niggers." She was heavy with child, and she touched her stomach, her fingers doing spider hops.

"It will be soon, won't it?" said Fanny, laying her hand on the young woman's stomach.

"Me no go field. Me lay roun'! Make plenty nigger babies for missis."

"No," said Fanny. "No! And don't use that word! Please!"

She hurried back in. Her head was swimming—where to begin? Where? Commit that list of names to paper, of course, while it was still fresh, now, right now, with not a minute to spare. She hurried past Mr. Oden and her husband to her writing table and quickly penned down the names she could remember—a half dozen. That was it. She stared at the list. But no: that woman with the willow branch—Teresa. She wrote that down. And then she returned to the table and handed Mr. Oden the list.

He let it drop on the table to one side of his plate.

"Listen," she said. "These poor women, they need help! They have very serious ailments."

Mr. Oden glanced at her, and then went on eating. "Thank you, ma'am. Petitions and petitions. Isn't that right, Mr. Butler?"

"That's right. They never end."

"Abigail, especially," said Fanny. "Please do help her. That poor old woman is running a fever. I felt of her forehead."

"Well," said Mr. Oden, with a laugh, "Abigail is always sick, isn't she, Mr. Butler? When's that old nigger not sick?"

Pierce forked a piece of fish into his mouth. "Always. The problem is, she's getting too old to work, to put in a decent day's labor. We'll have to retire her pretty soon."

"You retire them?"

"Of course we do. When they're too old to work."

And then she heard a commotion outside to the side of the house.

"They're lining up," said Mr. Oden. "Lining up, Mr. Butler."

"I know that."

"But let them sweat. Let them stir. Finish your supper."

"Indeed I will."

The hum of voices became a general babble of whimpers, groans, grumbles, and shrieks. Fanny's insides knotted up. She put down her fork.

Pierce delivered a piece of roast goose to his mouth. Two meats tonight, he had announced. He chewed quickly. He delivered another piece to his mouth.

The babble increased in volume.

"Goddamn if I can ever finish my supper!"

"You don't have to go yet, you know," said Mr. Oden. "They can wait. Who's massa—you or them?"

"Me, goddamn it. But they're beginning to annoy me."

"I'd not allow it," said Mr. Oden.

Pierce continued eating. The crowd outside was stirring even more. Human voices were reaching crescendos and then tapering off, and then, once again, increasing in volume. It reminded her of the swelling of the sea when a storm was brewing. She imagined the outside wall caving in.

Finally, Pierce rose from the table and left the room. Fanny followed him as he stepped into the petitioning area.

He turned to face her. "What is it you want?"

"To observe."

"No. Go on now. Go—"

"I want to see."

"No. Go sit with Mr. Oden."

"Perhaps I should just join them out there. Would you prefer that?"

He grabbed at her, but she was too fast.

"You had best be still. I'm not to hear a word from you."

"That depends."

"No, it doesn't."

He lifted the window several inches and then took a seat before it.

She sat to one side of the window.

He removed a ledger from a shelf below the window. Close by was a box of red woolen caps. He lifted the window with a loud screech.

The first petitioner, a young girl, about fifteen or sixteen, pressed herself against the window. Her eyes drooped over dirt-streaked cheeks.

"Now, what do have we here?" said Pierce.

"Me so bad tired. After baby. Have baby. So, so tired."

"Is that right? Your name?"

She gave it.

"Well, let's see." He opened his ledger and flipped through some pages. His stubby fingers pressed against one of the pages.

The young girl waited, a look of expectation in her eyes, of worry. Her hands rested on the windowsill, leaving smudges. Behind her was a disturbance, a rustling. The line was growing longer, more crowded, the petitioners impatient. They were pushing against each other.

"Ah!" said Pierce.

A finger went up to the young girl's mouth.

"Your lying-in is over. I thought as much." He held the ledger up and fingered it. "Here, you can see for yourself."

"She can't read, can she?"

He glanced at Fanny. "You hush!"

The young woman's eyes grew frantic, darting from one place to another. But she wasn't looking either of them directly in the eye. Her gaze was elsewhere, perhaps at the window itself, or perhaps at nothing at all.

"Me so awful tired . . . can't go field, massa . . . no field. *Pleeze.*"

"Sorry, but your time is up—savvy?"

"Please, massa. *Pleeze.*"

"No," said Pierce. "*No.* Keep begging, and we'll see where that gets you. You comprehend?" He reached in the box under the window and came forth with a red cap. He handed it to her.

Her eyes fell. She walked off, clutching the cap, limping a little, one hip lower than the other, gyrating in her dark gray woolen garb.

"Next?"

The line kept growing. Fanny counted more than thirty petitioners. One white-haired old man complained of a bad knee. A gray-haired old woman complained of a bad shoulder. A middle-age woman complained of bleeding.

"The doctor will be here soon," said Pierce.

"She must go to the Infirmary now," said Fanny. "Look at her. My god, Pierce—"

"What did I say to you?"

"You must report to the Infirmary right now!" shouted Fanny.

She nodded sadly and went off.

"Listen," said Pierce, turning to her.

"You listen. You listen to these people."

The petitioners were closing in.

"Got a bad foot," said one young man. "Toes—them rotting."

"Go to the Infirmary."

"Them say can't fix."

"Let's see what the doctor can do."

"Him say can't do nothing," said the young man.

"Then what do you expect me to do?" sneered Pierce. "You think I'm God?"

"Massa help," said the man. And then he noticed Fanny. "Missis help."

"You go to the Infirmary," said Pierce. "Right now. Do you understand?"

"Yes, massa." The young man moved on. He took a step at a time, privileging one foot over the other.

The next petitioner stepped forward: a rail-thin, white-haired old woman who looked to be in her eighties, or nineties, with a large growth on her face. It was so large that one side of her face utterly sagged, dragging her lip down.

"Yes, Betty? What is it now?"

"Me . . . me not able . . ."

"Not able to what? What are you not able to do?"

"Me can't," said the woman. "Me can't . . ."

"Can't *what*?"

"Jus' can't." She squinted at Pierce and then laid a hand on the window ledge. Her hand was almost on his. She did not seem aware of it. "Me can't. No more. Can't no more."

"I don't doubt that," said Pierce. "Now move on."

"Me can't."

"You best be on your way, Betty. Right now. You hear?" He handed her a red cap. The old woman reached for it, clutched it in her gnarled hand, and stumbled her way to the back of the line, stood there momentarily, and then stumbled toward the row of slave huts. She got lost in a throng of children running about, chasing a flock of ducks.

The line had grown even longer, and Pierce suddenly rose from his chair and said, "All done! That will be it for today. Petitioning is over. Come back tomorrow. Go now!"

A cry rose up.

He quickly brought down the petitioning window, almost smashing an old woman's fingers.

The line began to fall apart. The petitioners were making their way back, toward the row of slave huts.

Pierce put his ledger away, in a drawer below the window. He headed for the bedroom, and she followed him.

He reached in his pocket and drew out a key. He inserted it in his trunk by his side of the bed. Then he came forth with a bottle and a short whiskey glass. He poured the glass half full. Then he sat on the bed and took a long sip. "Care to join me?"

"No."

"What is it you want, Fanny? You think I'm a miracle worker?"

"What will you do for these people?"

"Me? It's not up to me. It's up to Mr. Oden."

"You're the owner."

"Mr. Oden's the overseer."

"And so it's up to Mr. Oden, entirely. Not to you at all."

"That's right."

"I gave him those names, and he hardly looked at them. He thinks it's all a joke."

Pierce sipped his whiskey, looking away, and then he

turned to look at her. "Fanny, you must attend to your own business. This plantation is my business, not yours. You pestered me and pestered me to come, and I forbade it, and then you suddenly arrive—on your own volition. But you're to remain silent about the running of this place. You can hear grievances, but that's all. I make policy. Mr. Oden carries it out. Are we clear?"

"Then it *is* up to you."

"The policy, yes—of course. But Mr. Oden is the overseer."

She pointed a finger at him. "I'll make it my business to do good here, regardless of what you say or do. I will follow my conscience. Perhaps you have none, but I do."

"I tire of your insults," he said, and took a drink of whiskey.

She left.

Early the next morning, at daybreak, she turned to the slave huts. They were in one long row, the first hut but a short way down from the overseer's shack. The door was ajar. She entered and several young children peered up at her. At first, in having stepped from the light into the dark, she had trouble focusing, but soon, once her vision had adjusted, she could. Young children were sitting up, some lying down, on mattresses leaking out moss, with tattered blankets half covering them, and babies crawling in the dirt, encrusting their feet and hands.

There was no fire in the fireplace, only dying embers.

"I'll be right back," she told the children.

She hurried to a wooded area several hundred feet from the overseer's shack. She began gathering twigs and breaking off rotten limbs. She returned to the hut with an armload. Then she went for firewood from the pile in the back of the overseer's shack. She went inside for an old copy of the Darien newspaper. She ripped pages into several small pieces.

When the twigs, with the aid of the paper, began to catch on fire, she gradually fed in the rotten wood, then wood from the wood pile, taking pleasure in watching the fire build and build. Soon the children were clapping, and she was clapping herself.

She bid them goodbye.

She went to the next hut. She did the same.

She went from slave hut to slave hut, making the rounds from the stand of timber to the wood pile, carrying the rest of the Darien newspaper with her. By the time she had finished lighting fires in each hut, the afternoon was growing on, and she could see the bluing of the sky and the sun fiery yellow but beginning to make its downward arc.

It was time to take care of those dirty little bodies. She started with the end hut, where she'd built her last fire and went from hut to hut, instructing. "Wash your faces and hands! Go now— get water!" In each hut, she sent two boys after river water, one with a piggin and the other with a large wooden bucket. She returned to the overseer's shack, searched about in a narrow closet, found a few tattered cloths, then went from hovel to hovel and instructed the older children to wash the younger ones, their faces, arms, hands, legs, and feet. She showed them how to scrub feet hard; they were so horribly dirty.

"Now, listen, my little dears," she told them. "You'll get a penny each if you keep yourself clean. Do you hear me?"

They seemed not to know what she meant.

She held a new Liberty Head penny up and flashed it around. The children's eyes brightened.

"I have children of my own," she said. "Do you know that? And I make them wash their faces daily. I make them wash all over!" She couldn't help but be pleased to bend the truth a little. It was Margery who did that.

"Missis," an older boy said, "you the missis."

"Yes, that's right. But I'm just a mother—that's all."

"Missis good lady," said a little girl.

She sloughed that off.

"Now I mean that about the penny. Keep yourself clean, and you'll reap a penny. It's a promise. And a promise from the missis is a promise you can count on!"

"Yes, missis," said the older boy.

And then it was a cascade of "Yes, missis!"

She set out for the overseer's shack. In a few places, not obscured by timber, she could see dark figures, almost like ants, making their way back in twisted lines from the flat field. The sky was darkening.

"You're running late, Mrs. Butler," said Mr. Oden.

She sat down. She fixed her attention on Pierce, then on Mr. Oden. "I've seen the slave huts. I've spent my day with them—the whole day."

"Is that right? And what did you see?" said Mr. Oden. "Enlighten us."

"I could scarcely have imagined."

Mary set forth a plate of fish with turnips and greens. She poured water from a carafe, and she said, "Would missis want coffee?"

"Yes, please."

"The missis wants coffee with every meal," said Pierce. "Let's get that right, you hear?"

"Yes, massa."

"I am quite sure I will survive without coffee," she said to Mary.

"Watch it," said Pierce.

"Dirty?" asked Mr. Oden.

"They are beyond dirty. They are a breeding place for pestilence and plague. And such conditions cannot continue, sir. They are shocking."

Mr. Oden laughed. "Well, ma'am, this is the way your

average nigger chooses to live. Just like back in Africa. And perhaps they are shocking, as you say—to whites, that is. But niggers, Mrs. Butler, they're not exactly the same breed. I'm not sure what it would take to make you see that, but I know it myself, having served as overseer for many a year, on this plantation and elsewhere."

"I will thank you not to use that word around me. I wouldn't think you would want to use it at all, but please do not use it around me. Second, I don't suppose they are the same breed. They are what you've made of them!"

Mr. Oden gave it another laugh. He forked turnip into his mouth. Then he began to chew, grinning at her. "You don't like that word, do you? Well, I suppose your husband did forewarn me. But beyond that little matter, as to what you've said, we've heard it before, haven't we, Mr. Butler? Is there any truth in it? I'm of the opinion *No*. No, there isn't."

"I'm of the same opinion," said Pierce.

"You *could* help these people," she said. "If you only would. Both of you. Have you no decency, no compassion?"

Mr. Oden dug into his food, going for the turnip greens. "That's where you're wrong, ma'am. They have what they need. And if you give them any more, they won't use it. They'll abuse it."

"How do you know?"

"Tried and true, Mrs. Butler, going on my own experience. Long experience. I'm what you might call overseer-wise."

"Well, I need supplies. Cloths to wash them, ample firewood, and decent blankets."

"They'll destroy those blankets. It's a waste of money."

"And they need firewood."

"That part is up to them. There's an axe on the pile out there."

"You expect them to do that after toiling in that sun all day?"

"Yes, Mrs. Butler. You wouldn't believe the strength of

264

some of those bucks. It's beyond your imagination. They grow them big in Africa, you know."

He lighted a cigar, rose from the table, and put on his tan hat. And then he left, whistling. Pierce followed him.

She ate her supper in silence.

A dozen women soon entered, one followed by another, through the narrow door. She remained at table, and they hovered around her. She could feel their warm breaths on her neck.

They began to complain of a litany of problems.

Over and over, she responded: "I will tell Mr. Butler, I promise. I promise I will tell Mr. Butler. Surely something can be done to help you." But she didn't believe what she was saying at all.

A whisper. "Massa not help . . ."

"He *must* help. I will require that he does help."

"Bones ache and ache. Head, it *hurt*."

"I'm sorry. I'm so sorry. There must be something you could take." Laudanum, she thought. These people need laudanum.

Later, she spoke to Pierce about it. Could he obtain some? Could he check with the doctor? "It could help relieve their suffering. The right measure of it, I mean."

"I don't think so."

"You don't? Why not?"

"Drugs? That's excessive. Use your head."

"Those dirty little hovels they live in and all their aches and pains—you won't spend a thing to alleviate their misery?"

"Must you be so theatrical?" He went to his trunk and drew out his bottle. He poured a whiskey glass half full. He drank it down, and then he poured another.

"Why must you drink like that?"

265

"It helps," he said, sipping.

"With what?"

"Why don't you go away and leave me alone?"

"Why don't you give up this life if it bothers you so?"

"It's you who bother me!"

She entered the two-story, whitewashed Infirmary. There was little light, and coming out of the bright sun, she could not see at first. But she could hear plainly enough the whining, the moaning, the screams and cries.

Birthing.

She found a chair and carried it to the outside wall. She went for a high, glazed window and lifted it to let in some light. She did the same with the other windows.

Rose, the midwife, was coaching two young women with heavily swollen abdomens. They were panting, moaning, and letting out long, wailing screams.

She went about, taking in the devastating sights of the sick: women lying about in the dirt, shivering, with rags for blankets, babies screaming and shrieking on the dirt floor.

"Missis! Missis!"

"Yes?"

"Me so glad to see you!"

"Yes. I know. I know."

Some women were huddling on settles before dying embers.

She hurried upstairs. Sick men lay about, groaning. No fire.

She hurried back downstairs and confronted Rose. "Where is the firewood?"

"No wood left, missis."

"Then I'll go get it."

"Oh, no, missis, me get wood." She got up from a birthing woman.

Fanny shook her head. "No—of course not! You attend to that woman."

"You got nigger enough—"

She kept going. She would not hear that.

She headed to the woods, making her way through the brush. Rattlesnakes. One could die so easily, from just one bite. Such a devilish thing, she thought, a product surely of the Fall. She doubted there would be rattlesnakes in Heaven. No, she thought, but here they lie waiting in the thick scrub for victims. How many poor slaves had died from one bite in a mission to gather firewood?

She went for sticks and twigs, more newspaper, and then she hurried back to the woodpile behind the overseer's shack for an armload of wood.

"Missis no carry wood!" shrieked Rose. "You got nigger enough for that!"

Fanny dropped the wood into a pile. "I *will* carry the wood. And please, you are not to use that disgusting word! I will not hear it ever again! Do you understand?"

"Yes, missis."

She made two more trips and carried back two more armloads of firewood. She built fires on both the first and second floors.

She returned to the pile of firewood. She gathered up another armload to keep both fires going. She was just turning in the direction of the Infirmary when she noticed Mr. Oden standing there, watching her. His tan hat was shoved down over his forehead.

"Where are you off to with that, Mrs. Butler?"

"To the Infirmary."

"No, ma'am. Slaves cut their own, as I made clear. Remember?" He pointed at the stand of timber, where she'd just been. "In that woods right over there. Not from our own

267

pile, ma'am."

"But they have none."

"Then they'll have reason to cut some, won't they?"

"After a day in that field?"

"We covered that. It's policy, ma'am."

"Well, it ought to be changed!"

"Mrs. Butler. Mrs. Butler."

She dropped the armload of wood.

He disappeared into the overseer's shack.

She gathered up another armload and headed back to the Infirmary.

When she got back to the overseer's shack, she found fleas on her ankles, and she had to remove her shoes.

Pierce was asleep.

She grabbed him by the shoulders. "Wake up! You wake up!"

"What?"

"Wake up."

"What now?"

"The Infirmary. It is miserable and hellish. You must correct this immediately."

He rubbed his eyes and turned over. "Leave me alone, please. Will you?"

"No. You listen!"

She recognized how frantic she sounded. But how could she not be frantic? How could she just matter-of-factly report what she'd seen?

He let out a sigh. "Clean your own doorstep. Leave mine alone."

She wanted to smack him, but she just left.

2
Supplies

She spotted Jack, busily pounding a large piece of iron on an anvil, the ends ember red. It appeared to be a plow blade. When he noticed her, he immediately dropped his forging hammer.

"Yes, missis." He hurried toward her.

She shook her head. No. First, he must finish what he was doing. She was fine waiting. She would come back a bit later—she had not meant to take him from his work.

He looked confused. "Massa say."

How could she countermand massa? "It's no matter. I have a few things to attend to first." She told him she would be back soon, in perhaps an hour. He knew what the space of an hour was like, didn't he?

"Yes, missis! Me send nigger?"

"No! I'll come. And please—" She gave up.

She went back to the overseer's shack and spent an hour working on her journal. And then, once again, she set out for the blacksmith's shop. Like before, Jack was pounding a piece of red-hot iron. He immediately put it down and joined her.

They headed for the landing.

How was she to walk with him? Was he to walk behind her? How far behind?

It mattered very little since the landing was close by, and Jack was soon at her side, bending over, getting hold of the rope that moored the canoe, which was bobbing up and down in the swift current of Butler River.

"This here's the *Dolphin*," he said. "Me call it our trusty *Dolphin*."

"That's an interesting name."

"Got seat cushions, massa, him use—you want?"

"No, no. I'm hardy."

He laughed, and then looked embarrassed, worried. "Me row you wherever you want."

"To Darien. That's where I want to go."

He waited, and she realized she was now to get into the canoe—ahead of him. He hadn't wanted to say it, as though he were telling missis what to do. He would get in second. It was his place, and he knew it.

She got in, the canoe rocking in the water, and for a moment she feared flipping over.

Jack slipped in, took up the oars, and she leaned back as the canoe slid over the murky water. They were crossing the river, past a long sandbar, banked with reeds, and she could see a cut ahead, which they'd be entering soon—from her map, this was General's Cut, dug by Oglethorpe, through General's Island.

Jack worked at the oars, his powerful muscles rippling. It was a lovely winter morning, a good day to be out, but she planned a short visit to Darien because Jack perhaps had duties in the blacksmith's shop, but more to the point, what would he do while she was in town? She must make her appearance at a shop or two and leave quickly.

"Does Mr. Butler have work for you to do—work you'll be missing?"

"Oh, no, missis. Massa, him want me to take you walks on water—him said buncha times."

"Is that so?"

"Oh, yes, missis. Jack, him please massa."

How revolting! How self-diminishing! And yet what else could Jack think? But Jack was right: Pierce wanted her as far away from plantation work, as far away from his toiling slaves, as possible. If he could keep her from witnessing the tyranny of slavery, she wouldn't have what she needed for her next book—

and wouldn't he surely know she was writing one?

They entered General's Cut, and she could see to her left, coming up, a huge rice mill—steam-operated.

"Big monster," said Jack.

General's Cut was a narrow one, twisting to the northeast, the banks covered thick with lush vegetation. Water birds sprang forth.

"Can I take a hand?"

Jack didn't seem to hear her. She asked again, and he turned quickly. "Missis row?"

"Yes, Jack. I want to. I would very much enjoy doing so."

"Massa—"

"Massa doesn't know everything. And he doesn't have to know everything. It'll be our little secret." But she was suddenly sorry she had said this. How could she jeopardize Jack by giving him such ideas, by making him think like a rebellious slave? She mustn't. She started to say something to correct what she had just said, but Jack was already speaking.

"You got nigger—"

"Hush that! Don't use that word—not around me. Never use that word, not even in your own mind. Do you see, Jack?"

"Yes, missis."

She hastened to row. It was hard at first, hard on muscles she hadn't used in some time, if ever, but it felt good—very good. She knew Pierce's idea: a genteel woman never exerted herself. This was below the dignity of her station. He'd prefer that she lie around weak and helpless and in need of his ministrations, whenever he felt like administering them. Isn't that what all men of his station wanted? "You must beware of this," Catharine had told her. "Being a genteel woman has its downsides. Be as weak as possible for your man—that's one of them."

Jack sat back, and when she turned to look at him a time or two, he smiled uneasily.

She felt the oar growing heavy in her hand against the swift current. She began to tire more than she'd imagined she would, and Jack soon took over. They entered the Darien River, veered to the north, and the docks came into view. They soon came to a wooden pier, the supporting posts slimy with river water, and Jack hopped out and tied up the *Dolphin*.

She walked ahead, Jack falling behind several feet, for in Darien, even more than at Butler Plantation, she knew she must not be seen walking abreast with Jack as though he were her equal. It would not be she who would pay for this infraction of white supremacy, but Jack. Did she want Jack flogged for his presumption of walking alongside a white woman? Hadn't she read enough stories in the newspaper to clue her in? He kept several paces behind her, and once, when she slowed to avoid a depression in the ground, she looked back and saw that he too had stopped. He stood there. She went on.

In ten minutes they were in the Darien business district.

At a dry goods store, she allowed Jack in, but he stood at the door as she approached the proprietor, a balding man with a paunch. She inquired about blankets.

The man smiled, nervously. "Your nigger there, ma'am, he gonna have to stay outside. The nigger store's up a few blocks—if he's got money to spend. Only this ain't Saturday, so—"

She turned to Jack. He obediently went for the door, opened it, and disappeared outside.

"Now," she said, "blankets. I want blankets."

"Yes, ma'am! Yes, ma'am! This is for your own bedstead, I'm assuming, or your husband's?"

"Neither. For my husband's slaves."

He stared at her. "Slaves?"

"Yes, that's right."

"Well, ma'am, I don't carry that sort of thing here—this is more for the husband or wife—or children. You got children?"

272

"Yes."

"Let me show you something fine in their line." He planted a cigar in his mouth.

She shook her head. "Not today. Do you have cloths?"

"Cloths? Why, we sure do. Some fine, embroidered cotton cloths—oh, yes, ma'am. Come look. Come." He directed her to a shelf stacked high with them. "This is for your husband, you, or the children?"

"My slaves. As with the blankets."

A pained look came over his brow. "Ma'am, I never turn away shoppers, especially nice looking women like you, but I do want to be honest. You need to go to a shop that deals with slave goods. We don't carry that sort of thing here. Now, Mr. Donnelly up the street—he sure does. Ours is the finer sort of cloths, fine bedding, and fine towels too. How about some of that for the lady? Could I kindly show you our selection?"

"No thank you. I'll go to Mr. Donnelly's."

"I understand. You do come back, ma'am. You're—?"

"Mrs. Fanny Butler."

"Mrs. Butler! Oh, my, oh my! Well, Mrs. Butler, I do declare. And I do apologize. You see, we've got some new customers come down from the North, Maryland, places like that, acquired them a few niggers and I didn't know—I wasn't sure—I didn't know Mr. Butler was bringing his wife—I didn't see anything in the paper—"

"He didn't."

He again stared at her, but he went on: "Oh, well, now, do come back. We got all sorts of items for bedding, bathing—all sorts of fine linen, too—you just really sure you don't want to see? A woman can find all kinds of fineries here to please her husband."

"No, sir. Not right now."

"I understand. But hear, you say hello to Mr. Butler—okay? Do that for me, will you?"

She made no answer.

He went on: "Oh—and my name's Mr. Scott. Well, you can see that from the name on the store! Right out front!" He pointed.

Jack was standing there.

"Yes, sir. I'll be going now," said Fanny.

"Ma'am, it's a pleasure. A distinct pleasure."

"Thank you."

She stopped off at Donnelly's, with Jack in tow. He stood outside while she entered the shop. She decided she'd make the visit a short one so he didn't have to stand around outside with nothing to do, looking down as soon as some white man or woman came by, directing his eyes at the cobblestone sidewalk or, if called upon, having to answer quickly—and answer just right. And who knew what that might call for? And what if someone stole him? Now and then she turned to look out the window just to be sure he was still there.

She could order blankets and cloths, Mr. Donnelly assured her, but he needed the money upfront. Surely Mr. Butler had an account here at the store if he could find it—he thought he did. "Well, no," he said after he thumbed through a thick record book, "I guess that's another Butler, not your husband. But he should come in and open an account for his plantation—and soon. Now, the previous overseer, he took care of that, and that's probably the way to handle that business," said Mr. Donnelly, closing the book, "so your busy husband don't have to fool with it."

"But I myself can't do it?"

He shook his head. "No, ma'am. I'm very sorry to say, but no—I have a strict policy to deal with owners only—or overseers, ma'am. Overseers are fine, as I say, but—well, the store has run into problems of one kind or another when we veered off that particular path. You understand, don't you?"

274

She turned again to look for Jack. He was right there at the window.

"That your nigger there?"

She didn't answer. She wanted to hit the man. She turned to go.

"Fine looking nigger," shouted Mr. Donnelly.

She turned and faced him. "I don't call him that," she said.

He laughed. "Not so good looking, huh? Well, not to a white woman, I'd venture. And that's good—that's just as it should be. Because, my god, the . . . well, you do get my meaning, don't you?"

She headed for the door. "Yes, I do. Unfortunately, I do."

"Pardon, ma'am?"

Outside, Jack smiled at her.

"Are you hungry?"

"Yes, missis. Me dreadfully hungry."

"It's a long way back. We need to eat, both of us."

"Yes, missis."

She had passed a restaurant called Darien Fine Dining. But where was Jack to go? He could certainly not go in there. He was certainly not welcome in an establishment like that. She was sure he was not welcome in any eating place, café or restaurant, in Darien. He was not supposed to eat, probably. Not in Darien, for sure.

He looked curiously at her. And then he deflected his eyes, as though he suspected she was about to call him down. And then suddenly he said, "Massa, him leave me in boat when him go eat. And sometimes him bring me back a bit of this or that to eat."

"What would that be? That Mr. Butler brings back to you?"

"A hunka bread. A hunka meat—sometimes. But mostly a hunka bread."

"Oh. But what do you do back at the canoe?"

"Oh," he laughed. "Plenty a niggers at the landing. They's doing this and that. Plenty to talk to. Laugh and carry on."

She didn't want to insult him by asking exactly what he meant. She assumed it was innocent and wouldn't land him in trouble.

"Okay, but do be careful. You go on back, and I'll bring you something to eat. I won't be gone long. All right?"

"Yes, missis. Yes, missis!" He turned to go.

And then it occurred to her. "You'd better follow me."

She headed back to the landing with him. Like before, he seemed to know he must walk several paces behind her. When they got there, just as Jack had said, there were several Negroes waiting and talking. She reached in her purse. She took out one of her pens, with a new nib. She took out a piece of paper and wrote: *My nigger . . .*

No.

She stopped.

She couldn't write that word, even to protect Jack.

She ripped the paper in half. On the other half, she wrote: *Mr. Butler's slave named Jack I'm allowing to wait for me on the landing, while I eat at Darien Fine Dining. He will be in my canoe. - Mrs. Pierce Butler.*

"You take that, and no one will trouble you."

"Thank you, missis."

"I wish you could go eat with me. Perhaps the time will come when you can." And then she added: "I am certain that time will come."

"Thank you, missis."

She turned and headed back toward the business district.

In a half hour she had eaten and was heading back for the landing, carrying meat and bread wrapped in paper. A hundred feet away, she could see Jack laughing with another black man. He could now eat, but she felt like she was bringing scraps to a dog.

She rowed while he ate.

It was growing dark when Jack brought the boat into the landing at Butler Plantation, Settlement One. Tomorrow she would go in search of provisions. Tomorrow she would get Jack to take her to Settlement Two.

∽

Early the next morning she and Jack took the canoe south on the Butler River past the rice mill, down to where the Butler emptied into the Altamaha, then converged with the Champney. She rowed a good distance, but then she could row no more, her arms growing tired, her whole body weak and achy from exertion. Jack took over, and he paddled up the Champney to a landing.

"This here's Settlement Two."

"Let's stop here, then."

They gained the landing, and Jack stepped out and tied the boat to a mooring. He assisted Fanny in getting out of the canoe. Then she was on her way, and he followed. They headed in the direction of a shack on a small rise of land. As they approached it, Fanny could see a long line of hovels beyond this, and the rice fields in the short distance, much like Settlement One. She could hear voices, deep, resonant, but higher-pitched voices in a kind of hum. Poor black people singing, toiling, as they met their quotas, or tried to.

The overseer's shack was somewhat larger than Mr. Oden's. Still, it was awfully plain and dreary looking. "I want to visit a little," she told Jack. "Do you want to go with me or go back to the boat?"

"Go with missis. Boat, it real hard stay in it all day."

She wondered what he'd do. Wouldn't it be better to stay in the canoe? "I can leave you a note in case anyone bothers you."

"Go with missis—if okay."

"It's okay." But he would need a note, still, and so she wrote him one out, as before.

He graciously took it, smiling at her.

Fanny knocked. Jack stood directly behind her. "Here." And she directed him to stand next to her. There were no steps—only bare ground.

She could hear a scurrying inside, hard soles on floorboards, something rustling, perhaps a woman's dress. And then she heard, "I'm coming. I'm coming." A nervous female voice, almost frantic.

A woman perhaps fifty opened the door. She was wearing a very fine brown cape with bonnet, and a silver pendant necklace. "Yes, Mrs.—"

"Butler."

"Oh, my. Oh, my! Please do come in. I was hoping for a visit from you."

"You were?"

"Yes, Mrs. Butler." She held the door wide open.

"Thank you." She stepped in, and the woman said, "Oh, Mrs. Butler, I am sorry, but your nigger has to stay outside. Or perhaps you require his services?"

"He is *not* my *nigger*. He's Jack."

"Pardon?"

"He rowed me over."

"Yes. I see." She turned to Jack. "*Shoo*," she said. "You get outside, you, and the missis and I will chat." She gave Fanny a conspiratorial look. "You have to be firm with them, don't you?"

"You won't allow him in?"

"No. No, ma'am." She moved toward Fanny and whispered, "They stink." Her breathing grew heavy. She confronted Jack. "Listen, you—outside."

"As you wish," said Fanny.

The woman looked confused.

Fanny waited for Jack to exit and then shut the door.

"Will he be all right out there?"

"I reckon so. Unless my husband sees him idling."

"I left him a note."

"If my husband looks at it."

"When's your husband arrive?"

"Any time now."

"Perhaps you should write him a note, too—if you would."

"Yes, Mrs. Butler. I will do so."

She waited while the woman wrote something out. She handed it to Fanny.

Mrs. Butler's nigger is permitted to sit idle until Mrs. Butler calls for his services.

Fanny wadded it up. "As I said, he's *Jack*—did you hear me?"

"Pardon? You wish me to say that in the note?"

"Yes, I do. Please indulge me."

"Very well." The woman again took pen to paper, and she wrote, and then handed the note to Fanny.

Mrs. Butler's boy Jack is permitted to sit idle until Mrs. Butler calls for his services.

"I suppose that will have to do." Fanny excused herself and took the note out to Jack, who had sat down at the side of the house. "Here, in case someone comes along. It's from the overseer's wife."

"Thank you, missis."

"You're welcome, Jack. I won't be long."

Back inside, the woman said, "That's all taken care of, then?"

"Yes."

"Please—do have a seat." She directed Fanny to a hard

chair and sat down herself on another hard chair, facing Fanny. She sat very erect and folded her hands in her lap, almost in an attitude of prayer.

"I don't know your name," said Fanny.

"Oh, dear. Well, I'm Mrs. Robert Lawrence. And so, as we both know, my husband works for yours. And I know his overseer in Settlement One—Mr. Oden. A very fine man, Mr. Oden. My husband speaks very highly of him. They've gone hunting together on more than one occasion."

"I wasn't aware of that."

"Mr. Lawrence thinks highly of your husband, too. They play cards. Dear God, who knows how much those two take each other for! I wouldn't want to know. Mrs. Butler—"

"Yes?"

"How long will you be here at Butler Plantation?"

"For another month or so, and then we go to St. Simons Island."

"Oh, what a lovely place, I'm quite sure, but how is your visit here? How do you keep yourself busy?"

"I am busy trying to improve the lot of Mr. Butler's slaves. To do that, I need some provisions. I need cloths and blankets. Do you have any you could spare?"

The woman seemed to reflect on this. "Oh, no . . . we have nothing of that kind. None to spare."

"I must have these. And some laudanum."

"Laudanum?"

"For their pains."

"Yes, well," said Mrs. Lawrence. She looked around the room as though searching for the mentioned medicine. It was an exceedingly plain room, much like Mr. Oden's front room, only it had two extra hard chairs besides those at the table. "I find I have so little to do. I want nothing of these nasty niggers. At least I don't have to work. I thank God for that. Well, just little things now and then. Boss the cook around! My husband thankfully is a good provider. And he's quite fortunate to be in Mr. Butler's employ—St. Simons? Ah, the ocean! A breath of fresh air! Perhaps Mr. Lawrence could be reassigned?"

"I wouldn't know about that."

"I'm not an unappreciative woman, Mrs. Butler. But I'm so shut in. I never see a soul. Perhaps St. Simons would be better than this!"

"I wouldn't know. I've not been there."

"Would you like something to eat? Perhaps some meat and bread, and some cake and wine?"

At first she was about to say no, but she was hungry. "Yes—that sounds delicious." She thought of Jack sitting outside with that note granting him permission to do so. At least he was getting a rest from his labors, and perhaps, she thought, some cake in the offing.

"I'll get us a nigger woman to put the food on. This cake I have—it's from Darien, from one of their finest bakeries, and the meat—pork, slaughtered by one of the niggers right here in our settlement."

Fanny glared at her.

Mrs. Lawrence flinched. "Oh . . . oh, yes, Mr. Lawrence did tell me—you're from England. Aren't you?"

"Yes. And I'm not all that hungry, really," said Fanny, rising from her chair.

"Oh, dear—Mrs. Butler, please, please don't take offense at the way I speak. I hardly . . . I hardly ever have a bit of company, and . . . it means something to me that you've stopped by." She wiped her eye. "Please . . . may we start afresh?"

Fanny sat down. "I suppose we may."

"That food I spoke of?"

"Yes?"

"The Negroes . . . may I call them that?"

"Yes, I suppose so."

"Well, the Negroes, I meant to say, they'll get our food on plates, and so forth. I do hope you're hungry. I am. Of course, I'm always hungry. So is my husband."

"I don't think we need slave help," said Fanny. "Surely we can put a few things on our plates without such as that. Can we not?"

Mrs. Lawrence stood still, looking nonplussed.

"Oh, dear Lord, well . . . as long as Mr. Lawrence doesn't . . . he doesn't show up and see us . . . dear Lord. Well, I guess. I suppose so."

She went for plates and set them on the table. She went for forks and knives. And Fanny saw cloth napkins close by and laid one in each of the two settings Mrs. Lawrence had made. And then Mrs. Lawrence went for the bread. She delivered it to the table on a large plate, painted with a homey rural scene, with beehives in light blue. "This was baked fresh yesterday, along with the cake. Mr. Lawrence had business in Darien."

"It looks very tasty."

Mrs. Lawrence pointed up. "That wine. I can't reach it. We'll need to get a nigger . . . I'm sorry, *Negro*, in here to get it. Don't you think?"

"I'll do it."

"Dearest God—no, no, I—"

Fanny scooted a chair from the table to the wall. Up above on a shelf were several bottles of wine: red, white, and two of them burgundy in color. "Which?" she asked.

"The red," said Mrs. Lawrence. She looked perturbed. Her voice had grown brittle, but shaky.

Fanny brought it down, handed it to Mrs. Lawrence, and stepped off the chair. She scooted it back to the table.

"I'm glad Mr. Lawrence didn't see that!" cried Mrs. Lawrence.

"Oh? And why is that?"

"Because, a white woman . . . dear God!"

"I hope he would have lived."

"But would I? I guess in England, it's much different, isn't it?"

282

"This looks very good," said Fanny.

"Thank you, Mrs. Butler."

"Just call me Fanny."

"Oh."

They ate the meat, the bread, drank the wine, and Mrs. Lawrence got up and brought the cake to the table. It was a two-layer white cake with raisins.

"It's very nice," said Fanny.

"And now for the best part," said Mrs. Lawrence.

After they had eaten, and had a bit of conversation—Mrs. Lawrence speaking mainly of the Sea Islands, how delightful St. Simons would surely be for the Butlers, and how she would like, at some point, to move there herself if there was a spot for Mr. Lawrence—Fanny bid her goodbye. And then she thought once more of Jack.

"I'm wondering. Could you cut me a piece of cake for the way back? I get so hungry rowing. I know it's an odd request, but if you have a piece to spare."

"Pardon? *You* row? Did you say?"

"It's very good exercise."

"I see. But your husband . . . surely . . . well . . . certainly I will. Of course. Please take a seat, and I will bring another piece out to you. A nice, big one."

She was gone for several minutes, much longer than it would take to cut a piece of cake and wrap it in paper. Fanny wanted to see what the woman was doing, but she didn't want to be caught snooping.

Finally, Mrs. Lawrence arrived. She was holding a package wrapped in white paper. "I've put a fork in with this. And a cloth to wipe."

"Oh, you needn't have, but thank you. I'll return them."

"You need not. But Mrs. Butler—?"

"Yes?"

"I hope you enjoy the cake."

"I will."

She walked Fanny to the door. She looked out. "Is your Negro boy here? I don't see him."

"I'm sure he's here."

Mrs. Lawrence scowled. She whispered to Fanny. "Maybe you don't feel the same, but from my point of view they are necessary. You couldn't run your plantation without them. But they are so foul, so loathsome."

"Good day," said Fanny. "Thank you for the cake."

"Wait!" said Mrs. Lawrence.

Fanny turned around. "What?"

The woman's lips were trembling. "Don't tell your husband, would you not? About anything that happened here today?"

"What happened?"

"Well . . . about you on that chair? About me, about you—about no Negro help . . . would you not? I trust that you will not."

"My husband would understand. He knows my ways."

"English," said Mrs. Lawrence. "English!" She broke into a laugh.

Jack was sitting against the side of the overseer's shack. He looked comfortable, and she hated to disturb him. But he wasn't safe here. She was certain of that, and now she felt bad about leaving him all to himself. She knew she had taken too long, and she should have chosen being rude to the overseer's wife instead of putting Jack in jeopardy. And was a piece of cake really worth the risk?

"It's time to go back," she told him.

Once they were in the canoe, she gave him the cake. One thing was clear: Mrs. Lawrence wouldn't have cut a piece of cake for the likes of Jack!

While Jack ate, she swung the canoe out in the middle of the river, shifting directions, and headed on back. She was getting stronger, better. She thought she could love rowing. She wanted to build herself up, strengthen her muscles, handle the canoe coming and going. The water had its power, it wanted, wanted, as Trelawny had said, but she wanted, too, and she must master it, and in the process discover her own power.

It struck her to ask something, and she suddenly did: "Would you want your freedom, Jack? If you could obtain it?"

She knew she shouldn't have asked him this, but didn't he deserve his freedom? And shouldn't he at least imagine it? And shouldn't he have her well-wishing, for she did wish him well. She did wish him free.

He looked quite baffled. What to say? What not to say? It could get back to massa, or to Mr. Oden. Or even missis herself—she might be offended. How be sure? No, she thought, I should not have asked such a question as that. I was grievously wrong to do so.

"Oh, no . . . me no want to be free. No."

She said nothing at first. She had said too much already. But here she was with another human being, one whom she couldn't help like and appreciate, one who seemed to enjoy being with her. And so she went on: "Why not?"

He hesitated. She rowed. Finally, in a soft, uneven voice, he said: "Because me happy here."

It angered her. Maybe it shouldn't, but it did. "But wouldn't you be happier if you were free?"

"Oh, no—what would massa do? How him run this place?"

"I see. But maybe he could hire you to run it?"

"No—me no need money. The only thing me would like, if could get it . . ."

"Yes?"

"A pig. To slaughter. To have pig meat. Or shoot birds."

"I doubt you could get the gun," said Fanny.

"Can't have the pig either," said Jack.

❧

In the next few days, she tried the other two settlements, but no one had any provisions to spare. And so she watched for an opportunity.

She took careful notice as Pierce opened his trunk, took out his liquor, poured it into his glass, and sat back and sighed. He tended to go sleepy-eyed after he'd had a few, and more than once, he had fallen asleep—the trunk open, the key in his lap.

She must get that key.

She watched for an opportunity, several days passing, and finally the time came.

When he began to snore, she very carefully took the key up, and then very carefully opened the trunk.

He continued to snore.

She reached in, grabbed the leather bag of money, and drew out, piece by piece, all the money she thought she might need—and a bit more.

Then she closed the trunk and restored the key to his lap.

Jack came out of the blacksmith's hut, carrying his hammer. "Yes, missis. Me take you walks on water?"

"Yes, Jack—please. To Darien."

He laughed. "Darien. Darien good!"

He let the hammer fall to the ground, and they headed toward the river. There floated the *Dolphin*, rocking in the water. Fanny took the oars.

"Oh, missis. You got nigger—"

"I will do the rowing." She moved them slowly, steadily away from shore. The oars were hard work, and she was not powerful like Jack, whose arm and neck muscles knotted up when he went at them. But she swore she would last longer this time than the time before. She would get a little better every time.

"Missis do good job," said Jack.

She wished he wouldn't call her that. But she despaired of what else he might call her and what this might lead to. After she had rowed perhaps a tenth of a mile, she decided to pump him for a little information. "What happens to the really old slaves? When they can't work?"

"Woodville. Them go there."

"Where is that?"

"It on Carrs . . . way down there, bottom of de worl'."

"What happens there?"

"Them die."

"They get sent off to die?"

"Them no longer do the work. Them have to die."

"That is horrible."

Jack didn't say anything.

She rowed until she could row no more, and then let him take over.

She wrote Jack a note. He stayed in the canoe while she went into Darien and posted a few letters. Then she spent an hour looking around for stationery and pen nibs.

She spent another hour purchasing cloths and blankets. She had to pay extra to have them delivered to Butler Plantation. She had bought one hundred cloths and fifty blankets. She had a modest amount of cash remaining.

When she got back, Jack wasn't there. She looked all around. Had he gone into town on his own? No, he couldn't have. It wasn't a Saturday. No, Jack wouldn't be that foolish.

She became quite concerned.

A tall, thin white man lounged in a boat close by, smoking a cigar. A bottle of whiskey was parked in his lap. He had longish sideburns, much like Pierce's, and he was reading a newspaper, and now and then shaking it. An old black man with a grizzled beard was fanning him.

He looked Fanny's way. "That there your canoe, ma'am?"

"Yes."

"Sheriff Bob, he got your nigger."

"What? What did he do?"

"Do? Don't know, ma'am. Maybe he smarted off. Sheriff Bob, he don't go for no nigger smarting off."

"Where is this Sheriff Bob?"

He flicked his cigar. "You go into town, see, and you stay on the main street. End of the third block—no, fourth. Four blocks. Just past a nice little saddle shop. That's where the jail is. Now, if you have a hard time finding it, you just ask anybody. They can tell you. You out of the area, I take it. Who we talking to?"

"Fanny Butler."

"Butler. John? Pierce?"

"The second."

"Well, I do declare, and so I have the pleasure of Mrs. Pierce Butler this fine day."

"I suppose you do."

"My name, if you're curious, or you're not, is Ralph Barnaby."

"Barnaby—"

"That's right. One of the Barnaby brothers. You probably know Jasper, the big religious fella. Baptist church?"

"No. I've not met him."

"Well, don't judge all Barnabys by Jasper Barnaby. We ain't all the same." He held up his bottle of whiskey.

"All right. I won't." And she turned, once again, toward Darien. From what the man had said, it was a block down from the post office on the opposite side of the street. While she'd been looking for writing supplies, and purchasing cloths and blankets for the poor slaves, there was Jack being arrested by the sheriff and herded into his jail. She'd written him a note. What was the problem?

She came to the jail. It was a plain stone building about the size of the overseer's shack. She entered, the door a creaky one, and a hunched-over man with his back to her was looking out a side window.

"Excuse me," she said.

He turned slowly around and squinted at her. He seemed to need to adjust his vision. "Ma'am?"

"Are you Sheriff Bob?"

He laughed. "No, no! Sheriff, he's out right now. Ma'am, what is it you're a-needin'?"

"I'm Mrs. Butler. I need my Jack. Sheriff Bob brought him in this morning—I think."

"Your nigger boy?"

She wanted to slap this Southern cracker. *Fanny, you had better not offend them when you go into Darien. They're the law. They're hired to enforce the law. And they do.*

"My *Jack*."

"Back in the cage, ma'am. Bob figured him for a runaway."

"No, sir. He is not a runaway. He's my Jack."

He grinned. His face was plain and pasty, like uncooked dough. "You sound like you're pretty goddamned fond a-that nigger. Must think he's a damn fine nigger. Well, Bob, he was under a different impression."

"Do you know who you're talking to, sir?"

"I think you done said 'Mrs. Butler.' That's what I recall least ways." He was leaning his hunched-over body on his desk and peering up at her.

"I am Mr. Pierce Butler's wife."

"Don't say. Well, goddamn."

"That's right."

"Ma'am, I don't mean any disrespect. But I'm sure your husband, Mr. Butler, he'd want us to stop a runaway nigger of his. He's one of the key men about these parts that's worked hard on the slave patrol. You ask Bob, see if I'm not right."

"Well, I am telling you that Jack, back there in your iron cage, is my boy. Commissioned by Mr. Butler to take me around from place to place in a canoe. And if you contact my husband, he will tell you that. Do you want a lady like me to have to row herself all the way back to Butler Plantation in the dark? Mr. Butler certainly doesn't want that. Do you and Sheriff Bob want that?"

He seemed to reflect on this. He poked a wad of chewing tobacco in his mouth. And then he advanced toward her. "Ma'am, I ain't even introduced myself. My name's Tom." He reached out and grabbed her hand and shook it. "Tom Orange."

"Well, Mr. Orange, I do wish you'd free my boy Jack because I surely do need him to row me back to the plantation. Before it gets dark. I certainly don't like that river in the dark."

"Heavens, no! Know what you mean there, ma'am. Know what you mean. And as much as I'd like to be at your service, I got to wait till Sheriff Bob himself shows. He's the one in charge. He's the one that runs things around here." He grabbed a paper off his desk and held it up. "Right here is them arrest papers. Now, I can't just go and let a nigger go free without Bob's John Hancock. Don't you see?"

"That makes it very inconvenient for me. Now doesn't it?"

He looked closely at her. "Your nigger there had no papers on him. Not a one."

"Papers."

"No, ma'am. No pass, ma'am. A nigger doesn't have that, and it's right off to jail with his carcass. Sheriff Bob, he moves swiftly on a thing like that."

"Mr. Butler said nothing at all about a pass, Mr. Orange."

"Well, ma'am, if your husband knows anything at all, he knows a nigger leaving the plantation has got to be carrying a pass—if he ain't attended by a white man. Lucky Bob didn't shoot him."

"That's real lucky."

"No need for sarcasm, ma'am. Just doing our job." He leaned over and spit in a bucket.

"When do you expect Sheriff Bob back?"

"Could be this evening. Could be tomorrow morning."

"What! Then how am I to get back?"

He looked at her, and then grinned, with yellowish brown teeth. "We'll get us a local man to hire you out a nigger. Nobody around here expects a woman to row herself back—that ain't us. But it'll cost you. Probably two to three bucks."

"I'll row myself back for that."

"Oh, no, ma'am. Naw."

"I want to see Jack. If you would just please accommodate me."

He shrugged. He spit again into that bucket. "Guess I could show you your own nigger, ma'am, but don't you take too long. Bob, he don't go for that much—he's back there for a reason, you know."

"Yes, you told me."

"Well, then, ma'am, I'll let you back there—for five minutes. Five minutes tops. That's the limit."

"Yes, sir."

"Oh, shoot, ma'am, you needn't call me that. Just call me Tom. Everybody around here does."

"Okay, Tom."

"Right this way, Mrs. Butler. Right this way."

Hunched over, he took a large key and inserted it into the locked door a few feet behind and to the left of his desk.

And then he swung the door half open, and he led her down a row of cells, where black men sat on narrow benches, or clung to bars, staring at her as she went by. They passed a half dozen of these cells and came to the end. There sat Jack.

"Jack," she said. "Jack . . ."

"Missis. Me do nothing, missis. Me do nothing. Sheriff Bob, him—"

"You shut your goddamned mouth!" shouted Tom. "Or it'll go bad for you. Sheriff Bob, he done his duty. You broke the law, nigger, so you just shut your goddamned mouth."

"Yes, massa."

"See you don't open that mouth again against Sheriff Bob."

"Yes, massa."

"I'll leave him to you," said Tom, winking at her, and he turned to go. "Five minutes, ma'am. Five minutes."

"Yes, Tom."

"He ain't a bad nigger. Got a good body for the field, ma'am."

"He's a blacksmith."

"Well, shoot. I'd of thought so, looking at him. Break a man's neck he get the chance, wouldn't he?" He again winked at her.

"No, he would not."

"Well! Then you got the nigger tamed, huh? Five minutes, ma'am." And he took off.

She waited until Tom was gone, and she said, "Jack—I'm so sorry. It was my fault. If I had only hurried back. But I had no idea—"

"Me not run off," said Jack, advancing toward her. "Sit in the boat. Sheriff Bob, him come and grab me. Take lash—" He turned around and showed her his back, his shirt shredded, with bloody gashes scored all across it.

"Oh, dear God!"

"Sheriff Bob, he ain't a bad man. No pass, him say. Me break the law."

"Did Mr. Butler make you out a pass?"

"No, missis. Massa, him make out no pass."

"Then it's not your fault. It's mine, Jack. For not knowing about it." She started to cry.

"Oh, no, missis. It ain't your fault. Missis be good to Jack."

"I'm afraid not," she said, crying.

"Missis be good."

"How many lashes, Jack? You tell me. How many lashes from Sheriff Bob?"

"Lost count, missis. Over and over."

She wiped her tears. She grew infuriated. "Well, I'll have a few words with Sheriff Bob about this, Jack. I'll have some strong words with Sheriff Bob."

He nodded.

"Missis good lady."

"I want you back home. I want you back right now. You do not belong here. You've done nothing wrong. Nothing at all."

"Missis good lady," said Jack, gripping the bars.

"I'm afraid missis is not as good as she could be." She wiped her eyes. She saw Tom Orange waiting outside the door into the office. "I must go now. But I will get you out of that cage. Soon. I promise!"

"Yes, missis."

And she went back past the jail cells toward the deputy.

Back in the office, Tom said, "What's it going to be, ma'am?"

"I'll wait here for Sheriff Bob."

"Naw. No telling when he'll be back, ma'am."

"I'll wait anyway."

"Well, then, you go ahead, ma'am."

"I will."

She sat on a bench while Tom hunched over papers at his desk, smoking a cigar. Now and then a man would stop by, and Tom would laugh and joke around, leaning back in his chair, propping his boots up on the desk and going into a paroxysm of laughter. Late in the evening, about suppertime, a large, stocky man came in clearing his throat. "Well, Tom, you sure do look comfy."

"Sheriff," said Tom.

"Enjoying that cigar?"

"Yes, sir," said Tom. He put some papers down and got his feet on the floor. "This here is Mrs. Butler. She wants her nigger back. Name of Jack."

Fanny rose from the bench.

"Well, now, Mrs. Butler, it's a distinct pleasure." He reached out to shake her hand.

She allowed it. It was a firm, tight handshake. It could break bones. And then he withdrew.

"You're wanting your nigger Jack back. No doubt. No doubt." He stared down at her. "But I'll need Mr. Butler to come over and spring him. Is what I need. I guess you can understand that. I know he's a busy man, but I can't let that nigger go without his John Hancock."

"I'll sign the paper, or whatever it is you need," said Fanny. "Mr. Butler failed to give him a pass."

He shook his head. "Your signing won't make a lick of difference, ma'am. A pass from the owner—that's what's required."

"I'm as good as his owner. I'll sign. So please."

"No, ma'am, won't work, as much as I'd like it to. No. Because see, he's not your nigger—he's your husband's. Unless you got papers on you signing him over to you, well, then, that'd be a different story. Do you?"

"No."

He inched close to her, towering over her. He was about Mr. Oden's size, or a little taller. Jack, muscular or not, wouldn't have a chance with this man. "See, here's the thing. It's a legal issue. I can't set a man's nigger free without his okay. Maybe your husband, he wants him here for a bit of discipline—not carrying his pass on him. Incidentally, you're lucky, ma'am, somebody else didn't get to that nigger boy of yours before I caught up with him. He's in protective custody here, you see. But all that to the side, I need to know the will of your husband on this matter, and the only way I know that is if he's here in the flesh and signing the form."

Fanny stepped back from him. "He's not going to be very pleased about having to travel all the way from Butler Plantation to Darien to do this. As you said yourself, he's a busy man."

"I know it, I know it, but my hands are tied on this, ma'am. I'd let your boy go right this minute if it was up to me."

"I think it *is* up to you."

"Ma'am?"

"You hurt him, didn't you? You lashed that poor child on the back. I saw it—the blood. You have done a terrible thing, sir."

He flinched a little. He again inched close to her. "And I wish I hadn't had to do that, ma'am. But he needed a bit of correction."

"What was he doing?"

He stiffened. "He was traveling without a pass, as I plainly said. That's as good as being a runaway in my book."

Tom adjusted his boots on the desk again. "Ma'am, Bob, he's a fair man, but he's also an officer of the law. Don't you forget that."

Sheriff Bob turned to Tom, "Go and get a nigger for her, Tom, right now, and we'll get her back home in an hour or so."

"I don't want one of your so-called 'niggers,'" said Fanny.

The two men exchanged looks. Then they looked back at her. "What?" said Sheriff Bob.

"I think you heard me plainly enough."

"Well, ma'am," said Sheriff Bob, "I don't know exactly what to say." He turned to Tom. "You know what to say?"

"I heard tales," said Tom. "I'm not ordinarily one to repeat gossip. I let that up to the women folk, but I did hear tales."

"That's right," said Sheriff Bob. "But ma'am, if you'll excuse us, that's what we call them down here in Georgia.

Maybe where you come from, that's not what they call them. But we're stuck with what we call them down here, no offense. All right? No offense."

"I do take offense at such language. I have always taken offense at it, and I will continue to do so."

"English woman," said Tom. "That's the deal there."

"Well, I think I know a thing like that and don't have to be told," said Sheriff Bob, laughing. "You must feel like a fish out of water, ma'am, being so far away from your fair country."

"I'll bet Mr. Butler calls them that," said Tom.

"Now then," said Sheriff Bob. "You're going to need a boy to take you back to the plantation, ma'am, regardless of what we call him. Boy, buck, nigger—words we use around these parts. Regardless what we call him, you're going to need you a black man to take you back to your husband, aren't you?"

She shook her head. "I'll stay here with Jack. You can put me back in one of those fine cages of yours. That'll suit me just fine."

"*Ma'am?*"

"Sheriff ain't about to put you in one of them cages," said Tom. "That ain't a-gonna happen, ma'am. You treat the law with respect—now, you listen here."

"Well, I'm not going back without Jack."

Sheriff Bob seemed to consider this. He raised a tentative finger at Tom. "I guess we could provide a night's lodging in the hotel . . . can't blame a woman for not wanting to go back all by herself on that river. In the dark with some hired-out nigger. No, who's to blame her for that?"

Tom rose from his desk. "I'll go check on a room. It's a fine, fine hotel, ma'am, Darien's best. Hotel plus boarding house. Old lady's husband died, what was it, Bob?"

"About ten years back. Yes, Mrs. Mosely, she runs a fine, fine hotel—plus, as Tom here says, a fine, fine boarding house. Everything's as clean as can be, and on top of it, the finest food in Darien. Better than your restaurants or cafes— at least to my taste, no offense to the rest of them."

"Same here," said Tom.

He was making his way to the door.

"You needn't bother. You're wasting your time," said Fanny, retaking her seat on the bench.

Tom stopped and turned to look at her. "What?"

"I'm staying right here. Until you give me Jack back."

Tom squinted at the sheriff.

"Ma'am," said Sheriff Bob, "that's not going to work."

"I'm afraid it'll simply have to work."

He laughed. "You can see yourself, there ain't no place here, other than that bench you parked yourself on. A lady can't sit on that all the livelong night!" He turned to Tom. "You escort Mrs. Butler here to the hotel."

She sat fast. "I'm not going anywhere."

Sheriff Bob looked down at her. "Ma'am."

"Yes?"

"She's a hard woman, ain't she?" said Tom.

"Yeah, yeah," said Sheriff Bob. "But look, ma'am, maybe we're going at this the wrong way. The hotel's lonely, I understand—you don't know a soul there. Maybe you'd rather stay at my place. The wife, she'd be more than happy to feed you, fix you a nice bath, give you a comfortable bed for the night. She'd probably even talk your ear off. And then, well, we'll see about your boy back there first thing in the morning. Right, Tom?"

"That's right, Sheriff."

"I think," said Fanny, "I've been clear enough with you. I'm not moving. Do you lack ears to hear?"

Sheriff Bob looked like she'd spit on him. "Ma'am, if you get difficult with us, we'll have no choice, you know."

"Choice meaning?"

Sheriff Bob laughed. "You know, Tom, this woman's

smart. Ain't she?"

"Guess they raise them smart in England, Bob."

"Guess so." He put a finger up to his lips. And then he went to one of the two windows, and looked out. After several moments, he turned to Tom. "Go spring that nigger, but make him comprehend. You got it?"

A nasty grin plastered Tom's lips. He started for the jail.

Fanny quickly rose. "You touch him again, and it will go bad for you."

"Tom," said Sheriff Bob. He pointed with a long, bony finger.

"Yes, sir," said Tom. He inserted the key in the door. He got it open.

Fanny darted for it, pushing her way past him. Into the jail.

"Well, if that don't!" cried Tom. He lingered in the open doorway. "Bob?"

"Give her the goddamned nigger! Hell fire!"

She waited while Tom went down the short passage by the other cells, came to Jack's, and inserted a key in Jack's cage, and let him out. When Jack came to her, she took him by the hand. She gripped his hand tightly.

"That the way you treat a nigger?" yelled Tom. "What are you, some goddamned nigger lover? You some goddamned nigger lover, ain't ya?"

She swung around. "You hush! I've heard enough of you for one day."

Tom reddened. "Well, goddamned."

"And quit using the Lord's name in vain."

She led Jack out of the jail through the open door into the office. She continued to grip his hand tightly. She passed Sheriff Bob, went to the door, didn't look back, and headed into the street with Jack.

They hurried together to the landing, her gripping his hand all the way.

When they were in the canoe and paddling their way back to the General's Cut, Fanny said, "You may not go back to Darien. That's it for Darien."

"Yes, missis."

"You call me Fanny. Okay?"

"Missis?"

"When we're together. Just then. Okay?"

"Yes, missis."

"Fanny," she said. "*Fanny.*"

Jack, rowing, lay a comforting hand on hers.

A few days later, at the supper meal, Mr. Oden announced the arrival of a shipment from Darien.

"What sort of shipment?" said Pierce.

"A rather large shipment." He gave Fanny a quick glance. "They're in the storage building. Stacked up. One hundred cloths, fifty blankets. Now, how is it that this happened?" He turned from her husband to her. A little grin worked on his lips.

"Fanny?"

"I ordered them. That is how we are now graced with them." She took a sip of her coffee.

"Indeed. And where did you get the money for this?"

"It fell from the sky."

"Fanny."

"Yes?"

"You tell me how you came up with the money to make an order like that." His face was reddening.

That grin from Mr. Oden was helping fuel it. Pierce Butler could not brook being intimidated, especially in the company of men. He would certainly not like for his overseer to be amused by something at his own cost. Couldn't a man control his wife? What was wrong with him?

"I suppose," said Fanny, "the elves brought them. Is there any other possible explanation?"

"Goddamn it, you tell me where!" He smashed his fist on the table, rattling the coffee cups. Mr. Oden's coffee spilled.

Mary, with a carafe of water, stepped back.

"I'll leave that up to you," she said. "You find out yourself."

He narrowed his eyes on her. "I'll whip a nigger a day for your little prank. Maybe two. How's that?"

She shook her head. No.

"Well?"

"Out of your trunk. That stash of cash for your whiskey, my dear husband. Right out of your precious little cargo."

"What? That's locked. How'd you get the key?"

"I have my ways."

"Fanny."

"On your lap when you were drunk. Is that all you can do is sleep and drink? There was your key, and I was pleased to use it for a good purpose. You wouldn't do a thing, and so I did. There you have it."

The table was quiet for a few moments. Pierce staring at her. Mr. Oden grinning.

Then Pierce pointed a finger at her.

"You've done nothing. Because, my dear wife, it's all going back. Every cloth, every blanket. You've wasted your time—that's what you've done."

"Well, at least I tried."

"Did you? We'll see where that gets you."

The next day, Sheriff Bob arrived.

"There she is," said Pierce. "My thieving wife."

"We've met before, haven't we, Mrs. Butler?"

"Yes, we have."

"I want her arrested. I want her jailed."

Sheriff Bob glanced at him, then at her. "You really want

that, Mr. Butler?"

"She's a thief. She needs to be brought to justice. Now doesn't she?"

Sheriff Bob went over to her husband and quietly huddled with him. But she could hear the whispering. She could hear Sheriff Bob say how this wouldn't look good in the community. How this wouldn't be good for him, not in the least, and maybe the best would be to send her packing, on her way—back home. What was she doing down here but making trouble anyway?

"Do it," said Pierce.

And then Pierce left the room and came back and rejoined the sheriff. She saw him pass the sheriff a wad of money.

Sheriff Bob returned with handcuffs. "Ma'am, I wish I didn't have to do this, but it's my duty. Hands out."

She complied.

He inserted a key and locked both cuffs.

He marched her to the door, with a fatherly sort of hand on her shoulder. And then he turned. "So long, Mr. Butler. You have a good day, sir."

"I will now."

She was now freed of the handcuffs, in the custody of Sheriff Bob, with Jack paddling the canoe. She wanted to paddle, but Sheriff Bob said, "You try that, and it'll go bad for that nigger boy of yours."

When they got to Darien, Sheriff Bob escorted her to the jail, told her to take a seat on that same bench where she'd sat before, and then shortly afterwards, he said, "You're going to my house. That's the deal here. We'll see if you can act like a civilized lady and not be an embarrassment to yourself and your husband. And to me and my wife."

He walked her up the street from the landing. "It's a nice house, and my wife will make you comfortable. Just be polite, is all I ask."

"Do you have a cell waiting for me there, Sheriff?"

"Don't be ridiculous."

"Oh, but I demand a cell. I'm a criminal, after all."

He leaned toward her. "Yes, ma'am you are, and I'm sure we'll find a way to deal with you."

When they got to his home, a two-story frame house with a wrap-around porch, the sheriff assisted her up the porch steps with a hand gripping her elbow, and then he opened the door and waited until she had entered.

He yelled out for his wife. "Betsy! Company!"

An hour later, she was eating with them, being treated like a guest, only she wasn't.

"I'm paying your way back home," he said.

"You are? Well, I'm not ready to go home."

"You may not be, but this is what your husband wants, and this is what we're doing."

"I'll only return," she said. "I'll use the money for the slaves."

He turned to his wife. "Imagine being the husband of a woman like this."

She detected a slight grin on his wife's part. She was a beanpole of a woman with a freckled face. She said, "More coffee?"

"Yes. I would like some," said Fanny.

"It's nice to have company," she said.

"On a different basis," said Sheriff Bob. "Isn't that right?"

"Yes, dear," said his wife.

"Some things you can't fix," said Sheriff Bob. "Get her a bath, and get her to bed," he said to his wife. "She's leaving early tomorrow morning."

"To where?" said Fanny.

He shook his head.

The next morning, shortly after breakfast, Sheriff Bob accompanied her to the landing. "See that black man? He'll be rowing you back. Behave yourself. I don't want to see you in these parts ever again. Is that understood?"

"You can handcuff me when you do," she said.

"I feel sorry for your poor husband. And you're such a nice looking woman." He paused, looking closely at her. "It's a pity, really."

"You think so?"

"Yes, I do."

She was soon in the boat and going back, back.

3
The Liberator

"You're back," he said. "So he couldn't get rid of you. Well, I hope you learned your lesson."

"Oh, I learned it. You have before you an utterly reformed wife."

"Sarcasm. He apparently didn't lick that out of you."

She went to the dining table to work on her journal.

He was asleep when she went to her trunk to store her journal away. She climbed the steep stairs and knocked on Margery's door.

She heard the latch scraping, and there stood Margery. The young woman put her finger to her lips. She whispered at her, pointing at the two little girls on the bed. They were taking their afternoon nap. How sweet they looked. They were not lying in the dirt, but in a comfortable bed. This made her feel guilty, but why should her children pay for their father's sins?

"I'll go," she whispered. She made her way back down the steep steps, carefully, very carefully. One could be laid up with a broken leg with steps like these.

In a few hours, Margery appeared at her writing table, Fan wiggling in her arms, and Sally pulling at her hand. The children were ready now, she announced, and Fanny rose from her table and again locked away her journal.

She followed Sally outside to play while Margery held Fan. The yard of the overseer's shack was bare, with the periphery edged in scrub. The sun was high overhead with white cloud cover, and it felt like it might grow cool in the evening, the wind picking up a little. For a January day, it was quite warm compared to up in Philadelphia.

Sally soon grew busy ordering around three little slave

children. "You do it now because I'm the one who gives the commands," she yelled.

"Yes, missis," they shouted.

She threw the ball. "Go! Fetch it!"

A little black boy got it and hurried back with it. He handed the ball to Sally. "Here, missis."

Sally threw again. "Now—fetch! Go fetch it!"

When one of them lingered, getting occupied in something else, Sally yelled, "Now! Stupid!"

The little boy hurried after the ball and returned with it, giggling.

"Sally," snapped Fanny. "Stop that. Right this minute!" She grabbed the ball from her.

"No!"

"No is right."

"Give it to me! It's mine!"

"Not now it's not. Come. Come with me."

She pointed at the house, signaling Margery. She didn't want Fan to see this. She didn't want it to seep inside her little head, were that possible.

Margery headed inside with Fan.

"I was having fun. And they were having fun!"

"No!" said Fanny.

The black children hurried after them, laughing, their eyes dancing. "Missis, missis!" they cried, circling them, and reaching up, pleading. It was true, they were having fun. They liked Sally, the little missis, that terrible little white tyrant.

"If you won't order them around," said Fanny.

"Why not? They like it!"

"I don't care! You're not to do it. It's wrong, and it's utterly disgusting, and I won't have it!"

"But I want to!"

"No. We're going in now."

"No!" Sally pulled away.

"Yes."

"I hate you!"

"No you don't."

"Yes I do!"

"You're being horrible. And I don't like it."

"No!"

"I'm not raising a tyrant," said Fanny.

They got back inside.

"Don't let her go outside," she said to Margery, who stood by the door, with a squirming Fan.

"No, ma'am."

Sally started for the door.

"Stay!" shouted Fanny. "You're not to go out there. Not until you act right."

"We're friends!" shouted Sally. And she began to cry.

"That's not friendship," said Fanny, taking her in her arms. "Don't you see?"

"They like me."

"Because you're their *missis*?"

"Yes." Her lips went pouty.

"If you won't be their missis, you can play with them."

"No!"

"Well, then," Fanny said, "you'll have to stay inside."

"I hate you, then," said Sally.

"Please, honey. No, you don't."

"I hate you a whole lot!"

Fanny began to cry. "Take her," she said to Margery. "Take her upstairs, please."

She caught Pierce napping. Again. She shook him.

"Huh? What? What the hell—"

"I'm leaving. You got your wish! I want to be free of this godforsaken place. And I'm taking the children with me."

"What is it? What is it now, Fanny? What is it now that's so important that you must once again disturb my sleep? What?"

"Our daughter is being corrupted. I will not stand by and allow this to happen."

"Sarah?"

"Ordering little black children around."

He laughed. He sat up. "Fanny, Fanny. You must understand the nature of what's going on here, that's all."

"You inform me, then. Be so kind as to enlighten me on this."

"I will. It's quite simple. Think rationally about it—for just a moment. Get beyond your silly feelings. It's good for little Sarah. To know her authority with the little Negroes, and them to know their place. She's learning to adopt the role fitting to her station in life as a white woman of some standing—something you, unfortunately, haven't learned."

You want her to be a little tyrant, then?"

"Call it what you want, but it's God's plan."

"No. It's the devil's."

"According to your abolitionist nonsense, and I won't be bothered with it. Go. Get yourself off. Leave me be. I don't want to hear it."

"I won't risk my child thinking like you."

"You brought her."

"Yes, and it was a mistake. A terrible one."

She went outside and walked for a while on the dike, watching as the sun shone through the moss and crept behind the thick brush of woods, and above her the brilliant blue sky, laced with drifting white clouds, filled with turkey buzzards gliding on the air currents, rising, dipping. They were returning home, a day's work done. If you were dead, they would feast on your remains.

It was after midnight, and she was about to retire to bed. Pierce was staying overnight in one of the other settlements.

He'd been doing so for the past several days.

"Why?" she had asked.

"Supervision."

"Is that right?"

"Yes, that's right." He pushed by her.

"Cards? Gambling?"

"So what if I am? You're not my mother."

"I'm glad of that."

He grunted something, and he was soon gone.

She was relieved that he was gone. She'd rather sleep alone. But where was he sleeping? And who was he sleeping with? She didn't want to know.

"Whiskey helps one sleep, doesn't it?"

"I sleep fine, Mr. Oden."

He poured himself more. "Call me James."

"I'll call you Mr. Oden."

"Ah, Fanny . . ."

"Goodnight," she said.

When she had pulled on her nightgown and lain in bed, looking up at the white moonlight illuminating the perfectly black sky, she thought carefully how she would do all she could to advance her mission of good, and how she might manage her time. How tomorrow morning she would begin a rigorous program, one combining all her efforts so far: a careful cleansing of each child, a close attention to the needs of each hut, and a concerted effort to improve the Infirmary.

All without the necessary provisions.

Perhaps it was just a matter of making sure things didn't get worse. How could you make them better?

A noise of boots.

"Fanny?"

"Mr. Oden!"

"James, please."

He approached her bed. He sat down beside her, and before she could react, he had her hand in his.

She jerked free.

But he grasped her hand again. "Fanny, listen. Listen to me. You're an attractive young woman. You must know that."

"Go!" she cried. "Go!"

"Why?"

"Go, or I'll tell my husband!"

"Fanny, my dear. What kind of husband leaves his wife to sleep alone? And almost every single night?"

"That's hardly any of your concern. Now go!"

"If you want a real man, Fanny, I am at your service."

His hand patted her blanket, over her thigh, and she twisted in bed. She tried to shove him off, but he was too big, too stocky, too strong.

"Please. Please just go. Won't you?"

He was silent. Just his breathing.

"It's a mistake, Fanny. I've had many a woman. Most women take to James Oden."

"Not me! Leave me alone. I'll not put up with this another moment. I swear!"

He left. She heard him whistling in the other room, and then his own door closing. She lay there. She cringed. How could this slaver ever imagine her dreaming of a new start with the likes of him?

A loud knocking. A frantic voice. Delirium.

Pierce was back, once again sleeping next to her. He groaned. "Who in the hell dares bother me at this hour? They had better have a good goddamn reason."

Another knock. Two knocks. Hard ones.

"Goddamn it, I'm coming!"

He was lighting the lamp. She got up, too.

A black woman stood at the petitioning quarter's window. At first, Fanny didn't recognize her, but then she saw: Teresa, the slave woman with the willow branch.

In a huff, Pierce lifted the window. "What in hell's name are you doing here at this hour?"

"Me speak to missis," she cried out.

"What? You had best go away, nigger—and come back during petitioning hours. Is that clear?"

"I'm here," said Fanny. "What can I do?"

"You go to bed," said Pierce.

She pushed him away. "No. I'll see what she wants. You go to bed."

"I will. You're goddamned right I will."

"How can I help you, Teresa?"

"Me can't work no more. All dem babies, and dead babies, and me back broken. Me can't do it no more. Please, please. It hurt so. So bad, it hurt. Hurt to bend over . . . like this."

"I know, I know. So please. Please don't then—don't do that."

"Can't go field, can't go."

"I know. I'm so very sorry. Dear God, you shouldn't be—"

"Me can't—no more."

"I understand, but give me a little time. Please, just a little . . ." She whispered at the woman, "Mr. Butler and I will confer about this matter—all right?"

"Yes, missis."

She watched as Teresa slumped away, leaning on that willow cane. Above her, the moon was waxing, rising from a bed of white, feathery clouds. She could see the poor woman as she made her way back to the line of hovels. She watched until she could no longer see her.

She advanced toward the bed. "Now, you listen. This Teresa—"

"Snuff the lamp."

"That poor woman is truly a pathetic case. How can she possibly work? Her bones might snap!"

"Extinguish the lamp."

"I'll not do such a thing—not until you listen."

He got up. He shook a remonstrative finger at her. "Don't stick your ugly nose in my business anymore!"

He put out the lamp.

She got dressed. She left the room.

Mr. Oden was at the dining table with a lamp. "Couldn't sleep, Mrs. Butler?" He seemed not to bear a grudge toward her for not accepting his sexual advances. Should she credit him with that?

"No. I was disturbed. And I *am* disturbed!"

"Something about these nights, isn't it? Winter nights. I can't sleep on winter nights. I don't know why." He ripped into a hunk of duck with his long, white teeth. He chewed quickly.

"I have a concern—about a woman named Teresa."

"Oh, you do." He eyed her. "What's that concern?"

She went ahead. She told him about Teresa, whom she'd mentioned when she'd first arrived—she'd written her name down on a list. Did he recall? The poor woman's back was literally at the breaking point. She had not been able to recover from so many babies, too many babies for one woman, and who knows how many miscarriages? And so she was begging him, please, to put the poor woman on reduced work—or really, to be humane, no work. "You do want to do the humane thing, don't you? You do care about people a little, don't you?" She tried to modulate her voice so that she would not appear to be lecturing him, but only pleading with him.

He ripped off another hunk of duck. "Humane? What's humane? Different people think differently about that, ma'am. They come up with different ideas about such lofty things as that. But I take my orders from your husband. He's the judge on what's humane around here. Whatever Mr. Butler says is humane, that's what's humane."

"Well, that lets you off, then, doesn't it? That permits you to do anything."

He chewed, swallowed. "Mrs. Butler, I think you're messing in an area where your nose don't belong. I think you're trying to do my job for me. But I'm the one who's got to do that job."

"Let me suggest, then: *Don't* do your job."

He laughed. "My god, you are a feisty woman!"

He gave her a leer, but she wouldn't let that disturb her. "Maybe I am. Maybe that's what it takes to be a woman in this world, and not just a piece of meat."

He laughed again. He shook his head.

She went back to her room.

She tried to sleep but couldn't. Finally, she must have dropped off. She awoke late the next morning, and Pierce was gone.

The next evening when she was out walking, with lantern in hand, she saw a thin black woman, bent way over, clutching a stick, approaching her, stumbling.

Teresa.

"Missis."

"Yes, Teresa. What is it?"

"Get whippin', missis—get bad whippin'!"

"What?"

"Twelve . . . twelve lash."

"No," said Fanny. "No."

"Mr. Oden, him say not tell you me troubles. Me aches, me pains."

"Mr. Oden!"

"Lie to you, him say."

"No. No, you didn't."

"Spread lies, him say."

She started to place a hand on Teresa's shoulder but stopped herself. Her hand was shaking. "Let me see. Please. Allow me. Would you?"

Teresa nodded.

Fanny carefully pulled up her top garment.

"Oh!"

"Oh! I'm very, very sorry. Oh, dear god."

She held the lantern up so that it illuminated the woman's back. She stood back, jolted. Deep cuts covered her back like ruts in a wet clay road, red and runny.

"Hurt, *hurt*," cried Teresa. "Hurt so bad! But me go out this morning to field—and it hurt, hurt, *hurt*. Each time me move back—oh!"

She put her face next to Teresa's. "I am deeply, deeply sorry."

"Hurt, hurt so *bad*, missis."

"I will see about this—I assure you, I will see about this. You can count on that."

She looked for Mr. Oden. She couldn't find him any-where, not in the field, not in the house. She went up and down the row of hovels. Where?

Until past midnight, she waited. Where was this overseer with his sleep problems of a winter night? Was he walking about in the dark? Where might he go?

The following morning, he arrived at breakfast, looking perturbed, jittery, anxious.

Pierce was still in bed. He had climbed into bed in the early morning dark.

She sat down. She took a moment. "You, Mr. Oden, look just terrible."

"Couldn't sleep. Not a wink. It's these winter nights, Mrs. Butler, I'm telling you. Something in the atmosphere, somewhere—moon, stars, something. Maybe the astrological signs—you believe in all that? I do, I think. Why shouldn't we believe it—it goes way back, now doesn't it? Ah, those signs. Maybe it is that. You reckon? Coffee's essential." He bent over, sipping it. It was steaming hot.

"Maybe you suffer from guilt, sir."

"Hmm? You think so, do you? From what, ma'am?"

"I think you know."

"Tell me." He set his coffee cup down.

"Committing an atrocity against a very poor, crippled woman by the name of Teresa. You recall Teresa?"

"Yes, I do."

She was ready. She would let him know. She spoke slowly, firmly, of how he had cruelly punished this poor, broken woman for Fanny's speaking out on her behalf. Of how she had seen deep, horrible cuts on the woman's back. To her, it was unthinkable that a man would do this to a woman, or to anyone, and clearly he had done it. Had he no compassion at all? Had he no decency? Had he no conscience?

He sat forward, his eyes red. She had struck a nerve. "Let's do be clear about something, Mrs. Butler. I do not need to account for my behavior to you—not a whit of it. To your husband in there—dozing away—yes, I do. Because I work for him. But just so you know, it's not as that nigger woman says. She was whipped because she outright refused to work. If she went out to the field, she had me to know, she'd come right back because her back hurt too much to work. Insolence. That's why she was flogged—insolence and disobedience. Plain and simple."

"Oh, I see. And you wouldn't listen to her. You wouldn't admit to yourself that she's too broken down for field work. Do you not have eyes?"

He grunted. "Yes, ma'am, I do have eyes, and it was my judgment that she was just fine."

"Well, apparently you are lacking in judgment, sir, the most basic kind, the kind every human—even to be considered human—must have."

He suddenly laughed. "You do have a tongue, don't you?"

"When I need it."

"You're no ordinary woman, Mrs. Butler, I'll give you that. Yet you did come down here on your own steam. Now didn't you?"

"Indeed I did."

She rose from the table.

At her writing desk, she noted the Teresa episode in her journal. She wrote up the entire incident. And then she began to cry because she decided it was all her fault. She should never have encouraged that poor soul. "I am their bane," she thought. "They would make it better without me." She wrote in her journal:

> I am their curse, their hell. Just consider what my
> sympathy has cost that poor soul. But no, what am
> I saying? I must continue on. I must do everything
> I can to improve their lot.

Later, she headed for the field. When she arrived, she saw a multitude of black people bent over, striking the ground with hoes. She spotted the black driver on his horse, whip swinging at his side. Suddenly he trotted his horse in the direction of several young black workers, and then he stopped, watched, and moved on. He cracked his whip.

Pierce was making his way toward her. "What exactly are you doing here?"

"Watching. I am observing my darkies toiling for me."

"Don't be silly. Go on now. Go."

"No. I like it right here."

"Oh, is that right? Well, you're not wanted here."

"By whom?"

"By me."

"What would you have me do then?"

"Go with Jack. Explore the island. Sit in your room. Read. Write. Those things you do at home. You choose to your little heart's content, but stay clear of here."

"And why is that?"

"Need I explain?"

Mr. Oden was approaching them.

"Maybe I'll do a little hoeing myself," she said. She approached the driver. She made her request.

"See massa," he said, softly. "See massa."

She made sure both Pierce and Mr. Oden overheard her. "I want a hoe! Surely someone here can provide me a hoe!"

"You are embarrassing me," snarled Pierce, his voice screeching. He grabbed her by the arm.

She swung around. She slapped him hard. It was the hardest slap she'd ever given him.

He fell back.

Mr. Oden was laughing—to himself. "What a woman!"

"I'll take a hoe. Give me one now!"

"You will not!" shouted Pierce.

"Give her a hoe," said Mr. Oden. "Let's see what she can do."

"The hell I will," said Pierce, and he hurried off the field.

She walked the narrow dike, past the landing. On one side ran the Butler River, on the other high sedges. She was mesmerized by the rank vegetation, the ivy with its intricate vein work and its rich greenish brown color, garlanding the low evergreen bushes. Through a thicket of cypress and evergreen, she had fragmentary glimpses of the rice fields and workers hoeing. She heard a loud crack, like a gunshot, muffled from here, but a discernible crack.

Afterwards, she wrote in her journal:

My husband is that whip. My husband is a crim-

inal. Mr. Oden is his henchman. Here, quartered with my poor children, under the same roof, are two criminals, whose crimes are perfectly legal.

❦

At breakfast, Pierce Butler and Mr. Oden sometimes spoke of card games—of winning, of losing. Of money owed.

"You owe me for last time," said Mr. Oden. "No, make that for the last two times. He's a terrible card player," he said to Fanny, in a conspiratorial manner. "And he's slow to pay. Isn't that right, Mr. Butler?"

"You'll get your goddamned money. In due time."

This morning it was just she and Mr. Oden. When Mary had cleared the breakfast table, Fanny took up her reading materials. There was more room here than in that small space that functioned as a bedroom.

She had just received a copy of *The Liberator*.

"What is it you have there?" asked Mr. Oden, sipping coffee.

"Something you wouldn't approve of."

"Is it fit for a lady?"

"It depends on what kind of lady you have in mind."

"What is it?"

"*The Liberator.*"

"Oh, my god. That? Mrs. Butler, my goodness." He was shaking his head.

"You're familiar with it?"

"Don't you think I would be? What plantation man wouldn't? You want a Nat Turner with a gang of killers hacking you to pieces? It's a shame a man like that stirs up so much trouble."

"How is it that *he* stirs up trouble? Cruel tyrants like you stir it up. He is only naming it. He's the messenger with the bad news, sir."

He laughed. "Such a northern woman, you are—a downright abolitionist! You could be arrested for possessing that vile thing spread before you—you know that?"

"Arrest me, then."

"Not me."

"Report me. Go ahead."

"Ha! Mr. Butler told me all about you. Of course I know how much you disapprove of me, Mrs. Butler, but you don't have to be so frank about it."

"Why shouldn't I be? The whole existence of Butler Plantation greatly disturbs me, and you're a central part of it."

"Nobody made you come down here, you know."

"No, they didn't. It was my choice. And it was a good one because I see more clearly than I'd ever if I hadn't come."

"You think me a bad man, but I'm not. I'm given a job to do, and I do it as well as I can."

"What you do, sir, is odious. Some jobs you shouldn't perform well."

He stared at her, and then he winked at her. He came around the table, stood next to her. He grabbed *The Liberator*, held it up before him. "Um. The Slave Power, is it? That's what he calls it?"

She grabbed it back. "Isn't that precisely what it is?"

"Fanny, Fanny. Slavery is here to stay, my dear. It's the law."

"Bad things can be changed. That includes bad laws."

He leaned over and kissed her cheek. "Must we quarrel—dear?"

She swung at him—but missed.

He laughed.

She left the room and went to her own desk in her small compartment. She wrote in her journal:

I had my abolitionist ideas about slavery before I came here, but those ideas were very abstract. Yes,

I could imagine men and women whipped by cruel slave masters, I had read plenty about this, and I imagined the slaves half starved, but I did not feel the matter deep in my very soul. I did not have the sensory experience, and the sensory is a far cry from the abstract. A pall has been cast over this place—and over me. I feel death everywhere, deep in my spirit, and yet they go on, and on, slaving for massa and missis.

Mr. Oden sat before a glass of water, his plate empty. He took a sip, then a long gulp. "I'm telling you some nigger's poisoning the food. You had best listen. You hear?"

"I'm not sick," said Pierce.

"I can't eat. The food tastes funny. And it smells." He went over it again, as he had for the past three days, of how one of the slaves, a criminal type, with vengeance in his heart, had put bad, very bad, things in the mush. Grave dirt, most likely. Maybe this man—but it could be a woman—didn't put that much grave dirt in. But then you started tasting it, even when you weren't eating. It had a way of lingering. You could smell it. And then you started feeling bad, real bad. And then you died. He'd seen it happen on a plantation in Louisiana. "I'm a sick man. I'm a dead man."

"You don't look so good," said Pierce. "I'll have to say."

Mr. Oden clutched his stomach. "I've got it bad, real bad."

"Perhaps you should see the doctor," said Fanny.

"You think so? You think he could help? There's your *Liberator*, ma'am. They get ideas—huh? Maybe you don't know that, but I do!"

She said nothing. He was sick. He was at a disadvantage.

319

"I can arrange to have him come," said Pierce. "Or take you to him."

"What would he know, being a man of science? He doesn't know these Africans' ways, now does he?"

"I expect he knows."

"I expect he doesn't. You oversee a few plantations like I have, and you come to see things a medical man never sees. No, sir!"

"It may be Mary," said Pierce.

"Mary would not do that," said Fanny.

"I'll be watching her," said Mr. Oden. "And others. It's that Teresa nigger woman. The one I had whipped. You know it is. They'll kill you if they get a chance. You think I don't know that?"

"Come," said Pierce. He beckoned for her to follow.

They went past the rice mill, then to a weedy enclosure on the edge of a swamp. Small wooden slabs, slanted, rose out of the ground. Mr. Oden was leaning over, stirring the soil with a stick.

"Find anything?" asked Pierce.

"There's loose soil here. This criminal nigger, right here, he went after the driver with his hoe, and he got what he deserved, you bet he did, fifty lashes—that was last fall. This is where it's coming from. Right here."

He dug at the dirt.

"It all looks the same to me," said Pierce.

"You don't know them like I do," said Mr. Oden. "You'd be surprised how good they are at fooling the white man."

"I really don't think anyone has put anything in your food," said Fanny.

"They don't have to, ma'am. Goofer dust. They cast spells with it."

"Are you that superstitious?"

"You'll learn to be superstitious around these niggers, Mrs. Butler. Or you won't survive."

She said nothing.

When the two men left, she ambled about the graveyard, gazing at the numerous wooden slabs sticking out of the Georgia clay, with the dead slaves' names, dates, and ages etched in large print. She ran her finger over one.

Robert
Died in 1827
Aged 70

There were many infant deaths, and many young people's, and she thought they were the lucky ones. Those who were taken from this grim existence at the age of one or two, or even ten or twelve, those who wouldn't have to serve massa and missis for the rest of their earthly lives but were settled in the ground, out of their reach forever—they were the lucky ones. How about the dead ones? Did they go to Heaven? How could they not? Most of them did believe in God and much more, she thought, than Pierce and Mr. Oden could ever believe. The poor slaves had nothing else to believe in.

The next evening the doctor was in Mr. Oden's quarters, and Fanny listened from her place behind the partition.

"How does that feel, sir? Is there any pain?"

"Yes, it hurts."

Silence.

And then the doctor's quiet, resonant voice: "You may have an ulcer, sir."

"Ulcer? Is that so? What can you do for it?"

"I could bleed you, sir."

"No. You're not doing that."

"Or blister."

"No!"

"You'll have to handle it on your own, then, Mr. Oden.

Eat plenty of soft foods, several feedings a day. And drink milk. That's my advice. You have a milk cow?"

"No."

"I'd suggest getting one."

"Milk cow?"

"Yes, sir."

A silence, then boots moving on the floor, a door being opened.

"Goodbye, Mr. Oden. If I may be of more service, do let me know. My door is always open to you."

"Thank you, doctor."

The door banged closed.

"Ulcer," shouted Mr. Oden. "Now what . . . what do you think caused that? Oh, the doctor can say that, but what in hell *caused* it?"

Pierce and she exited their small room.

"You didn't tell the man about the hoodoo," said Pierce.

"You think a doctor like him wants to hear that? A man of science thinks it's mere tripe! But I can tell you, a man like me has spent plenty of time with these savages from Africa, and he knows better. He knows a thing or two. You bet."

"And so it's the magic that made the ulcer," said Fanny.

"You dispute that?"

"Yes."

"Go ahead and dispute it then. Just maybe you'll be next."

She heard noises under the floor. A rumbling noise, followed by the sound of something brushing against wood, then a loud bump, followed by curses. She stood in the dining area, waiting. Mr. Oden soon came in brushing dirt off his clothes and face. He removed his tan hat, half crushed, and set it on the table.

"A sorry lot, that is."

"You were under the house? What for?"

"Charms, Mrs. Butler. Charms. Something you don't believe in."

"Oh? And what would such a thing look like?"

"Cat-skin bag stuffed with rattlesnake fang, grave dirt, other noxious stuff. Seen any cats?"

"No."

"Good. But that doesn't mean there aren't any—or weren't any."

"Would you mind explaining?"

"African witchcraft. I looked for it, but no sign."

"Well, I'm certainly glad we're safe from that."

"You scoff."

He slid the cedar bathing tub from up against the wall into his little living space. And then he went outside. In a half hour several young black men began carrying in steaming buckets of water. Eventually Mr. Oden's door went shut, the sound of the latch rubbing against it, and then water splashing. He suddenly began to sing:

> *Maxwellton braes are bonnie,*
> *Where early fa's the dew,*
> *And 'twas there that Annie Laurie*
> *Gave me her promise true.*
> *Gave me her promise true . . . .*

She liked his voice. She was sorry when he quit singing. She didn't dare ask him to sing more, though.

The next morning, she sat at the table with her journal.

Mr. Oden entered. "Where is Mary?"

"I haven't seen her. I suppose she'll be here any minute now."

"Well, I need my coffee now. Not an hour from now!"

"I could make it for you."

He laughed. "Would you?" he said, with his grin.

"Mr. Oden."

"Haven't you heard that a white woman doesn't make coffee here at Butler Plantation? I'd venture to say you don't make it at home."

She noticed him clutching his stomach. "Is coffee good for that?"

"I suspect you'd think not, but a man can't make it through the day without his coffee."

"Or his liquor?"

"That's right, ma'am."

She bent over her journal. There were a few more ideas she wanted to add. She wrote:

> *So often we think we know something when we know only the half. Who knows what the other half is here, at Negroland?*

"What are you writing? Personal diary?"

"I suppose you might call it that."

"What would you call it?"

"A journal I'm keeping."

"Ah!"

"Why do you say that?"

"This is a fine place to keep a journal, ma'am. There is much to learn. You'll find that you know very little about the running of this operation. Look around all you want. Take your notes. You might as well get an education while you're down here. After all, what else is there to do? Isn't that right?"

"Thank you. I'll do that. But Mr. Butler, I am quite sure, would disapprove. Don't you think?"

"Of what? An education?"

"Of my keeping a journal."

"Oh, would he? And why is that?"

"Because I might say something bad about his plantation."

"I suppose you will, won't you?"

"I'll be honest. I'm not going to lie."

He grunted. "Where's goddamned Mary?"

"I'm sure you don't have to call her that."

"Well, ma'am, I do get a bit riled when I don't have my morning coffee." He sat back and looked long at her. "I kept a journal once."

"Did you?"

"Yes, ma'am. But on a different plantation than this. Over in Louisiana. Now that's different there, Mrs. Butler. Slaves have it a whole lot worse in Louisiana, or maybe you don't know that. Here, slaves have it pretty good as slave life goes. We don't work our slaves to death, and we don't whip them to death. We're kind here, and if you look around and take notice, they like massa. They know it could be worse, and they don't want it to get worse."

"Is that liking? Or is that just fear?"

"Fear's part of it, ma'am. It has to be. But they like massa too. They respect him—almost like a father. Me? They see me like a big brother—one with authority. You see?"

She put her pen down. "If that's true, then why are you so worried about being poisoned? About those charms and oaths?"

He removed his tan hat and set it on the table. "Mrs. Butler, maybe you don't know, but there are always a few troublemakers, a man, or it could be a woman, who has a score to settle. Maybe they don't like some stripes they took. Maybe they think life owes them something. Or maybe they've just got the devil in them. You have to keep a watchful eye."

"Only a few carry a grudge?"

"That's right. But they can influence others, the kind who'd never rebel on their own. Nat Turner—there's your example. You see?"

Mary arrived with the coffee.

"Well, it's about time," said Mr. Oden, "I thought I was

going to have to go find you out. Where were you?"

"Fixing the coffee, massa."

"Well, it had better be good. Let's see if it is."

She slowly poured him a cup of coffee in a thick white mug. When she got near the top, he waved a hand. She quickly withdrew the pot. He took a quick drink. He coughed and spit at the floor. "What the goddamned hell? What's in this stuff?"

Mary looked at the floor. "Coffee, massa."

"Why's it taste so godawful bad?"

"Me sorry, massa. Me wanta make it good."

"You're *sorry*. I'll make you sorry. Now, woman, you take this coffee here, and you dump it out there." He pointed at the door. "But not where I'm going to have to pick up the mud when I make my walk to the field."

"Yes, massa."

"And then you fix some real coffee, and you bring it to me pronto. Is that clear?"

"Yes, massa."

"Okay. Then be about your business. And be quick about it."

"Yes, massa."

Mary headed out the door with the coffee. Mr. Oden watched her. He shook his head. He ran a finger at his temple. "It's Mary. That nigger's out to poison me."

"Was that necessary?"

"What?"

"Treating her like that. And talking about her like that."

He shook his head. "Mrs. Butler, you know so little about these slaves. You have to put things in perspective and realize the kind of thing we're dealing with here."

"And what is that?"

"The kind of creature we've got here, ma'am. That's what it comes down to. It's something your rich English blood can't even imagine. Your husband knows, but that's because he's a Southerner. The same as his grandfather, the Major. And what he doesn't know, I teach him. But I doubt you're willing to learn. Are you?"

"I am repulsed by what I just witnessed and what you just said."

"Go ahead and be repulsed. You know what? You wouldn't make it for a day, coddling these niggers. You and your northern *Liberator* . . . but maybe you just don't know. I've been an overseer of many a plantation, as I think I've mentioned, darlin,' and I do."

"Then I suppose you've learned to be a tyrannical man. That's not good for your soul, you know. Surely, that sin is weighing on you. Don't you feel it?"

He snorted. "Call it what you want, Mrs. Butler, but it's what has to be done. Give a nigger an inch, and that nigger will poison you."

"So you blame Mary for your bad digestion."

"I'll be looking into it."

"Maybe if you paid her, she'd do a better job."

He laughed. "She's a slave, ma'am. It's against the law."

"And why is she a slave?"

"Because that's her condition. If she bought her way out of slavery, well, then we'd be talking different. But she's not a free black, and so speaking of wages is absolutely silly."

"Sad, isn't it?"

"What's that?"

"I'll leave that to you." She went back to her journal.

The coffee arrived. Mary poured Mr. Oden a cup, and he took a sip. "Now that's good, Mary. That's a very good job. Goddamn, I can't imagine what you did with it before. What was that?"

"Me don't know, massa."

"Well, don't do it again. You hear?"

"Yes, massa."

"Okay, be about your business."

"Yes, massa."

Mary moved off, and soon was out the door. Mr. Oden smiled. "I'm not so bad of a man, now am I, Mrs. Butler?"

"Are you proud of yourself?"

He placed a sudden hand on hers and squeezed. "Fanny."

This time she didn't pull loose. She let her hand lie limp, lifeless.

"Don't be a hard woman."

She rose from the table, taking up her journal. "I must go," she said.

One Sunday evening as the pale blue sky to the west was streaked red-orange over the Butler River, Ned began running up and down from the row of slave huts to the rice mill and back. Up and down, up and down. Fanny stood outside the overseer's shack, watching him, and then later Pierce and Mr. Oden joined her.

"Something wrong with that nigger?" said Pierce. "What's wrong, do you think?"

"Let's wait and see," said Mr. Oden.

And then Ned was almost upon them, coming upon the overseer's shack. Fanny could see his crazed face, his wild eyes, his hands flailing about. And now he was stopping, standing, and yelling at them: "Dis here nigger, him bound for Canaan!—dis here nigger!"

Mr. Oden watched, and then a grin came over him. "Thinks he can run it? More like he's bound for hell. He's worth about eight hundred, a nigger that big."

Ned ran on. "Bound for Cannan!" he yelled.

"You'll have to catch him," said Pierce. "He's fast on those feet. Look at him go."

"You let me handle things," said Mr. Oden. "He's mine."

Pierce said nothing.

They went in for supper. When they came back out, Ned was still running, yelling.

Around the side of the building petitioners were lining up at the window.

"Are you putting up with that?" said Pierce. "They're hearing that."

"I'm not putting up with anything. You'll see."

"I've got my own affairs to take care of," said Pierce. And he went back inside. Soon, Fanny could hear the petitioners making their pleas. Her husband's voice had a noncommittal air about it, though at times it grew sharp.

Fanny and Mr. Oden remained standing in front of the overseer's shack, watching Ned run. "What's wrong with that poor man?" she asked.

"Sometimes they go crazy."

"Perhaps he needs medical attention."

"Oh, yes, ma'am. He'll need it all right. When I finish with him."

"Don't be vile. Why don't you find out what's troubling him?"

"Don't judge a matter you don't understand."

"I think I'm quite capable of judging."

He laid a hand on her arm. "Mrs. Butler, how obstinate you are."

She pulled loose. "It's you who are obstinate."

"What do you know about that nigger? Do you know the first thing?"

"Do you?"

"I know a thing or two about him," said Mr. Oden, and about that time, here came Ned again running hard toward them. It looked like he was going to run straight into Mr. Oden, but then he veered off that course, and once again ran by them.

"Canaan!" he yelled. "Dis here nigger! Bound for Canaan!"

"And what's that? What's that you know?"

"I know he'll be sorry soon enough. He might get to Canaan earlier than he figures."

Once Mr. Oden had gone in, slave women began gathering around her. Ned continued his running, his yelling, and the slave women were whispering to each other. They eyed him as he passed by them, ran up to the rice mill, turned and ran straight back toward them, yelling, "Bound for Canaan!"

"Missis help," said one. "Missis help Ned."

Fanny looked around at the women.

"Ned," she said. "What's wrong with Ned?"

A young woman heavy with child said, "His Sadie, her been a-lyin' in. Missis go see Sadie in Eeenfermary."

"I will," said Fanny. "I will do that." And then she listened to all the ills from one woman to another, none of which she could do a single thing about.

There was Sadie with her newborn, wrapped in a dirty, ragged blanket.

"What's wrong with your Ned?" Fanny asked. "Why is he running and running, yelling and yelling?"

"Mr. Oden, him say massa sell Ned. Ned, him bad!"

"No," said Fanny. "No. I will speak to Mr. Oden about this. He will do no such thing."

Rose stood looking.

"Go about your business," said Fanny. "See to Sadie's needs."

"Yes, missis."

"I'm going to see Mr. Oden right this minute." She stepped outside the Infirmary. Up ahead, she could see the women slaves still gathered out in front of the overseer's shack. When she got there, she went by them, saying. "I have business to conduct."

Mr. Oden was sitting at the table cleaning his weapon.

She sat down across from him. "Do you know Ned's Sadie?"

"Yes, I do."

"You told her my husband was planning to sell Ned?"

"Yes, I did."

"Is he?"

"If Ned keeps acting that way, he just might have to."

"But when did you tell Ned this?"

He kept at his gun. "That's none of your business, Mrs. Butler. What I do, when I do it, anything about the running of this plantation. It's all nothing to do with you. Isn't that clear by now?"

"I want to know right this minute why he's acting that way. You tell me."

He looked up. "I don't think you heard me."

"I did hear you."

"Well, Mrs. Butler, didn't I tell you? The nigger's gone crazy."

"We'll see," she said.

"I believe we will," said Mr. Oden, holding his pistol up to the light.

She could hear Pierce whistling. When she went back to their small living space, she found him on the bed with his head propped up on a few pillows. He was having a drink.

"Are you so unfeeling that you would sell Ned off?"

"Who said anything about selling that nigger?"

"Mr. Oden."

"Well, that's his prerogative. It may be necessary."

Even in here she could hear Ned yelling, only now it sounded more like a scream. There was a shriek to it now, the word *Can-aan* like a piercing wail. She passed Mr. Oden still at the table. She quickly opened the door and went outside. It was getting dark, and there ran Ned circling back from the rice mill. He was heading directly for her.

She stood in the middle of the road. He slowed and began to run at a slow trot, then to a walk, and finally he stopped—

his eyes on the overseer's shack, then on her, then on the women slaves, who were gathering around her, closing in on her.

"Don't run any longer. And don't shout. Your wife needs you."

"Massa sell," he said.

"No. No one will sell you."

He looked at her and his mouth fell open. Saliva was dribbling down his chin giving him an uncanny likeness to a mad dog. "Oh, missis! Missis save Ned!"

His attention suddenly shifted from Fanny to Mr. Oden, who stood by watching, his gun raised.

Ned returned to running, heading toward the slave hovels. But now he wasn't yelling.

Mr. Oden went inside.

She stood before him. "I do trust that you will not sell Ned. I want your word."

"That's up to your husband."

"Not according to him. You leave that poor man alone."

He brought his whip out and laid it on the table. "Go ahead, Mrs. Butler. Go ahead."

"What?"

"You take it, and you run this place."

She took the whip and slung it across the room. "No thank you."

Back in her living quarters she confronted Pierce. "If you sell Ned, you'll be sorry," she said.

"I'm about to sell you," he said, and he burped. And then he laughed.

She turned away and took out her journal. It occurred to her that Pierce Butler was almost better drunk than not.

As Fanny approached the field the next morning, she heard gunshots, cracking loud, reverberating. And then she realized those weren't gunshots. There was Mr. Oden, standing idly by. Several feet away a black man was standing over

Ned chained to a log, raising his whip.

Ned's shirt was in tatters, blood seeping between the strips of shredded fabric.

"Give me that," said Fanny.

The driver hesitated.

She yanked it out of his hand. "You go away," she yelled. "What is wrong with you?"

Mr. Oden went for her.

"No," she said, raising the whip. "He goes to the Infirmary."

"Mrs. Butler!"

"No!" She swung her whip.

Mr. Oden stepped back.

Then he took a key out of his pocket, bent down, and removed a lock off the chain. He turned to the driver. "Infirmary. Get him out of here."

She watched as the driver rounded up three black men. They soon were carrying Ned's limp body off the field.

And then Mr. Oden moved up close to her. His eyes looked yellowish, watery, his face sick and wan. "You think you've got the answers. Don't you? But something you don't know about your poor nigger Ned. That nigger practices curses. Did you know that? His granny knows all about that from way over in Africa. And that's why my bad stomach. So don't be feeling sorry for the likes of your dear old nigger Ned."

"I pity you," she said. She hurried toward the Infirmary.

Minutes later she was seeing about Ned, lying in the dirt, with no blanket. She ordered warm water, and soon she was bathing his wounds. He cried out as she very carefully took a cloth and doused his back, covered with bloody gashes. His Sadie lay next to him with her newborn.

The next morning they had visitors, Mr. and Mrs. Jasper

Barnaby. Mr. Barnaby was a large man with a generous mid-section, his thick gray hair and his bushy sideburns giving him the look of an English country gentleman. He leaned on a gold-tipped cane. Mrs. Barnaby was tall and bony, exceedingly thin looking. There was a severity about her face which made her seem about to condemn something. Fanny wondered what.

"Mr. and Mrs. Barnaby," said Pierce. "This is my wife, Fanny."

The woman stepped forward and gripped Fanny's hand tightly. "I am Emily Barnaby."

"You two women talk church," said Mr. Barnaby, "and Mr. Butler and myself, we'll go see about a nigger."

Fanny's hand was still within Mrs. Barnaby's tight grip, but she quickly pulled loose. She made it out the door in time to join Pierce and Mr. Barnaby, who were moving step by step, Mr. Barnaby limping, toward the line of slave huts.

Mr. Barnaby spotted her. "Well, ma'am . . . what is this? Where's my poor wife?"

"Your poor wife's back in the shack, sir."

"What's she doing back there, Mrs. Butler?"

"I wouldn't know."

Pierce stopped. "Go back, Fanny. Mr. Barnaby and I have business to conduct."

"No thank you."

Mr. Barnaby rested on his cane. "Your wife always like this?"

"Like what?"

"Where's that nigger?"

"In the Infirmary."

"Infirmary!"

Mr. Barnaby limped along on his cane. They eventually came to it.

Rose had Ned's head lifted onto her lap.

"Her ain't doin' no good, missis."

"Where's that nigger?"

"Ned there," said Pierce. "He's the one. I'll sell him low."

"*Him?*" Mr. Barnaby poked Ned with his cane. "Why there ain't a thing left of that buck. Look at that back there. He caint work. You ain't gettin' a lick of work outta that nigger. I caint pay a cent on him. What'd he do?"

"Insubordination."

"I caint throw good money at that." He turned to go.

"Wait a minute," said Pierce, grabbing his arm. "He'll heal. He's a damn fine worker. And after what we did to him, he won't be the kind of nigger that'll give you any trouble. He's a reformed nigger."

Mr. Barnaby snorted. "You say, do you? That nigger's given up. You won't get a lick out of him no matter how hard you swing that whip."

He left, and Fanny and Pierce followed.

Mrs. Barnaby rose from the table when they entered the shack. "You tell them about church?"

"No, dear, that's your business."

Pierce remained standing. Fanny did too.

"Well," said Mrs. Barnaby, "We'd like to invite you to our Baptist church. We have some very fine pews close up front. At an affordable price."

"We attend elsewhere," said Fanny. "The Unitarian." Though they hadn't, not down here.

"The Unitarian?" said Mrs. Barnaby. "That's real small. Congregation fifty—if that. Isn't it?"

"And so?"

"We've had our eye on that for the longest time," said Mr. Barnaby, "tryin' to get it to merge with our Baptist."

"Baptist and Unitarian?"

"Yes, ma'am, that may seem odd to you. But, you see, Baptist is heavy on salvation. And the dear Lord knows we need it. We all do, niggers too. We planning on building a nigger church to boot. Get them freed of their sins, saved, don't you know? What's to be saved in the Unitarian?"

"Fallen," said Mrs. Barnaby. "Fallen. It's the crucified Lord that we must depend on. Is it not?"

"We're not that kind of religion," said Pierce.

"Pews ain't as much in our Baptist," said Mr. Barnaby.

"Is that right?" said Pierce. "Well, I must be about my work. Good day to the two of you."

"You think about it," said Mr. Barnaby.

"You pray about it," said Mrs. Barnaby.

"You don't buy my nigger," said Pierce, "and I don't buy your pews."

"Lord," laughed Mr. Barnaby, "there's a Christian attitude for you!"

"We won't trouble you any further," said Mrs. Barnaby.

"You'd sell Ned to *him*?"

"I won't be selling him to anyone," said Pierce. "If you can't sell a nigger to Mr. Barnaby, you can't sell him."

"Is that right?"

"Yes, it is. And I blame you for that."

"Oh you do?"

"Yes, I do. Because old Ned would never have given up if it hadn't been for you. Bucks like that keep going unless you coddle them to death. And look at his wench. How long will she make it?"

"You've got a filthy mouth, don't you?"

He scowled. "I'll be gone a few days to other settlements."

"And what will you do there?"

"What's it to you? None of your business, now is it?" He took a long drink of his whiskey, and then he was gone.

He was back, but he wasn't showing up for bed.

She caught him in the field.

"Where have you been? I want an explanation."

"What did I say about your presence here? And how many times do I have to say it?"

"*Where?*"

"*Fanny.*"

"I asked you where you've been. Where?"

"Busy."

"Busy doing what?"

"Fanny—"

"What?"

"Playing cards."

"Is that all?"

"You shut your mouth."

"You have such lust for that, don't you? Who is it this time?"

"I don't appreciate your sauciness, my dear wife. But I suppose I'm stuck with it, aren't I?"

"Yes, you are."

Now he moved in close, his mouth against her ear. "Do you know the meaning of *divorce*?"

She moved away. "Yes."

"You think about the kids. You think about that."

She glared at him. "You think about me. What I might be capable of."

"I do!" he shouted as she made her way off the field.

4
Night Trips

She was at work on her journal when Margery hurried to her, hands trembling. "You need to come up, Mrs. Butler. Please, and hurry."

"What's wrong?"

"Sally. She's complaining of an ache."

"Where?"

"Her stomach. She hurts—bad. Just terrible."

Fanny got up from her writing table and hurried after Margery up the steep steps. On the upper floor, Margery pushed open the door and went in. Fanny followed. There sat Sally holding her stomach, crying.

"What's wrong, darling? What's wrong?"

"Tummy. Tummy. It hurts."

"Oh, oh, dearest little one. Let me hold you."

Sally cried and cried, and Fanny said to Margery, "What could it be?"

"Maybe the doctor," said Margery. "Maybe send someone to get the doctor."

"We'll have to if she doesn't feel better soon."

By nightfall, Sally was crying hard, and screaming at times.

Pierce and she were attending to her.

And then, suddenly, she stopped. She was very quiet. Utterly still.

"Maybe it's the water," he said. "It might be the water."

"But it's boiled. How can it be the water?"

"The food, maybe."

"Oh, my, oh dear God."

"The slaves," he said. "Poison."

"No," she said. "Please. Don't."

"Mr. Oden. He told us. Plain and simple. Did we listen?" He turned to Margery. "Has she been—"

"What?"

"Vomiting?"

"No, sir. Nothing."

"It's not cholera, then. I don't think. We had better go for the doctor."

Sally's face had turned ashen white. Fanny had never seen her look so drained of blood. She usually had a flush of color about her. This child was sinking, and sinking fast.

"We must take her. Now. We cannot wait."

"At night like this?"

"Yes. Of course. Look at her, Pierce. We must not delay!"

"I suppose we could get Jack to boat us over."

"Do then! We *must* hurry."

"We'll hope we can raise the doctor," said Pierce, grabbing Sally up into his arms. She was whimpering, and she had grown almost silent, which worried Fanny even more.

"Raise him? What do you mean?"

He headed out the door. "Is he home? We hope so."

"Oh, dear God. Oh, dear, dear God."

"You'd better call on God," said Pierce, "to take care of the devil." And he hurried down the steps. There wasn't the slightest hesitation, but she worried, of a sudden, that he would trip and send Sally flying out of his arms onto the steps below.

She rushed down the steps.

"Hold her," he said.

She took Sally, who felt cold to the touch, and she worried that cold was worse, much worse, than hot.

In ten minutes Pierce pushed open the front door and yelled. "Now—we're ready!"

She hurried out the door, hugging Sally against her, limp

and lifeless, and she rushed after Pierce carrying a lantern, throwing shards of orange light against the edge of the water.

They came to a boat, tied at the dock. "Get that rope," shouted Pierce at Jack.

"Yes, massa."

Pierce and Jack climbed in.

"Hand me Sally," Pierce said.

She did so, and then climbed into the boat, which rocked from side to side.

"Me get you there real fas', missis," said Jack. He dropped the oar in the water, and the boat slid down the river.

The moon was full tonight, engorged, bright yellow against black, the heavens filled with stars, aggregating in pools of brilliant white light. They crossed the Butler River to the General's Cut, and they were soon in that canal.

Jack was hard at the oar. The water lapped against the boat, rhythmically, soothingly, and yet she could not be soothed, not yet—not until Sally was in the hands of the doctor and pronounced well. A minor thing, he would say with a smile, a gastronomic disturbance—nothing to fret about. That was all. But what if it was? What if it was some foul, noxious fumes from the swamp, the miasma surrounding them? Couldn't it get into one's breath and blood?

Pierce still held Sally, and Fanny reached out toward him. "Give her to me. She needs her mother."

He handed Sally to her.

And she took her in her arms and felt her cold body. Perhaps it was the night partly. It was growing colder as it did at nights, for after all it was winter. And so perhaps that was it more than the effect of whatever it was she'd eaten or drunk or whatever it was that had overcome her. She did not want to think poison, spells, or curses. Dear God, she prayed, don't let me fall into thinking that. I do not believe in such nonsense. But the child felt so odd, her skin so strange to the touch. She lightly ran her finger on her forehead and on the back of her neck. It wasn't right. It felt like cool marble.

"Can't we hurry? Jack, can't we?"

"Yes, missis. Me get you there real fas'." He worked at the oars, and they slid over the water.

"Pierce," she said.

"Yes." He was looking vacantly at her. She could see his dull eyes clearly in the light of the moon.

"Maybe you should help Jack."

"What?"

"You heard me. Maybe you should help, or take Sally, and I will."

"I will not, and you will not. Jack is doing fine."

"She doesn't feel right."

"We'll be there soon."

"We could lose her."

"We won't lose her. She'll be fine."

"We must pray."

"Go ahead," he said.

"Our dear Father," she began. And then she prayed silently, whispering her pleas. She wept openly. Sally stirred and then fell once again into a state of limpness, so lifeless that Fanny thought surely she was dead. And now she said silently, more to herself than to God: *I cannot give her up. I won't give her up.*

This child, she thought, this child that took me nearly two days to bring into the world, in great pain and travail, how can you take her so quickly? How can you be so heartless and cruel?

It would be wrong. It would not be just.

"We comin' to it," said Jack. "We comin' to it now. See them lights up thataway? Thas Darien. It sure is. Little miss Sally, her see the doctor anytime soon now."

"Hush," said Pierce.

She said nothing.

They pulled up to the dock, and Pierce got out quickly,

jumped up to the landing and reached out for Sally.

"Here, missis, you stan', I hold you, you take little Sally up, and you han' her to massa there. That all right, missis?"

"Yes."

And she stood, or tried to stand, but she couldn't because the boat rocked too much. Jack was standing too, with his hands positioned around her waist. She feared Pierce seeing this, but though his eyes were on her, on Jack, on both of them, he said nothing.

"Dock's up there kinda high, ain't it?" said Jack. "Here, missis, give me Sally. I get her up to massa."

She hesitated. "No," she said. "No—"

But he'd already grabbed Sally and was handing her to Pierce.

"Goddamn you!" shouted Pierce.

"What?" said Fanny.

"Goddamn you, nigger. You listen—you hear? When a white man or woman gives you an order, you heed it—hear? You disobey again, and it'll be a different matter."

"Yes, massa."

"Goddamn you."

"Pierce, please. Please don't."

But he wasn't listening. He was running off with Sally, bouncing her about in his arms.

And now Fanny got up to the landing.

She looked down at Jack in the boat. "You don't pay him any attention. He has no idea what he's saying. He has no idea about anything. I am very, very sorry, Jack."

Jack laughed. "Oh, massa, he know. He know a lot."

She shook her head. She quickly wrote Jack a note. If Sheriff Bob came, it would do little good, but at least Pierce was here with her this time. She took off. Pierce had disappeared with Sally into the night.

It had grown colder, and she rushed along, pulling the coat tight against her neck. She came upon him, standing outside a two-story stone house. He was knocking. Hard knocks, three at a time.

"Goddamned," he yelled. "Goddamned, is the man home or not?"

"Softer, please," she said. "Sally . . . how is she?"

"I don't know."

"Let me have her."

He handed her Sally, and he again knocked—pounding his fist on the door.

Sally felt cold but moist now to the touch. Something had happened. Something was oozing out of her, an essence of some kind. Fanny touched the back of her neck, which was warmer—and then hot.

The door suddenly opened.

"Yes—oh, Mr. Butler. Oh, what do we have here?"

"Emergency," said Pierce and shoved his way past the doctor through the half-opened door.

"Please," said Fanny, "please help us. Our daughter, our little daughter—she's very, very ill."

"Come," he beckoned. He stepped to one side. He had on a silk and velvet gold-colored robe, very French looking.

She stepped into the house. A lamp was burning.

"I knocked and knocked," said Pierce.

"I'm a heavy sleeper," said the doctor. "It would take the Judgment Day to wake me."

"Please," said Fanny, and held Sally up to him.

He took her in his arms. "Now, let's see what we have here." He laid Sally on his sofa, and he stood and looked down at her. Then he bent over and felt her. He put his ear down to her mouth and listened.

"When did this begin?"

"This afternoon."

"And how was it then?"

"A stomach ache. But it grew much worse."

"Just the ache."

"Yes."

"No vomiting."

"No."

"No loose bowels?"

"No."

The doctor gave her a look. We could use leeches, if she'd abide it."

"Do what you have to do."

The doctor took each of them by the arm. He guided them over to the window, where the moon was bright yellow through the moss-covered trees.

"She doesn't look good. I would prepare."

"What are you saying?" said Pierce.

"You could lose her. I expect if she makes the night, you won't lose her. But there's no guarantee."

"Hell. What *is* it?"

"I don't know. One can't be sure about these matters. It's in the hands of the Almighty, isn't it? We can't know about these things, can we?"

"Goddamned niggers, is what it is!"

"What?"

"Goddamned witchery!"

"No, no, Mr. Butler—don't believe that stuff. Let's see about the child. There's not a moment to lose. I'd recommend leeches. She won't know what's going on because there's not a lot of sign of, you know, awareness, but if she comes around, a little, then we can decide on our next step. Maybe it'll be leeches, maybe bleeding, maybe blistering, maybe none of those. We'll just see. We'll just watch and wait."

He took each by the hand. Fanny felt his warm grasp.

She began to weep. "We shouldn't have to go through this. Why do we have to go through this?"

"Everybody does," said the doctor. "At one time or another. Everybody. Every creature under God's heaven is slated for it."

"I need a drink, a stiff drink," said Pierce.

"I have some wine," said the doctor.

"Nothing stronger? I could use something stronger, Doc."

"I'll fix you a glass of wine. It's all I have, is some wine. It's good for the digestion, you know."

She couldn't sleep. She heard Pierce asleep in a room close by, snoring, while the doctor was a few rooms away applying leeches—if that's what he had decided on.

She prayed and prayed. But she couldn't help but despair. *What did I do to deserve this? Haven't I tried to be a decent human being? Am I to be afflicted for your divine pleasure?*

Morning came. Sally lay stone-silent on the teal rosewood sofa, covered by a blanket.

Dead. She is dead.

She hurried over to her. She touched her forehead. The child whimpered. "Sally," she said.

The child said nothing.

"Sally?"

She put her face against the child's chest, buried herself in her, and cried. And then later, perhaps an hour later, the doctor came in, stirring, in his robe. It seemed much too bright, too gaudy, for this doleful occasion.

"Let's see," he said. "Let's take a look."

Fanny moved away, and he bent over her.

"Well," he said.

"How is she?"

"Well, not good. I'd hoped for better results, Mrs. Butler. But we'll try, we'll try. We'll keep trying."

Fanny moved off to look out the window. A bright, early-morning sun was dancing in the trees, lambent flames of light licking the limbs as they moved and swayed with the wind. She could hear noises from the river—shouts of men, a barge horn blowing, the world coming alive. It was the time for breakfast, for ham, eggs, coffee. But she had no desire at all for food or drink.

"Please step this way," said the doctor.

"What?"

"Now—if you would, Mrs. Butler," he said.

She hurried over. "Yes?"

He placed a hand gently on her arm. Then he shook his head. "I'm sorry, but you must say goodbye, Mrs. Butler, because your child will not make it. You see her face—right there—that slackness?" He lightly grazed her cheek with a long, gnarled finger. "That's the way they look when their soul is about to ascend to Heaven." He grasped her hand tightly. "I'm sorry. I'm very sorry."

"Pierce!" she cried.

He did not come.

"I'll go get him," said the doctor.

She waited, coaxing Sally, touching her face, caressing her arms.

Pierce was hurrying in with the doctor behind him.

"*Pierce*," she wept. "Our little Sally. Our precious little Sally. No, no, no, no, no."

"No," he shouted. "No! Goddamn you!" He began to cry. "What kind of God are you? What kind of . . ." He turned to the doctor and grasped him by the arm. "What kind? What *kind*?"

"No, Mr. Butler, no," said the doctor, "please—we mustn't, not this way."

"Goddamn you!" screamed Pierce. "Goddamn you—and your niggers! I'll get them for this! I'll whip them to death!"

"No, no, no," cried Fanny. And she hurried away. "No, dear God, no."

She felt hands rubbing her shoulder. She turned. And then the doctor took her warmly by the hand.

"We must never, ever, give up on God," he said. "It's all

we have, ma'am. That's all we really have."

"But I must have Sally. I must!"

"I don't know," said the doctor. "I don't know about these things, Mrs. Butler, or understand them. I see so much, and yet I understand so little of it."

She lay down with her. She would close herself around her little child, protect her. She could hear Pierce screaming and crying in the other room. He continued to curse God. He was hurling curses at slave magic. He swore he would get even. "Yes!" he cried. "I will get even, you goddamned niggers! You watch!"

She tried not to hear. She tried to close her ears to everything, the sounds of the river traffic, the wind rattling the window, the doctor's pacing. She held her child as tightly against her as she could. *I will not bury you. Oh, no, I will not bury you in the cold ground. Not here, not in this foul, dark place.*

She fell asleep after a while. Her dreams were troubled.

"Mrs. Butler," said a voice. "Mrs. Butler."

"What?"

"Now."

The doctor was pulling her away from Sally.

"No, no," she cried. "Another minute. Please . . . please."

"Look at her," said the doctor.

She pulled away. The child was whimpering. Her color looked different. A flushness was spreading on her cheeks, like the sun itself rising.

"I was wrong," said the doctor. "I was wrong. I was wrong to say what I said. Can you forgive, Mrs. Butler? Can you ever forgive?"

He looked suddenly foolish standing there, his balding head, his glasses sliding down his short, squat nose. That foolish gold-colored robe. He had reached forward and grabbed up the child. And now he held her against his chest. "It must have been your prayers, Mrs. Butler. It wasn't his curses."

He half-smiled.

"Oh, Sally!" she cried.

❧

She'd seen Pierce heading out at night on foot, toward the slave hovels. Late one night she went in search of him, lantern in hand, heading down the row. A raucous babble filled the evening air. Slaves had gathered in front of hovels, talking, laughing, singing, dancing. One yelled out, "Me so glad to see you, missis! Me so glad!"

"I know," she said. "Thank you."

She returned to the shack.

Another night. Another little trip, she thought.

She delivered on her penny plan.

The children grasped their shiny Liberty Head pennies with happy faces.

"You deserve it," she told them. Faces cleaner, arms, hands, feet—all cleaner. But then she despaired when she thought of how little this could possibly matter. When she turned over the patients in the Infirmary to take a close look at their bodies, she continued to see the evidence of stripes— deep, terrible cuts. The threat of infection—dear God, how would these ever heal? She bathed them, got the dirt out. Again, again, like a dreadful leitmotif in a tragic orchestral piece, they let out painful yelps and screams.

I am hurting them, she thought. I am only adding to their misery and suffering.

❧

Pierce was busy rummaging in his trunk. He pulled out a gun. He fitted a holster around his waist and buckled up.

"Why are you getting that? What's going on?"

"There's been a killing—over at Settlement Three."

"Who?"

"A rabid old nigger stuck a knife in the driver."

Before she could say something, he holstered his weapon and left.

Her husband was gone for a few days. When he returned late one morning, he said nothing about the killing or what he'd done, and she didn't ask. He went on with his, by now, usual routine, gone from their bed every single night, back early some mornings, sometimes drunk, sometimes not.

Why some nights drunk, other nights not?

"Because, like anyone else sometimes I enjoy imbibing; other times I don't. It's as simple as that, Fanny. Doesn't that make sense?"

"Well, I prefer your coming in not drunk. I don't like the stink. And either go to bed or don't."

"I'm not all that drunk," he said. "Now am I? And I don't see that you have much to say about that bed of ours. I'll come in when I please."

"Just don't come in stinking drunk," she said.

"If that's what it takes," he said.

"*What* takes?"

He didn't answer her.

One night, when he slipped out, she decided to take her lantern and follow him. As she made her way down the row of huts, kids jumped out of their red clay yards and caused a stir.

"Missis, where you going?"

"Just walking."

"Where missis walking? Me go, take care of missis!"

"No, that's fine. Missis can walk by herself."

Whispering back to their shouting.

Pierce, a few hundred feet ahead, had turned around now

and was standing there on the dirt path watching her. The evening breeze was blowing loose moss and leaves about.

She turned in a different direction, away from Pierce, and headed along the drainage ditch to the rear of the huts.

Evening after evening, she attempted to track him, but he invariably stopped, looked back, and caught her. He said nothing, but he wouldn't move forward until she'd turned back.

∾

One evening when an orange crescent moon stood in the blackening sky, with a light wind lifting strands of her hair, a dozen or so women lined up before her, complaining, as always, of aches and pains. And then a gray-haired woman pushed her way through the crowd and, looking her straight in the eye, said, "Me seen things a-comin'. Me seen!"

"What? What have you seen?"

"Worl' . . . it comin' to end. Me seen that."

The woman was very close to her. Her skin was making contact with Fanny's skin. "When is it coming to an end?"

"Things," said the old woman. "The worl'—it comin' to end. Me seen it."

"Where?"

"Up in the yellow moon," she said, pointing. "Nights, me seen it. Stars fill de sky. Me go up there—take big trip—in de dark, de black. Up dere!"

"What's your name?"

The old woman muttered something.

"What?" asked Fanny.

"Her name's Psyche," said one of the women. "'Cause of what she be."

"Psyche," said Fanny. "What will happen? Can you tell us?"

The old woman nodded. "All de peoples. All dem. Dem

all dere. Worl', it gonna end. Dem be good. No work for massa no more."

"No work for massa?"

"No, missis. No work no more."

And she didn't. She hadn't, said Mr. Oden, for seven days running. And he had lashed her himself a dozen times or more. "But you can't reach that nigger. Her back's covered with strips of flesh hanging out. Still, she's got in mind the world's going to end. And it's catching. I had to take the lash to a half dozen this morning." He was speaking to her, not Pierce. He was in the middle of chewing a huge piece of fish.

"You are telling me this," said Fanny. "You have the audacity to tell me this?"

His eyes flashed at her. "Yes, ma'am. I am. Just so you know."

"Know what?"

"Know that when this Psyche nigger comes whining to you, that there's a reason, a good one."

"You don't have to account for yourself," said Pierce.

"No. I don't."

"You certainly do," said Fanny.

"Oh? To whom?"

"I'll leave that to your imagination."

She could hear the slaves lined up in the petitioning window to see Pierce. "When a slave doesn't work, he gets no food," said Pierce.

"It doesn't seem to bother them at all," said Mr. Oden. "They get religion like that, and you've got a big problem on your hands. You've got to crack the whip harder—it's the only way."

She said nothing. She had already said it. She rose from the table and went outside. A crowd of women were waiting for her.

She began to follow Mr. Oden. From hut to hut each morning, she followed him. Grown men, grown women, old men and old women were staying behind in their huts, surrounded by children. Mr. Oden would pull them out of their hut and threaten them with whippings unless they reported to the field. She would move in between him and them. She would try to pull the whip out of his hand, but he was much too strong. "No!" she would yell. "No, you may not use that horrible thing! No!" She would push him, shove him. And he would relent. But not relent. Because shortly afterwards, when she was walking up and down the slave row, she would hear screams and cries coming from the huts. And she would run hard to stop him, but by the time she had arrived, it was too late. There they were, four or five men and women, their backs bloodied.

And there was Mr. Oden, his whip handy, red blood dripping off of it.

One morning she managed to get the whip out of his hand, and she struck him, struck him, and struck him until he got the whip away from her.

"You're quite a woman, Mrs. Butler. Quite a woman! I do admire your ferocity!"

"I'll get my own whip," she shouted, "if I have to!"

"I'm sure you can purchase one in Darien," he said, whispering at her. "But you can bet you won't have it for long."

He headed out to the field.

"Did you get all of them whipped?" she yelled.

She went from hut to hut. He had missed some. There were at least a dozen men and women in those huts who wouldn't show up for work.

"Worl' endin'," said one old man. "Worl' endin'. No work for massa no more. Massa, him goin' devil."

"I think you're right about that," said Fanny.

"Missis?" he questioned.

"Yes—to the devil. Indeed."

"You struck Mr. Oden?"

"Yes, I did."

"He's got cuts all over him."

"Well, I would say he deserves it. He got a little of his own medicine."

"He's a cheat at cards," said Pierce. "Maybe he did."

"A cheat? How so?"

"You'd have to know something about cards."

"So you don't mind that I struck him."

"Hell with him, but I'd say you'd better watch it with a man like that."

"A dangerous man?"

"What overseer isn't? It takes a dangerous man to run a place like this."

"And what kind of place is it?"

He shook his head. "That Psyche?"

"What about her?"

"She's no problem now."

"Why?"

"Ask Mr. Oden."

He was standing outside the shack.

"What's this about Psyche?"

"What's your question?"

"What have you done with her?"

"You planning on taking the whip to me again?"

"No."

"I don't owe you an explanation, ma'am. That's between me and your husband."

"He said to ask you."

He took a few moments. "All right. Woodville."

"And what will happen to her there?"

"Not a thing."

"Is she there now?"

"That she is, ma'am." He went for her hand.

She quickly moved away.

"A hard-to-get woman," he said, grinning.

She got hold of Jack. "Take me to Woodville."

"Woodville. Oh, missis. Me don't like Woodville."

"Why?"

"Bad, bad place. Niggers, them die there. Bad, real bad place."

"Why?"

"Nothin' to eat. Snakes. Rattlin' types. Peoples, them die fast in Woodville."

"Take me."

"Oh, no, missis. Missis no wanta go Woodville."

"I'll get some mush first," she said. "Meet me at the canoe."

In a half hour they were canoeing toward Woodville. They rowed down the Butler River to where it joined with the Altamaha, then circled to the west up the Champney River to where it joined the South Altamaha, and went down that river to the southern tip of Carrs Island to the Woodville landing.

They got out of the canoe, Fanny carrying mush in a wooden bucket, and they came upon a small settlement with a row of a half dozen minuscule huts and a shack the size of an overseer's shack.

"Why the shack?"

"That be where some overseer they go when the malaria get bad. White man, him can't take the malaria. Not like nigger."

"Jack," she said, and shook her head.

She began going from hut to hut looking for Psyche. Old men and women, so decrepit they could barely stand, much less walk, met her gaze as she looked in their filthy hovels.

No one spoke. They stared at her silently, just eyes really, emaciated bodies worked to death.

In the last hut, she came upon Psyche. The old woman met them, her body the obvious result of many lashes. She seemed not to notice. Her walk was a little jerky, but her smile was strong.

"End of de worl'," she said. "End de worl'. All dem peoples, dem no longer work for de massa. Them's off to big place in de sky. Big, big place. Take big trip in de dark. They all happy dere."

"I know. I realize that," said Fanny. She wanted to say: *It will be that way, eventually, but not here, not now.* She touched the woman's arm. "Do you want some mush?"

Psyche didn't seem to hear her. "I see de white light," she said. "I seen it las' night, be standin' out dere, where de snakes is, in de timber, and I seen it. White light. It comin'. No work for massa, no more. None of dem. You see? Comin'. Comin'. Soon, it be a-comin.'"

"Yes," said Fanny. "I think it will come soon. I think you are right, Psyche."

She gave her a little hug and then looked for a bowl. "Do you have a bowl?" she asked. "For this mush?"

"A-comin'. That light. It tell me. Comin' soon. No work for massa den. No." A large smile burst on her withered face.

"I'll leave the mush here," said Fanny. "You eat it. You must eat it to keep up your strength." She set the bucket of mush on the ground. There wasn't a single thing in that hut for this old woman. Just the ground itself. Dirt. Nothing to lie on. No place to build a fire.

Why eat? Why not just die? What was the point?

She started to leave.

"You come back, visit Psyche," she said.

"You eat the mush," said Fanny.

The woman didn't seem to hear her.

355

They set off in the canoe for Butler Plantation. "That ole woman, her crazy," said Jack. "Got buncha niggers whipped."

"She's not as crazy as she may seem," said Fanny.

"No, missis."

"We'll have to bring more mush each day. Not just for Psyche—for all of them."

"Them eat insects," said Jack.

"No. They will not eat insects."

"That's all them have," said Jack.

"We'll see that they have more."

One evening as Fanny stood by watching Pierce in his petitioning line, she overheard a woman half whispering, whimpering. Then pleading.

"Massa say," said the woman. "Massa say!"

"Hush," said Pierce. "You hush now."

Fanny moved up closer to Pierce, standing where she could see the young woman and see her well. She was more white than black, about twenty, slender, well-proportioned, with a very pretty face and nice white teeth.

And now the young woman was grasping Pierce's hand. And crying, then shouting, "Massa promise. Massa *promise.*"

His hand came down hard on the window sill. "I did not promise! I did not promise a single, *goddamned* thing."

The woman fled in tears.

The next woman came to stand before him.

"Go on. I'm done this evening."

"But massa—"

"You heard me. I'm closing up now."

"But me sick," said the woman.

"Go to the Infirmary."

"But me can't work. Bones cold, tired, body aching bad and terrible."

"Infirmary!" He was closing the window.

"Please, massa . . ."

"You want this window down on your hand?"

Fanny grabbed his shoulder.

"Who was that young woman, Pierce?"

He jerked away. "What woman?"

"The one speaking of a *promise*."

"How would I know? I don't know them all. There's legions of them."

"Come now. What's her name? You know."

"No—I don't know. Why are you pestering me?"

She pointed a finger at him. "You had better not."

"What?"

"You know. With that girl. You had better not."

Early the next morning she headed for the fields. By seven it had already warmed up. She felt the humidity, and the way the day would wear on and on, and one would tire out and need rest and food and wouldn't be able to work any longer but would still have to work, until sundown or until one had completed one's appointed tasks—one's quotas. The whip would keep one at it. Hard work was better than the whip. It appeared that there were no more followers of Psyche. For the past several days, she'd heard no screaming coming from the huts.

She stopped and watched the slaves hoeing away. She waited until she finally saw her. How white she was. Yes, it was her, and Fanny knew.

She watched the driver making his way around the field on his horse. Now and then he'd crack the whip. He'd crack it loud.

She went up to him. He stopped on his horse.

"What me do for missis?" he asked.

"You're Frank. You're the driver."

"Yes, missis."

"I wish to speak to that woman—over there, the young one."

"Which woman, missis?"

"I don't know her name. The very white one. She's between those two old women. You see? She's stopped hoeing. Her."

"Leah, missis?"

"So that's her name. I want to speak to her."

He shook his head. "Mr. Oden, him say no—she got quota. They all got quota. Her no got time take it with you. You see Mr. Oden about it," he said.

"I can't speak to her?"

He looked worried. His eyes went down. "Her not get quota, get lashes."

She watched Leah working. "You would do it?"

He nodded. "Her get quota or get lashes."

"To that poor young girl."

"Her get quota," said Frank. "Or lashes."

She left the field.

She came back at sundown, when the slaves were heading in from the fields. She spotted Leah. She followed her, at a short distance, and she saw her enter a hut. It was the second to last hut on the row. She went directly to it.

She knocked on the warped door.

No response.

She peeked in. There were several black people in there—including Leah.

"I need to speak to you," she said, beckoning her.

"Yes, missis." Leah got up from the dirt floor and quickly came to her.

"Let's talk outside."

Leah stepped out of the hut. She was about her own height. She was very beautiful.

"Tell me," said Fanny, "what is going on with my husband?"

Leah stared at her. Fanny could see fear in her eyes. She had done something wrong. She would now be punished.

"Me no do nothing, missis."

"I know you didn't. But you were upset with him. I saw it. You took hold of his hand."

"No, no—me sorry! Never touch massa. Never!"

"I'm sure. But did massa touch you?"

Leah looked down at the ground. It wasn't a question she wished to answer—clearly, there were pitfalls. What if she said yes, and missis got angry? What if missis carried it back to massa? What would massa do? How many lashes? Massa could whip a slave as much as he wanted. Five hundred times if he wanted. To death if he wanted. No black man or woman could accuse him. No white jury would find him guilty. Leah would surely know that. Those two old women in the hut would have raised her on that fact.

"Me be good," she whimpered, and she leaned against the slave hut and seemed to fold in on herself.

"But did my husband touch you—in places he shouldn't touch you?"

Leah contemplated this for a short while. She looked about, at slaves walking up and down the row. Night was falling fast. "No." She shook her head.

"What did my husband promise you?"

"Him no promise . . ."

"You can tell me. What was it?"

"Him no promise anything."

"I won't tell him what you have to say. You tell me. You tell me what he said, about the promise. I'm your friend, Leah. I want to be."

She looked closely at Leah. *Am I not a fraud for saying*

that?

Leah looked down. "Him no promise."

"You can trust me, Leah." She pulled the young woman close so that they were looking at each other, eye to eye.

Leah started to pull away. How could a slave woman embrace missis? But Fanny held her tight. Leah seemed to melt into her.

"Be him woman," said Leah. "Be massa woman."

"His woman."

"Me no be bad," said Leah, and she began to sob.

She pictured it:

How she was heading in the direction of Leah's hut. How she was carrying her lantern.

A night wind was picking up.

She would approach the hovel. She would stand outside and listen. There would be moaning, grunting, panting noises, and she would recognize them. Oh, yes, she would.

She would step inside.

Where had all the black people gone? Told to scat? For how long?

With the lantern, she would see the two of them, unclothed. Pierce pulling a dirty blanket up to cover himself. She wouldn't want to see this, so she would hurry off.

Pierce was again occupying his petitioning spot.

"I want to speak to you," said Fanny.

"You do, do you? What about?"

"I'm telling you again."

"Telling me what again?"

"If you have something going with that girl Leah, you had better stop it."

Several women were lining up now. Pierce was making ready with his ledger. "I'm busy, Fanny."

"I'm telling you."

He turned from her. His attention was now on the first petitioner.

"Now, then," said Pierce. "What seems to ail us this evening?"

She began to go to Leah to take time with her. She stood outside her hut with her. She wanted to find out all about her. About what Pierce did to her. She would open herself up to the gritty details. Hadn't she done so with Jane Hannigan? But Leah didn't want to speak openly about it.

"Did he give you money?" she asked.

"No," said Leah. "No, him no give money. No."

"But you were his woman. Isn't that right?"

Leah looked down.

But Fanny lifted her chin, carefully. She waited.

Leah was now looking at her. "Him woman," she said, softly.

"I am against him," said Fanny, "and for you."

But was she? Was she enough for Leah that she would risk her children?

Leah looked down again. Fanny wanted to lift her up. She wanted to remove her, for no woman, black or white, should be *him woman*, unless she chose to be so.

"I'm 'him woman,' too," she thought. "In that, you and I are one."

When darkness came one evening, she asked Leah to come out again.

"Touch me," said Fanny.

Leah jolted. "What, missis?"

"Touch me. You can touch me." She put her hand out. "Here, take my hand into yours."

Leah hesitated. "Missis, me not—"

"I'm not your missis. I'm Fanny. Fanny Kemble. It makes you uncomfortable to touch white skin?"

"No, missis. Me love white skin."

"No you don't. My skin is no better than yours. It's just skin."

"No, missis. You skin white and good."

"No. You mustn't believe that."

Leah looked down at the ground.

"What do you see down there?"

She looked up, but she didn't look in Fanny's eyes.

"Look at me straight here," said Fanny. She touched each eye. "I don't own you, Leah. My husband *thinks* he owns you, but he doesn't really. No one can own another person."

Leah again looked down at the ground. And then she whipped her head around and looked in the direction of the fields, which were by now quite dark.

There was a foreboding stillness in the air.

"Me not free. Not want to be free."

"Yes, you do want to be free. Every person on the face of the earth wants to be free. A terrible injustice has been done to you, and I want to take you with me. Do you want to go?"

"Go—with missis?"

"With me. Fanny Kemble. Yes—I'm leaving here, and I'm taking you with me—if you'll go."

"Run off?"

"Yes. It's the only way."

She stood there. Fearful, her chin trembling. "Massa—"

"I know all about massa," said Fanny. "But you have no life here. You are my husband's slab of meat. Isn't that right?"

"Whip," she said. "Lashes."

"You have no life," said Fanny. "No life. You are nothing here, and you deserve more. All the people on this plantation do, but I can't take them all. I'll take you. That's all I can take—you and Jack."

"Jack?"

"Maybe you don't know Jack?"

Leah stared at her. "Whip," she said. "Lashes."

"Do you have a husband?"

Leah shook her head.

"We must go," said Fanny. "It's time to go."

"Yes, missis."

"Fanny. Do call me 'Fanny.' I will come and get you. You wait."

"Yes, missis."

And then she went to the blacksmith's shop, where she knew she would find young Jack.

Back at the shack, Pierce was gone. He'd be gone all night, she knew. He'd go on to another woman—there were plenty besides Leah, and he would try as many as he could, from settlement to settlement. He would be looking for the whitest ones. He had four settlements to choose from—and then St. Simons after that. But how was he any different than the owners and overseers who preceded him?

She climbed the narrow stairs. She knocked on the door. She heard the latch being moved—dull wood on wood.

"Oh, hello, Mrs. Butler."

"Margery."

The children were on the bed.

"Read!" shouted Sally.

Margery took her up and grabbed Fan and settled down on the bed. The lamp light illuminated the children's faces.

"Have them ready. Their things gathered up. Do so immediately."

"Ready, ma'am?"

"Yes. Soon, I will come up to get them."

"Where are you going, ma'am?"

"Never mind. Just have them ready."

"Yes, ma'am."

Fanny went for the door.

"Don't fail me."

"They'll be ready," said Margery.

"Good."

In her room, she sat down on the bed and studied Pierce's trunk. The key. Where was it?

She got up and checked his bedside stand. She pulled at the drawer—locked. A key to the drawer to get the key in the drawer for the trunk. Everything in this world operates by keys. Where is the key to your heart? Where is the key to this drawer? She pulled at the drawer. A simple dresser drawer, in a piece of furniture handcrafted by artisans here in Settlement One. Quality workmanship. So solid. Nicely planed to a smooth finish sans stain. She yanked. No, she must pry. Pry. Which meant a tool of some sort.

There was that axe on the woodpile.

Yes, there was.

She went out and got it and came in with it, swinging.

Mr. Oden sat working at the table. "What's that you've got?"

"An axe. What does it look like?"

"What do you need an axe for?"

"I'm going to chop my foot off. Hobble myself."

"Ha! Funny." He went back to his work.

She carried it into her room.

She approached the nightstand. She got the axe blade inserted in a crevice on one side of the drawer. She began to pry. Careful now. Don't damage it. A fine piece of furniture.

Nothing.

Try the other side. She got the axe blade inserted in a crevice on the other side. She pried. Careful, oh so careful.

Nothing.

She looked up. There stood Mr. Oden.

"You've still got your foot, I see."

"Yes, I do."

"What's the problem? What the hell're you doing?"

"I need to get this drawer open."

"For what?"

"That's my business."

"Locked, huh?"

"Yes."

"And you don't have the key."

"No."

"Is that your drawer?"

"Yes, it's my drawer."

"No it's not."

"How do you know?"

"I just do. I'm not dumb, Mrs. Butler."

"I'm getting into this drawer," said Fanny. "One way or the other."

"Stealing from your husband again, huh?"

"Call it what you want."

He grinned. "He'll be calling the sheriff again, won't he?"

"I suppose he will."

"A woman with steel nerves. Tell me what you want, and I might be of assistance."

She stared at him. "Really?"

"I think I told you. I like a woman with spunk." He gave her another leer.

She ignored it. "There's money I'm after. It's mine."

"What do you need money for?"

"Why does anyone need money?"

"He won't give you any, huh?"

"No. And a woman's got to shop, now doesn't she?"

"Hell, bust it in. Give it to me." He went for the axe.

"What are you about to do?"

"Beat the goddamn thing in. Stand back now."

She moved away.

He took a swing, and then a second. The drawer caved in, splintering. He pulled the drawer free. He reached in and rummaged around. He held it up—the key. "Is this what you're looking for?"

"Yes."

"I know about that, Mrs. Butler. I know all about your husband." He pointed at the trunk. "Fits that trunk, doesn't it?"

"Yes—I suppose it does."

"Goddamn right it does. And I know what he keeps in there. Because he's reached in there a few times to pay me off, when he bothered to pay me off, when I didn't threaten to beat his goddamned brains in. Right now, the way I've calculated it, the man owes me a hundred dollars. Gambling debts, Mrs. Butler. You may not like his poker habits, but if you owe a debt, you pay it. So you go ahead and open that trunk there, get into that stash of his, and give me my money, and our little business here will be at an end. And while you're doing that, I'll get hold of a piece of replacement furniture for this fine piece here."

He left.

She got into the trunk, found his leather bag, and opened it. And then she grabbed up the thick wad of banknotes. She flashed through it—all of it issued by the Bank of Pennsylvania and the Bank of the United States. She took it all and a pile of coins.

I'll leave him a Liberty Head penny. We'll see how far he gets on that.

She grabbed his gun. She found a box of bullets.

She loaded the gun.

Then she pocketed the gun and extra bullets in her purse. She strapped it over her arm.

In minutes Mr. Oden came back with an identical bedside stand. He grabbed up the smashed one.

She handed him a hundred. And then she handed him a few twenties.

"Well, now, nice doing business with you, ma'am!" He left, smirking.

She took the axe back out to the woodpile.

Back inside, she retrieved her journal from her trunk,

some pen nibs from her desk, then wondered about that brown trunk. Should she? No, she must jettison it. She would buy a new one when the time came.

"We're going home. You can go with us or stay here. But we're leaving."

"What about Mr. Butler? Does he know?"

"No, he doesn't."

"I'm going with you," said Margery. "I'm not staying here by myself."

"No—I wouldn't think you'd want to."

Outside was a sliver of green moon like a slice of unripe melon. She hurried to Leah. She was waiting outside the hut.

"Missis . . ."

"We must go."

"Now, missis?"

"Yes—now."

She rushed her down the row of slave huts, past the over-seer's shack, to the river's edge, where Margery and the two children waited at the landing. And there stood Jack.

Dark, dark, dark, the water lapping, but that sliver of melon moon struck her as infinitely gorgeous, and a good omen. She whispered at Jack. "Get the boat untied."

"Got bigger boat," said Jack. "Canoe, it not big enough."

"I know," said Fanny. She looked around, but in the darkness there was no one.

Jack made his way down to the boat. They waited.

Fan started to cry.

"*Hush*," said Margery. Sally was laughing, and let out a squeal. "You must be quiet," said Margery, "or bad things will happen. Be quiet, child."

"Mama," said Sally, grabbing at Fanny.

"We must be absolutely, absolutely quiet," said Fanny. "We are going on an adventure. And if you are on an adventure, you must be quiet."

They made their way down to where Jack was taking the oars. Fanny took the two children, and Margery got in, and then she reached for the children. Leah got in. Fanny got in last and took a second set of oars.

5
Escape

Soon the boat was moving down the river. She couldn't paddle it very fast, and now and then she had to stop to rest. But Jack kept at it.

She made the turns, along with Jack. They were soon in General's Cut, heading to the Darien River. And then in an hour or less, lights visible. Lanterns. Candles in windows. A bonfire. Darien. Canes rattling in the swamp close by.

Once they got to Doboy—to the wharf there—they could hop a sea-going vessel to Charleston, and on up north.

Soon the water became turbid. Her arms were giving out. Sally squealed.

"Be still," she said. "Be still now."

She turned to Jack. She whispered, "I'm giving you a gun. It's loaded. In case we get separated—only then."

"Gun," he said, rowing. "Gun."

"Yes, in case we get separated. You'll need it. You'll be fighting for your life. All right?"

"Yes, missis."

"Fanny."

"Yes," he said.

She handed him the gun. She waited a moment, and then she plunged in her purse for the extra bullets. "These, too," she said. "Put out your hand."

"Yes, missis."

He extended his hand.

"Bullets," she said, letting them fall into the palm of his hand. "Extra ones. Grasp them tightly. Then put them some-where. Do you have somewhere to put them?"

"Yes, missis."

They were approaching Doboy. Up ahead was a boat, lit

by lanterns, casting yellow puddles on the dark water.

"Fanny!"

"Yes?"

"Someone's coming."

"I see them."

"Jack," she said. "Keep paddling. Do not stop. Do you have the gun? Is it out of sight—but is it ready? Can you get it out fast?"

"Yes, missis."

She could see men's faces in the yellow glow. "Get down," she told Leah, and she felt the girl's body moving so that she was lying down. Jack kept rowing. She kept rowing.

A shout: "Who goes!"

"Be quiet," said Fanny. "I will handle this."

She snuffed out her lantern.

"Who goes!"

In a few minutes, the other boat pulled up alongside them. Several men gawked at them. They let out ribald laughs. One was cradling a long rifle. He said, "What you gals doing out here at this hour—huh? I see you got your nigger with you." Then another man said, "Yup, got their nigger with them. Hey, two goddamned niggers. Look at that."

Now, a big man, large-gutted, rose in the light of a lantern and slumped into their boat, rocking it. He let out a loud hawking spit. A deep clearing of the throat.

"Hey, gal," he said to Leah. "You get up now. Don't you hide yourself from your Uncle Travis like that. Hey, gal!"

Leah moved quickly to a sitting position.

"Good looking nigger gal," he said to Fanny.

"What do you want?"

"Well, missy," drawled the fat man. "This here's the slave patrol. And so what you doing with that black-as-night nigger boy at the oars and this here half-white gal hiding her sweet little self from her Uncle Travis?"

"We're off to Doboy."

"And what business you got in Doboy?"

"Business."

"I asked, ma'am, *what* business?"

"Are you intending to impede a white woman's progress on this river?"

The fat man nodded slowly. "Yes, ma'am, I am. Until you tell me what business you got going to Doboy here at this time a-night."

"Now why would I want to tell you that? These are my two niggers, and why don't you let me and my family take our niggers with us and not have to explain every little thing."

"Because, ma'am, as I told ye, this is the slave patrol, and what I see here I'm not taking a-liking to."

"What do you see?"

"This ain't a family is what I see. Where's the man?"

"Who's at the oars?" said Fanny. "He looks like a man to me."

The fat man let out a snort. "You hitched to that nigger, are ye?"

"No."

"Well, then, ma'am, where's your own man, your husband?"

"Back on the plantation."

"And what are ye a-doin' *not* on that plantation?"

"I guess you just have to know, don't you?"

"Yes, ma'am, I do. And you'd better tell me."

"Well, Uncle Travis—"

"That's a time. That's my name."

"We're off to Doboy to catch a boat to Charleston, since you just have to know."

"You goin' to Charleston, are ye?"

"Yes. That's what I just said. Didn't I?"

He turned to look at his men, and then he looked back at her. "And what be your business in Charleston, ma'am?"

"Visiting relatives."

"Vising relatives. Ain't that dandy? And what relatives might that be?"

Sally said, "I wanta go to Charleston."

"That's where we're going, honey," said Fanny.

"I like Charleston!" said Sally.

Fan whimpered.

"Who're them relatives?" asked the fat man.

"In-laws."

"Ma'am, you're just gonna hafta be more specific for your Uncle Travis. He's got a job to do. And if he don't do his job, well, hell's to pay. So, let's ask ourselves again, who're them in-laws there in Charleston you're about to visit?"

"Specific?" said Fanny. "You're awfully, just terribly nosy, Uncle Travis."

"Paid to be, ma'am."

"What do they pay you?"

"Not enough, ma'am. Do they, boys?"

"Hell no," yelled one. And there was a rousing chorus. She saw one of the men had a large bottle he was drinking from. And then he was passing it around.

"If you just must, absolutely *must* know, I'm vising relatives of my sister-in-law, Gabriella Butler. Now does knowing that fact please you?"

"Well, goddamn, a Butler. Now who are you, missy?"

"I'm not 'missy.' I'm Mrs. Fanny Butler, and I'm off on a vacation my husband said I well deserved after spending a good bit of time at Butler Plantation. The kids are squirmy, and I'm just terribly bored and need some big city life. Don't you see? But what would that be like without help? So my husband just insisted: 'Now you be sure to take your niggers with you. At least two.' So that's what you see, Uncle Travis. That's what we have here."

"Little white nigger gal there, too," he said, motioning at Leah.

"Yes, sir—to cook."

372

"Well, damn, but that don't sound like one hell of a fine story. You boys hear all that?"

"Yeah, we heard. We ain't deaf."

"River's real noisy," said the fat man. He looked at Fanny for a long moment, and then said, "Goddamn it if I believe that little tale of yours, missy. You must take your Uncle Travis here for a simpleton. Ain't that right?"

"No. Indeed not. I take you for a man who's about to be jailed for stopping a very important man's wife from catching her ship to Charleston. I take you for a man who's going to be very sorry he gave the dickens to Mrs. Fanny Butler, wife of the second largest slaveholder in the entire state of Georgia. That's what I take you for."

The fat man arranged a chew in his mouth. "You say?"

"That's exactly what I say."

"You got any money for this here trip?"

"Yes, of course."

"Well, then, maybe you wanta pay your toll right here, right now."

"Toll?"

"Toll, ma'am. That's right."

"No. I do not wish to pay a toll. You say your name is Travis? I will be letting my husband know all about you, sir. Every little thing."

In the light of the moon, the chew in the fat man's mouth was bulging his jaw. He leaned back, sighed, and then quickly turned his head and spit into the river. He yelled out at the men in the boat. "These here gals, they's the hardest, ain't they?" Then he grinned at Fanny. "Why don't you give me that little nigger gal there, and we'll call it even-steven."

"No! You had better leave me alone, sir, or I will see you publicly whipped!"

"Whipped?"

"Yes, sir. Flogged. Fifty lashes. My husband is very quick with the whip. As he should be if you want to keep your niggers in line. And he wouldn't spare it for a sight like you, wanting to steal a nigger woman like this away from him."

"Yeah," drawled the fat man. "We oughta shoot you is what we oughta do."

"You go ahead. You shoot us all."

The fat man let out a howl. "This here gal's crazy!"

"What I want," said Fanny, "what I demand, is that you let me, my children, their nursemaid, and my two niggers alone. And let us go."

Silence. The fat man staring at her. And then: "I heard things about you. You bet I did."

"Oh, and what is that?"

"You a nigger lover, ma'am, and everything you been a-ladlin' out to your Uncle Travis's been pure lyin'. Falsehoods, ma'am. And you think me and these boys here're gonna stand by and be fooled. Well, we ain't. Now, you can put aside all that 'my niggers' stuff and tell me the truth. And if you don't, I'm a-gonna be hauling the whole passel of you to Sheriff Bob. Is what I'm about to do, ma'am."

"Stealing a man's niggers!" shouted out the man with the long rifle.

"All right," said Fanny. "I will tell you, then."

"You'd best, missy."

"All right. My husband has allowed me to take these two slaves with me on my trip to Charleston. I don't see why that is all that hard to comprehend. And if you don't start comprehending it very quickly, I'm going to miss my boat."

"Why'd you call them 'niggers,' then. Why'd you put on for us like that, missy?"

"I'm not your *missy*."

"*Mrs. Butler*. Hell fire."

"That's better. You ask? Because that's what you call them down here. Maybe it's having an effect on me."

"English woman, we heard a-plenty," said the fat man.

"If you delay me any longer, I'm going to miss my boat,"

said Fanny. "Do you really want that?"

"You be running off with them two niggers," said the fat man, and "you about to do worse than miss your goddamn boat. You about to end up in jail stealing a man's niggers."

"I'm not running off with them. As I've told you. And told you. And told you. Are you so thick-headed you still do not comprehend?"

"Where's the passes, then?"

"Passes? What passes?"

"Travelin' passes for these here two slaves. That's the passes."

"My husband gave me no such passes."

"No, ma'am, I venture to say he didn't."

"Perhaps he just didn't know he was supposed to."

The fat man grinned, and then turned and spit into the water. He waited a while, not saying a thing. The men in the other boat were taking drinks from a bottle and cursing. "Okay, you pay us for our services, and we'll see you make that there boat."

"Pay you? That's a laugh," she said. "You mean to extort us?"

"Say what?"

"I'm to bribe you, am I? That's what you want?"

"Slave patrol don't operate on good will."

"I'll bet. How much?"

"What do you say, boys?"

"Ten!"

"Ten? Goddamn. We ain't working for nothing. Hundred," said the fat man.

"*Hundred?*"

"That's what I said. If my ears is right."

"That is outrageous! I shall tell my husband how you are nothing but highway robbers."

"You won't be tellin' your husband nothing," he said.

"And we both know it."

She went for her purse. She removed a hundred and handed to the fat man.

"Ah!" he cried. "That'll do, won't it, boys?"

And he got out of the boat. And into the patrol boat.

Jack took the oars and started moving.

She heard the rifle cock, and then a blast ripped into the trees across the river.

"You all, you have a nice trip now!"

She didn't look back. But she could hear riotous laughing and carrying on until the noise of the river drowned them out.

"I was so afraid," said Margery.

"I was too," said Fanny.

Jack handed her the gun.

"No," she said, "we're not there yet. You keep it."

In Doboy she found a two-story hotel within a hundred feet of the landing. All six of them entered the lobby area, where a skinny, pimply desk clerk stood, waiting behind a short counter. He was a young man, no older than twenty, and he looked sleepy-eyed. "Niggers ain't allowed in this hotel, ma'am." He turned to Jack and Leah. "You there, out that door!"

"Wait!" said Fanny. "I require their services."

She turned to Jack and Leah, who were about to leave.

"Hotel policy, ma'am," said the clerk. "Niggers ain't allowed."

She leaned toward him. "Where can they stay?"

"Got a shed out back."

"How do they get fed?"

"Bring them some mush later. That's the deal there, ma'am. Just following policy."

"What if I don't like that policy? You know, other hotels I've stayed in have allowed all of us a place to say—in the hotel. They understand a gentlewoman's needs and wants. And they do not hesitate to meet those needs and wants."

"Where would that be?" said the clerk, his eyes twitching. "Which hotels?"

"Oh, in Savannah and Charleston, too. Fine hotels, where a lady's treated just right."

"This ain't either of them places. This here's Doboy. We do it our way down here in Doboy. We ain't a big city, ma'am."

"Is this the South or not?"

"Yes, ma'am."

"Well, sir, even in Maryland they treat a lady better than this."

"Maryland."

"Yes, that's where I'm from. I've been visiting relatives all around the area, and now I find I'm treated like I don't how ladies are treated, when they're treated like ladies."

"Maryland."

"You heard me right. We have our slaves up there, too, you know. We're not the South, but you wouldn't know it. I wonder," she said, "if I could pay a little extra for a little extra service. To receive the kind of service a lady needs."

The desk clerk looked at her, his eyes more intent. "What'd you have in mind, ma'am?"

"Oh, say, ten dollars?"

"God bless!"

"Yes, and I *would* bring God into it because He's in everything, isn't He, including looking out for a lady's slave help when she needs it. Like at night if she needs a drink of water, or the chamber pot emptied for her little children—don't you see?"

"Yes, ma'am. Ten?"

"That's right." She went for her purse and removed a ten. The lodging was a dollar, which she thought was rather steep for a village as tiny as Doboy, Georgia. The desk clerk took hold of the ten and seemed unsure what to do with it. "That's a tip for you," she said.

"Tip."

"Yes."

"God bless you, ma'am." He nodded at Jack and Leah. "I'll fix them up a room."

"A man with a woman?"

"Well," he said. He whispered at her.

"How dare you!" she cried.

"I'm real sorry!" he said. "Two rooms, one each."

"I would think," said Fanny, "that ten dollars would buy at least that."

"It's two dollars apiece for them rooms," said the clerk.

"Their rooms are double mine? What are you thinking?"

"Dollar apiece, ma'am."

"Well, that's better."

Just before retiring, there was a knock on her door.

She went to it. It was Jack. "The gun," he whispered.

"Come in."

He came in, and she closed the door.

"Yes," she said, and took it, and the bullets he dropped in her hand.

"I hope I don't need this," she thought.

She knew it before, but she knew it better when she took passage north.

When you get on a ship headed for Charleston, you face more opposition as soon as they see those dark skins or, if half white like Leah, evidence of Negro descent. As soon as they see a young man, a young woman, a Jack, a Leah— they want to know right off: are they free, or are they slave? *Where's the papers on them? Do you have ownership papers? Or passes signed by the owner? You don't? We'll need papers, ma'am. Who are you now? Who?*

And more of the same.

But money talks. Yes, she thought, it sure does. You hand out a hundred—that silences a man who wouldn't otherwise be silenced. Two cabins, one for each of them. An additional twenty dollars, just to Charleston. It takes a lot.

Wait, she mused, until Pierce discovers he's been fleeced. But Mr. Oden won't say. He won't tell on you. Pierce's overseer has had his fill of that man, that's plain to see.

Underway, you knock on their cabin doors, now and then, to make sure they're okay. You check, sure, but not too much. You check when no one's around to see you check.

You ticket yourself and your whole party to New York, and then from there, to Nova Scotia. Only in New York harbor, there are more questions. Down there in those two cabins, sequestered away, two runaway slaves—or are they personal slaves of Fanny Forester, resident of Maryland, with her two children and nursemaid, on a family trip?

"Taking your slaves to Nova Scotia, are you, ma'am? Why is that?"

"We're vacationing there, sir."

"Vacationing in Nova Scotia."

"That's right."

"Better watch for kidnappers, ma'am."

She could see the glint in the man's eye. Had she made a mistake? "I'll soon be going back to Maryland with them," she said. "Baltimore."

"Ticket to Nova Scotia or Baltimore?"

"The former. What will it take for you to leave me to my own doings?"

A long pause. Eyes on her. Maybe he won't answer that question. But finally: "What is it you're willing to pay?"

"Fifty."

"Fifty? I'm going to need two hundred, ma'am."

"Two hundred. Surely," she said, "you must think me a fool."

"Job doesn't pay much, ma'am. And those slaves of yours—no papers—they're worth a whole pot of money more than that. Aren't they now?"

"You intend to steal two hundred from me?"

"It's a business arrangement, ma'am. That's all it is."

"I'll pay one hundred and not a penny more, and I will take a receipt for the money, and the agreement spelled out," said Fanny.

"I don't know about that, ma'am. I don't think so."

"Well," she said, whispering at him, "you think about it. There's more money if I, Fanny Forester, don't suddenly discover those two missing. It's a bird in the hand—think of it that way. But if they disappear . . . ah, well! . . . no more money greasing those palms of yours. Do you follow?"

"Yes, ma'am."

"And I want the finest service for them. Because I'm willing to pay."

"Thank you, ma'am."

And so, more and more, the purse. The money. The bribes.

But two very nice cabins below. One for Jack, one for Leah. One for her and Margery and the two children. Dear husband, you never guessed, did you, that your money—stolen from me, wrenched right out of my soul, would be used to aid two of your so-called "niggers" in living in style, but how could you imagine such a thing? Your mostly white woman concubine—the woman you chose to rape, almost before my very eyes—a woman as close as you could get to an actual white woman on Butler Plantation, and your Jack, a useful boy to run errands for you, to occupy your pest of a wife's time, and finally to aid her in her flight and theirs too—how could you imagine all that? How could you?

And finally to Nova Scotia, free soil. That first night in her hotel, she went down to the ocean and pitched the gun way out. Then the bullets, one by one. She stood there. "There's an end to that. We have left those savages behind."

Before retiring, she wrote in her journal:

The winter moon shows in my hotel window. It's pale white, colored in shapes of gray, like a map of the world. Escaping, we are, all six of us, out of that dungeon of the South, that rank cellar where ignorant, brutal people lord it over others—torturing them based on nothing more than cupidity, a perverted desire for power, and a sick sense of hatred for their skin color. Their hatred is all-consuming, and they are victims of their own darkness. A long voyage, yes, but free air. The free air of freedom for every one of you, including my dear, dear children, uncorrupted no longer by the pestilent air of Butler Plantation—which your mother so wrongfully exposed you to.

And Margery, one could see how excited she was by the prospect of a new land. How could she not be? How could she not feel, like her, the immense pull of it? Fanny could see it in her eyes, feel it vibrantly in her girlish presence.

And Leah, such a beautiful young woman, dressed in new clothes. How European she looked. How Parisian!

And Jack, in his fine suit. How strong, how becoming he looked. One could not imagine him a slave.

The six of them a family now.

"You must not call me 'missis' any longer," she said to Leah and Jack as they sat in a small café on the sea coast. From where they sat, one could see the ocean beating against clay-colored rocks. One could hear the howl of spring storms on the rise. "I am Fanny—Fanny Kemble. You must both choose last names. What will they be?"

Leah looked confused. She had never had a last name. It was a category she could hardly imagine.

"Me," said Jack, "me be called Jack Short."

"Because you're short?"

"Yes, ma'am."

"You think about that name. So much is involved in a name. Perhaps you should try out different names. Perhaps another name will come to you, eventually. Leah?"

"Me don't know," said Leah. "Missis name us."

"Fanny. Call me Fanny, please."

"Fanny," said Leah. But she was whispering it.

"You call me Fanny because I'm your friend. I was never your missis. I hope you will come to see that. *Am* I your friend?"

"Yes," said Leah, softly.

She sat Baby Fan before her. She must control her tongue with Sally, lest the subject of her father come up. But she could speak to Fan. She must tell her. She said, in a soft, soothing voice, "You will go first to England—and then points hence from there. Or perhaps back here, at some future stage, but that I cannot possibly know."

And then she remembered Fan in her father's arms. There was something between them. She sensed something: a father wanting his daughter, a daughter wanting her father. "You can't have him," she thought.

In a few days, they left their small hotel, where she had again booked three rooms. They took a coach to the wharf where Fanny would now book passage to England. She posted a letter to Edward Trelawny:

Dearest Edward,

*I, my nursemaid, Margery, my two children, and
my two escaped slaves are now about to board a
ship to England. I hope to see you when we arrive. I hope to escape from the wrath of my devious
husband somewhere, perhaps in Venice. I am, you
know, a water creature, an undine. He would never think of Venice—never. And I imagine it in all
its glory, with its rich history of the literary greats,
Goethe, Byron, Shelley.*
*But for now, I simply want to apprise you of my
return to native soil.*
Ah, how I have missed it!
*Ah, how I have missed you as well. Will you be
waiting to see me?*
Yours,
Fanny

Sally wanted to know, "When will Father be with us
again?"

"Your father is busy at his plantation. Perhaps he will
join us at some future date."

"In England?"

"Yes, perhaps."

"Will we go to Butler Place?" asked Sally. "And meet him
there?"

"No, child, it will have to be England."

She began to cry. She wanted her father. And who could
blame her? What did she know? "Will they be our family?"
she asked, pointing first at Leah, and then at Jack. "Them?"

"Yes," said Fanny. "They will."

"But they're black," she said, pouting.

"Is that a big thing?"

She saw Leah smiling. And then Leah took Sally's hands.
Sally grabbed Leah tightly, and then hugged her.

"You will have a second sister," said Fanny, "who will

love you dearly. As long as you do not command her to do something. As long as you are not a little tyrant."

"But they loved me," said Sally.

"I know they did. But was it real love?"

"Yes!"

"We will see," said Fanny.

Now the sea rose before them, the sea which continued to pound the brown rocks where they would soon board the ship, the sea she had taken years before, and was now returning. That steamboat tied up along the pier would soon take them out—under an opaque sky, beyond the white lighthouse on the snow-covered knoll, deep into the interminable reaches of the world.

Acknowledgments

The section "Wedding Journey," was first published as "Newport" in *Pennsylvania Literary Journal*, May, 2019.

I am indebted to the following for my research for this novel: Margaret Armstrong, *Fanny Kemble: A Passionate Victorian* (Macmillan, 1938); Margaret Armstrong, *Trelawny: A Man's Life* (Macmillan, 1940); Malcolm Bell, Jr., *Major Butler's Legacy: Five Generations of a Slaveholding Family* (The University of Georgia Press, 1987); Catherine Clinton, *Fanny Kemble's Civil Wars* (Simon & Schuster, 2000); Deirdre Davis, *Fanny Kemble: A Performed Life* (University of Pennsylvania Press, 2007); Barbara Ehrenreich and Deirdre English, *For Her Own Good: Two Centuries of the Experts' Advice to Women* (Anchor, 2005); Anne Farrow, Joel Lang, and Jenifer Frank, *Complicity: How the North Promoted, Prolonged, and Profited from Slavery* (Ballantine Books, 2006); Rebecca Jenkins, *Fanny Kemble: The Reluctant Celebrity* (Simon & Schuster, 1988); Julie Roy Jeffrey, *The Great Silent Army of Abolitionism* (University of North Caroline Press, 1998); Frances Anne Kemble, *Journal of a Residence on a Georgian Plantation* (University of Georgia Press, 1984); Fanny Kemble, *The American Journals* (Weidenfeld and Nicolson, 1990); Fanny Kemble, *Records of a Later Life* (Henry Holt & Co., 1882); Barbara Penner, *Newlyweds on Tour: Honeymooning in Nineteenth-Century America* (University Press of New England, 2009); Valerie Kossew Pichanick, *Harriet Martineau: The Woman and Her Work, 1802-76* (The University of Michigan Press, 1980); John Anthony Scott, *Fanny Kemble's America* (Thomas Y. Crowell, 1973); Edward Trelawny, *Recollections of the Last Days of Shel-*

ley & Bryon (Carrol & Graf, 2000); Fanny Kemble Wister, *Fanny: The American Kemble* (South Pass Press, 1972); Constance Wright, *Fanny Kemble and the Lovely Land* (Robert Hale, 1972): and Bertram Wyatt-Brown, *Southern Honor: Ethics & Behavior in the Old South* (Oxford University Press, 2007).

I especially thank the following persons for their substantial encouragement and help in writing this novel: Mary Jane Smith, Stephanie Cowell, Dennis Must, and Walter Cummins.

About the Author

 Jack Smith has published five novels: *Run* (2020), *Miss Manners for War Criminals* (2017), *Being* (2016), *Icon* (2014), and *Hog to Hog*, which won the 2007 George Garrett Fiction Prize and was published by Texas Review Press in 2008. He has published stories in a number of literary magazines, including *Southern Review*, *North American Review*, *Texas Review*, *In Posse Review*, *Word Riot*, and *Night Train*. His reviews have appeared widely in such publications as *Ploughshares*, *Georgia Review*, *American Book Review*, *Prairie Schooner*, *Mid-American Review*, *Pleiades*, *The Missouri Review*, and *Environment* magazine. He has published numerous articles in *Novel & Short Story Writer's Market* and is a regular contributor to *The Writer* magazine. He has published two books on creative writing: *Write and Revise for Publication: A 6-Month Plan for Crafting an Exceptional Novel and Other Works of Fiction* (Writer's Digest Books, 2013; Penguin Random House) and *Inventing the World: The Fiction Writer's Guidebook to Craft and Process* (Serving House Books, 2018). Besides his writing, Smith was fiction editor of *The Green Hills Literary Lantern*, an online literary magazine published by Truman State University, for 25 years. He presently teaches for Writers.com.

www.ingramcontent.com/pod-product-compliance
Lightning Source LLC
Chambersburg PA
CBHW030624250626
47154CB00006B/1915